The Last Checkmate

A NOVEL

GABRIELLA SAAB

wm

WILLIAM MORROW

An Imprint of HarperCollins*Publishers*

P.S.™ is a trademark of HarperCollins Publishers.

THE LAST CHECKMATE. Copyright © 2021 by Gabriella Saab. All rights reserved. Printed in the United States of America. No part of this book may be used or reproduced in any manner whatsoever without written permission except in the case of brief quotations embodied in critical articles and reviews. For information, address HarperCollins Publishers, 195 Broadway, New York, NY 10007.

HarperCollins books may be purchased for educational, business, or sales promotional use. For information, please email the Special Markets Department at SPsales@harpercollins.com.

FIRST EDITION

Designed by Diahann Sturge

Pawn chess piece © Channarong Pherngjanda / Shutterstock, Inc.

Library of Congress Cataloging-in-Publication Data has been applied for.

ISBN 978-0-06-314193-3 (paperback)
ISBN 978-0-06-314338-8 (library edition)
ISBN 978-0-06-320542-0 (international edition)

21 22 23 24 25 LSC 10 9 8 7 6 5 4 3 2 1

For Poppy: my grandfather, my godfather, and my biggest fan.
I love and miss you with all my heart.

 Chapter 1

Auschwitz, 20 April 1945

THREE MONTHS AGO, I escaped the prison that held my body, but I haven't found freedom from the one that holds my soul. It's as if I never shed the blue-and-gray-striped uniform or set foot beyond the electrified barbed wire fences. The liberation I seek requires escape of a different sort, one I can achieve only now that I've returned.

A drizzle falls around me, adding an eerie haze to the gray, foggy morning. Not unlike the first day I stood in this exact spot, staring at the dark metal sign beckoning me from the distance.

ARBEIT MACHT FREI.

I remove the letter from my small handbag and read over the words I've memorized, then pull the gun out and examine it. A Luger P08, just like the one my father kept as a trophy following the Great War. The one he'd taught me how to use.

I drop the handbag onto the wet ground, straighten my shirtwaist, and tuck the pistol into my skirt pocket. With each footstep against the gravel, the scent of fresh earth mingles with the rain, but I swear I detect traces of decaying corpses and smoke from cigarettes, guns, and the crematoria. Shuddering, I wrap my arms around my waist and take a breath to assure myself that the air is clean.

Once I pass through the gate, I stop. No curses, taunts, or slurs, no cracking whips or thudding clubs, no barking dogs, no tramping jackboots, no orchestra playing German marches.

Auschwitz is abandoned.

When the loud voice in my head deters me, the little whisper reminds me that this is the day I've awaited, and if I don't see it through I may never have another chance. I continue down the empty street, past the kitchen and the camp brothel. Turn by Block 14 and come upon my destination, my hand against my other pocket to feel the rosary beads tucked inside.

The roll-call square. Our meeting place. And he's already here.

The bastard stands by the wooden shelter booth, and he looks no different than I remember. Hardly taller than I, slight and unimpressive. He's in his SS uniform, crisp and pressed even in the rain, jackboots shiny despite a few splatters of mud. His pistol hangs at his side. And his beady eyes lock upon me when I halt a few meters away.

"Prisoner 16671," Fritzsch says. "I prefer you in stripes."

Despite the many times I've been addressed by that sequence, the way he says *one-six-six-seven-one* steals my voice. I brush my thumb over the tattoo along my forearm, such a sharp contrast to my pale skin, and pass over the five round scars above the tattoo. The simple gesture coaxes my tongue into forming words.

"My name is Maria Florkowska."

He chuckles. "You still haven't learned to control that mouth of yours, have you, Polack?"

The endgame has begun. My wits are my king, pain my queen, the gun my rook, and I am the pawn. My pieces are in place on this giant chessboard. White pawn faces black king.

Fritzsch beckons me with a jerk of his head and indicates the small table set up in the middle of the square. I'd recognize the checkered board and its pieces anywhere. Our footsteps against the gravel are the only sound until I prepare to sit behind the white pieces; then his voice stops me.

"Have you forgotten the terms of our arrangement? If you're going to bore me, I see no need for a final game."

As he moves to block my path, one hand rests on his pistol, and I take a slow breath. Somehow I feel like the girl surrounded by men in this roll-call square, all eyes on her while she engages in chess games against the man who would lodge a bullet in her skull just as soon as place her in checkmate.

The silence hangs heavy between us until I manage to break it. "What should I do?"

A hum of approval rumbles in his throat; I loathe myself for putting it there. "Compliance serves you far better than impertinence," he says, and I watch his feet as he steps closer. "Other side."

He's taking my white pieces and my first-move advantage as easily as he took everything else from me. But I don't need an advantage to defeat him.

I move to the opposite side of the board and study the water droplets glistening on the black pieces. Fritzsch will open with the Queen's Gambit. I know he will, because it's my favorite opening. He'll be sure to take that, too.

And he does. Queen's pawn to D4. The solitary white pawn stands two squares ahead of its row, already seeking control of the center of the board. When my black queen's pawn meets his in the center, he responds with a second pawn to the left of his first, finishing the opening.

Fritzsch rests his forearms on the table. "Your move, 16671."

I swallow the *Jawohl, Herr Lagerführer* rising to my throat. He's not my camp deputy anymore. I won't address him as such.

When I stay silent, the corner of his mouth tightens, and the heat of satisfaction courses through my body, mingling with the chill of this dreary morning. As I examine the board, I keep both hands in his view—the pistol remains tucked inside my skirt pocket, heavy as it rests against my lap.

Fritzsch watches while I reach for my next pawn, eyes alight as if he expects me to speak. Something inside urges me to comply, if only to get away from him, from this place, but I can't, not yet. Not until the time is right. Then I will demand the answers I seek, but if I let the questions consume me now, if I lose focus—

After I make my play, I smooth my damp skirt, giving myself a reason to hide my hands under the table. The trembles can't start. This game is too important. My hands are steady for now, but the slightest change is all it takes.

Finish the game, Maria.

Chess is my game. It's always been my game.

And after all this time, this game will end my way.

Chapter 2

Warsaw, 27 May 1941

EVER SINCE MY family and I were confined to Pawiak Prison, one phrase had reverberated in my mind: *The Gestapo will come for me.*

Huddled in the corner of our cell, I hugged my knees against my chest and brushed my thumb over my split bottom lip. At first I thought maybe the German secret police would decide I wasn't worth their time. One look at my blond braid and wide eyes, and they'd deem me harmless.

But it was too late for that. They already had proof of what I'd done.

On the single metal bed with its thin mattress, Zofia hugged Mama's arm. A prisoner had just stumbled past our cell, but my little sister hadn't released Mama or stopped staring at the bars on the door. The man's pleas for mercy echoed in my ears, pleas that had earned him kicks and shoves as the guards ushered him away. At last Mama coaxed Zofia into loosening her grip, then wrestled with her golden curls, likely hoping to distract her.

Karol, on the other hand, seemed to have forgotten the scene we'd witnessed. He got up from the filthy floor and hurried to my father at the opposite edge of the cot.

"I want to play with my toy soldiers when we get home, Tata," he said.

"Will your soldiers defeat the Nazis?"

"They always do," Karol said with a grin. "Can we go home now?"

"Soon," Tata replied. "Soon." But he exchanged a glance with Mama, the same one they'd started giving each other when the Nazis invaded. The one filled with doubt.

I wondered how much they resented me. They didn't act like it, but they must have—if not for themselves, then for Zofia and Karol. My actions had gotten two innocent children sent to prison. We'd been held only a few days, but my parents' soft yet emphatic sighs, their futile comforts and encouragements, my sister's bored complaints and brother's hungry cries, all reminded me that I was responsible for our misery.

As Karol clambered onto Tata's lap, a new sound caught my attention. Footsteps.

My parents reached for each other—a small, simple gesture, but they made it as one. Moving at the same time, the same speed, perfectly in sync. Two halves of a whole. Their hands touched for a moment before they looked at me. I wished they hadn't, because upon seeing the look in their eyes I hugged my knees tighter.

Mama sent Zofia and Karol to the far side of the bed, as if the rusty metal frame could protect them, while Tata stood. When he put too much weight on his bad leg, he winced and pressed his palm against the wall to stabilize himself. It was all he could do without his cane. Silence filled the tiny space while the booted footsteps drew nearer, then our cell door creaked open and revealed two guards. One pointed at me, a gesture that made my heart plummet almost as much as the words that accompanied it.

"You, out."

All along, I'd told myself that, when the guards came for me, I'd obey to keep them from manhandling me. But suddenly I couldn't move.

Tata lunged. I wasn't sure how he managed to stay on his feet, but he did until a guard struck him and knocked him to the floor.

Mama held me to her chest, between herself and the wall, shielding me. "Don't touch her!" she shouted. Her shrieks reverberated in the small space and continued even when her head jerked back. Her arms tightened around me, but I glimpsed the guard holding her by the hair, and he wrenched us away from the wall and tugged me from her grasp.

I twisted and writhed—a gut instinct, though there was no point—while they hauled me out of the cell as if my struggles were a minor inconvenience, and then they slammed the door and clamped heavy cuffs around my wrists. My family's screams faded as they took me away. An ominous thought crept into my mind, and I wondered if I'd ever come back.

Thuds and clinks echoed alongside each footstep as we traveled down the long, cold hallways. Even my own breathing was loud. The air smelled like metal, blood, sweat, and God knew what else. If suffering had a smell, it would have smelled like this place.

When one guard opened a door, the other pushed me over the threshold. I emerged into a world awash in piercing light and stumbled blindly until another shove brought darkness back. Blinking, I found myself in a van, sitting on a low wooden bench along one side. A large black canvas hood stretched over the space, blocking my view of the outside, and the sudden pitch of the vehicle as it started to move almost threw me from my seat. The prisoners packed around me prevented me from losing my balance as the van rumbled through the streets of Warsaw.

The drive didn't take long. When a merciless grip pulled me

out, I stood before *Aleja Szucha* 25—the Gestapo headquarters on Szucha Avenue.

I squeezed my eyes shut, unable to bear the sunshine or the massive building with billowing Nazi flags, harsh red against gray stone. One guard said something about Polish swine and marching, so I followed the Pawiak inmates through the courtyard, inside, and downstairs, descending into damnation. Each step down the narrow, dingy gray halls took me deeper into the bowels of Szucha until we reached an empty cell. A guard grabbed me, sniggering when I shied away, but he removed my handcuffs and told me to file toward "the tram"—I assumed he meant the row of single wooden seats, one behind the other, facing the back wall.

The iron door clanged shut. The tiny space reeked of blood and urine, the smells of terror, so pungent I stifled a gag, and the wooden floor was slick with both.

I was the youngest prisoner.

I sat on a small, hard seat behind a woman whose left arm was swollen, bruised, and hanging at her side. Broken, probably. I stared at the back of her head, afraid to move, afraid to breathe.

From the corner of my eye—I didn't dare turn my head—I noticed something etched into the black paint beside me. Maybe a name. Maybe a heroic message about freedom or independence. Maybe nail marks from a prisoner as he was dragged away for another interrogation, a prisoner terrified that he'd break this time.

Another sound pierced the shallow breaths around me. I lifted my eyes to a small open window, where I heard fervent voices from upstairs. An interrogator's yelling, a prisoner's petrified murmur, then cracks, screams, and sobs. Listening to torture was almost worse than the thought of experiencing it.

One by one, the guards summoned prisoners from the cell. In a vain attempt to stay calm, I closed my eyes and took deep breaths.

In and out, slow and controlled. All it did was fill my nostrils with the tang of the blood and urine on the sticky floor and the stench of filthy, unwashed bodies. Every time another guard came to fetch a prisoner, my heart raced with renewed terror as I expected them to call my name.

But when I heard it, my racing heart came to an abrupt halt. "Maria Florkowska."

A rush of lightheadedness crashed over me. My body felt rooted to the tram, facing forward, always forward, and suddenly I would've given anything to stay seated for the rest of my life rather than go into an interrogation room. But I had to protect my family and the resistance. I sent up a quick prayer for strength and rose.

Upstairs, I sat at a rectangular table with my back to Hitler's portrait. Two guards stood nearby while I assessed my surroundings. Stationed behind a desk in the corner, an impassive woman rested her fingers on a typewriter keyboard. Otherwise the room was sparse—except the far wall, lined with whips, rubber truncheons, and other instruments of torture.

Under the table, I clasped my hands together in an effort to stop them from shaking.

The door opened to announce my interrogator's arrival. Sturmbannführer Ebner, the same man who had arrested us.

After the German invasion of 1939, when it had been safe to emerge from our apartment building's basement, I'd seen a dead horse splayed outside. Birds had torn into its carcass, stripping flesh, muscle, and sinew from bone, staining the ground red, leaving the mangled form to rot. As Ebner sat across from me, I took in his features, from his premature baldness to his aquiline nose, and I couldn't shake the image of those birds and that carcass.

"My name is Wolfgang Ebner." His voice was light, as if we were old friends getting reacquainted. "Yours is Maria Florkowska, isn't it?"

I hated the sound of my name coming out of his mouth, but I didn't confirm or deny it. When the typewriter dinged, I jumped and hoped Ebner didn't notice.

"Should I call you Helena Pilarczyk instead?"

The words held a faint trace of sarcasm, and a green identification card landed on the table. My false *Kennkarte*. He opened it to reveal the fabricated information and forged government stamps surrounding my photograph and signature. When I didn't speak, Ebner moved the Kennkarte aside.

"As I recall, you speak excellent German, but I can bring in an interpreter if you'd prefer to resolve this matter in your native tongue."

An interpreter would have lengthened the process, when all I wanted was for it to end. "I've been fluent my whole life," I replied. Somehow I managed to keep my voice level.

Ebner nodded and produced a pack of cigarettes. He lit one and took a slow, pensive drag, then released the gray smoke. As it filled the space between us, he offered the pack to me. When I didn't acknowledge it, he put it back in his pocket.

"All I need is the truth. If you cooperate, we'll get along just fine."

I almost heard Irena's voice in my head—*Dammit, Maria, how many times did I warn you about what those bastards will do to you?* My fellow resistance member had filled my mind with tales of Gestapo brutality, and her vivid descriptions washed away Ebner's false reassurance.

The typewriter let out another shrill ping while Ebner smoked and waited for me to say something. When my mouth stayed closed, his expression didn't change, but a gleam of annoyance flickered in his eyes. He blinked and chased it away.

"I presume you are aware of the penalty for aiding Jews," he said. And I *was* aware, of course, but was he really threatening such a minor member of the resistance with severe punishment, even death? He set a second document before me. "You delivered blank baptismal certificates for the Polish underground resistance?"

The proof was right in front of us, so there was no point in denying it. I nodded.

"How did you keep your work a secret from your family?"

"When you were a boy, did your parents know every time you disobeyed them?"

He chuckled. "No, I suppose they didn't."

My lie must have been far more convincing than it felt. If Ebner believed my parents had been unaware of my resistance work, surely I could convince him they hadn't been involved alongside me. Whatever it took to spare my family an interrogation.

Ebner dropped his cigarette stub onto the floor and ground it under his boot heel to extinguish the smoldering embers. He placed the certificate next to my Kennkarte and leaned closer, slow and calculated, eyes alight, prepared to ensnare his prey. Although I tried not to move, I gripped the edge of my seat.

"For whom are you working?"

His voice remained even, but all I heard was the unspoken threat behind the question. A selfish part of me tried to force its way to the surface, desperate to prevent what would come if I stayed quiet, but I pushed it back. I wouldn't let the Gestapo turn me into a traitor.

My fingers ached, unable to loosen their hold on my seat. Ebner retained the power to do anything to me. To my family. Sitting in the tram, I'd overheard how the Gestapo rewarded prisoners who didn't give the answers they sought. And my time was coming; I knew it was.

"My family lives in Berlin," Ebner said as he settled into his chair. "It's difficult being away from them."

This man was putting me, a girl, through Gestapo interrogation. Did he really think I'd believe he was sentimental?

"My wife, Brigitte, is a housewife. Hans is near your age, and he wants to become a lawyer. Anneliese is younger and says she'll get married and have beautiful Aryan babies, but first, she'll own a store which sells dolls, dresses, and chocolates." He flashed an amused smile.

Discovering he had children left me with a small ray of hope; in the next instant it faded. I knew better than to trust him. The tactic was a good one, I gave him that. But not good enough.

"If you answer my questions, I will arrange for your release. And your family's. Now, surely you can tell me who gave you your orders."

The bribe sounded so genuine. If I hadn't suspected that it was a bluff, he would have convinced me. Naturally I wanted my family released, but, even if I betrayed the resistance and confessed, somehow I didn't think Ebner would let us go.

When I didn't comply, he jerked his head in a nod, issuing a silent order. Before I could guess what it was, the guards lifted me as if I weighed nothing, and my chair clattered against the floor. They disregarded my struggles and tore off my skirt. Why were they taking off my clothing? It was happening too fast, much too fast. So fast that I had no time to resist.

Irena was right. They aren't taking pity on me because I'm young.

The guards stripped me of everything except undergarments—a small, unexpected blessing—and slammed my back against the wall. They searched my clothing first, then tossed it aside and discovered the small seams in my brassiere, betraying hidden pockets.

The pockets are empty. I wanted to scream the words, but I could scream them only inside my mind. *Don't search them, please don't search them.*

But I knew they would, and they did. They searched my entire body and probed the pockets thoroughly, relishing my flinches and struggles while Ebner watched in silence. After they groped me, I was too breathless to struggle. I glanced at the woman in the corner, praying she'd come to my aid, but she placed a fresh sheet of paper in the typewriter and paid me no mind. I shrank back, acutely aware of my near nakedness among these wicked people.

It's an intimidation tactic. Don't let them know it's working.

My breath came in shallow gasps, though I tried to steady it while Ebner skirted the table and fallen chair on his way toward me. He absorbed every centimeter of my small, exposed frame. As he approached, a tremor seized my body—whether from cold, terror, shame, or all three, I didn't know. Gone was his pretense of camaraderie. I was his enemy, not a child; just a resistance member who hadn't fallen for his wiles. Someone he would break.

He grasped my jaw and raised my head, yelling and spitting while his tobacco-laden breath filled my nostrils. He demanded to know whom I served, insisting that he'd uncover the truth if he had to pry every damn word out of my Polack mouth. Even if I'd been willing to answer, the tirade left my throat too dry for words, and when he released me he crossed to the far wall. The one with the torture instruments.

I twitched against my captors and prayed that the pathetic gesture would break their holds so I could flee from the hell I was about to endure.

It didn't, of course.

Ebner caressed the metal rod, the chains, the whip, and I dug my fingernails into my palms. At last he made his choice. A club. More merciful than the whip, I supposed, though I couldn't swallow the bile in my throat. When he reached me, I turned aside, but he caught my chin and made me face him. My unsteady breaths were the only sound until he touched the club to my temple, and worse than the solid weapon against my skin were the words that followed.

"Every prisoner pleads for death, but until I have answers, I don't grant it. Remember that when you beg me to shoot you."

Though Ebner's voice reached my ears, it was Irena's I heard.

By the time they're finished with you, you'll be begging them to put a bullet in your skull.

* * *

Two and a Half Months Earlier
Warsaw, 14 March 1941

The steady thump of Tata's cane against the cobblestone sidewalk broke the quiet hovering over the Mokotów district. The morning sun was reflected in the silver handle, worn smooth from daily use following Tata's service in the Great War. I drew a strange comfort from the shuffle of his limping gait and the rhythmic tap of his cane. His physical strength had been compromised, but his strength of character was the part of him that no injury could steal.

Ominous field-gray uniforms caught my eye—*Schutzstaffel*, the National Socialist Party's Protection Squadron, or SS. Across the street, two officers smoked cigarettes and carried on a conversation. When Mama noticed them, she looked over her shoulder at Tata. It was a look I'd caught them sharing ever since the invasion. Concern and doubt, interlaced in glances so fleeting they'd be easy to overlook if I hadn't grown accustomed to them. As we approached the end of our block, I rushed to Zofia's side, awaiting the inevitable. Sure enough, she stumbled and yelped. I laughed and caught her arm to steady her.

"You trip over those loose cobblestones every time, Zofia."

She cast a bitter glance at the stones scattered around us. "Someone needs to fix them."

In response, I pulled one of her golden curls, then released it so it sprang back into a tight coil. She giggled and waved me away. A hole lay beneath the cluster of cobblestones, but we kicked them back to re-cover it. Once the trap was laid for the next unsuspecting victim, Tata scooped up Karol, who stole the wide brimmed gray fedora from our father's head and placed it on his own.

"Zofia, Karol, have fun at Park Dreszera and listen to your father." Mama adjusted their coats before glancing at me. "Maria and I are picking up rations, so we'll see you at home."

As our mother kissed my siblings goodbye, Tata offered me a wink. He had shared many discreet winks with me these past few days, ever since I revealed that I was privy to his and Mama's secret. Since I had eavesdropped on their whispered conversations late at night while my siblings were sleeping; discovered anti-Nazi pamphlets distributed by the Polish resistance hidden in our apartment; found identifications naming my parents Antoni and Stanisława Pilarczyk, not Aleksander and Natalia Florkowski. Since I had asked to join the Polish underground alongside them, to help free my home from the invaders who persecuted Jews, non-Jewish Poles like my family, anyone who was not Aryan or defied the Third *Reich*.

Mama and I *were* picking up rations, it was true. But not until after my first day of resistance work.

"Do you want to play chess with me when we get home?" I asked Zofia, while Mama checked her handbag to ensure she'd brought the ration cards.

She made a disgusted face. "Chess is boring."

"That's because you won't let me teach you how to play." I attempted to tug a curl again, but she slapped my hand away and darted out of reach.

"I'll play chess with you, Maria. Zofia, you can set up Monopoly," Mama said. A few years before the war, my father had returned from a trip to Germany and surprised us with the game, an American import; ever since, it had been my sister's favorite.

We parted ways. As Mama and I sidestepped patches of snow and ice, we passed apartments and shops that had survived the bombings, but gaping holes indicated less fortunate buildings. Nazi propaganda contaminated every wall and storefront, and each bloodred poster featured a loathsome black swastika against a white circle. A street vendor offered Mama a brooch from his collection of trinkets, but she politely declined without slowing her pace.

Once inside a small gray apartment building in the Mokotów district, we discreetly followed a narrow hallway covered in cheerful yellow paint. Mama rushed to the last door on the right, knocked three times, waited, and knocked twice more. An unusual pattern, one I hadn't heard her use before. A short woman opened the door, and Mama shoved me inside.

Though I'd learned that Mrs. Sienkiewicz was a prominent resistance figure, it was difficult to grasp because I knew her as my mother's friend. She welcomed us with a beaming smile and fresh ersatz tea. I drank mine to be polite, though I wished the unpleasant mixture were real tea. I sat next to Mama on the sofa and studied a large portrait over the mantel. It depicted Mrs. Sienkiewicz and her late husband on their wedding day—she in a beautiful white lace dress, he in a decorated Polish army uniform.

"This is dangerous work, Maria, as I'm sure you understand," Mrs. Sienkiewicz said. "Until you're familiar with what we do, you'll have a companion at all times."

That was the last thing I'd expected to hear. Mama eyed me with disapproval, probably warning me not to look so sullen. At least the arrangement was temporary, and I supposed it would be beneficial to learn from someone. Once I'd proved myself, I could work alone. Mrs. Sienkiewicz disappeared to fetch my companion. She returned with her daughter.

Irena stepped into the room behind her mother and frowned at the sight of me. "Shit."

Not quite the reaction I was hoping for from a colleague, but not unexpected when that colleague was Irena.

Mrs. Sienkiewicz grabbed her daughter's forearm. "Language."

I couldn't pretend that I didn't share Irena's feelings; the idea of working with her didn't appeal to me, either. Irena had always acted as if our three-year age difference were three hundred, even prior to the war, when we'd sat through endless dinners with our parents. She listened while the adults expressed fears that war was brewing, discussed Nazi Germany's *Anschluss*, a plan to unify with Austria; I, eleven years old at the time, hated the thought of my father returning to military service, though he insisted it was impossible for him to fight. I had no reason to fear he would be sent away, where he might be injured again. Despite his reassurances, the incessant talk of increasing strife in Europe always prompted me to escape to my chessboard.

On that spring day in 1938, after the conversation about the

Anschluss, Irena had followed me into my family's living room, where my racing heart was already slowing as I plotted my opening strategy. "One day, when you're older, you'll understand there are more important things to worry about than that damn game," she said, leaving me no time to reply before returning to her place at the dining table.

Perhaps she mistook my focus on chess for indifference toward the risk her father and so many others would undertake should war come to Poland; still, I bristled at the way she had spat *when you're older*, as though youth were synonymous with ignorance. As for the so-called game, she had refused the few times I had offered to teach her how to play, yet I was the ignorant one?

But the same condescending glower she'd given me that day returned now.

"Maria is the new recruit?" Irena looked at her mother as if she'd been betrayed. "Mama, you said I'd be teaching a new member, not becoming a nanny."

I sipped my ersatz tea, but it was as bitter as the retort that rose in my throat. Keeping the words within the confines of my mind wasn't as satisfying, but I refused to wither beneath her scowl. "I'll learn quickly," I replied instead.

"Allow me to give you your first lesson." Irena sat on the coffee table in front of me and clapped both hands onto my knees. I recoiled, before making a conscious effort not to give her the satisfaction. She leaned closer until I could see a tiny gold crucifix around her neck and count each delicate link in its chain. "There's a special place in hell for resistance members who get caught. It's called Pawiak Prison. And if all secret policemen were devils, the Gestapo would be Satan himself. Those bastards won't take pity on you because you're young, and by the time they're finished with you, you'll be begging them to put a bullet in your skull—"

"Enough." Mrs. Sienkiewicz's cheeks looked as if they'd been painted with an entire pot of rouge. Before she could say more, Irena stood and marched into the kitchen.

A sudden chill swept over me after Irena's successful efforts to terrify me, and I resented her even more for it. I was well aware of the dangers I'd face. No need for the reminder.

Mrs. Sienkiewicz sighed. "Please forgive Irena's behavior, and her swearing. I've tried everything to make her stop, but since we joined this cause after her father . . ." Her voice faded, then she cleared her throat. "Maria, if Irena is inappropriate while you're working together, let me know and I'll talk to her."

Did she think I was stupid enough to tattle? I valued my life, thank you. "I'll keep that in mind," I said aloud.

"And don't worry, dear, she'll come around." The uncertainty in her tone didn't instill much confidence.

She joined Irena in the kitchen, and I concentrated on the muffled conversation carrying through the walls, on Irena's complaints that she'd be encumbered by me, a child.

Mama sat with her lips pressed together while I placed my teacup on the silver tray and ran a finger over the sofa's floral upholstery. Irena's disparaging gaze and caustic tongue would place me under constant scrutiny. She'd analyze me the way I analyzed a chessboard, seeking weaknesses to inhibit my opponent. I didn't intend to lose to her. As an established resistance member, she had the initial advantage, but she'd need more than that to overcome me.

After Mrs. Sienkiewicz coaxed Irena back into the living room, Mama embraced me, her grasp tight, breaths unsteady. I inhaled her familiar scent—geranium, her favorite flower. When she kissed the top of my head, the tautness in her body eased.

"Be careful," she whispered as she tucked a loose strand of hair behind my ear, probably to distract me from her glassy eyes.

Mrs. Sienkiewicz wrapped a comforting arm around Mama's shoulders and led her from the apartment, off to complete their own resistance errands. The door closed with a gentle click, and a tense silence hung in the room until Irena broke it.

"Don't expect a damn thing from me. The work comes first, not the people."

"Glad I can count on you, Irena."

"It's Marta, you idiot." She pulled her false work permit and Kennkarte from her handbag and waved them to emphasize her alias. We exchanged identification documents. "Helena Pilarczyk," she said, reading mine aloud. It was a good name. I liked it—not as much as I liked Maria Florkowska, but I liked it. Irena snatched her card, shoved mine into my hands, and left without waiting for me.

"What's our first errand?" I asked as I hurried to match her long strides.

"If I wanted you to ask questions, I would've said so."

A knot of anger tightened in my stomach, but I stayed silent. We walked past dilapidated bakeries and battle-scarred churches, bare parks and meager storefronts. Some fought for a semblance of their former splendor; others had given up. The crowd swelled as we moved toward the city center. I expected Irena to lead me to a streetcar so we could make the journey in half the time, but she didn't. She darted down the street and wove in and out among passersby; whether or not I kept up didn't seem to matter.

At last we turned on to Hoża Street, one of my favorites due to its multitude of trees, covered with green leaves and vibrant blooms during springtime. A few buds were cautiously starting to emerge, but maintaining Irena's pace didn't leave me time to admire them. I followed her toward a cluster of buildings, the provincial house of the Franciscan Sisters of the Family of Mary. Irena bypassed the black gate nestled within the redbrick wall, stopped before a small wooden door, and pressed the doorbell.

"Marta Naganowska is here to see Mother Matylda," she said.

The door opened to reveal a young sister clad in a black habit with a deep purple rope around her waist and a rosary at her hip. She led us into a cobblestone courtyard, flanked on three sides by the convent. A few trees were scattered amid the white stucco and rust-colored brick buildings, and in a large, circular flowerbed a white statue of Saint Joseph holding the Child Jesus surveyed the lush space. It was quiet and tranquil, a retreat nestled within the city. We went into a small room. There, seated at a square wooden table and engaged in a fervent telephone call, was Mother Matylda.

The elderly mother provincial didn't look up when we entered. "You're certain you'll accept God's blessing?" She adjusted the large black crucifix around her neck, then ran a finger over the three round buds that adorned each arm. After a moment she closed her eyes, and her shoulders heaved with a small sigh. "I'm so glad, my friend."

While Irena toyed with her own crucifix, I noticed a small notebook on the table. It covered a cluster of documents, but one was askew. I moved toward the bookshelf beside her, as if examining titles by various saints and theologians. I flipped through a worn copy of Augustine's *Confessions* and peeked at the paper. A baptismal certificate, partially completed with personal information. Intrigued, I stepped closer, but a sharp cough almost made me drop the book. I hugged it to my chest and whirled to find Irena pointing to the vacant space beside her. I narrowed my eyes, but returned the book and joined her.

At last Mother Matylda hung up the telephone, scribbled in her notebook, and gave Irena a bright smile. "Marta, how wonderful to see you. And you've brought a friend."

Irena didn't seem fond of Mother Matylda's use of the word *friend*, but she didn't dispute it. Instead she waved a dismissive hand in my direction. "Helena." She reached into her blouse, produced a slip of paper from her brassiere, and handed it over. "I have a prayer request, Reverend Mother. My mother is sick."

Mother Matylda accepted the small paper. "May God grant her health and a long life," she murmured as she unfolded the paper and placed it on the table. I strained my eyes to glimpse its contents. In Mrs. Sienkiewicz's elegant script was a list of names, and one stood out to me. Stanisława Pilarczyk, my mother's alias.

The paper stayed on my mind as we returned to the Sienkiewiczes' apartment. Irena tossed her coat over the back of an armchair and dropped into it, paying me no heed. My feet felt three sizes too big for my shoes, so I curled my toes to alleviate the throbbing. We must have walked eight kilometers. I wasn't sure why she was opposed to streetcars.

"You keep messages in your bra?" I asked at last.

Irena studied her nails. "All resistance girls have padded bras with pockets in them."

"And that's your method for smuggling information to religious sisters?"

"I'm taking advantage of the gifts God gave me." Irena looked up long enough to smirk at me. "You should get a bra like that, you know. Does that bother you? Because if you're too prudish to hide information wherever necessary, you might as well quit now." She chuckled as she kicked off her oxfords and tucked her feet under her in the chair.

I'm glad you find yourself so amusing, I thought, though I didn't voice the words aloud. Instead I moved closer to her chair, but she got up and crossed toward the mantel. "You gave Mother Matylda a coded message, didn't you?"

"Figure it out, if you're so damn smart."

"You're supposed to be teaching me, and you're doing a terrible job."

"I *am* teaching you. I told you about the bra you'll need to wear, and I'm telling you to figure out the message for yourself."

With a huff, I paced around the room and settled beside the writing desk in the corner. A thin film of dust covered the typewriter, as if it hadn't been used in a few days, and a paperweight rested atop a stack of papers. I picked up a pencil and tapped a finger against its dull point. Rather than running errands with a helpful resistance member, I would be carrying out mine in Irena's difficult company.

"Irena." When she heard her real name, she glared and returned to her chair, and I enjoyed my small victory before continuing. "Tell me why Mother Matylda was creating baptismal certificates and why my mother's alias was on that paper."

"Good Lord," she muttered, but she shooed me into the chair across from hers. "How the hell do you expect the sisters to disguise Jewish children without certificates? They have to prepare the documents so resistance members can smuggle children from the ghetto."

"Mama is taking a child to the sisters?"

"Tomorrow, which is what I indicated by saying my mother was sick. The child will be taken to a Catholic family or one of the sisters' orphanages outside Warsaw. When Mother Matylda asks someone if they'll accept God's blessing, she's asking if they'll care for the Jewish child. As for you, you'll go with me to deliver messages and funds, but you won't touch confidential information until you're deemed worthy—if that day ever comes."

The words stung, though I shouldn't have let them. Despite her proclivity for reminding me of my inferiority, every scathing remark fueled my determination to prove myself.

"At the start of the war, you were only fifteen when you joined early resistance activities," I reminded her.

"Yes, but I had been staying informed, not hiding behind a chessboard. One more thing." Irena leaned closer to me and dropped her voice. "All resistance members risk their lives, but I don't intend to lose mine for anyone. You'll do what I tell you, and if you cross me or jeopardize me, I will make your life hell. Am I clear?"

More threats. Unlike her story about what the Gestapo did to resistance members sent to Pawiak, this warning didn't scare me.

My favorite chess piece was the pawn. A strange choice, perhaps, because pawns weren't the most important, but, when one reached the opposite end of the board, it had the unique ability to transform into a more powerful piece. Suddenly a meager pawn shifted the entire balance.

In this game, I was a pawn, and every moment with Irena taught me more about how to shift the balance. I moved to the edge of my chair and clapped my hands upon her knees, mirroring her actions of the morning. Her pleased smirk disappeared, but she didn't blink when I tightened my grip and flashed the sweetest smile I could muster.

"Clear as can be."

Her jaw remained set, but the look in her eyes was satisfying enough, as if we were in the midst of a chess game and my play had dashed her intended strategy. Soon, she would realize I was no longer the little girl who shied away from the war, and that every moment I had spent playing chess had taught me how to strategize and outwit the opponents I would face in this work.

Before she could respond, a key turned in the door, announcing Mama and Mrs. Sienkiewicz's return.

Irena got up. "Until next time, Helena."

"Resistance work is over." I stood and lifted my chin. "It's Maria."

* * *

Warsaw, 27 May 1941

As I curled onto the floor in the interrogation room, I wondered how long Ebner would leave me this time before he started again. My forehead was damp with sweat, my face streaked with remnants of salty tears, and my shaking hands wiped away evidence of both as best I could. The acrid taste of vomit lingered in my mouth.

He could hear *I don't know* and *believe me* and *please* only so many times before he tired of me. And then what?

When the guards picked me up, I tensed, but they returned me to my chair. I slumped against the table, grateful for the respite, and the typewriter dinged again. *Click, click, ding!* Over and over while the woman responsible did nothing but transcribe. Mouth closed, face blank, empty of either detestation or compassion. Even through a particularly aggressive series of blows, when I'd made eye contact with her and screamed for help, she'd ignored me.

Ebner sat across from me, and his bloodshot eyes held no sympathy, no regret, just anger and frustration. His cheeks were ruddy, sleeves pushed up, hair disheveled, upper lip and hairline beaded with sweat. Hours of threatening and beating a child took their toll.

During my interrogation, I'd kept my resistance knowledge in a refuge deep within the recesses of my mind. Now I was tired, so tired, and desperate for a glass of water. When Ebner's chair creaked, I prayed it was over, but the sinister gleam in his eyes said otherwise.

"Fetch the family," he said to the guards. "Maybe they can help us jog the girl's memory. Start with the boy."

He's bluffing; please, God, let him be bluffing. They wouldn't torture a four-year-old. But I'd witnessed firsthand what they could do, and I knew they would.

"Wait, please wait!"

At my cry, Ebner slammed both hands on the table so hard it made me recoil. "You think you're so fucking brave, sitting here like a damn mute?" He was beside me in an instant, and he grabbed my hair and forced my head back. Needles of agony sliced across my scalp, and his enraged face hovered centimeters from mine. "Start talking, you little Polack bitch, or I'll cuff your ass to this chair and you'll watch while your entire family pays for your silence."

My family was his checkmate against me. The last move I had was to confess to something, anything, to keep him from playing it.

"Messages." It was all I managed before my voice caught. When Ebner returned to his seat, my lie came out in a frantic tumble. "I got messages from the resistance. I don't know who wrote them, they weren't signed—"

He leaned closer, and I shrank away and hugged my bare midsection, foolishly believing the gesture would protect me. "What did they say?" he asked.

"They told me where to pick up or leave the documents, and once I had a message asking for the information they needed to make my false papers, but that's all." I paused to catch my breath, and Ebner stood. I should've watched what he was doing, but I was too shaken, too worried about forgetting the story I'd crafted or letting the truth slip—

Something rattled and clanked when it hit the table; at once, I drew back. Handcuffs.

Dear God, my plan isn't good enough.

Either Ebner was about to shackle me and send the guards for my family, or he'd placed the cuffs there to scare me; I didn't know. All I knew was that failure was not an option; betrayal was not an option. I had to stay in control; I had to convince him.

"Who recruited you?"

I fought past the sobs constricting my throat and forced my response out. "A message was lying in the street and I picked it up to see what it was. Someone must have dropped it, so I left a note in the location mentioned, and I told them how to reach me so I could help."

Ebner grabbed my bruised shoulders, and a strange, gasping sound emerged from my throat while he gave me a swift shake. "Who told you what to do? Give me a fucking name."

"I can't. The signature indicated it was from the resistance, but it didn't include names."

"Where did you take your documents?"

"To the cobblestones, loose cobblestones at the end of our block. I hid the certificates under them, and that's where I picked up messages."

When his lips curled into a cynical sneer, a fresh onslaught of emotion hit me, as merciless and painful as his club.

"It's the truth, I swear to God—"

A sudden blow to the cheek halted my cries and reopened the cut on my lip. As the fog around my mind lifted, he drew me closer. "Stop sniveling. And if one damn word was a lie . . ."

I shook my head in vehement refusal, but all I managed was one more desperate sob. "Please let me and my family go home." I choked on more tears and didn't bother trying to speak further. Ebner released me, and I drew my bare feet onto my chair.

Silence stretched across the room, broken by the typewriter's taps and the debilitating sobs I couldn't control. Bawling like an inconsolable child, I pressed my forehead against my knees, trying to obey his command to quiet my weeping. He lit a cigarette and took a long puff, and the horrible smoke invaded my nostrils.

"Well, I'm glad you decided to cooperate, Maria. It's a shame it took so long."

All this time, I'd convinced myself Ebner wouldn't release us, but now I'd given him a confession. Maybe there was mercy somewhere within this wicked man. I blinked away my tears and met his unsympathetic gaze while he brought the cigarette to his lips.

"I answered your questions, Herr Sturmbannführer." The voice that came from my mouth was shaky and raw, unrecognizable as my own. "Will you send me and my family home?"

Ebner placed his cigarettes and matches on the table. "I said I'd release you if you cooperated, didn't I?" he asked, so I nodded. Then he dipped his head toward the guards.

One grabbed my right arm, keeping me restrained, and stretched my left forearm out on the table. It happened so quickly that I didn't have time to struggle before Ebner's lit cigarette met my skin. Searing pain ripped a scream from my throat, but he applied more pressure before tossing it away and accepting another, which the second guard had already ignited.

"Let this be a lesson to you, Maria." He pressed the second cigarette below the first mark and raised his voice above my cry. "You spent hours being disobedient, proving you had no regard for my generous offer." He took a third cigarette while I writhed, but the guard held me in place, and Ebner continued the line of burns down my forearm. "Once you started behaving, it was too late. Our deal was already off." As the fourth cigarette met my skin, I heard the guard striking another match, which made me shriek almost as much as the pain did. "You could have accepted my offer and gotten yourself and your family released, but you didn't." The fifth cigarette pulled a gasping sob from my lips, and Ebner lifted his eyes to mine. "You stupid girl."

He brought the cigarette to his mouth, then the guard released me.

Five burns, five red and white circles of angry, melted flesh in a perfect line along my forearm. One for each person in my family, including myself.

As I cradled my damaged arm against my chest, the smell of my own burned flesh mingled with the stench of cigarette smoke. My stomach jolted. Yellow bile clawed up my throat and splattered against the floor.

A guard tossed something toward me, and I flinched, but the soft thump of fabric against wood announced the return of my blessed clothing. I snatched them and dressed as quickly as my aching body would allow. The buttons had popped off my shirtwaist when the guards ripped it away, but my sweater covered the ruined garment. Once dressed, I didn't have time to wipe blood or moisture from my face before rough hands closed over my arms.

As I stumbled back to the tram, my burns throbbed. If I'd cooperated right away, my family and I could have gone home

No, I couldn't fall for Ebner's lies. He was never going to send us home. My family was a tactic in this vicious game. His best one.

Once we returned to Pawiak, the guards took me inside. In an odd way, I was grateful for their firm grips. The pain had subsided into a dull ache, but I didn't have the strength to drag my battered body down the hall. I had to compose myself before we reached the cell.

I was questioned, that's all. Just questioned.

While I concentrated on placing one foot in front of the other, I offered a silent prayer of thanks that Ebner hadn't broken any bones and the signs of my interrogation were beneath my clothing.

Before the war, I thanked God for things like my family, friends, and sunshine, but if something affected those blessings, I lamented my misfortune. I had the audacity to ask God why He let rain chase away my sunshine, as if a thunderstorm were the worst thing that could happen to a girl. But far worse things could happen to a girl: getting her entire family arrested, being interrogated by the Gestapo, having no power to prevent whatever lay ahead. All I had was rain, and I didn't know if the sunshine would ever return. So I'd find blessings amid the thunder and lightning.

When our cell came into view, I saw my family waiting in tense silence while Mama paced back and forth. She'd probably been pacing since I'd left. The sour stench of sweat, urine, and vomit surrounded me and mingled with the tang of blood and smoke. The smells of Szucha. I couldn't mask them, but I wouldn't give away anything else.

Karol was the first to notice me, and his face lit up. "Maria is back."

The guards shoved me inside. When I landed on the floor, Mama was beside me in a heartbeat before she lunged at the guards with a bloodcurdling shriek. "Bastards!"

It was wishful thinking, believing I could convince my parents that I'd been merely questioned.

Once we went to the Warsaw Zoo and watched the zookeeper feed the lions. As the man approached the enclosure, one lion sprang at him through the bars. If not for those bars, I was certain the zookeeper would have been dead.

Mama's blond hair had been pinned into its usual elegant updo, but that had been destroyed in the scuffle accompanying our arrest. Her hair now cascaded in unruly waves around her face, framing wild eyes and lips curled into a snarl, and she reminded me of that lion. She reached for the guards' throats and probably would have torn them out, but they slammed the door. She grabbed the bars, demanding the cowards come back and face her, but their footsteps faded as they disappeared down the hall.

Tata clutched the bars for a moment, then approached Mama, but she shoved him away, sank to her knees, and pressed her forehead against the door.

Mama never swore—not when she knew we were listening—and Zofia's eyes widened.

"What happened, Maria?" she asked, her voice tremulous. "Where have you been?"

If I lay motionless much longer, I didn't think I'd ever move again. "Private questioning," I murmured, though I didn't look at her as I sat up. "Mama's upset because they pushed me."

Maybe Zofia believed me. Or maybe she wondered if the outburst wasn't as unwarranted as I'd made it appear.

"What's wrong with you?"

Though I'd suspected she'd ask that question, it still wasn't easy to hear. "I'm tired," I said as Mama returned to my side, but a tremor slipped into my voice.

"But you—"

Mama lifted her head toward my sister. "Zofia Florkowska, not another word."

Zofia took a startled step back, bit her quivering bottom lip, and retreated to the small bed. Tata sat beside her and kissed her cheek. He glanced at Mama, who opened her mouth, but before she could speak, Karol hurried to her side. He was gnawing on his shirt collar, a habit that indicated he was deep in thought, though he knew better than to chew on his clothing.

"What's a bastard?"

"That's not a polite word, Karol," Tata said.

"Then why did Mama say it?"

"I'm sorry, darling, but they—" Mama's voice caught. "They pushed your sister."

"That wasn't nice of them," Karol said, then he darted toward the roach he'd been watching before Mama's expletive distracted him. He followed it as it scuttled into the corner.

Tata brushed a tear from Zofia's face. "Will you keep an eye on your brother?"

While she joined Karol, Tata sat on the floor beside me and Mama. We rested our backs against the wall, which placed pressure on my bruises, but I was too tired to mind. I rubbed a thin crust of dried blood from my hand. Maybe my parents hadn't noticed it.

"Darling, please," Mama whispered, but they could infer enough as it was.

I blinked through tears as Tata placed a gentle hand over mine. "When they threatened to bring the rest of you in there, I gave them false information."

My parents were silent. Mama kissed a tear from my cheek, then rushed to the door and stood with her back to us. Both hands ran through her hair and clutched it until her knuckles turned white. Her shoulders heaved, then she crossed the room and guided Zofia into her lap.

As I wiped a final stray tear, Tata placed something in my palm. It was a small piece of his bread ration mixed with a bit of mud, and shaped to resemble a tiny chess piece—a pawn, half the size of my smallest finger. I closed my hand around it, intertwined my arm with his, and gave him a grateful squeeze. I rested my head on his shoulder and surrendered to exhaustion, and I was almost asleep when his familiar whisper reached my ears.

"You are strong and brave, my Maria."

Even though I was slipping deeper into slumber, I still heard the quiver in his voice.

 Chapter 3

Warsaw, 28 May 1941

WHEN I WOKE, hushed voices greeted my ears. Mama and Tata were in the middle of a fervent conversation, so I did one of the things I did best—feigned slumber and eavesdropped.

"This cell is filthy, they hardly feed us, I snapped at poor Zofia, I taught Karol to curse, and Maria . . ." Mama fell silent before continuing. "We have to tell the Gestapo what we know."

"We're not going to be traitors, Natalia."

"What choice do we have? How else can we protect our children?"

"If we admit the truth, they'll realize Maria lied, and they'll punish her. Either way, they won't release us, but since she confessed, those bastards have no reason to question her again."

"*Question* her." She repeated the words in a sharp hiss. "They didn't *question* her. Dear God, Aleksander, they tortured her." A muffled sob followed her words, and I imagined Tata pulling her into his arms. I heard him kiss her, probably on the top of her head, because that's where he always kissed her when she was upset. Their heavy breaths were all I heard until Mama spoke in a small, sad whisper.

"I want to kill them."

"So do I, Nati."

The nickname tended to calm her, but I thought Tata knew it wouldn't work this time.

He told Mama they had only a couple of hours before the guards would come to wake us, so they should sleep while they could. After a while, their breaths grew rhythmic and steady. I sat up. My parents reclined against the far wall, and Karol and Zofia were nestled on the bed. I watched them until Zofia stirred. She glanced my way, as if she didn't know what to make of me anymore, then she sat on the floor near the bed and twirled her hair around her finger.

Though it hurt to move, I crawled closer until I was next to her, but she focused on a hole in her pale blue dress. "Zofia, if you'd known I was working for the resistance—"

"I wouldn't have told anyone."

"I hated keeping it from you, but if you'd known and they'd found out . . ." My voice died, and the hostility in her eyes softened.

"They would have questioned me, too. And when they questioned you, something bad happened."

I nodded, and she didn't pry further. For so long, I'd wanted nothing more than to be honest with her, even though lying meant keeping her safe. Now I had the honesty I wanted, but suddenly I wished we could stay hidden behind the deception. When protected by a wall of lies, it was easier to pretend the truth wasn't lurking on the other side. Now the wall was down and the truth exposed. I couldn't protect my sister from it any longer.

I gave one of her curls a light tug, the gesture that usually

made her giggle and slap my hand away. This time, Zofia intertwined her arm with mine and rested her head on my shoulder.

* * *

With nothing for us to do but sit in a cell, the day crawled by,
leaving me copious amounts of time to think. I sat in my corner,
terrified Ebner would realize I'd fabricated my confession.

Movement angered my bruises, so I tried not to shift. I wondered what Irena had done when I missed the errand I should've
run with her yesterday. It wasn't like me to be late, much less miss
resistance work. She'd probably stopped by our apartment and
discovered everyone gone. When an entire family went missing,
the conclusion was clear.

Dammit, Maria.

From the corner of my eye, I noticed Mama turning toward me,
but I didn't acknowledge her. I couldn't bear to look at my parents.
Tata's hair was haphazard, his brown tweed suit disheveled, his
chin stubbled. Mama's high cheekbones had lost their rosy glow,
her black shirtwaist dress was wrinkled, and small runs traveled
down each nylon stocking and disappeared into low slingback
heels. But it wasn't their appearances that shattered me. It was
their eyes. They reflected a sadness that had never been there before. It wasn't hopelessness, not yet, but close. And in my parents,
that scared me most of all.

Footsteps echoed down the silent hall, and I scrambled to my feet
when our cell door swung open, revealing Ebner and four guards.

*Oh, God, he knows I lied, and now he'll torture my family to
make me tell the truth.*

I wrapped my arms around my midsection as if I were back in
the interrogation room, stripped to almost nothing, his eyes all

over me. The tobacco smoke drifted from his breath and enveloped me . . .

I blinked and noticed I'd gathered my sweater in my hands, as if my grip could keep it from leaving my body. I loosened my hold, then moved closer to Zofia and Karol. An empty promise rose in my throat, a promise that I'd keep my siblings safe. Maybe I should have voiced it, empty or not, but I couldn't bear to lie anymore. Instead I stayed silent and wrapped my arms around them. It felt like less of a lie that way.

"Take the prisoners to transport," Ebner said.

That's not what the guards had said before taking me to interrogation, and for that reason alone I was relieved. We shuffled out of the cell. My parents tried to stand tall, but their shoulders slumped, depleted, and Tata leaned on Mama while she staggered beneath his weight. The guards didn't help or provide him with a cane   not that I expected otherwise. I brought up the rear, and my siblings stayed between us. Outside, guards ushered prisoners into large trucks that roared with life, swallowed inmates whole, and belched hot, black smoke from their tailpipes.

We climbed into the belly of our designated beast, and I imagined five chess pieces being captured, one by one.

Benches ran along either side, similar to the vehicle that had taken me to Szucha. We found a few remaining seats while more prisoners filled the empty space in the center, then the truck began to move.

"Are we going home?" Karol asked from his perch on Mama's lap.

She straightened his suspenders and kissed his cheek. "Not yet, my love."

"Where are we going?"

"You'll see when we get there."

In silence, I listened to the truck rattle down the cobblestone streets. When it stopped, we'd reached the railway station, where a train waited. Mama and Tata gave each other the look, the one full of concern. This time, something else joined it.

Hopelessness.

I clutched Tata's arm and held tight to the tiny pawn he'd made me. Pawiak prisoners surrounded us, so many that it was difficult to move, more difficult to breathe. Impatient soldiers herded us into empty railcars with boarded windows while prisoners elbowed me, stepped on my toes, and crushed me until I fought for air. Surely they didn't intend to fit so many into one small space.

But they did. More Pawiak prisoners filed into the railcar and tramped across the lime-covered floor. After squeezing between my parents, I noticed two buckets in the corner. One was full of water, the other was empty. A waste bucket. At the sight, I cringed and resolved not to use it, no matter how long we were trapped. Even Pawiak was more civilized—we'd had designated times to relieve ourselves.

When the doors slammed, I wanted to throw myself against them and break free so I could stay in Warsaw, go back to our cozy apartment on Bałuckiego Street in the Mokotów district, and be a successful resistance member again. I would have chosen even Pawiak over boarding the train. But the train wailed and screeched in protest as it began hauling its monstrous form down the tracks, reminding me that I didn't have a choice.

* * *

Three Months Earlier
Warsaw, 15 March 1941

Someday, someone other than Vera Menchik would win the Women's World Chess Championship; if I were going to be the second female world champion, I had to practice. After dedicating my day to chess, I finished my final game in the evening, when my siblings were asleep; then a few raps on the door announced Irena's arrival.

As Tata welcomed her into the living room, Mama brewed ersatz tea and set the teapot, cups, and saucers on the coffee table. The crisp white porcelain reflected the lamplight while the gold trim glinted beneath its warm glow. Tata was the only one who poured a cup.

Irena sat on the sofa, keeping distance between us. I ran my fingers over the intricate mahogany arms, fluffed a cobalt velvet cushion, and picked up a black knight from my chessboard, all in an effort to distract myself from the stifling tension. At last Tata set his untouched teacup down and cleared his throat.

"Irena, have you learned how to play chess yet?"

"No."

More silence. I put the knight back and selected a white bishop.

He made a second attempt. "You've been doing this a long time, haven't you, Irena? Do you have any good stories? A memorable errand, or a close call with a Nazi, perhaps?"

She considered the query. "Once, a soldier caught me during curfew, so I pretended he'd stopped me on my way home from work. I proved it with my fake permit and gave the bastard hell until he let me go."

Tata fought to control an amused grin. "An impressive escape," he said, then he turned to Mama. "Don't you agree, Natalia?"

She sat with one leg crossed over the other, arms folded. When he prompted her, she closed her eyes, pinched the bridge of her nose, and sighed.

After I spent a few more minutes fiddling with my chess pieces, the clock chimed eleven times. I peered out the window and watched as trucks equipped with loudspeakers rattled down the street, announcing that curfew was in effect. I'd never broken curfew before. Such blatant rebellion sent tingles across my skin, but Irena's critical voice crept into my head. I silenced it. Distractions hindered me in chess, and they would hinder me within the resistance. When mistakes were made, that's how the game was lost.

Irena got up and gave my parents a tight-lipped smile in farewell before letting herself out. By the time I followed, she was halfway down the stairs.

"Slow down," I said as I jogged to catch up.

"Talk louder, why don't you? The Germans in Hamburg only heard part of that."

I refused to dignify the snide remark with a reply. Irena kept to the shadows, making it even more difficult to follow her. She darted down a side street, unnoticed by me until I'd walked five steps in the wrong direction. I altered my course.

"Are we dropping something off?" I asked when I reached her again.

"Do you realize how annoying you are?"

"I'm trying to learn."

"Fine, if you want a damn lesson so much, here it is: You're annoying."

Without waiting for my reply, Irena made another turn. Every movement was stealthy and sharp, but she remained light on her feet, blending in with the night. She was concentrated and purposeful, and, if she weren't so irritating, I'd almost have been impressed.

"For a teacher's daughter, you're not very good at teaching," I said after a moment.

"Thank God. Teaching is Mama's passion, not mine. I'm more like my father."

"Did he curse as much as you do?" I stole a sly glance at her; instead of the eye roll I anticipated, Irena chuckled.

"Always, assuming Mama wasn't around."

A faraway look crossed her face as she adjusted the chain on her necklace. She'd spoken with some degree of civility. Clearly that was unintentional, because she put on another burst of speed and darted down the next street.

I dodged a patch of icy snow. "You know, I'm more likely to be spotted if you keep making me run after you, and you can't look out for me if you're ignoring me." I gave her a triumphant grin. "Checkmate."

"What did you say?"

"Checkmate. It's how you end a chess game. The king is the most important piece, and when you place your opponent's king in checkmate, the king is threatened with capture no matter which way he moves. Your opponent has no way to avoid the checkmate, so they lose. A check, on the other hand, means the king can avoid capture by—"

"I stopped listening two hours ago."

With an exasperated sigh, I tucked a loose strand of hair behind my ear. "Never mind. The point is, you have to let me keep up." I darted in front of her, forcing her to halt. "I win."

Irena scoffed. "Shut up, Helena. We have a long night ahead, and if you keep bitching, I'm going to leave you. Now, move your ass out of my way, or should I move it for you?"

I indicated the empty street with a flourish. "Lead the way, Marta."

She pushed past me, moving as briskly as before.

It was strange, walking around Warsaw when the city was so quiet. Bright, colorful squares were empty, lush parks inhabited only by nighttime creatures, storefronts dark and unwelcoming. I was used to bustling crowds, rumbling traffic, the clatter of horse-drawn carriages, cries of street vendors—and soldiers' barks and the thuds of their shiny boots. When the Poles who loved this city were confined to their homes, even the rustle of clothing sounded as loud as the roar of bombers flying low over the ground.

While my thoughts wandered, my pace slowed, but Irena's hadn't. As I scanned the dark street, a shadowy figure rounded the corner ahead. I pulled my coarse wool coat around myself to ward off a chilly breeze, then started jogging, treading lightly to silence the thud of my footfalls. Once I turned the corner where Irena had disappeared, I froze.

Down the block, an SS man detained her while another tossed items from her handbag.

At once, I pressed against the rough stucco building beside me and melted into the shadows, but a combination of curiosity and concern took over. I peered around the corner and listened as the empty street carried their voices to me.

"I told you, I'm going home from work. Get the hell off me and give me that." Irena attempted to wrestle one arm free, but the man holding her twisted it further behind her back. She stifled a cry, spitting a curse through gritted teeth.

The seconds crawled by while the soldier rifled through her belongings. I waited for him to produce her falsified employment papers to reinforce her lie. To let her go.

But when he turned the handbag over and dumped out its remaining contents, he made one single, horrible announcement. "No work permit."

Irena stiffened. "You're wrong, it's . . . I . . ." she stammered, voice weaker than before. She started again, this time faster and with more force. "I must have left it there. For the last time, let go of me!"

This was bad, really bad. Irena was giving them hell, as she put it, but it wasn't working like it had in the story she'd told my parents. I had a terrible feeling no amount of struggling or swearing would work on these soldiers. Over the course of our time together, she had never made a mistake, but, if she had forgotten to carry her work permit, she didn't have permission to be out this late.

The SS man dropped her handbag on the ground. "Last chance."

Although Irena scowled, disdain failed to mask the fear lacing her words. "I'm going home."

"Well, you can't work without your lost permit. We'll escort you to your place of employment so you can retrieve it, and your employer can verify your story. But if you'd rather tell the truth and admit you've broken the law, I might tell the Gestapo to go easier on you."

Irena's feeble twitches ceased, then she strained against her captor while her chest heaved faster, faster. He kicked her behind the knees, suppressing her rebellion, and when her knees hit the ground the other soldier stepped closer. She flinched and turned aside before he captured her jaw and twisted her head up.

I retreated deeper into my hiding place. Home, I needed to go home. Irena told me to put the resistance work first, not the members, so I wasn't obligated to intervene. I had to leave.

But I didn't. I had a plan.

Gathering my courage, I stepped around the corner and let out a startled cry. "Marta?"

The soldier released Irena's face and whirled toward the sound of my voice while I rushed down the street toward them. When he drew his gun, I skidded to a halt. For a fleeting moment, I regretted everything I'd just done, but, if I could focus, this could work. It had to work.

I'm just a child. A silly girl who has been wandering aimlessly, alone and scared. Not a resistance member acutely aware of the gun pointed at her.

I turned to the man holding Irena, who remained on her knees. "Please stop, that's my cousin. I'm sorry, Marta, I didn't mean to—"

"What are you doing out after curfew?" the soldier with the gun asked. The weapon remained steady in his hand, but his eyes flickered to it. The brief gesture led me to believe my age had taken him by surprise. He was pointing his gun at a girl.

"I didn't mean to be out this long. I was visiting a friend, and I left her apartment before curfew, honest I did, but I got lost going home. When I didn't come back on time, I knew my parents would ask my cousin to find me." I indicated Irena with a nod, though she looked as if she'd shoot me herself if I didn't shut up. "Please don't hurt her. She was trying to help me."

The soldier turned to Irena. "If she's telling the truth, why did you lie?"

Irena took a moment to pull her eyes away from the gun. All I needed her to do was corroborate my story. A tense silence hovered in the air as I waited for her to speak.

Please, Irena, make him believe the story.

"Of course she's telling the truth, but I didn't think you'd believe I broke the law just to look for her. Once I take this idiot back to my aunt and uncle's, I will make damn sure this never happens again." She directed a dark look my way. The threat wasn't for the soldier's benefit.

I took a cautious step closer. "I'm sorry, I really am. Please don't arrest us."

The soldier's eyes shifted from me to Irena. When he moved in front of her, she drew back until he pressed his pistol barrel beneath her chin, and she froze while everything in me stopped.

He watched her fluttering chest, then whirled and grabbed my shoulders. I gasped, expecting the blow or handcuffs or bullet that would follow.

"Next time, you won't get a second chance."

The menacing growl left me unable to give more than a tiny nod. He released me while his companion shoved Irena out of his grasp. With a sharp breath, she caught herself on her hands and knees. The soldiers marched away, and I watched them go until trembling hands latched on to my arm and dragged me down the street, ignoring my stumbling efforts to keep up. Irena's fury would be next, the anticipation of a reprimand like that of bombs before they are dropped. The distant rumble of an airplane. The piercing whistle as the projectile cut through the sky. Those were the only warnings before the world erupted.

When we rounded the next corner, she pulled me down the nearest alley and transferred her ironlike grip to my shoulders. "What the hell was that, Maria? Why didn't you go home?"

I took in the frenzied haze in her eyes, her disheveled clothes and bloodied knees, and finally managed to find my voice around my dry throat. "I couldn't let them arrest you."

She released me, shaking her head. "I'm not going to thank you for being a fucking idiot. Your concerns should be keeping the work safe and staying alive, and if you don't get that through your thick head and learn to fend for yourself—"

"Yes, fending for yourself worked so well for you a moment ago," I replied, glaring at her. "The Gestapo would have interrogated you."

"That's not your concern. You would've been free to continue working."

"But since I intervened, we're both free."

"And the next time you do that, we both might be arrested."

"Or we both could be free again."

"Dammit, Maria, you can't even recognize your own incompetence." Rigid with tension, Irena turned and took a few steps away.

Somehow those words struck something within me, something she'd never touched so deeply before. "Is that what you think? That I'm incompetent for helping instead of leaving?" I asked as loudly as I dared. "Well, do you want to know what I think? You say self-preservation is what's best for the resistance, but that's your excuse. Self-preservation is what's best for *you*, because you don't care about anyone but yourself."

Irena stiffened even more. Silence surrounded us, thick and suffocating, smoke after an explosion. Chaos one moment, stillness the next.

To steady the fury pumping through my veins, I inhaled the cool night air, pretending it smelled crisp and clean, not like the garbage and mildew in this filthy alley. At last Irena closed the distance between us until her tall, thin frame loomed over me. I stood my ground, but, when she spoke, her voice was sharper than the frigid gusts tearing across my skin.

"If you ever try another fucking intervention, we're finished. And if I hear another damn word out of your mouth tonight, you'll wish you'd left me with those soldiers."

She didn't wait for a reply—I wasn't supposed to say another damn word anyway—and instead walked toward the street. I stayed where I was, watching her go. Irena had broken her own rule about using our real names during resistance activities. I wanted to tell her so, but I decided not to provoke her. It seemed I'd provoked her enough for one evening.

* * *

Auschwitz, 29 May 1941

The train rumbled along the tracks all night, the railcar dark as Warsaw's unlit streets during curfew. Mama told us to drink the disgusting water from the communal pail, despite my fears of the drink forcing me to use the waste bucket. I already stood in a railcar, shoved against strangers, being transported like goods for trade; I could at least retain what little dignity remained. But Mama insisted.

By the time the train stopped, it felt as if we'd been trapped for decades. When the doors swung open, they revealed SS men, who ushered us onto a platform. Mama got out first, followed by Zofia and Karol, and I stayed behind to help Tata. As we neared the door, I grabbed his hand to pull him to a stop. When he looked at me, I couldn't look back.

"Tata, I'm so—"

He cupped my face in his warm hands, so I swallowed the tears threatening to spill out. "True freedom comes from bravery, strength, and goodness. The only one who can take those from you is you." After I nodded slowly, he took my wrist and rotated it, so I opened my palm to reveal the pawn he'd given me. With a smile, he closed my fingers over it and kissed my forehead.

"*Raus!*" someone shouted.

Tata and I continued toward the exit. It was a big step down to the platform, so he sat, took Mama's hand, and landed on his good leg. They both offered me a hand as I followed.

Outside, I'd expected to have more room, but it was still crowded and reeked of passengers covered in sweat, human waste, and filth. The gray morning carried a heavy chill while chaos unfolded before my eyes. Soldiers bellowed and beat the new arrivals with guns and whips, and crazed men in striped uniforms did the same, urging everyone along.

Karol reached for me, so I lifted him into my arms and contained a gasp when his weight angered the bruises around my midsection. "Look," he whispered. He pointed toward two soldiers who were shoving prisoners to hurry them along. "Bastards."

I masked my laugh with a cough before adopting as stern an expression as I could muster. "Karol, don't say that word."

"That's what Mama said when the guard pushed you, remember?"

I placed a finger over his lips and dropped my voice. "You're right, but the soldiers will be angry if they hear you say so. Why don't you and I keep it a secret?"

He nodded, seeming excited by the idea, and I kissed his cheek before putting him down and grabbing his hand. Zofia edged closer to me, eyes wide as she took in our surroundings.

"Where are we?" she whispered.

I readjusted my grip on my little chess piece and scanned the mass of bodies until I noticed a sign. "Oświęcim."

The Germans called it Auschwitz.

As we followed the other Pawiak prisoners down the platform, the SS soldiers ordered the men to separate from the women and children. I gathered the hem of Tata's wool jacket in my hands, but a shared glance between my parents settled my concerns.

"Would you allow us to stay together?" Mama asked the nearest soldier.

In response, the soldier spat at her feet, and Tata tensed. Mama grabbed his sleeve while the SS man looked us over with disdain.

"I don't give a damn if you stay together or not. You're going to the same place anyway," he said. Something about the way he said it gave me pause, but I wasn't sure why. "Move down the platform." He shoved her in the proper direction before marching away.

Tata caught Mama's arm without losing his own balance, and

I rushed forward to stabilize them. Mama took Zofia's hand and wrapped her arm around Tata's waist while he picked Karol up.

"Stay close," she said, and we kept going.

How was I supposed to stay close? Countless people swarmed around me, coming between me and my family as everyone lined up in rows. Thank goodness my father was tall. I focused on the back of Tata's head and pushed toward him. As I fought the crowd, someone jostled me, and my tiny pawn slipped from my grasp.

I darted after it, shuffling around feet clad in oxfords and pumps and loafers until I almost collided with shiny jackboots. Gasping, I straightened and found myself standing before an SS officer.

He held my pawn between his fingers.

Somehow it hadn't broken when it fell. He examined it while I waited for him to acknowledge me, but I wished he'd hurry so I could get back in line.

Everything about him was small and pinched—slight build, beady eyes, thin lips, narrow face. I imagined one of Karol's toy soldiers had come to life; the mental image would have made me laugh if not for the look on this man's face. When he lifted his eyes to mine, they were hardened by revulsion, as if he'd never seen anything more inferior than the girl before him. At the same time, his lips were parted in a way that seemed far too eager.

"Do you play chess?" he asked. He looked to a nearby guard and gestured, probably to tell him to translate, but I nodded. He clenched his jaw, perhaps insulted by my knowledge of his native tongue, and dropped my pawn into my palm.

I stepped back, but I wasn't in line at all. And my family was nowhere in sight.

I turned in a full circle. Surely they couldn't be far; I'd walked only a few steps to retrieve my chess piece. Nothing looked familiar, I couldn't remember which direction the soldier had sent us in, and I could hardly see over the crowd. People bumped into me and pushed me aside, making it impossible to stay in one place, and I clutched my fists to my chest, my heart hammering beneath them.

We're going to the same place, like that soldier said. If I don't find my family now, I'll find them when we get there.

The reminder was comforting, but every passing minute separated us more. Maybe they'd already reached our final destination. The SS officer was watching me, so I turned back to him. I couldn't bear the look on his face; instead I stared at the ground and spoke in a small voice.

"Could you tell me where to go? I was supposed to stay with my family, but now I'm lost, and I—" I broke off with a shaky breath. "Please, I have to find them."

After a brief pause, he snapped his fingers at another SS soldier and nodded toward me. The soldier looked confused, probably because he was leading a group of men; still, he didn't dispute the unspoken order. He waved me into his group, so I obliged.

For a moment, I thought I saw Tata, but my hopes were crushed as quickly as they'd risen. Not him. But we were going to the same place. How I got there wasn't important, only that I rejoined my family.

As I followed the men, I looked over my shoulder. The SS officer watched us go with that same hunger on his face, and I closed my hand tighter around my tiny pawn. Another SS man called out to him, and the sound of his name floated across the platform and reached my ears. Fritzsch. I had a feeling I should remember it.

Chapter 4

Auschwitz, 20 April 1945

I NEVER TAKE LONG to make my play. Fritzsch, on the other hand, surveys the board as if he's forgotten all the rules and must review them with every turn. He must know how annoyed I get when he takes his time during our chess matches, which is probably why he does it.

At last one hand hovers over a knight, then he seems to change his mind, and he adjusts the cigarette between his lips. I chew on the inside of my cheek and clasp my hands together to keep from fidgeting.

"Do you remember when you first came here?"

His question stirs the part of me I'm determined to keep suppressed, the part I have no control over. A response would risk awakening it, so to settle myself, I release a small sigh and wipe the rainwater from my eyes.

Chuckling, he toys with the black pawn he captured on his last turn. "You were a little runt of a creature, weren't you?"

Words, that's all they are. Just words.

"Your move." My voice is taut, charged with a current as strong as the one that once ran through these barbed-wire fences.

"It's been four years, so you would have been—how old? Fourteen, perhaps fifteen?" Fritzsch tosses his cigarette butt onto the gravel. "Tell me, 16671, what is it like?"

"What is what like?"

He sits up straighter and rests his forearms on the table. "Returning to Auschwitz."

The slightest provocation is all it takes to unleash the current inside me.

How can I put into words what it's like to return to a place like this?

Fritzsch waits, lips parted in anticipation, but I'll be damned if I give him what he wants. The current surges through me, but, before it can manifest into shaking hands or a snap of rage, I imagine the rush slowing, calming, receding into the depths. As I lean over the Deutsche Bundesform chess set and lower my voice, the pistol in my pocket feels as heavy and crushing as my memories of this place.

"Unless you intend to resign, it's your move."

For a moment, Fritzsch doesn't react. At last he relents, draws back, and moves his knight after all, but he holds the black pawn by the neck and twists it between his fingers, back and forth, back and forth. I bite the inside of my cheek harder. Though the current is buried again, its tingles of energy remain.

"It's as if we never left, isn't it?"

The words sound almost accusatory, as if he's prompting me to say more, to reveal why I've returned to this place when I was desperate for so long to escape from it. I keep my mouth shut. He's not going to force me into a play I'm not ready to make. Once I confess why I've come—if I lose control—he will have no more need for this game. For me. The past will seize me no matter how I combat it; I've spent three months fighting it, and not once have I won.

He will not rush me, will not bring those memories to the surface before I'm ready to battle them. I will cling to control as tightly as a lost little girl once clung to a chess piece from her father.

But he's right. Returning to Auschwitz makes me feel as if I never left. This is where it all took place, the reality that became the memories. Sometimes it's impossible to distinguish one from the other.

Being here is like the first day I arrived, and every day that followed.

It's hell. Absolute hell.

Chapter 5

Auschwitz, 29 May 1941

S*CHNELL!" THE* SS guard shouted as I marched with the group of men away from the railway platform. He raised his whip, but I moved faster and concealed myself within the throng.

Cold settled over me. I wasn't sure if it was from the rain that had started to fall or my lingering unease after my interaction with Fritzsch, but I wrapped my arms around myself to ward it off. Keeping my eyes open for my family's group, I clutched my tiny pawn as we approached what appeared to be a gate flanked by a barbed-wire fence. Once we drew closer, I made out the words on the metal sign over the entrance.

ARBEIT MACHT FREI. Work sets you free.

Irena had never mentioned the Gestapo sending resistance members to a place like this. Maybe she had no idea a place like this existed.

* * *

Six Weeks Earlier
Warsaw, 12 April 1941

A tiny bell over the door jingled in greeting when Irena and I entered the small haberdashery, our final resistance errand for the day. Various patrons were in the midst of browsing, so we did the same. Dark wooden shelves brimming with men's shirts lined the walls, and we wandered past racks of colorful neckties, leather belts, and hats before lingering at an assortment of sewing accessories.

Behind the counter, the clerk, Mr. Niemczyk, accepted payment from an elderly man, but a young couple examining neckties drew my attention. A swastika pin gleamed on the man's lapel, and the woman bore the same symbol pinned to her breast. *Volksdeutsche*.

Upon this realization, I drew closer to Irena, my heart ticking almost as loudly as the bronze clock mounted on the wall. While the woman browsed the selections, her eyes drifted toward us. Perhaps she wondered why two young girls were shopping in a men's clothing store. She refocused on her companion, but I didn't miss the pointed look they shared.

Another one of Irena's cardinal rules: expect Volksdeutsche to be collaborators. Those with German heritage but not citizenship—since they lived outside Germany—were afforded the opportunity to sign the *Deutsche Volksliste* in support of the Third Reich's policies for Germanization in occupied territories. Volksdeutsche living in Poland, even ones with Polish blood, who professed loyalty to the Reich were also notorious for betraying their countrymen to the Gestapo.

If Irena had noticed the couple, she gave no indication. We trailed closer to the hats, the two hovering in our vicinity. Though they attempted subtlety, it wasn't difficult to guess their intentions. I imagined they would linger to confirm their suspicions about us. We couldn't fulfill our task without them noticing, so we had to get rid of them.

They were hardly five meters away, close enough to overhear what I planned to do. Traces of leather and wood permeated the air, so I took a slow breath, letting the sweet aroma settle my nerves. None of the plans I'd enacted during my resistance work had failed me yet, and I'd make sure this one didn't, either. I waited until Irena put down one hat and selected another, then I threw my head back into a groan.

"Would you just pick one?"

She almost dropped the hat and swore under her breath, but, before she could recover, I proceeded.

"Do we have to waste so much time shopping for Patryk? I wasted enough time listening to you flirt with him this morning."

Her eyes grew as round as the hat's rim before they sharpened in both understanding and annoyance. After so many weeks of working together, no doubt she recognized the imaginary young man I always referenced whenever we needed a convincing story. It was my favorite resistance scheme—and her least favorite. Fortunately, she always played along.

Irena lifted the hat for closer inspection, her gaze flickering toward the Volksdeutsche. "The more you complain, the longer I'm going to take."

"Oh, is that why we spent so long at the café? Because I was complaining that you were making us late for errands?" I asked, crossing my arms while she turned back to the shelf. "Or was it because you two couldn't stop kissing?"

For that, I earned a particularly irritated frown. She wasted no time snapping her retort. "If you're so paranoid about the errands, finish them yourself."

"Maybe I will. I told Mama we wouldn't be long, and we still have to stop by the butcher shop. At this rate, we won't be home until curfew."

Mr. Niemczyk cleared his throat in response to our raised voices, but he knew why we'd come, so I imagined he knew what we were trying to do. As if to placate the clerk, I flashed a winning smile at him—though I didn't miss the aggravated glances from the Volksdeutsche—then picked up a black homburg and shoved it into Irena's hands.

"Here, buy this one and let's go."

She pushed it away. "No, I don't like that one."

"Settle down and do not tamper with the merchandise," Mr. Niemczyk spoke up, but our volume only escalated.

I waved a frustrated hand at the fedoras. "Pick one of those and stop being so particular."

"Stop being so damn annoying."

"You're the one wasting our entire day because of a stupid boy!"

Over our dispute, I caught a few indistinct mutters from the Volksdeutsche; then the man handed his neckties to Mr. Niemczyk and shook his head in refusal. Motioning for the woman to follow, he led the way to the door.

"Forgive the disturbance," Mr. Niemczyk said, stretching an apologetic hand after them.

When the little bell over the door ceased jingling, Irena and I fell silent. Alone at last. We waited another moment, making sure no one else was coming in, then hurried to the counter.

"Sorry we cost you a customer," she said, giving me a pointed look. From her handbag, she produced an envelope and a copy of the *Biuletyn Informacjny* and passed both to him.

As he folded the resistance newspaper, opened the envelope,

and pulled out the stack of zloty, Mr. Niemczyk shrugged. "If I forfeit a sale to protect you and your work, it's an honor."

She eyed the door before leaning closer to him. "The baby?" she murmured. A note of concern laced her words, absent her usual sharpness.

"Better," he replied with a smile. "He's filled out a little, and my children adore him. After I use this money to purchase goods on the black market, we'll be able to feed him even more."

I exchanged a relieved glance with Irena. Mama had dropped off the Jewish child in question, and upon her return later that night she'd paced around the living room, fretting about how thin he was. The positive report would ease her concerns, knowing the funds enabled Mr. Niemczyk to utilize the secret civilian market to support his family with more than the paltry rations and goods the Germans allotted.

Mr. Niemczyk dipped his head toward the door. "Run along before you scare off any more of my customers."

"I'll handle scaring off one more for you," Irena said. She turned to me, her eyebrows raised. "Anything else you'd care to say about Patryk?"

The name was enough to make me giggle, despite its sarcastic edge. I darted toward the exit. She followed at my heels, but the bell chimed, announcing another patron and saving me from her rebuke—for the time being, anyway. I hurried outside and barely made it a few meters down the empty street before I burst into laughter.

"Have you lost your mind?" Irena called out as she followed me to where I'd stopped outside a barbershop. "Why do you always do that?"

After a moment, I composed myself. "The Volksdeutsche were watching us and seemed to suspect something, so I knew a fake argument would make them lose interest. And it worked, didn't it, cousin?"

"If it hadn't? Good Lord, Maria, they could've lied to the nearest SS man simply to get us arrested and shut us up."

"Calm down, Irena. Don't make me start complaining about Patryk again."

Her anger dissipated, and with a faint but fond smile she leaned against the shop window. "Patryk was my father's name." She was quiet, then sighed and reverted to being critical. "Of all the stories you could've developed, you couldn't think of anything better than turning me into a lovesick idiot?"

"It's easy and believable. Checkmate," I replied, grinning. "Admit it, that was fun."

Irena lost her grasp on her attempted reprimand, and she shook her head. "You're an idiot, but somehow your stupid plan got them to leave so we could deliver those funds, so I guess you're not as incompetent as I thought. I didn't say you were competent," she added when she noticed my chin lifting. "Just not completely *in*competent."

"Well, I guess you're not as awful as I thought. Not nice. But not completely awful."

"Watch yourself. I still have the power to make your life hell, Helena Pilarczyk."

"And I can tell your mother how much you curse around me. You're not the only one with power, Marta Naganowska."

Narrowing her eyes, Irena started down the street, though not before I caught the smile she tried to hide. I masked my own grin and jogged to catch up. She heaved an exasperated sigh when I reappeared beside her.

As we walked, I basked in satisfaction. Another successful day of resistance errands. My pieces were in position, my strategy was set, and the opening phase was transitioning into the middle-game. In this phase, white and black struck with full force, utilizing every skill to capture the opponent's king. It was the most dangerous phase of every chess game. But also the most exciting.

By now, the Jewish ghetto entrance was in sight. The gate opened to allow a German car to pass, and I caught sight of another world, one whose inhabitants were forced to wear a white band bearing a blue Star of David. Three dark-haired, bearded men rode in a rickshaw pedaled by a fourth; a handful of disheveled children darted past a scrawny figure sprawled on the sidewalk. Dead or too sick to move, I wasn't certain. Near the still form, someone huddled beneath a pile of rags. Based on the size of the hand reaching toward the crowd, I assumed it was a woman. Beyond the beggar, soldiers detained a man who looked like a rabbi, and they trimmed his long gray beard while he remained solemn and dignified through the degradation.

The gate closed, entrapping the Jews, while a sharp pang of sorrow pierced my heart. One ideology spread like a disease and spawned such wickedness. Prior to the war, I'd witnessed various instances of hatred or oppression, but none as vile and senseless as this.

* * *

Auschwitz, 29 May 1941

I narrowed my eyes against the rainfall as I followed the group of male prisoners through the gate. Along the uneven road, we passed redbrick buildings labeled with black signs and white letters. The soldiers ushered us into Block 26, where men in striped garments wielded clubs like those on the railway platform. Inside, I looked for my family, but the only prisoners were the men from my group, and some were already in various stages of undress, preparing to accept their new prison garb. My family's group must have already passed through. As I surveyed the scene, a man a few meters from me peeled off his undershirt and shorts and stood there, naked.

For a moment, I was too startled to look away; when I did, I discovered everyone was undressing. Completely. Without putting anything else on.

Some men huddled together for warmth and support, others shivered alone. This place stripped human beings of clothing and possessions and left them cowering in nakedness. What sort of prison was this?

One of the men in stripes approached me. A white armband bearing the word KAPO in black capital letters encircled his bicep, but I had no idea what it meant. I expected him to be surprised to see a girl among the men instead of with the women and children, wherever they were, but he didn't look surprised. There was no emotion in his eyes at all.

"Take off your clothes," he said.

I hugged my midsection while my fingers gripped my sweater as if they'd never loosen, just as in Pawiak. I hated undressing in front of my own sister, my flesh and blood, and the people in this room were strangers—men, so many men.

"Now."

The order startled me into focus, and I took a hasty step back. "Wait, please, may I . . . may I have other clothing first?"

A new sound, deep and callous. Laughter. Why was he laughing at my query? It wasn't meant to be amusing.

When I still hadn't complied, he cast humor aside and took a threatening step toward me. "Take off your damn clothes, or I'll take them off for you."

After a few agonizing seconds, I swallowed hard, fought hot tears, and loosened my grip on my sweater. Anything to keep his hands off me. I fumbled with buttons and clasps, every movement a betrayal. Once the deed was done, I stood, naked, milky white skin splotched with harsh blues and purples, in front of a strange man old enough to be my father. Cheeks hot, eyes downcast, I crossed my arms over my bruised breasts to retain some modesty. It did no good.

The man snatched my clothes and tossed them onto a pile, but I kept the pawn from Tata hidden in my fist.

He wouldn't take that from me.

Someone handed me a card with a number written on it—my new name, so I was told—but *one-six-six-seven-one* didn't roll off the tongue quite as easily as *Maria*.

Some men attempted to cover themselves, others didn't bother, and we funneled past three young SS men watching us walk by. Nothing alleviated the most horrid vulnerability I'd ever known, this nakedness among strangers. The men were united in their exposure, but I bore it alone, the single female suffering this misery, the single body that didn't match those surrounding her. As I walked, warmed only by the heat of shame, all I wanted was to be inconspicuous, to be small and invisible.

I watched the ankles in front of me, arms across my chest, until a firm hand closed around my wrist. The hand pulled me toward its owner, bringing me face-to-face with one of the young SS men.

"No need for modesty, sweetheart."

He captured my other wrist and, despite my resistance, easily pulled my arms away from my body. I froze, unable to escape, unable to shield myself.

He assessed me with a sweeping glance. "There, isn't that much more comfortable?"

All I could do was stare at the *Totenkopf* emblems on his cap and collar. Two more pairs of eyes, two more eerie grins.

His companions took my arms, and one laughed. "This one's young even for you, Protz. What's a girl doing here?"

I hated Fritzsch for sending me with the men.

This wasn't happening; it wasn't. His hands weren't on my chest, they weren't sliding down my waist to my hips, he wasn't smiling as I flinched or pulling me closer. But I couldn't deny the guttural order that accompanied the finger tracing down my cheek.

"Come with me, little one."

Struggle, scream, beg. For God's sake, do something, anything.

But I didn't.

As Protz pulled me toward an adjoining room, everything inside me said to protest, and every part of me tried and failed to obey. Resisting wouldn't have worked anyway: he was too strong; he had a gun. One hand gripped my arm while the other rested on his belt.

"Protz."

He paused a few meters from his destination. I couldn't comprehend the new voice, the one instructing Protz to go somewhere and do something. I couldn't even breathe.

"Damn, that's a shame, isn't it? Until next time, love." Protz sent me back toward the prisoners with an enthusiastic slap on my behind.

Accompanied by his sniggers, I staggered away, crossed my arms over my chest, and let the crowd sweep me along. I was too numb to do anything but follow, too disgusted with myself and my own helplessness.

"Get moving, girl." The order came from the same guard with the strange armband who had made me undress.

But I was frozen again. More people in striped clothes were armed with scissors and razors. Before my eyes, entire bodies were shaved and tolerated thorough physical examinations, all in mortified silence. The same thing was about to happen to me. Where was my family? I had to find my family.

Someone pulled me backward with a swift, painful jerk and pressed something hard under my chin, forcing my head back until I met a vicious gaze. "It looks like someone already gave you a beating, and unless you obey orders, I will give you another." The prisoner with the armband shoved me at a man wielding scissors.

I stopped before him, painfully aware of my exposure, but his face was blank. I supposed that should have made me feel better, but it didn't.

The prisoner placed a hand on my trembling shoulders, guided me toward a stool, and sat me down. He wasn't rough, but he wasn't gentle, and I wished the ground would open up and swallow me. "Listen to the kapos," he murmured. "They may be prisoners, too, but they work as supervisors, so they have something the rest of us don't have—power."

More SS guards patrolled the room and watched the horrible procedure. The man lifted my braid, and metal scraped against metal as he opened the scissors. My hair was all I had left linking me to the girl I'd been before. The girl I would never be again.

"Please." It was a useless plea, but I couldn't help it.

Even if my plea hadn't been useless, I was too late. The man sliced through my hair and set the detached braid down, trading the scissors for the razor.

"I'll try not to cut you too much, but I have to be quick," he said, and the cold blade touched the back of my neck. "I have a quota to meet."

Once, Karol found a dead beetle on the kitchen floor. He dissected it and studied its legs, exoskeleton, and insides, leaving no part of the unfortunate creature unscrutinized. Now, as strange men shaved and probed me, I felt like Karol's beetle. When the humiliation was over, I touched the fuzz remaining on my head. It was all I had left to call hair. If I didn't touch it and ignored the chill on my neck, I could almost pretend I still had my long blond locks. But there was no point in fooling myself.

Zofia would hate this. If there was one thing she loved about herself, it was her curls.

Disinfectant stung terribly against the cuts covering my body, but after all the places strange hands, eyes, and instruments had violated me, not even the fiery purge of the cleanser made me feel clean again. Someone shoved a gray-and-blue-striped garment into my hands. The hideous, coarse uniform was a welcome sight, and I tugged it on as quickly as possible. I would never take clothing for granted again.

My uniform was too big, but no one seemed to care. A red triangle with a *P* inside was emblazoned on the left breast, and below the letter was a white strip of fabric with my number, 16671, in black. My new name. I pretended the headscarf hid the baldness, but it probably accentuated it; then I stepped into a pair of cumbersome wooden clogs.

In the next room, I attempted to fill out a registration form, but my hand wouldn't stop shaking, the scribbles barely legible. Another man in stripes took a few photographs of each new prisoner, then the guards ushered us outside.

Surely the worst was over now. I fell to the back of the throng as we marched across the expansive grounds. This place looked more like a camp than a prison. The rain fell steadily, and I narrowed my eyes against it to look for my family. With our shaved heads and matching uniforms, it was impossible to tell anyone apart, but my hope was to see a man, woman, and two children together.

A lone prisoner walked down the street, one with a headscarf instead of a cap. A woman. Thank God, finally another woman. As she drew closer, I slowed my pace, then touched her arm to catch her attention. She drew back, staring at me with dark eyes set in hollow sockets and framed by a gaunt face. She was thin, far too thin.

"You're a girl." The incredulous murmur carried a slight accent, one I used to hear all the time before the war.

So are you, I wanted to respond. I'd had enough of being the only girl among the men. Once I reconnected with my parents and siblings, my next mission was to find more women. Her uniform was marked with a *P* and two superimposed triangles, one red like mine and another yellow, forming a Star of David. Her number was 15177. I guessed that meant she was a Polish Jew, and she looked maybe ten years older than me. It was hard to tell.

"Do you know where I can find my family? We arrived today, but I got separated from their group, so I think they were registered ahead of me. Have you seen them? Tata is tall and walks with a limp, Mama is a bit taller than me, then my little sister and brother . . ." My voice died, unable to formulate words around the lump in my throat, put there by the woman's guarded expression.

The Jewish woman cast a furtive glance over her shoulder and dropped her gaze. "You'll see your family soon." She left without waiting for a reply.

If there was one skill I'd gained from studying opponents during chess games, it was how to read people. The clues that someone was lying were subtle—a change in pitch, a nostril flare, inability to maintain eye contact. Those indicators weren't always reliable, but I could usually tell when they were. In this case, the signs were as obvious as the kapo's club that cracked across my shoulders and forced me into motion.

The woman had lied. I wasn't going to see my family. Where had they been sent? A different camp? A prison? Would they be coming back? I rolled the tiny chess piece around in my palm, wishing I'd never dropped it so I could've stayed with the correct group.

As I walked and attempted to ignore the damp, itchy uniform chafing my bare skin, I noticed an open iron gate leading to a courtyard between Blocks 10 and 11. Even though I'd learned my lesson about falling behind, the sight left me too weak to move.

A truck waited near the gate, and prisoners piled dead bodies onto it. At the far end of the courtyard, a gray wall stood in front of a brick wall, and that seemed to be where the prisoners were fetching the corpses from. Naked bodies were tossed onto the pile like sticks being gathered for firewood. I didn't know which horrified me more: the irreverence for the dead or the indifference with which the prisoners completed their task.

A graying SS officer supervised from a few meters away, but, when I stepped toward the truck, he didn't stop me. The sharp, metallic smell of blood reached my nostrils, and I clutched my stomach to suppress a sudden wave of nausea.

"What happened to them?" I asked no one in particular.

A man carrying a body jerked his head to indicate the gray wall inside the courtyard. "Resistance members and Polish political prisoners are taken to the wall for execution."

Execution. These people hadn't died; they'd been killed. The lump in my throat expanded. "That's me and my family. Are we going to be—?"

"No, if you've been registered, you've been deemed fit to work. I wouldn't call that luck, but at least you aren't dead yet," the prisoner said with a dark chuckle.

He carried a man's body, and I noticed a small bloody hole in the back of the corpse's head. Again, my stomach rose up in rebellion; I quelled it with the greatest difficulty. The prisoner set the body on the truck and accidentally displaced another, which landed in a crumpled heap on the wet ground. He tossed it back with a swift, mechanical motion.

"Some political prisoners are allowed to work; others are shot, especially the sick, disabled, elderly, women, and children. I wouldn't wish this place upon the scum of the earth, let alone a child. If they kept you, they must be eager for more laborers, regardless of who they are."

The litany of the unfit rang in my ears.

Tata is crippled. Mama is a woman. Zofia and Karol are children. I'm a child.

You're going to the same place anyway.

The rain fell harder and soaked through my thin uniform. My whole body quivered, but not from the damp cold.

I didn't want to look at the people in the truck, I couldn't; but I had to. So I did. And that was when I noticed familiar blond curls nestled among the pile of bodies.

Once I'd located Zofia, I found the rest of my family clustered around her. Mama, Tata, Zofia, Karol. Dead. My entire family was dead because the Gestapo had caught me.

Something inside me shattered, sent me to my knees, a sharp, stabbing agony pummeling my chest. I'd have given anything to trade that pain for a thousand of Ebner's clubs, to face Gestapo interrogation over and over again, whatever it took to change what I'd done.

Bring them back, dear God, please bring them back.

A rough grip pulled me to my feet. "Fall out of line again and you'll wish you'd been sent to the wall like those Polacks." The raspy voice let the threat sink in before its owner dragged me back to the group and pushed me along.

The wall had been meant for me as well. Had I not gotten lost, Fritzsch wouldn't have sent me to registration. I should have been with them. No, they should have been safe at home. I got caught, but they paid the price. My parents, my sister, my brother—slaughtered, hair matted with crimson blood, piled among strangers.

A shout ordered us into Block 18. When the door slammed behind us, I didn't bother taking in my surroundings. I was trembling and suffocating, and I had to get away. I rushed to the farthest corner of the room, away from my fellow prisoners, and I collapsed.

Fierce, painful sobs strangled me, and the tears burned as they streaked down my cheeks. The flames of guilt and desolation were more agonizing than any pain I'd ever experienced. My entire family was dead.

Now I knew what hell was. Prison wasn't hell; torture wasn't hell. Auschwitz was hell.

"I knew I saw a girl."

The man's voice was beside me. No one had weapons, but my mind issued a warning—there were countless men in this room and one of me; every single man could be like Protz.

At once, I sat up and swung a closed fist in the voice's direction, and something crunched and gave way beneath the impact. With a yelp, the man brought both hands to his face before looking at me through wide eyes, which narrowed into a glare. When he lifted his head, blood streamed from his crooked nose.

"What the hell is wrong with you?"

I tightened my fist in anticipation, but he got up and walked away, muttering something about me being out of my mind. I curled into myself again. The uncontrollable sobs didn't stop, and my hand throbbed, but the pain was negligible compared to the agony within.

"Things may look bleak, but keep your chin up. You're not alone."

Such words were a common sentiment, vain platitudes used in a useless attempt to provide comfort, but something was different. The new voice was so soothing, I didn't even consider throwing a punch, and the words weren't empty, but filled with simple confidence.

"What's your name?"

Although I didn't lift my head, I calmed myself enough to answer in a whisper. "One-six-six-seven-one."

"Pardon?"

"My name is 16671." I spit the number out as my tears welled up afresh. It was the only name fit for me anymore. Bearing the name my parents bestowed upon me was an honor I no longer deserved.

Despite my hostility, the man chuckled. "Well, then, by your logic, my name is 16670. Pleased to meet you."

I peeked at his uniform. His prisoner number was the one right before mine, and he wore a red triangle with a *P* on the breast. He dropped to one knee, closer to my eye level, but kept a respectful distance, as if assuring me he meant no harm.

"I'm a Franciscan friar. My monastery printed anti-Nazi publications, so I and some of my brothers were arrested. Why are you here?"

Such a simple question, yet such a complex answer. Because I got my family arrested, because I got lost, because my family was dead. I swallowed the tears and wiped the moisture from my cheeks. "I worked for the resistance in Warsaw." He didn't need the entire truth.

"You must be a very brave girl," he murmured, but, of all the words I'd have used to describe myself, *brave* wasn't one. "My name is Father Maksymilian Kolbe."

The priest had a slight cleft chin and a handful of distinct lines and razor cuts on his face. He must have had a beard before being shaved—which would have made sense, considering he was a friar—and he seemed a few years older than my father. He regarded me with such kindness, kindness I could have wiped away if I told him the truth. A sincerity swelled behind his eyes, but, no matter how much I trusted him, I couldn't reveal what I'd done.

Still, he waited for my reply. For me to tell him my name. But I'd already told him what to call me.

Maria Florkowska was a stupid child who'd thought she could transform a meager pawn into a mighty queen. She was a fool, a pawn in a game she'd never win, outwitted, outplayed, and out maneuvered by opponents far more intelligent and powerful. Her family had paid with their lives while she became a *häftling*, Prisoner 16671.

And Prisoner 16671 was nothing. I was nothing.

"My given name was Maria. My resistance name was Helena. My new name is Prisoner 16671." My voice was gruff and sharp and angry, so angry.

Father Kolbe dipped his head into a small nod. "I see."

He turned to comfort a man who was cursing and lamenting his fate. I looked around long enough to confirm that I was the youngest in our block, and the sole female prisoner. I drew my knees up, pressed myself into the corner, and stared at the stripes on my uniform. When the distraught man fell quiet, Father Kolbe spoke with a few others, then sat next to me. I didn't look up.

"My given name is Raymund, but when I professed my vows,

I received two new names. The first is Maksymilian. The second is Maria, after the Immaculata, the immaculate Virgin Mother of God. The name holds a dear place in my heart, and even small joys make a difference in times like these. If you wouldn't mind, may I call you Maria?"

The name wasn't mine anymore, so I should have refused, but he looked so hopeful. I could make an exception, simply because it comforted him. I nodded my assent.

"How old are you, Maria?" Father Kolbe asked, then he chuckled. "Forgive me, but they took my spectacles."

"Fourteen."

"Is anyone here with you? A friend, perhaps, or your family?"

At the mention of my family, the tears returned, so I shook my head to hide them. It wasn't a lie, exactly.

"Well, following arrest, my brothers and I were separated. I didn't arrive with anyone, either, so we're alike in that sense, you and I. Shall we be friends?"

He wouldn't have offered to be my friend if he'd known my family was dead, lying in a truck in this very camp. Dead because I got us captured. I should have punished myself by refusing him, but his offer of friendship was all I had, the only chance to take my mind away from my sins.

I didn't trust my voice, so all I did was nod once.

His small smile was so warm, so empathetic. "That's settled, then. Friends."

Chapter 6

Auschwitz, 30 May 1941

I T WAS BARELY after midnight following an entire day in
Block 18, and I'd spent my time dwelling on my new existence.
Prisoner 16671, orphaned and alone except for a kind priest who
didn't know anything about me or what I'd brought upon my
family.

Steady breaths and light snores pierced the eerie silence. I
hadn't slept at all. I'd stayed on a lice-infested straw pallet on the
floor, staring into the darkness, clinging to the tiny pawn from
my father. When we'd settled down for the night, the two men
crammed on either side of me had assured me I had no reason to
fear them, but no amount of reassurance made me feel safe.

How could anyone sleep after the horrors we'd gone through?
We'd had various panics and outbursts since arriving in our
block, but now it was quiet. Maybe the others had accepted our
situation or were too exhausted to care, or maybe they hadn't seen
their own family amid a pile of bodies.

I closed my eyes, because it was just as dark with them open.
Even if I'd wanted to sleep, I couldn't. The horrific day filled my
head, though I tried to think of happy, carefree memories of life

before the war. I could almost smell the tantalizing aroma of fresh bread in the oven while my family and I gathered in the living room to listen to our favorite radio programs and play board games, but I couldn't cling to it long.

The memories faded, replaced by a chessboard, familiar and calming, a respite from the atrocities plaguing me. The pieces were black and red, and I closed my fingers around a red pawn's slender neck. My grip slipped, the paint fresh and wet. I studied the bright scarlet filling the grooves of my fingertips while a metallic odor hit my nostrils. Blood.

Gasping, I scrubbed my hand on my plaid skirt, except it wasn't my plaid skirt; it was a striped uniform. I grabbed a black pawn, but it was sticky and covered my fingers in dark, coagulated blood, and I looked across the board to find not one opponent but hundreds—naked bodies, piled on a truck. At once, I found them. Or maybe they found me. Mama, Tata, Zofia, Karol. Their eyes, which once shone with vivacity and love, now vacant and lifeless, staring at me, accusing me, reminding me this was my fault, all my fault.

Sobbing screams woke me, and it took a moment to realize they were my own. I'd fallen asleep even though I thought I'd never sleep again.

"Shut up!" an angry, groggy voice shouted.

The reprimand must have been directed at me, and some inmates complained about the disruption, but I couldn't control the sobs.

"Shhh, you're all right, Maria."

"My family—"

The gasping cry emerged before I stopped myself from saying more. *Don't. Don't tell him what happened.*

Father Kolbe helped me up and guided me toward the wall, and we sat with our backs against it in the midst of the sleeping forms. He wrapped an arm around my shaking shoulders and allowed me to cry.

"Would it make you feel better if you told me about your family?" he whispered once my sobs faded into hiccups, but I shook my head in refusal. "Very well, we'll sit here until you're ready to go back to sleep."

"I'm not going back to sleep."

"In that case, we'll sit for as long as you'd like." Despite my panic, Father Kolbe's voice remained calm. "Have faith, child. Even though your family isn't here, they're always with you spiritually. And you're always with them."

His words dispelled a bit of the anxiety coursing through my body. I didn't reply, and Father Kolbe was silent before he started murmuring familiar words. He was praying the rosary. My family and I would gather in the living room to recite this same prayer every night before bed. The rosary's large and small beads were a tangible reminder of each Our Father and Hail Mary passing over my lips while I contemplated Jesus Christ's life. Now, I could almost imagine that Father Kolbe's voice was my father's, could almost feel the beads between my fingers.

Thoughts of my family would make me start crying again. Instead I concentrated on staying awake and listening to Father Kolbe's prayer, but nothing alleviated the weight in my chest.

I ached, inside and out, heart and mind, body and soul. It was an ache that would never subside. In this game, my opponent surrounded me on all sides, allowing no foreseeable escape.

Listen to the prayers, think of the prayers. Don't sleep. Stay awake, just stay awake.

Despite my resolution, Father Kolbe's gentle recitation lulled me into slumber. This time, my dreams were peaceful.

* * *

Impatient shouts roused me. When I lifted my head from Father Kolbe's shoulder, he stood, offered me his hand, and helped me to my feet. Through the darkness, I could see his bloodshot eyes beneath drooping eyelids, though he offered me a soft smile. I wondered if he'd gotten any sleep after I woke everyone.

Outside, on a large parade ground stretching between Blocks 16 and 17, soldiers instructed us to line up in rows of ten for *appell*, as they said in German. Some Poles didn't seem to understand the order, but the guards' clubs spoke a universal language. My uniform did little to ward off the morning chill, but anyone who moved or complained was struck, so I tried not to succumb to shivers. I stood near the front, next to Father Kolbe, still and silent, while the guards counted the prisoners.

"All here, Herr Lagerführer," one man reported after we'd been standing for ages.

The *lagerführer* stepped into view, a man in a field-gray uniform.

Fritzsch.

I couldn't bear to look at him, so I turned my attention to the stoic officer beside him. Thanks to the dark circles under his hooded eyes and the lines around his wide nose, pursed mouth, and broad forehead, he looked old, older than his age would likely predict. A Luger P08 sat on his hip, similar to the one Tata kept in the closet with his army uniform from the Great War. When he'd taught me how to clean and load the weapon, he'd told me how he saved his comrade-in-arms from a German bullet, so he'd kept the German's pistol. Tata had shown me how to fire it, too, and he'd promised to let me shoot it someday. That day never came.

This wasn't the time for tears. I couldn't think of my family.

Determined to keep my thoughts guarded, I refocused on the man next to Fritzsch. He ordered one prisoner to move a few centimeters left to straighten the line. The häftling obliged, but I didn't notice much difference.

"My name is Rudolf Höss, *kommandant* of Auschwitz," he said, once satisfied with our formation. "Every morning, you will line up in the square for roll call, like you are now. Once each prisoner is accounted for, you will report to your work detail. You will obey commands promptly and labor with precision and efficiency. From this day forward, I turn you over to my camp deputy, Karl Fritzsch. I trust he will adequately maintain the standards I have regarding how my camp is to be run."

As Höss concluded, his voice didn't carry the same confidence in Fritzsch that his words did. He started to walk away and scanned the crowd one final time; then he stopped.

"Is that a girl?"

All eyes turned to me, the one in a headscarf. Next to me, Father Kolbe tensed. It was kind of him, but not even his concern was enough to keep my heart from springing into my throat. Now more than ever, I wished the earth would swallow me.

A frantic SS man consulted a handful of papers. "There must have been a mistake, Herr Kommandant."

"I don't have time for mistakes!" Höss shouted, interrupting the man's splutters. "I need men—workers, hard workers—and a girl isn't fit for labor. Take care of this, Fritzsch." Red-faced, he walked away, barking something about the sheer stupidity that ran rampant among those assigned to his camp.

When the kommandant was gone, I stared at the gravel, unable to look into Fritzsch's eyes as they scraped over me and peeled everything away until I disintegrated into visceral terror. He'd sent me through registration just to send me to the execution wall. I was sure of it. All the female prisoners had been sent there except the Jewish woman I'd met, and she must have been spared because she served some purpose. Fear coiled around me, squeezing until I was certain it would kill me before the bullet had a chance. I tightened my fist around the tiny pawn.

The sound of approaching footsteps reached my ears, and I didn't have to look up to know it was him. First I saw his feet, then his open palm. He must have realized I was holding something.

I didn't have a choice. I dropped the pawn Tata had made for me into Fritzsch's hand.

Although I expected him to walk away, he didn't. Once I lifted my head, Fritzsch looked at me with that same eagerness I'd seen when we met on the arrival platform, as if he were a child and I was his new favorite toy.

"There's no mistake. Daughter of intelligentsia, are you, Polack?" His cynical assumption was correct; my parents had been university graduates. I had lived under Nazi occupation long enough to know they despised intellectual Poles, planned to reduce us to a race of uneducated workers. "Unfit for labor," he went on, assessing me. "Unfit for survival. Unfit for anything except this . . . for a time." He gripped the pawn's slender neck between his thumb and index finger, twisted it back and forth, back and forth, slow and calculated. His fingers whitened as he squeezed harder, harder.

A sudden snap made me flinch, then the decapitated pawn lay at my feet. My father's last gift.

While I stared at my pawn and combatted the tightness in my throat, Fritzsch returned to his companions. I didn't hear what they said, but a few guards scattered in various directions. When they returned, one carried a small table, another two chairs, and another a box. They brought the items before me, shooed the prisoners aside, and ordered me to sit. I took a quick look at the bewildered faces surrounding me while Fritzsch pointed to one inmate a few meters away.

"Do you know how to play chess?"

The man's eyes widened, but, after he understood the question, he let out a visible breath and nodded. "I'm a decent player, Herr Lagerführer."

Fritzsch instructed him to sit across from me. Once he was settled, the guard holding the box placed it in front of us. A chess set.

Following a nod from Fritzsch, I swallowed hard to settle my pounding heart and glanced at Father Kolbe, then opened the box and removed the pieces from the two interior compartments. According to the stamp inside, the set was a Deutsche Bundesform. How fitting that we were being forced to play with a set manufactured by the Nazis.

The sturdy pieces were nowhere near as delicate and ornate as my Staunton set at home. Once I'd set up the white pieces, I made my opening play, queen's pawn two spaces forward. I decided to concentrate my attack on black's weak square, defended only by its king. Black moved his queen's pawn to meet mine, so I positioned my light-squared bishop along the left diagonal, testing my plan. If my opponent failed to defend his king, I'd develop my queen early—a risky and often foolish move, but one I was willing to utilize if my opponent proved careless.

The man scrutinized the center of the board and seemed focused on establishing control there, not defending his king. Excellent. He developed the black knight to my left, which didn't hinder my strategy at all. I developed my queen so she and my bishop both had a direct line of attack to black's weak square, an attack devastating for the black king. Black continued concentrating on the center with his second knight, losing his opportunity to defend himself.

White queen took black pawn on the weak square, white bishop was in place for attack, and the black king couldn't move without fear of capture. Queen's pawn to D4, light-squared bishop to C4, queen to H5, queen to F7.

Four simple moves, one opponent's carelessness.

I set the captured black pawn on the table and looked up from the board. "Checkmate."

The häftling opened his mouth, as if preparing to dispute me, then closed it while the guards erupted into laughter and shouts. I offered him the black pawn I'd captured, so he extended his hand to accept it.

Suddenly Fritzsch drew his pistol in a swift, fluid motion and shot my opponent in the forehead.

People gasped, some screamed—maybe I screamed—while the man collapsed, but, when Fritzsch turned to me, everyone fell silent. My only consolation was knowing that the prisoner's death had been instantaneous, so surely mine would be the same.

Instead of firing a second time, Fritzsch returned his gun to its holster and gave me an approving nod. "Well done."

My ears rang from the gunshot. The dead man had fallen from his chair onto the ground. The hole in his forehead was small, an expert shot, and blood trickled from the wound and surrounded his head. Eyes blank, face slack. One moment alive, the next dead.

Fritzsch took a few steps toward the onlookers. His words floated on the frigid breeze, something about if anyone else would like to play against me, but I couldn't focus, not on his challenge, not on anything. Another noise broke the silence—laughter, except it couldn't be. No one would be laughing at death.

As the guards' laughter faded, my own shuddering breaths filled my ears. Near me, Father Kolbe murmured a prayer for the repose of the dead man's soul. I thought he told me to avert my eyes, but I was transfixed by shock and morbid curiosity. I'd never witnessed a murder before.

When I was learning how to play chess with my father, sometimes I'd choose a move, then realize I should have selected another. Discouraged and frustrated, I'd ask Tata if I could change my play, start the game over, or quit altogether. He'd never let me. *Finish the game, Maria.* That was his response every time, no matter my persistence.

All I could do was obey. Sometimes I'd emerge victorious, despite my errors. Other times the mistakes cost me the game. Those losses were the most bitter.

"Prisoner 16671."

My name sounded harsh and grating on Fritzsch's tongue, and I closed my eyes as he drew closer. *God, please change his mind and let him shoot me, let it be quick, take me away from this place.*

"Remove the body."

Surely I'd misheard him. When I opened my eyes, Fritzsch jerked his head toward a nearby block. The rising sun washed the bricks in crimson light and illuminated a dark heap propped against the building, a tangle of arms and legs and torsos. Corpses.

Let me quit, Tata, please let me quit.

Before I could do more than blanch, Father Kolbe stepped forward, removed his striped cap, and spoke in clear, precise German. "Herr Lagerführer, would you permit me to assist?"

Fritzsch's gloved fist collided with Father Kolbe's jaw, and I gasped, but the priest made no sound. Fritzsch turned to me. "Do you need this pathetic bastard's assistance?"

Despite the question, something told me I had no choice in my answer unless I wanted more bodies added to the death count. I shook my head.

Father Kolbe dipped his head in concession. As he returned to his place, I swore his lips moved, could almost hear a faint prayer.

Something inside propelled me toward the dead man, though I wished I could trade places with him. Never did I imagine I'd envy a corpse. I got out of my chair, lifted his ankles in trembling hands, and, with awkward, labored efforts, trudged toward the pile of bodies while everyone watched. As I crossed the square, my attempts transitioned from staccato tugs into a slow, continuous drag across the dirt and gravel, but I kept moving. I had to keep moving.

When I reached the corpses, I stopped.

Pawiak had smelled like suffering, but Auschwitz smelled like death. A repugnant stench permeated the air around the naked bodies. I left the man beside the pile of rotting, maggot-infested corpses and buried my nose in the crook of my arm to stifle a gag. Although I didn't have the strength to run, I stumbled away. When I was far enough to breathe again, I gathered my uniform in my hands, hands that had touched a dead body.

Once I returned to Father Kolbe's side, I bit the inside of my cheek, praying pain would distract me, but pain wasn't strong enough to keep me from noticing the blood-splattered chessboard or Fritzsch's eyes on me.

I fell to my hands and knees, unable and unwilling to fight my heaving stomach this time. Vomit spewed onto the gravel and splashed my uniform and skin. My body purged itself of every-thing it once held vital until nothing remained. I was hollow, use-less. Nothing but a number.

Chapter 7

Auschwitz, 20 April 1945

DESPITE HAVING TO play with the black pieces, I'm satisfied with my development so far. Fritzsch and I remain evenly matched, both with secure defenses around our kings, both setting up strong attacks.

As I contemplate my next play, a sudden clatter breaks both the steady thrum of rainfall and my concentration. I gasp and snap my head up. On Fritzsch's side of the board, a few pieces lie on their sides.

"My fault," he says as he rights them.

I release a slow breath to calm the fluttering in my chest, then I return my attention to the board and evaluate my pieces. Silence settles over us until I reach for a pawn. The clatter comes again, and I draw back with another sharp breath.

"Damn this rain. It makes everything more slippery, doesn't it?" Fritzsch picks up the pieces once more. "Why so skittish? A few falling chess pieces shouldn't—"

"Let me focus."

The snap comes out before I can stop it, but I can't fathom why I've done it, why I've demonstrated such blatant insolence toward Fritzsch, of all guards.

"Forgive me, Herr Lagerführer."

I swallow the words back, but it's too late. My tongue has betrayed me. He's not my superior, I know he's not, but my mind debates me and claims Fritzsch holds the power. It's not true, not anymore . . .

Closing my eyes to sort through the chaos does little good. The lines between memory and reality are blurred and indistinguishable.

When I hear Fritzsch shifting in his seat, I open my eyes to find him studying me. He gestures to the board, indicating that I should proceed, so I select my pawn and capture one of his in the center of the board. This time, when I hear his chuckles, I make sure the fury stays contained before I look up. Control is essential if I'm going to play my best.

"You play with such intensity," he says. "You treat chess as if every move were a matter of life or death."

There's no point in pretending I missed the jab, but I won't yield to it. Instead I sit back and pick up the two pawns I've captured so far, occupying my hands, hoping it will keep the quivers away.

Chapter 8

Auschwitz, 17 June 1941

HARSH SEARCHLIGHTS ATOP the guard towers pierced the dark, ominous sky to illuminate the roll-call square surrounded by Blocks 16, 17, and the camp kitchen. It wasn't time for roll call yet, but Fritzsch had summoned me anyway. When I arrived, he'd already set up the chessboard a few meters away from the wooden shelter booth near the kitchen, and various guards were gathered to watch.

"Check. Your move, 16671."

The sound of Fritzsch's voice broke my concentration, and I combatted a twinge of frustration. I knew it was my move, but I forced the response he was waiting to hear. "Yes, Herr Lager-führer."

A thin haze of cigarette smoke hovered in the air, acrid and op-pressive. The guards formed a circle around us, some watching in tense silence, others conversing and predicting our next moves. I their circus act; they my ringmasters.

On my side of the board, my white king was surrounded by a strong defense, but I needed to get out of check. As I moved my king one space to the left, the searchlights fell across a faded bruise on my wrist. My bruises from Gestapo interrogation had almost disappeared, and I'd watched them transition through various shades of yellow, purple, blue, and black. A sad, twisted part of me wished they'd never heal. They were a physical reminder of my last days with my family. Now even that was being taken from me.

All I had left were my cigarette burns. As Fritzsch placed a black rook next to his king in the far right corner, I slipped my fingers into my sleeve to feel the uneven skin. They'd evolved from oozing blisters to scabs and now scars, ugly and a deep, vicious red. I was strangely grateful for them. These were scars that would never heal.

I didn't expect the pain of my family's death to go away, like my bruises. Anger and grief were intense and debilitating, warping everything beyond recognition. The prison that held my body was trivial by comparison. My true prison was the one that held my soul.

A clatter pierced the quiet morning. At once, I drew back. Fritzsch had a few captured pieces in his hands, and he dropped a second one. "Your move."

"Yes, Herr Lagerführer," I whispered, trying to prevent another reaction when he let a third piece hit the table.

Fritzsch and I both had most pieces in play, but I could already see my win. All that remained was the bait, a pawn he eagerly took. My trap had worked. I moved my queen and captured the pawn shielding his king.

"Checkmate."

It took our audience a moment to realize why I'd won; when they did, they erupted into cheers or groans and settled whatever exorbitant bets they'd placed on our game.

My victory didn't hold its usual satisfaction. It wasn't playing in front of a crowd that bothered me—after all, I'd once dreamt of competing in championships. It was knowing that, whether I played against Fritzsch, another guard, or a prisoner selected as my opponent, whether we were alone or on display for the entire camp, chess had transformed into something I was forced to do. Nothing more. I was Fritzsch's living, breathing game, one he'd keep playing until he got bored or he won. Whichever came first.

When Fritzsch produced a fresh cigarette, a young guard struck a match and offered it to him. "Forgive me for betting against you, Herr Lagerführer, but since you won a few days ago, I suspected she had learned her lesson."

Fritzsch didn't match the soldier's grim smile; he regarded me as he always did—seeking my reaction.

Sour bile nearly rose to my throat, mimicking our last game; I focused on the chessboard until it had transformed into a black-and-white blur. Following his win that morning, Fritzsch had suddenly grabbed my dominant wrist, slammed my hand down, and pressed his pistol to it.

The barrel pinned me in place, fingers splayed across the board, soon to be joined by mangled flesh and rivulets of blood. I had played terribly; Fritzsch made concentration impossible, analyzing me, speaking to me, dropping so many pieces onto the board. Poor gameplay made for a dull game, its price my chess-playing hand.

Fritzsch had told me once that, when he was a boy, his family had moved too much for him to receive a consistent education, but he had learned to play chess. Perhaps he sought to prove that my upbringing made me no better at this game than he, did me no good in this place where I held no power and he held all.

The morning air turned noxious, the silence tight, cutting into me, slicing my breaths into short tremors. As he applied more pressure to the gun, he assessed me as he had after my arrival, as though confirming his initial impression. *Unfit.*

Then he removed the pistol.

Sometimes there were such consequences—hours of unceasing gameplay until I had won enough to satisfy him, a bullet through my opponent's skull. Other times nothing happened. Fritzsch wrote the rules however he pleased, but the most important rule remained unchanged: one game would eventually be my last.

I closed my hand into a fist to bury the memory. After Fritzsch indicated that I should get up, the guards cleared the chessboard, table, and chairs before dispersing for roll call. While he smoked, I stifled a yawn. The workday hadn't begun, but I already wished it was over.

"Did you know Kommandant Höss plays chess? I suggested he challenge you to a match." Fritzsch flicked ashes from his cigarette as he strolled back and forth. "He hasn't done so yet, has he? Perhaps it's because he's unhappy I let you live."

The morning was silent aside from the distant tramp of boots as the guards prepared to rouse the prisoners. A light breeze carried a steady stream of Fritzsch's cigarette smoke over me, and I held my breath against it.

He paused before me, but I knew better than to look at him. "I assured the kommandant my decision was best for the Reich. You're beneficial for both the guards and the prisoners. The guards enjoy seeing how you fare against the men, and everyone enjoys your chess games. Public entertainment has a way of boosting morale—until the onlookers get bored. Then it becomes useless."

When he fell silent, I didn't know if I should answer or if he simply wanted me to be aware that my sole purpose was to provide amusement. I knew better than to speak out of turn, so I waited and hoped it was the right choice.

"It's been almost three weeks since you arrived, Prisoner 16671. We'll see how long you can entertain us."

If the suggestion of my impending death was supposed to frighten me, Fritzsch should have been disappointed. Death didn't scare me nearly as much as the idea of spending another moment in Auschwitz did.

Distant shouts reached my ears, followed by prisoners who poured from their blocks and hurried to the square to assemble for appell. Fritzsch dismissed me and moved to the front so he could watch the bedraggled crowd for signs of poor posture or moving lips. Once I located the members of my block, I took my usual place next to Father Kolbe, who didn't look surprised to find me already outside. This wasn't the first time Fritzsch had summoned me prior to roll call to start the day with a chess game. As we assumed formation, Father Kolbe caught my eye and flashed a small smile. Even in this living hell, somehow he remained joyful.

When everyone was in place, the sudden quiet sent a shiver down my spine, even though this morning was warm compared to others. Thousands of people were gathered in this square, yet the only sound was that of SS officers barking out numbers.

As the officers continued counting, I focused on the tall wooden sentry box in the distance. Stationed inside, the faint outline of a guard clutched a massive machine gun. One bullet, that's all. One bullet could have liberated me from one life sentence and condemned me to the next, from living hell to eternal damnation. Surely the suffering would be more bearable in the next inferno.

I curled my toes and clenched my teeth, irritable and impatient, until the gentle hum of a Marian hymn broke the quiet. Every time he whispered prayers or hymns, I was shocked by how quiet Father Kolbe managed to be. The only reason I could hear him was because I'd trained my ear to detect his reassuring murmur.

After appell, I concealed myself in the crowd, avoiding the kapos' blows and ignoring the guards' screams, and joined my labor assignment. Once in line, someone who didn't belong in my *kommando* pushed through the crowd—the other female inmate, Prisoner 15177.

"Where is the girl?"

No need to specify further.

I didn't intend to acknowledge her, but another prisoner shoved me toward her. I whirled on him with a glare. "Don't touch me."

"*Oy vey*, I asked where she was. I didn't say throw her at me," the Jewish woman said, frowning as she joined us.

The man smirked, as if amused by my fury and her displeasure. He forced his way into the center of the throng, securing sanctuary from the blows that would descend upon us while we marched.

The woman glanced over her shoulder, making sure the guards were distracted, and lowered her voice. "Well, I'm glad I finally found which kommando you joined. We need to talk."

If she thought I'd want to talk to her, she must not have remembered what she'd done.

"You lied to me. You told me I'd see my family soon, but you knew they were dead."

Before I could demand an admission of guilt, she raised her shoulders in a flippant shrug. "I didn't see the harm in letting you believe you'd see them again. In a place like this, even false hope is better than no hope at all."

At those words, I couldn't find my voice to respond. Any ray of hope was extinguished the moment I found my family at the death wall. Hope could have sustained me, but reality crushed me. Suddenly I found myself wishing I'd been able to cling to it a moment longer. But it was too late now that I'd become nothing. A dull, useless pawn, powerless, easily captured. Existence was meaningless for a thing identified by a number.

The day my family died, everything within me died alongside them. Death had already claimed my heart, mind, and soul, and my body was next. All I had to do was wait. And I grew more impatient each day.

"Why did they let you live?"

I took a breath to settle the sudden tightness in my chest. "Bad luck. And you?"

"I speak five languages—Yiddish, Polish, German, Czech, and French—and convinced them to let me work as a translator so a man with the same skills could be used for physical labor instead. If you're going to survive here, you need to learn some things." She stared pointedly at the wooden clogs on my swollen, blistered feet. "Shoes can be the difference between dying and living. Organize a new pair."

"Organize?"

"Steal, plunder, whatever you want to call it. The SS men have stockrooms where they keep items confiscated from transports. I can get some for you, but most people on the black market will require something in exchange."

So this place had a black market for additional resources, just like Warsaw. She paused long enough to ensure that the guards still hadn't noticed her before continuing.

"Inmates, kapos, and even some guards are willing to exchange goods or services if you make the right offer. Food. Money. Skills. Yourself." At this, I dropped my gaze, suppressing a shudder. She wore worn leather boots that looked as if they'd been nice at one time. Stolen from an innocent person who was dead now. The rules that governed this place—or lack thereof—astounded me. Her shoes reminded me there were people here who wanted to survive, people who still had something to live for. Given her offer, she must have been under the impression I was one of those people.

"I don't want new shoes, and I don't need your help."

"The second thing you need is an indoor labor assignment. Give me a few days—"

"I said I don't need your help."

"Yes, you do. Or did you find someone else who knows what it's like to be a woman in a men's camp?"

She let the words sink in and crossed her arms, but I wouldn't relent. I didn't want help, I didn't want friends, I didn't want anything other than to leave this place. Her kindness would have been better utilized on someone else.

After a moment, she sighed. "If you won't accept my help, fine, but if you change your mind, find me. My name is Hania. Hania Ofenchajm. What's yours?"

I gestured to the prisoner number on my chest. "See for yourself."

Hania was silent, then she cast a cautious glance around and stepped closer to me. "Prisoners who want to survive will stop at nothing to eliminate the weakest links and better their own odds. You and I are women, so how do you think they see us? We're a waste of space, a waste of clothes, a waste of rations. The moment you forget that is the moment you die."

She waited for me to respond, but I didn't. Although I admired her tenacity, I suspected she'd be disappointed to learn I didn't share it.

Before either of us could say more, the SS men ordered my kommando to march. Hania muttered something in Yiddish and hurried away.

I pushed her words aside as my kommando passed through the main gate, where the camp orchestra played a lively German march to accompany us on the arduous day ahead. The cheerful music made going to work harder. It was worse when we staggered back, encumbered by those who hadn't survived the day, marching in time to avoid our own bodies being added to the death count.

Some prisoners envied those who left the camp for work, but I thought leaving was worse than staying. In leaving, I glimpsed the outside world. After a mere few weeks, I'd already forgotten there were people who led an existence far different from my own. People who led normal lives. I was no longer part of the world beyond the barbed-wire fences, and I never would be again.

As we traveled along the main road, the sound of wheels displacing dirt and gravel reached my ears, and I located a boy who often rode his bicycle along my route. A shoddy bag stuffed with newspapers was slung across his back, and as usual he watched us as he pedaled by. His curiosity tended to focus on me, the girl among men, the prominent one despite the uniformity that reduced us to a singular, bland entity of shaved heads and striped uniforms. I tried not to look at him, but I couldn't help noticing when the fool dropped his bicycle alongside the road and fell into step with me.

"Did you work for the resistance?" he asked, before I'd processed the sheer stupidity of his actions. At least he was smart enough to keep his voice down. "Is that how you became a prisoner? I don't know anyone working for the resistance, unless they're working in secret—which is the whole point, I guess, so never mind, that was stupid."

The boy's remark wasn't the only stupid thing about him. He ran long fingers through his dark brown locks and tucked one hand into his pocket. His threadbare black pants were too short.

"You don't have to tell me," he said with a shrug. "I live in town, but I like riding along this route so I can watch the prisoners and—" He hesitated, and the next words came out more quickly. "Sorry,

I didn't mean that the way it sounded. It's just that I've never seen so many people in one place, and I don't see you unless you come out because no one is allowed near the camp. And as far as I know, there's never been a girl before you, so the first time I saw you . . . I don't know, I guess I've been meaning to say hello, that's all. To let you know if . . . if there's anything I can do to help . . ."

Rays of crimson and gold bled across the violet sky. I focused on the sunrise and the mass of marching bodies ahead. Another person offering help I didn't want or need—and if he, a civilian, thought speaking to me, a prisoner, was helpful, he was sorely mistaken.

"By the way, my name is Mateusz. What's yours?"

The guards were ahead of us, but it was only a matter of time before someone noticed him. I kept looking forward and spoke in a low voice. "Leave me alone."

Before Mateusz could respond, I heard the footsteps and sensed the figure looming beside me. I had no time to prepare myself before I was on the ground, with my eye throbbing and watering.

"Keep your mouth shut, 16671."

"She didn't do anything wrong," the stupid boy said.

Don't do it, I wanted to tell him as I rose to my knees, but he'd already extended a hand to help me up. Though I wasn't stupid enough to take it, the cold barrel of the guard's pistol pressed against my temple.

All I could think of was this hard, unforgiving metal against my skin. One simple motion stood between life and death. Was this the last thing my family had felt? Had the gun ever touched them?

I banished the horrible thoughts when Mateusz withdrew his hand and backed away, his face pale. He looked as if he wanted to protest, but he kept his mouth shut. He cast a final, guilty glance at me, his startling blue eyes moving over my scraped knees digging into the gritty road, the swell forming around my eye, the gun against my head. Then he retreated. Once he was about ten meters away, he turned his back.

The moment Mateusz turned, the guard pointed his pistol at the sky, fired, and kicked me to the ground. At the sound, Mateusz whirled in time to see me collapse, and he stared, mouth agape, paler than ever. Laughing at his own cruel prank, the guard allowed me to get up, then shoved me along. We caught up to the group. Though I didn't dare look behind me, I knew Mateusz's gaze never left me.

At last the guards ordered us to halt. We'd reached Kommandant Höss's home, a beautiful villa where he lived with his wife and four young children. Once, while working in his garden, I'd caught a glimpse of the kommandant. He'd invited Fritzsch to the villa for dinner. I'd watched as he kissed his wife and scooped the delighted children into his arms; Fritzsch had offered a bottle of wine to the adults and candies to the children. It was my most baffling day since I'd arrived in the camp. I couldn't understand how a man running such a twisted operation could assume the role of father and husband while his vicious subordinate played the polite dinner guest, yet there it was, right before me.

The prisoners and I spent hours under the hot sun. We shifted soil, laid flowerbeds, watered plants, and pulled weeds, making sure the kommandant's garden was in pristine condition. Before Auschwitz, I hadn't known much about plants or gardening, even though my mother loved flowers, but I was learning as quickly as I could. Work continued uninterrupted until the day was almost over, when I uprooted a crocus stem instead of a weed. The kapo's club was quick to point out the error of my ways.

After marching back to the camp, tired and dirty and sore, I

received my evening meal, one that made me long for the bundle
of questionable meat wrapped in butcher paper that Mama used
to bring home after picking up rations. I took my food back to
Block 18, where Father Kolbe greeted me with his usual smile and
led me past the men toward our pallets.

Most men in my block hardly glanced at me anymore, unless
it was a look of frustration or annoyance, as if my presence somehow inconvenienced them. Still, I kept close to Father Kolbe as we
passed. Although I remained vigilant and never felt completely
safe, Father Kolbe made me feel safer.

Before consuming his meager portion of dark, heavy bread and
gray, watery soup, Father Kolbe crossed himself, bowed his head,
and clasped his hands, blistered and calloused from his day on
the construction site. He didn't complain, though they must have
hurt terribly if they felt as bad as they looked.

I poked his arm. "Stop, you'll get punished." It was probably a
sin to interrupt someone in prayer, especially when that someone
was a priest.

Father Kolbe opened one eye and brought a finger to his lips.
"Shhh, I'm not finished." He smiled and closed it again.

By the time he lifted his head, I'd gulped down my soup. He
slipped half his bread to me. With considerable effort, I refrained
from shoving the additional portion into my mouth. Instead I
nudged him and tried to return it, but he pretended he didn't notice. I nudged him again, harder this time.

"You might as well eat it, Maria, because I'm not taking it back,"
he said, a mischievous twinkle in his eyes.

I couldn't resist a small smile. "Fine, but you need to eat, too,
Father Kolbe."

"I'll eat my soup."

"Right, of course. Be sure you don't overindulge."

With a chuckle, Father Kolbe gathered his food and joined a forlorn young man a few meters away. He'd share words of encouragement with the prisoner and likely give him the rest of his bread. That's what he usually did. I could attempt to dissuade him all I wanted, but he'd never stop.

As I lifted the bread to my lips, a shadow fell over me. A young prisoner stood above me, large and strong, and his greedy gaze was set on my remaining food. A whole ration and a half of bread.

"You won't last long here. Hand it over."

We're a waste of space, a waste of clothes, a waste of rations.

I clung to the bread with a viselike grip and opened my mouth to consume it all at once, but, before I could, the man caught my wrist. As he wrested the rations from my clutches, all I knew was the hunger that clawed my insides. Without bread, I had nothing left to sustain me until morning. I lunged for it, but when he raised a hand I recoiled and shielded my head and face. One eye was blackening, and I didn't need another. The blow didn't come. I lifted my head while the inmate walked toward his next victim: Father Kolbe.

As I suspected, Father Kolbe had passed his bread to the man beside him and was preparing to consume his soup. Before the first spoonful reached his mouth, the thief reached him.

"Rations shouldn't be wasted on the likes of you, old man." He extended his hand toward the bowl, but Father Kolbe was already offering it to him.

"You're young and strong, and you need the nourishment far more than I do, my brother." Father Kolbe's voice held no resentment. There was no fear, either, only kindness.

The young man needed no more encouragement. He transferred Father Kolbe's soup to his own bowl and walked away, looking pleased with his conquests. Father Kolbe returned to my side and offered me a small smile. He didn't say anything, un-aware I'd witnessed the exchange, unaware I was targeted by the same prisoner. I stared into my empty bowl while the anger surg-ing through my veins mixed with astonishment.

In a place where people fought over scraps like rabid dogs, this man retained his humanity. And I couldn't understand how or why.

* * *

After the evening meal, free time began—the only somewhat bearable part of the day. I hurried to the toilets and washrooms. Ugly ceramic sinks ran the length of the washroom, reminding me of troughs, and I moved to a spigot in the back corner. I cast a discreet glance over my shoulder before filling my bowl and lift-ing it to my lips. Maybe quenching my thirst would alleviate the emptiness in my stomach.

As I washed my uniform with a tiny piece of soap, I imagined Mama beside me with her clothes submerged in hot water. Back home, I'd sometimes found her armed with a bar of lye soap and a washboard, removing sewage filth from her skirt, blouse, stock-ings, and shoes. A sign she'd smuggled children from the ghetto the night before.

Mama would insist she could disinfect them herself, but I wouldn't leave without helping. Together we'd change the water numerous times, scrub every speck of filth from her clothing, and clean ourselves and the bathroom from top to bottom. Once fin-ished, I'd fetch Tata's clothes and mine so we could wash them and hang them to dry next to Mama's. Before long, Zofia and Kar-ol would appear with their own dirty clothes, complaining about how Mama refused to use the laundry down the street.

A guard ordered us to hurry, so I donned my damp uniform and departed, rebuking myself for thinking of my family. I knew better.

With each passing day, I was more determined to leave Auschwitz. How it would happen, I didn't know. As I passed the barbed-wire fence, I considered electrocution, but slipping by the guard towers would be difficult, and if the guards noticed me getting too close to the fence they'd shoot. If my end were to come by bullet, there were easier ways that didn't include the risk of electrocution if the guards didn't care to stop me. Despite my determination to leave this place, I wasn't certain I possessed enough courage to touch the fence when such a death seemed terrifying. Why chance it when I could just as easily prompt a guard to shoot me during roll call or labor? Maybe I'd stop eating, but, if I did, Father Kolbe would notice and insist I maintain my strength. With him sharing additional morsels, malnutrition wasn't as likely. I kept walking and tugged at the loose skin on my ripped palms. Maybe the wounds would get infected, or maybe I'd succumb to exhaustion or disease.

There was always Fritzsch. As soon as he lost interest in our games, he'd get rid of me.

All I knew was that I was tired, and I missed my family. I would leave Auschwitz, and there was only one way to leave—through the crematorium chimneys.

Finish the game, Maria.

I would plan my attacks and coax my opponent into the end-game I wanted, but my patience was as thin and worn as the uniform on my back.

When I returned to Block 18, I sat on a pallet, relishing the brief respite. Most inmates lingered outside the block during free time, so I took advantage of the extra indoor space while I could. In silence, I counted the bug bites covering me and discovered seven more since yesterday.

Before long, Father Kolbe entered the block and gave his usual smiles, blessings, and encouragement to the inmates. At last he placed his pallet across from mine and set something beside him, out of my sight. He drew a large square in the dirt on the floor, then added a series of lines, forming smaller squares within the large square. Once finished, he had eight rows of eight small squares. Next he picked up the items he'd placed next to him: a handful of gravel. He put the largest rock in the back row, on a middle square. The second largest went next to it. Two more were stationed on either side of the first two, and he continued in such fashion until the two smallest rocks were in the outside corners. In front of the row, he lined up eight pebbles.

Then he produced some twigs. He lined them up on the opposite side of his grid, arranging them by size as he'd done with the gravel. Once finished, he marked each horizontal row *A* through *H* and numbered the vertical rows 1 through 8. At last he surveyed his handiwork.

"Not the best, but it'll do. The twigs are the black pieces, the pebbles are the white ones. I know you play a good bit of chess these days, Maria, but should you ever care to play simply for enjoyment, I'm happy to oblige." Father Kolbe gave me a knowing smile. "I'm told I'm quite good."

Grinning, I positioned myself across from him, then clasped my hands together to keep myself from snatching up my first piece. No matter how much the old me yearned for a simple pleasure from her old life, I couldn't do it. It wasn't fair. Not after what had happened.

Maria Florkowska was reckless as she danced around the chessboard one move at a time, strategizing and reacting based on her opponent's counterattacks, never doubting she would emerge the victor. Prisoner 16671 knew one wrong move was all it took to cost her the entire game.

"You're the white pieces, I'm the black," Father Kolbe said, his eyes alight. "I must warn you, I play to win."

My reservations nagged me, filling my mind with angry shouts, but a small, persistent voice argued in return. Father Kolbe had gone to the trouble to do something kind for me, to bring enjoyment back to the game that had become nothing but my lifeline. He was my friend, my only friend, and it would have been cruel to spurn him. Both voices took turns trying to win me over before I silenced them with my decision.

I'd made an exception for Father Kolbe regarding my name, so I could make an exception here, too. Just this once.

My strategy sprang to my mind, clear and distinct: I'd open with the Queen's Gambit, and, if Father Kolbe countered with the Queen's Gambit Declined, I'd lead into the Rubinstein Attack. So I picked up my queen's pawn and moved it to D4.

This was chess the way the game was meant to be played. Two opponents coming together of their own free will to engage in a battle of wits. This was the chess that had been a part of me for so many years. Fritzsch could use the game to control my time here, but, when it came to me and the board, I would play as if nothing had changed, as if I weren't desperate to leave this place. As long as I lived, I would play chess, and play well.

And I did play well, but, the deeper we got into the game, the more agonizing each passing moment became. Father Kolbe had helped me so much this past month, and now he'd done this, for no reason other than to provide me with joy. All I'd done was keep secrets from him.

The realization was all-consuming, so much so that when the

second gong sounded and sent us into evening silence, I muttered a quick thanks for the game, gathered the pieces, and turned away. As we settled down for the night, I begged sleep to come immediately so the nagging thought would leave me alone, but it didn't work. There was only one way to escape the weight pressing upon me.

Father Kolbe had treated me with compassion. I could at least give him honesty in return.

After allowing a few minutes for people to fall asleep, I got up. If I waited longer, I'd lose my nerve. I reached across to Father Kolbe and tapped him on the shoulder, trying not to disturb the clusters of slumbering people.

We moved to the far corner of the room, where we sat while I gathered my courage. Even though he couldn't see my expression in the darkness, I imagined that Father Kolbe knew I had something important to say. He waited for me to speak. If I told him the truth, there would be no going back, but I couldn't bear the deceit any longer.

So I told him what I'd never told anyone else—the story of how my family and I were sent to Auschwitz, beginning with our arrest.

Chapter 9

Warsaw, 25 May 1941

"LET'S PLAY MONOPOLY, Maria," Zofia said, twirling her finger around a loose curl. She rolled a ball to Karol, but he missed it, so it continued past him toward Tata's chair. Tata sipped ersatz coffee and used his cane to guide the ball back to my siblings.

"Sorry, Zofia, I can't." I refrained from mentioning why, but she wouldn't need an explanation. If I refused her on a Sunday, the reason was always the same.

"Are you leaving for the convent? May I go, Mama?"

"No," Mama said too quickly. She grabbed the nearest dishrag and gathered crumbs from the table with meticulous care.

Ignoring Zofia's complaints, I went into my bedroom and pulled on a thin pale pink sweater over my white shirtwaist. I watched my reflection in the mirror as my fingers moved through the familiar pattern to secure my hair in a braid. Once finished, a few tiny strands refused to be tamed; otherwise, it was suitable. I straightened my green plaid skirt and made sure my Kennkarte was in my handbag, then fetched my basket from the kitchen, checked the false bottom to ensure the documents were inside, and arranged a couple of potatoes over the compartment. When I returned to the living room, Zofia was still prattling.

"Please, Mama? We take food to Mother Matylda every Sunday. Sometimes you go, sometimes Maria goes, but I never get to go." She inserted an extra dose of complaint into the words and cast an envious glance at me.

"I want to go with Maria and Zofia!" Karol exclaimed. He tugged on Mama's skirt, as if a trip to the convent were life's greatest joy.

Not him, too. I turned an accusatory eye on my sister and waved a hand toward Karol. "Now look what you've done."

She faltered over a suitable retort, mouth agape, and called on Mama to demand justice. I sat on the rug by the coffee table and scooped up a white rook from my chessboard. Smooth and sturdy, a tiny turret that held so much power. *More power than a pawn*, a loud voice in my head jeered, but a little whisper shooed it away. Power wasn't enough to win a chess game. Strategy was far more important.

"Plotting your famous rook endgame, are you, Akiba Rubinstein?"

At Tata's query, I smiled and put the rook back. From one of my favorite chess grand masters, I'd learned to take the endgame into account from the opening play. It was an interesting strategy, intense and aggressive, one that tended to serve me well. Rubinstein exercised a mastery of rook endgames, but my variations on his strategy favored the pawn.

While Tata returned his empty cup to the kitchen, I made an opening play with a white knight. Chess required all my attention and sharpened the edges of my mind like a sword against a whetstone. Queens and kings and bishops, knights and rooks and pawns. Each intermingled until the board was an intricate black-and-white web of my own design. Two opponents, black versus white, were united in a common quest for triumph, but were otherwise irreconcilable. One prevailed by overcoming the other. In the case of a stalemate, where neither player emerged victorious, only by playing additional games could the winner be established. Two enemies, one victor, and one ultimate way to determine who that victor would be. The checkmate.

But there would be no checkmate for me and my sister. We remained locked in a stalemate where neither Rubinstein's rook nor my pawn could affect the outcome.

"You don't have time to play Monopoly, but you have time for chess?"

I hadn't noticed Zofia approaching, but the scornful question came from right beside me and ruined my concentration. "I'm only playing for a few minutes before I leave. Be quiet so I can finish."

"You're going with Irena, aren't you?"

She voiced it as if I'd committed the most heinous crime imaginable. I surveyed the board and selected a rook. "No, but even if I were, that's none of your business. Stop bothering me."

It was the wrong thing to say, and I knew it as soon as I heard the words. I opened my mouth to make a desperate attempt to salvage the conversation, but Zofia erupted.

A sudden flash of movement, then a few chess pieces clattered against the table and fell to the floor. Gasping, I dove after them, but I'd hardly collected them before she knocked a few more off, encouraged by my protests. An angry shout—probably from Mama—rang in my ears in the midst of Zofia's third attack, and I pushed her back with the hand not clinging to chess pieces. Undeterred, she lunged again. I screamed at her to stop, blocked her with my arm, and wrestled her away, because if the little brat broke my chess pieces . . .

"Girls."

The quiet, firm tone was one we both knew better than to disobey. We froze. I clutched the chess pieces to my chest, refusing to loosen my grasp or lower the arm that held my sister back, and Zofia remained folded over me, one hand centimeters from the board. I tried not to wince upon meeting Tata's unrelenting gaze.

"That's enough."

Usually when his voice carried that particular note of warning, not even Zofia would persist. This time nothing could douse the flames of her temper, not even Tata's reprimand or Mama ordering me to the convent *now* and Zofia to the dishes *immediately*. With a furious huff, she pushed me away, stomped to our bedroom, and slammed the door behind her. The silence that followed was suffocating.

During my past few months of resistance work, I'd delved into the heart of lies, danger, and rebellion, a world far removed from my sister's. The war had forced us apart, but until the danger had passed I didn't see a way to remedy it. As I combatted the tears blurring my vision, I made sure none of the chess pieces had been damaged by Zofia's tantrum. Mama came to her knees beside me, and I ran my fingers over the black queen. My chess pieces were intact, but somehow I felt as if they weren't.

When Mama brushed a few stray hairs from my forehead, I spoke in a whisper. "Can't I tell her?"

She sighed and covered my hands with her own. "All we can do is pray this war ends soon."

A stalemate until things changed. If they ever did.

Mama kissed my cheek before going to our room to check on Zofia, so I gathered my belongings. Tata stood, put on his brown tweed jacket over the matching waistcoat, and donned his favorite fedora, gray with a blue Petersham ribbon. In the security of my mind, I begged him not to follow me, but he picked up his cane and dashed my hopes. If he wanted to speak to me alone after an argument, I had a feeling it meant punishment. Silence remained until we stepped out into the hall, then I seized my chance to argue my case.

"I'm sorry, Tata, but Zofia wouldn't leave me alone, and she almost broke my—"

He cleared his throat, so I fell silent. It was worth an attempt. The wait was agonizing, but I stared past him and focused on the apartment door labeled FLORKOWSKI, our family name. At last he sighed.

"Well," he said slowly, "I must say, you have impressive reflexes."

The words conjured a sudden smile, and Tata chuckled while I nestled into his comforting embrace. He held me close. One hand cradled my head as if I were small, and I almost wished I could go back to those times. When I was small, there wasn't a war. I didn't have to keep so many secrets from my sister.

"You understand why you've been so busy these past months. Zofia doesn't," Tata murmured. "She can't. All I ask is that you try to be more sensitive toward her feelings."

I sighed. "That would be easier if I could tell her the truth. But I'll do my best."

"Would you rather I go to the convent for you today?"

"Did the thief who stole Mama's handbag find your Kennkarten inside and return them?"

He chuckled. "No, but considering none of the information is accurate, I would have been impressed if he had. Our replacements should be ready in a few days, then we'll be able to work again." He kissed my forehead. "Be careful, my brave girl."

Instead of loosening my grasp, I clung to him a moment longer. His familiar scent was laced with faint traces of wax and pine, evidence of the polish he'd used on his cane that morning. The combination was oddly appealing. At last I lifted my head, and Tata brushed his thumb across my cheek, tracing the remnants of a tear stain.

Once he disappeared into the apartment, I pushed the argument aside and bounded down the stairs. The convent visit was exactly what I needed to lift my spirits. Outside, sunshine kissed my cheeks and lent a golden tint to the beige stucco of our four-story building, but the beautiful day was marred by a disgusting sight.

A large truck and two cars drove through the intersection. The sight brought me to a startled halt, and I lingered by the door while they parked. SS officers and men dressed like civilians swarmed onto the street like ants upon carrion. As one of the men got out of his car, he tucked something into an interior coat pocket. The sunlight glinted off a chain and silver disk.

A warrant badge.

I'd never seen one, but Irena and my parents had described them to me countless times. It was the only way to identify the people we feared most. Someone had betrayed my family, I was sure of it, otherwise the Gestapo wouldn't have come.

When the Gestapo agents didn't charge into my building, I loosened my grip on the doorknob. They stood by their vehicles while one consulted a piece of paper and said something about needing to go down one more block, but one of the SS officers scanned Bałuckiego Street until his sights locked on a new target—me.

"Come here."

Resistance members and Gestapo agents played a similar game. We hid our identities and completed our missions in secret while no one around us knew the truth of who we were. I'd probably passed countless Gestapo agents on the street without knowing it, perhaps had even been stopped by SS men who were also secret members, but this time I was fully aware of who had beckoned me.

Swallowing hard, I obliged and took small steps to buy time to think. The street was bare and quiet, magnifying the shuddering breaths that announced my panic like the loudspeakers in the square announced every German victory. They couldn't have suspected me of anything when all I'd done was leave the building . . .

I clutched my basket tighter to focus my thoughts. *Stay calm. Study them.*

There were six and, judging by the insignia that determined his rank and the number of medals on his uniform, the man who had spoken was in charge. As I drew closer, his unyielding gaze remained fixed on me.

"Identification," he said.

That particular order never got any easier to hear. I searched for my Kennkarte, delaying as long as possible. This officer wasn't a boy who prided himself on shiny jackboots, massive weapons, and titles. This was an officer whose mission was to crush the resistance. I needed to ensure that he didn't consider me a threat. After handing over my Kennkarte, I took a moment to gather myself, then inserted a level of lightness into my voice.

"If you'll forgive me, Herr Sturmbannführer, I'm on my way to—" Both my voice and my courage fled when he looked at me. I'd never had so much difficulty attempting to be calm before an officer. "To meet a friend."

"The basket."

Everything in me screamed in refusal. "Of course, but my—"

The *Sturmbannführer* nodded to another man, who snatched the basket. My plan wasn't working. I needed to figure out what I was doing wrong, and I needed to reclaim my possessions, but I was at a loss. All I could think about was the warrant badge.

The man shuffled through the basket. "Nothing, Sturmban-nführer Ebner."

I kept my eyes lowered so he wouldn't see my relief, but I was aware of him extending the basket toward me. Before he could return it, Ebner ripped it from his clutches, and I bit back a cry of protest.

"Name," Ebner said as he began a painstakingly thorough search.

"H-Helena." I paused, hoping it would banish the quaver from my voice. No one had ever interrogated me over the contents of my false papers. I'd memorized the information, of course, but it was difficult to recall any of it when my heart wouldn't stop thumping against my chest. "Helena Pilarczyk."

This time when Ebner looked at me, I forced myself to look back, and I saw what I was afraid I'd see.

Suspicion.

No, it was in my head, just in my head. He wasn't suspicious; his thoroughness and the warrant badge had unnerved me, that's all. Irena and I had gotten past soldiers countless times, and I'd done it alone, too. If I could do it before, I could do it now.

"Date of birth."

The longer I stayed, the more questions he'd ask, and the more he'd go through my belongings. I had to answer quickly. I had to think of a way to make them leave or convince them to let me go.

Don't panic, think. Study him. Ignore the guns pointed at you. Think.

"Date of birth."

The impatient snap made me realize I hadn't said a word, so I mumbled the falsified date and tried to develop an escape plan, but the thoughts didn't come. Nothing came, nothing but an overwhelming urgency that plagued my insides but didn't prompt me to action, not when Ebner dropped the basket and stomped on it, not when the weave splintered while pieces of potato oozed around his boot, not until he kicked the broken basket apart and the baptismal certificates scattered across the cobblestones.

Run.

It was foolish, it was desperate, it was all I could do. I put on a burst of speed, but I didn't make it three steps before an SS man raised his rifle butt. A heavy, blinding pain drove the air from my lungs and threw me to the ground. I coughed and gasped until an ironlike grip pulled me to my feet. Ebner was yelling, but I was too distracted by my pulsating gut to listen, so he grabbed my face and twisted it toward the handful of blank documents.

"Answer me, you stupid girl. Where did you get these, and where are you taking them?"

I could have spat in his face or begged for mercy, and neither would have made a difference. I was in no condition to be defiant, but I chose defiance anyway. It was all I had left.

"I don't know, Herr Sturmbannführer. I'm just a stupid girl."

The slap was almost worth it. Almost.

The stinging blow split my lip, and I was too busy spitting blood to hear what he said next; then the Gestapo agent spun me to face someone.

It was Mrs. Kruczek, our neighbor. She couldn't have picked a worse time to leave the apartment building, but it was too late. She stood frozen in the doorway, petrified, and clutched her baby, Jan, to her chest. I stared at her, pleading through silence.

Some of the guns pointed at me turned on Mrs. Kruczek. She gasped and held Jan tighter, as if her arms could have somehow fended off bullets.

"Identify this girl and where she lives, or all three of you will die."

Another man repeated Ebner's order in Polish. She had no choice. I knew she had no choice. But I kept praying anyway.

Please. Please don't. My family.

Mrs. Kruczek's glassy eyes met mine, as if issuing a silent apology, before she lowered them. Her voice shook so much she hardly got the words out. "Maria Florkowska. Second floor."

Think, think, for God's sake, think.

They dragged me past a sobbing Mrs. Kruczek, inside, and upstairs. Thank God Mama and Tata's false identifications had been stolen. My parents wouldn't be implicated, and Zofia and Karol were children. Surely the Gestapo didn't care about children, so they'd tell my family about my arrest, nothing more.

A heavy fist pounded on the door bearing my family name, but no one had the opportunity to respond before a booted foot delivered a swift, forceful kick. It caved with a splintering crack. They threw me inside, and I stumbled into my father's arms.

When I lifted my head, I noticed my own blood had stained his shirt. I had only a moment to meet Tata's horrified gaze before the men invaded and tore me from the security of his grasp. Their bellows mingled with Mama's scream.

The Gestapo agents turned over furniture, emptied cabinets and drawers, broke dishes, pulled up rugs, and demolished everything in their path. I thanked God Tata's resistance newspaper, the one piece of evidence they could have found, had already disappeared from its usual hiding place—beneath the seat cushion of his chair. One of the Gestapo agents flipped the coffee table over, and my chessboard crashed to the ground. The beautiful pieces scattered.

The sound of my name broke through the furious German shouts, and I found Mama with her back pressed against the wall. She clung to my siblings and implored me to come to her. Tata's

voice rose above the din, claiming he printed the baptismal certificates and distributed them himself and that his daughter had
taken the wrong basket by mistake, and I remained in the middle
of the chaotic scene, paralyzed.

An SS soldier turned to my father with a condescending sneer.
"You mean for us to believe you deliver documents?" To emphasize his point, he struck my father's bad leg.

Tata collapsed, and his cane clattered against the floor as a
groan escaped his clenched teeth. I screamed and darted toward
him, but another blow to the stomach brought me to the floor,
and I curled into myself, willing the agony to subside while the
world around me turned hazy. Mama's shriek sounded distant.
A foreign voice joined hers, followed by a sharp, deliberate
smack.

Hands found me, and, as the ache in my stomach dissipated, a
Gestapo agent hauled me down the stairs. I struggled, but he was
too strong. It was like fighting a stone pillar. He tossed me into the
truck, my hip taking the brunt of the impact, pain shooting down
my leg. As I sprawled across the empty floor, a thud landed beside
me, accompanied by a familiar gasp. Mama. More thuds followed,
indicating the rest of my family, and the door slammed shut.

The truck began to move. I pushed myself up and held one arm
across my throbbing stomach. Tata sat up, wincing as the movement angered his leg, then he helped Mama. She held Zofia and
Karol as if she'd never let them go, and their hiccupping sobs
joined into one. Mama nestled into Tata and gingerly touched the
bright red mark on her cheek.

"Dear God," she whispered. A small, desperate prayer.

What a fool I was. To think I'd almost convinced myself that
my family would be spared.

"They stopped on our street, and I saw one of them had a warrant badge. I didn't know what to do, and after they took the basket and found the certificates, they forced Mrs. Kruczek to identify me, and I'm sorry, I'm so sorry."

As my voice quivered, Tata guided me closer and wiped blood from my cut lip. "There's no shame in fear. You didn't do anything wrong, Maria."

His words weren't true, but I didn't say so. If I'd thought faster, I wouldn't have cost my entire family their freedom.

"Did we break the law?" Zofia murmured.

Tata placed an affectionate hand over hers. "This war has brought incredible cruelty upon Jewish people, so your sister, Mama, and I have been helping them. Helping innocents flee persecution is not wrong."

Zofia stared at me as if I were a stranger. No one spoke further, and I moved away from my family and into the far corner, crippled by the sheer magnitude of what I'd done.

When the truck stopped, the doors swung open, and we were greeted by a rifle barrel. The soldier wielding it motioned for us to get out. Mama scrambled out with shocking speed and rushed to another soldier who stood behind the first.

"Please, they're children, for God's sake."

He grabbed her arm before she could say more, and she stiffened and fell silent. Tata climbed out next and reached for Karol, who was closest to the door, but a soldier shoved my father back while another pulled Karol out of the truck.

I'd never heard my brother or my parents shriek the way they did, then Mama's cry rose above the rest.

"Let me hold him, please let me hold him!"

Her pleas grew louder and her struggles more frantic until her captor looked so irritated that he released her. She snatched Karol out of the other man's arms, held him against her chest, and spoke to him in a soft voice while he burrowed into her. When she looked at Tata, an escaped tear glistened against her cheek.

As two more soldiers came forward to collect us, Zofia's hand found mine. The soldiers let us proceed to the door on our own, probably to avoid another outburst from Mama. I gave Zofia's hand a small squeeze for comfort, even though I didn't feel capable of providing any. I knew exactly what sight would greet me when I stepped outside.

A wall of gray stone surrounded the massive complex. Even before the invasion, I'd always thought Pawiak was harsh and ugly, a blight upon a city of stunning beauty. Now it wasn't just a hideous building. It was a manifestation of all my fears.

There's a special place in hell for resistance members who get caught.

✣ ✣ ✣

Auschwitz, 17 June 1941

"My parents and siblings were shot as soon as we got to Auschwitz. I was selected for execution, too, but I strayed, and Fritzsch placed me with a group of workers. My family was killed while I survived because Fritzsch happens to enjoy chess."

As I finished my story, Father Kolbe didn't respond right away, and I was grateful for the dark. I didn't want to see the shock and disgust I imagined on his face. But when he spoke, his voice didn't match the expression in my mind.

"What happened to your family is horrific. Words can't express how much my heart aches for you, Maria."

"I didn't mean to leave them." My voice broke, but I was desperate to confess, desperate to transfer the weight of my sins to this poor, kind priest who had been foolish enough to befriend me. "When I got lost, I thought I'd find my family after registration. I didn't know one group was condemned to death while another wasn't. All this time, I've been using you, Father Kolbe, and I let you believe I'm someone I'm not, and I'm sorry."

"My beliefs about you aren't false, Maria, I assure you. And if our friendship allowed me to play a small part in alleviating your suffering, then I thank God for giving us that grace."

Thank goodness Father Kolbe couldn't see the tears on the brink of spilling down my cheeks. "I don't deserve God's grace."

"None of us do, yet He gives it to us anyway."

"Do you really believe that in a place like this?"

"It's in a place like this that I believe it most of all. How else could we find meaning amid such suffering?"

When we fell silent, the gentle patter of raindrops reached my ears. It was comforting somehow, and I wasn't sure why because very little comforted me anymore. Comfort had receded into my past, unattainable in this new world, a world of anything but comfort. Father Kolbe's presence was the only thing that transported me back to that state. To have the rain do the same was unusual, as if I were sitting by the window in my family's apartment in Warsaw, watching raindrops roll down the windowpane. But neither Father Kolbe nor the soothing rainfall was enough to change my mind.

Father Kolbe wouldn't approve of my decision, but I was tired of lying to him. He needed to hear the truth, the whole truth.

"I'm ready to leave." I intended to say more, but the words stopped coming. My decision was made; it had been for a long time, but I didn't anticipate it being so difficult to share.

The quiet surrounded us once again, a silence that pierced my heart until I could hardly withstand it. This time, instead of shock and disgust, I imagined fury on Father Kolbe's face, but even in my mind the image was ludicrous.

"That's not the answer, my friend."

"I'm sorry to disappoint you, Father Kolbe, and I don't expect you or God or anyone to have mercy on me, but I can't live with what I did to them," I replied, the words barely audible. "Besides, I was sent here to die anyway."

"Not like this."

I didn't know how to respond. I wished he'd yell at me, curse me, tell me I was damned for all eternity. For some reason, that would have made it easier to remain firm in my decision. Instead all I sensed was quiet empathy. Of course he wasn't trying to dissuade me through a fit of righteous anger. That wasn't Father Kolbe's way, but somehow his gentleness was harder to resist.

"Your life is a gift, even during terrible suffering. It's been a gift to me. Your family wouldn't want you to give it up."

It was strange to hear him speak of my family's wishes after I'd spent all this time suppressing my memories of them. Keeping them hidden was supposed to protect me from pain, but it had left me with nothing but emptiness. Now I allowed myself to picture my family, to let them fill my emptiness. During my time in Auschwitz, I'd detached myself from such recollections, watching from the outside. Remembering, but not remembering. This time, I was on the inside. *Mama. Tata. Zofia. Karol.*

Father Kolbe pressed something into my palm. I couldn't see it through the darkness, but I recognized the feeling of the smooth, round beads. A rosary.

"When I arrived, I asked a soldier if I could keep my rosary. Now I want you to have it. You're named after the Blessed Mother, and the rosary glorifies her Son's life—even His suffering and death. Within Christ's life, you'll find the strength to make peace within yourself and survive this place."

In the silence, my bony fingers moved along the beads and found the crucifix. I closed my hand around it, and the simple gesture broke every barrier within me. Everything I'd kept behind those barriers came tumbling out, and I sobbed as hard as I had when my family died. Father Kolbe's rosary pressed into my palm while recollections filled my head, memories of nights spent praying these familiar prayers with my family. Somehow the acute pain was more bearable. And somehow I felt less despicable than I had in weeks.

When my tears subsided, Father Kolbe's emaciated hand closed over mine. My grip on his rosary didn't loosen, and his gentle murmur filled every corner of the room.

"Live, Maria. Live for your family. Fight for your family. And survive for them."

* * *

I was under no illusions that death was guaranteed to leave me be. No one was safe from it. The chess pieces were set up on the board, and I faced an opponent more ruthless and unpredictable than any I'd ever confronted. We'd made our first moves, and the game was underway.

After my conversation with Father Kolbe, I'd stayed up most of the night sewing a small pocket with a button flap onto the underside of my uniform skirt. The next evening, as I marched back to camp from the workday, his rosary was tucked inside.

When I passed through the gate, Fritzsch stood by Block 24, where he usually waited for me if he wanted to end his day with a chess game. After a nod from Fritzsch, the guards waved me away, so I went to him.

"The same old chess game is getting tiresome."

At his abrupt greeting, I didn't know what he expected me to say. He could have been testing me. If entertaining him with chess was all I was good for, maybe he wanted to know if I'd welcome the implication of my death or beg for my life. I wasn't certain either would alter his decision when the time came. As long as Fritzsch was in control, my time in this place remained in his hands.

But only as long as Fritzsch was in control. If I survived this place, perhaps I would feel as if I had granted my family a small form of justice. And if I was going to survive this place, I had to survive Fritzsch.

"We could have a tournament."

His expression didn't change at my suggestion. Silence hovered between us for a moment, then he turned and walked away.

As I watched him go, something rose up inside me, a feeling I recognized from my days working for the resistance. My strategy had changed. Maybe I could win this game after all.

Chapter 10

Auschwitz, 26 July 1941

WHEN I HEARD the distant hum of voices outside, I collected the twigs and pebbles from the floor in Block 14, where Father Kolbe and I, among others, had recently moved. "We'll play again tonight," I whispered while he swept his hand over the filthy floor to erase our chessboard. "Next time, you can play with white and I'll play with black. You need the first-move advantage."

While I stifled a giggle, Father Kolbe raised a teasing eyebrow. "You do recall I won the game we just played, don't you?"

"And I won the game before that. You're a worthy opponent, Father Kolbe, but I hope you won't be too disappointed when I reclaim my title as victor."

"Is that a challenge?"

"A direct one."

"Accepted," he said, flashing a competitive grin as he helped me to my feet. "But if you win, I demand a rematch."

I clambered to my bunk, a welcome upgrade from the pallets of my last block. "I was hoping you'd say that."

Father Kolbe chuckled as he returned to his bunk, and I settled beneath my thin blanket. The moment I closed my eyes to feign slumber, the door swung open, followed by a guard's voice calling my number.

Rubbing my eyes as if I'd just woken up, I climbed down and hurried to the two guards waiting at the door. They didn't say anything, but I knew why they'd come. I followed them out into the dark morning and to the roll-call square, where the crowd had already gathered.

"Today marks the final day of our chess tournament," Fritzsch said when we arrived. "You know the rules, Prisoner 16671. After roll call, instead of joining your work detail, you will meet me here by the shelter booth. The first round will consist of five games between the guards. Those five winners will play against you."

While Fritzsch droned on about who would be competing today and other such trivial matters, I suppressed a sigh. Although this tournament had been my idea, I preferred my games against Father Kolbe to these incessant rounds against the guards, spending all day in the roll-call square with no one but Fritzsch and the SS men. I'd lost count of how many games I'd played each day, but the guards had relished it so much that Fritzsch had already promised to have another tournament soon. At least my plan was keeping me from manual labor—and above all, keeping me alive.

My two guards remained beside me. While Fritzsch continued speaking, one turned to the other and spoke in a low voice. "Who are you betting on?"

"I'm not watching the tournament today," his companion muttered as he lit a cigarette. "Not now that Kommandant Höss is back from Berlin. If he catches me slacking after what happened yesterday, he'll have my head."

"That's right, you told me about that," the first one said as he twirled his club. "Why the hell did the kommandant get so angry over a simple question?"

The other guard shrugged. "I welcomed him back and asked how his trip was, then he forbade me from prying into secret Reich matters and threatened to have me transferred. My family would never forgive me if that happened, so from now on, I'm following orders and keeping my mouth shut." He pulled out a pocket watch and checked the time. "I imagine Kommandant Höss will be here soon. Last night, he said something about spending today in the main camp."

"After roll call, we should advise Fritzsch to reschedule the tournament. God forbid anyone disobey the kommandant's orders," the other man said with a snigger.

As I listened to the conversation, my hand strayed toward the small pocket inside my uniform. I pressed my fingers against the fabric to feel the pale blue rosary beads and silver crucifix tucked inside.

Live. Fight. Survive.

I wanted to live. Every part of me wanted to live. Auschwitz had taken so much from me, but I wouldn't let it have me, too. Not if I could help it. This was a game I'd vowed to win. And the conversation between the guards had inspired the next phase of my strategy.

Once the rest of the prisoners joined us for roll call, I took my place next to Father Kolbe. Though I'd bought myself time with chess tournaments, those wouldn't be enough to wrest control away from Fritzsch—but with this next phase I'd just conceived, perhaps I'd found the solution. All I had to do was make it work before he decided I was no longer useful.

To my left, Father Kolbe hummed a piece by Schubert, one that accompanied a familiar Marian prayer. The *Ave Maria.*

The melody transported me home, and I closed my eyes. Mama was there, seated at her dressing table, armed with hairpins. While her fingers twisted and shaped her blond tresses, she watched her reflection and softly sang, as she often did when focused. Her tone was graceful, reverent, and her lips enunciated each Latin word while her meticulous fingers inserted hairpins into the elegant creation atop her head. Tata paused outside the doorway, listening, loath to disturb her. She smiled when she caught his eye in the mirror, but she didn't stop.

Father Kolbe's tune ended, carrying Mama's voice away and bringing me back to the roll-call square. I waited until Fritzsch's heavy footfalls reached my ears as he strolled through our ranks. Time to test my plan.

I took a breath to gather my courage and dropped my voice to a whisper. "My mother used to sing that hymn all the time."

Fritzsch came closer. I suspected he'd heard me. Though I didn't look at him, I felt him scrutinizing me. This had to happen if my plan was going to work, but that didn't make it any easier to draw a steady breath while the threat of his wrath loomed over me.

Fritzsch watched me, taking his time. "Prisoner 16671, were you speaking?"

"Yes, Herr Lagerführer." *Answer as simply as possible. Never offer details unless asked.*

"Which of these sorry bastards were you addressing?"

I tried to speak, swallowed hard, and tried again. "None of them, I . . . I was talking to myself."

It was the most pathetic lie I'd ever told, but that didn't matter. My plan didn't involve incriminating Father Kolbe. I'd just needed a reason to say something. From the corner of my eye, I saw Father Kolbe opening his mouth, but he didn't have a chance to intervene before Fritzsch's club met my stomach and sent me to the ground. I gritted my teeth against the familiar, pulsating pain, trying not to give him the satisfaction of my agonized cry, but of course I failed.

"For your disobedience," Fritzsch said. "And for your lie."

The blow to the ribs was sharp and excruciating, and all I could do was whimper. Drawing a breath made my eyes water, but Fritzsch bellowed at me to get up, and I had to obey. Once I was on my feet, he grabbed my face with his leather-gloved hand and forced me to meet his malicious gaze.

"Listen carefully, 16671. You're going to tell me which of these vermin you were talking to, or I will beat it out of you."

"Forgive me, Herr Lagerführer, it was my fault entirely," Father Kolbe spoke up. "No need to punish the girl."

How Father Kolbe always managed to sound so calm, I never knew, but I wished he would take his words back. This wasn't part of my plan. Fritzsch was supposed to catch me disobeying—only me. I'd forgotten to assume that, whether I'd spoken to Father Kolbe or not, of course he'd try to help. I couldn't have picked a worse opportunity to test this strategy.

After pushing me away, Fritzsch approached his new target. Father Kolbe didn't make a sound when Fritzsch struck him across the face, but it took everything in me to contain a protest.

"Both of you will stay after roll call," Fritzsch said. He marched away, striking prisoners as he went.

I didn't dare turn my head to look at Father Kolbe, but I apologized to him in the silence of my mind. Still, a flicker of hope rose into my chest. I wasn't certain if keeping prisoners after roll call went against the kommandant's wishes, but I imagined it did.

When roll call ended, we stayed in place while the prisoners swarmed around us and departed with their work details. Once everyone was gone, we were alone with Fritzsch. And Kommandant Höss was nowhere in sight.

It was far too late to take back my actions, but I regretted them. Maybe the guards had been wrong about the kommandant coming to the camp. I'd provoked Fritzsch into punishing me for no reason, and I'd brought my fate upon Father Kolbe, too.

Fritzsch looked between us. "You two are friends?"

I shook my head in immediate refusal, though I couldn't fathom why. Lying wasn't going to do me any good. Fritzsch nodded, then he hefted his club and approached Father Kolbe.

"Wait, no—I mean, yes. Yes, Herr Lagerführer." I let out a breath when Fritzsch paused moments before he struck. "We're friends."

"In that case, you've made my job easy." Fritzsch lowered the club and turned to me. "Choose his punishment. And he'll choose yours."

Beads of sweat trickled down my neck and brow, and not simply because the day was getting hotter with every passing moment. Before I could find words, Father Kolbe stepped forward.

"Herr Lagerführer, I take full responsibility and will accept the consequences for both of us."

"Keep your fucking mouth shut or I'll send you both to the gallows." Fritzsch shoved Father Kolbe back, so he fell into place and remained silent.

Fritzsch waited for me to speak, but I couldn't. What a stupid, reckless plan this was. I glanced at Father Kolbe, who gave me a small nod, as though assuring me he wouldn't hold my choice against me.

"The longer you take, the harsher I'm going to require the punishment to be." Fritzsch moved closer, eyes aglow as if we were in the middle of a chess game and he'd just placed me in check.

How was I supposed to choose? Two weeks of half rations? Our rations were pathetic enough as it was. A week in a standing cell in

Block 11? My feet throbbed at the end of every workday, so to lose the chance for relief would have been absolute misery. Twenty-five lashes? I had no idea how painful a flogging would be, but I never wanted to find out. And even if I'd been able to determine which was the most merciful option, I couldn't force any of them upon Father Kolbe.

"Why aren't the prisoners with their labor assignments?"

For a moment I thought the dizzying heat and my parched throat had made me imagine the new voice, but I hadn't. He'd come.

"The prisoners spoke during roll call, Herr Kommandant," Fritzsch said. "We're determining punishment."

"Keeping them from their labor assignments isn't going to improve their behavior," Kommandant Höss said, frowning as he joined us. "Your job is to punish them at an appropriate time, not to prevent them from working. All you've done is affect the efficiency of my operation." Höss turned to me and Father Kolbe. "Consider this your warning. You won't be granted leniency if you disobey again."

"Yes, Herr Kommandant," we replied in unison.

After telling Fritzsch to come to his office so they could discuss his trip to Berlin, Kommandant Höss glanced at us one last time. The furrow in his brow deepened when he settled on me. He pressed his lips together and marched away, shouting at a few guards to report to Fritzsch. When the guards obliged, Fritzsch looked to Father Kolbe.

"Prisoner 16670, what's your assignment?"

"Construction, Herr Lagerführer."

Fritzsch seemed pleased by this news. He ordered the guards to escort us both to the construction site, even though that wasn't my kommando, and we followed them from the camp. Construction should have terrified me, but I wasn't focused on the difficulty of the labor. My strategy had proved successful. I had to persevere to the main goal: I had to prompt Fritzsch into violating protocol when the kommandant was around to catch him. To survive for my family, I had to get Fritzsch transferred.

Chapter 11

Auschwitz, 20 April 1945

THE ALLIES ARE hunting people like you."

I don't know why I blurt out the words. Maybe I hope to catch Fritzsch off guard, unnerve him. The alliance of nations on the cusp of defeating Germany and its Axis partners will surely inflict consequences on them. They must intend to hold men like Fritzsch accountable. Perhaps he fears the fate awaiting him, so my threat should pique his interest. He looks up, turning one of the captured black knights over in his hand.

"Is that so?"

His tone is level, unconcerned, untouched by the fears I hoped to provoke—or perhaps simply refusing to reveal them to me. Still I nod, though I'm not certain there's any truth to my claim. But Fritzsch doesn't need to know that.

"Yes, and I doubt I'm the only former prisoner looking for you, either. Someone else will find you, just like I did."

I manage to sound far more confident than I feel. Even if he believes me, I'm certain Fritzsch won't admit it, but for a moment I could swear something changes in his face. It doesn't linger long enough for me to decipher it, but it gives me a small boost of encouragement.

Fritzsch scoffs. "The Allies are hunting men who served their country? Men who sought to rid the world of its vermin and make it a better place? And those same vermin think they have any power over those of us loyal to the Reich?"

This time I'm the one who scoffs while I move a bishop. "If those so-called vermin have no power over you, why did you bother meeting one here?"

Although Fritzsch doesn't respond, his fingers curl around the knight. Success is cool and calming, cleansing me of the turmoil rumbling inside me like the thunder rumbling in the distance. I'm in control. Not Fritzsch.

As he prepares to take his turn, he sighs and wipes rainwater from his face. "I'd hoped the rain would stop, but it hasn't, so we should move indoors. What do you think? Block 11, perhaps?"

A distant peal of thunder shakes the sky while the memories flare up again, attempting to wrest control from my clutches. I knew better than to provoke him, but I did it. I did it because I'm stupid and reckless.

"You can remember where your pieces were, can't you?" he asks, gesturing to the board. "Go on, take yours, and I'll take mine. We'll be more comfortable inside."

I rub my hand along the back of my neck and across my back, feeling the thick, raised skin that betrays the web of scars. Suddenly they throb as if they were fresh. "I'm not moving."

"Don't be difficult. I'd much prefer Block 11, wouldn't you?" Fritzsch gathers a few pieces; then he smiles. "We can set up in Cell 18."

Of course he'd suggest that. I knew he would, but when I hear the words something inside me feels like it's on the verge of collapse. I dig my fingernails into my palm, desperate to keep it contained. "You're not going anywhere near Cell 18."

"Aren't you going to get your pieces?"

"No, I'm not moving. I said I'm not moving—"

"No need to get excited," Fritzsch says, silencing the hysteria rising in my voice. "I thought you'd welcome the idea of taking shelter from the rain, but it was only a suggestion. A simple 'No, thank you, Herr Lagerführer' would suffice." He puts the pieces back, moves a pawn, and nods at me. "Your move."

My move. The scars across my back throb so much, I'm not sure I'll be able to make it.

Chapter 12

Auschwitz, 29 July 1941

THE EARLY MORNING sun peeked over the blocks on what was proving to be a sweltering day. But the suffocating heat wasn't what made it difficult for me to breathe—it was the guards' panicked shouts and recounts.

An inmate had escaped. An inmate from my block. Those who failed in their escape attempts were penalized, often killed; those who somehow managed to succeed left the rest of us behind to accept the consequences for them.

I did my best to remain inconspicuous, disregarding the sound of Fritzsch's curses. Once the guards finished roll call, he announced the punishment.

"The following ten prisoners from Block 14 are sentenced to immurement."

Confinement and starvation. What a horrible way to die. Fritzsch strolled up and down our ranks, assessing each petrified prisoner, selecting his victims one by one. As he called out numbers, guards pulled the poor, innocent inmates out of line and gathered them together to be escorted to their fate. I pitied them, but my mind was too clouded by a single plea to focus on pity.

Please don't call my number or Father Kolbe's.

The phrase banished all thought, and I repeated it over and over in my mind, as if my desperation could somehow control Fritzsch's decision. Surely he wouldn't select me. He had plans for future chess tournaments—unless he'd changed his mind and decided he was tired of me after all. No strategy had prepared me for this. I was bound by his camp, his rules, his timing; no matter how determined I was to have him transferred, to honor my family with my survival, his next move could destroy everything.

When Fritzsch reached my row, he had one person left to choose. With each step he took toward me, my silent plea grew in volume until it reached a full-fledged scream. *Please don't call my number or Father Kolbe's please don't—*

Fritzsch stopped when he reached me, and the screaming in my mind fell silent.

To meet his gaze would have been defiant, and defiance would have been the worst move to make. All I could do was stare at his jackboots, praying, willing him away, cursing my plea for doing no good even though I'd known it wouldn't. Fritzsch stood before me, motionless, and I felt his eyes scraping across my number while he took a breath.

With a chuckle, he moved past Father Kolbe beside me. I'd barely wrapped my head around our fortune before he announced the tenth and final prisoner sentenced to immurement.

"Prisoner 5659."

The last victim was a man near me, and when he heard his number his face turned white. He collapsed with a piercing wail. "My wife, my children . . . I'll never see them again."

When the cry left the devastated man's lips, Father Kolbe stepped forward without hesitation. He said something no one heard over the inmate's pleas for mercy, but Fritzsch noticed that Father Kolbe had moved out of line. He held up a hand, and the guard paused before collecting Prisoner 5659. Fritzsch told the weeping man to shut up, then regarded Father Kolbe with a sneer.

"What the hell do you want?" he asked, so Father Kolbe repeated himself in his calm, gentle manner.

"I'm a Catholic priest. I'd like to take this man's place, because he has a wife and children."

At this, everyone fell into stunned silence—the prisoners, the guards, and especially the young man. Even Fritzsch was rendered speechless. He took a moment to recover; once he had, he looked at Father Kolbe with renewed interest. "You're a Catholic priest?"

"I am, Herr Lagerführer."

Fritzsch exchanged a pleased glance with the other guards, kicked the dumbfounded young man, and ordered him back into line. "Replace 5659 with 16670. Take the prisoners to Block 11."

The trade happened so fast, I hadn't processed it before the guards led Father Kolbe away. He looked back at me. My dear, selfless friend. I could almost hear his soothing voice bidding me farewell, imploring me to understand. And I did. But, as he disappeared from view, the loud voice in my head screamed at him to take his choice back, kept screaming until the quiet voice pierced the devastation.

I would fight for every moment I had left with him.

My plan would work, I was sure of it. I knew Fritzsch, and I knew exactly how he would react to what I was about to do.

With a shriek, I fell on my knees before him. "Please, Herr Lagerführer, don't kill Father Kolbe, please!"

As I screamed and begged, Fritzsch kicked me away with a disgusted grunt, but nothing would deter me. More hysterical than ever, I crawled back, pleading in German and Polish, and clung to his ankles before he pulled out of my grasp.

"Shut up, you filthy Polack." Fritzsch picked me up by the shoulders and shook me, eyes alight with malicious pleasure. "You're reassigned to Block 11. You can watch 16670 die." He threw me to the ground, where I curled into a sobbing heap.

I knew it would work, you stupid, evil bastard.

Fritzsch ordered the prisoners to clear space around me and watch while he rewarded me further for my outburst. I had a feeling he'd be too impatient to wait for the public display of punishment that always accompanied evening roll call. I lifted my head to scan my audience of indifferent prisoners and amused SS officers. One officer stood out, an older man who appeared uncomfortable; he looked familiar, but I didn't have time to determine why.

I knew what was coming, the punishment I'd gambled on whether my plan worked or not. This was the only way to get what I wanted. Despite the terror of anticipation hanging over me, I would fight through it.

I was huddled on the ground, waiting to be medically cleared to withstand punishment, when Fritzsch's booted footsteps drew near. He grabbed the back of my collar and gathered the thin fabric in both hands. I cowered, expecting him to hoist me up; instead he pulled. The rip sounded like a death scream. Why had he torn my uniform?

His whip whistled through the air.

Pure, piercing agony tore across my back and wrenched a sound from my throat, a shriek unlike any I'd made before. Fritzsch wasn't following protocol at all. He was just eager to watch me bleed.

My Gestapo interrogation had been child's play compared to this. The pain was even worse than I'd feared. But I knew what was expected of me.

"*Eins. Zwei. Drei.*" With words that sounded more like sobs, I counted the lashes aloud, but upon my fourth blow my mind went blank. Four *in German, what's* four *in German? Hurry, I've known this language my whole life—*

A piercing whistle, the bite against my back. The fifth lash. I was too late. I'd lost count. And I knew what happened when the prisoner lost count.

"Start again!" Fritzsch shouted. The satisfaction in his voice was unmistakable.

Tears sprang to my eyes as the leather clawed my flesh, and the word fought to emerge through my gritted teeth. "*Eins.*"

We kept going, blow after torturous blow, while my gasping sobs and cries marked each new stripe. The pain was overwhelming, harsher than any I'd ever known, and I couldn't make another mistake, couldn't take much more of this.

As I counted the lashes, my mind traveled to when Sturmbannführer Ebner found the baptismal certificates in my basket, and when he threatened to torture my family to make me confess. He'd known he had bested me; now, as he inflicted my punishment with total disregard for protocol, Fritzsch thought he had, too. Once again, I was facing a man who believed he'd won. The difference was that Ebner *had* outwitted me, but Fritzsch had played right into my hands.

Fritzsch paused after my fifteenth lash. "Would you like to speak out of turn again, 16671?"

When I'd antagonized Sturmbannführer Ebner after he called me a stupid girl, it had been a small but satisfying act of rebellion.

Once again, I was in no position to provoke my captor. It hadn't been a wise choice then, and it wasn't a wise choice now. But my plans were always reckless.

It took considerable effort to lift my head and look at Fritzsch. With each step he took away from me, blood dripped from the whip clutched in his fist. My blood. As I stirred, one of the SS guards alerted Fritzsch, who paused and faced me. When I spoke, my voice was gruff, but it didn't waver.

"My name is Maria Florkowska."

I was ready for what would come next. Defiance was invigorating.

He descended upon me, delivering lashes so quickly I couldn't have counted them aloud even if I'd wanted to. As I screamed beneath the agonizing blows, newfound energy surged through me. I was living, and I was fighting.

"Fritzsch, what the hell are you doing?"

By the time the cry reached my ears, Fritzsch had fallen back. I thought the voice belonged to Kommandant Höss, but I wasn't certain. The pain made it impossible to focus.

"The Polack bitch has a mouth on her, Herr Kommandant." His voice held no remorse—not that I'd expected any.

"Then follow protocol to discipline her. I don't see a whipping block. Was she medically examined before the punishment was administered?"

"No, Herr Kommandant."

"For God's sake, I won't have incompetent officers in my camp. The next time you penalize a prisoner, follow protocol, do you understand?"

The world swam around me, a sea of searing anguish, but, as he spoke to someone else, the kommandant's voice began to fade. I assumed he was leaving. The guards ordered the prisoners to their labor assignments, and their footsteps grew fainter as they shuffled away—but a different set of footsteps grew louder.

A firm grip closed around my scrawny, torn shoulders and lifted me up, igniting the fire anew, and I screamed.

"Block 11 awaits, 16671." As the sneer brushed against my ear, a chill mingled with the scorching heat consuming my back. He threw me down, and everything continued to spin.

A slick warmth spread across my mangled back while remnants of sweat and salty tears streaked down my face. The pain was excruciating. But I would go to my new assignment.

I didn't even make it to my hands and knees before I collapsed. I had to get up, I had to get to Father Kolbe, I had to live and fight. But I was so tired and in so much pain, even though I didn't regret what I'd done. My plan had succeeded, and defying Fritzsch had armed me with renewed vigor. That same vigor told me to get up, and I would, I had to, but the sun beat me as eagerly as Fritzsch had, robbing me of what little energy I had left, and my mouth, lips, and throat were as parched as the hot, dusty ground beneath my cheek. Maybe I'd rest for a moment . . .

A shadow crossed over me, bringing me back to the present, reminding me to go to Father Kolbe. I dragged myself a few centimeters across the ground while the rough, blood-soaked gravel dug into my chest and palms and the painful effort made me retch. At the same time, I tensed, waiting for more blows to force me to my feet, but they never came. Instead the hands that touched me were gentle. They must have been Father Kolbe's—no, that was impossible, he was in Block 11. Maybe my mother's . . .

"Shhh, I'm not going to hurt you. Don't close your eyes, do you understand? Stay with me." A female voice. Not Mama's. This one was a bit deeper and accented. Familiar.

Somehow I ended up off the ground. Maybe I was walking,

maybe I was being dragged or carried, but I was changing locations one way or another. Amid the woman's comforting murmurs, one phrase stood out. *Don't worry.* Such an odd saying. In my experience, such a phrase meant that you should, in fact, worry. The realization should have been concerning, but I was too tired for concern. Instead I closed my eyes, even though the woman had told me not to.

Chapter 13

Auschwitz, 30 July 1941

WHEN I CAME to my senses, a sharp throb traveled across my back and shoulders. Something covered the pulsating sensation, something tight. Bandages. I opened my eyes and blinked as the world came into focus. I was on my stomach, lying on what must have been a thin mattress, in a large space crowded with other people. Some wore bandages; others were frail and sickly; others moved from bunk to bunk to examine the inhabitants. When had I been admitted to one of the hospital blocks?

Father Kolbe.

The thought sprang to the forefront of my mind, and I started to get up, but I paused with an agonized cry when the pain made my stomach turn.

"Don't move. You were flogged yesterday, remember?"

Slowly, I turned my head to locate the voice's owner. Standing at my bedside was Hania Ofenchajm, the young Jewish woman.

"I've been here for almost four months, and I've never seen a prisoner provoke the guards into giving additional lashes," she said. "That took a lot of *chutzpah*."

I had no idea what chutzpah meant, but I had a feeling she

wasn't paying me a compliment. My suspicions were confirmed by her disapproving frown.

"Out of every SS man you could have aggravated, you chose Fritzsch? The entire camp heard you carrying on about that priest. And if a flogging wasn't enough, you chose to be brazen, too? Did you expect that to win you anything other than harsher punishment?" Hania allowed me to mull over the queries, then she took a deep breath and softened her tone. "You can't take risks like that. Not if you want to survive."

She was right, of course. As intentional as my actions had been, I knew they were stupid. But I didn't regret them.

"What are you doing here?" The raspy, raw sound that came from my mouth took me aback. I cleared my throat, even though it wouldn't make an improvement.

"Translating and interpreting is a good job compared to others. It gives me additional privileges, such as the ability to move freely around the camp if I have responsibilities here rather than at the SS administrative offices. Today, I'm needed in the camp, so I slipped into the hospital to check on you."

Must have been nice, having the freedom to wander. I didn't dwell on it. "My name is Maria."

"So I heard in the roll-call square. Where are you from?"

"Warsaw."

She arched an eyebrow and flashed a pleased smile. "So am I. Did you work for the resistance? What kind of work did you do?"

"Different things, but mainly I helped a group of religious sisters who smuggled Jewish children from the ghetto."

"How long were you involved before you were caught?"

"A few months. From March until May." I paused, wincing as I shifted positions. "You brought me to the hospital, didn't you? Why?"

"I wasn't going to leave you bleeding to death in the roll-call square."

I looked at Hania, studying her features. Sharp cheekbones jutting above hollow cheeks. Probably in her early twenties, though she looked older. Thin, but not as thin as I was, which made sense because indoor labor assignments meant less strenuous conditions. Large, deep-set eyes as dark and rich as the stain on my father's wooden cane. The shorn hair peeking from under her headscarf was the same shade. Despite her thin form and aging beyond her years, she was beautiful. The guarded look in her eyes wasn't uncommon, so it didn't surprise or concern me. We shielded ourselves however we could.

"I told you to hold still," Hania said when I shifted again.

"Something is poking me through the mattress."

"Did you expect otherwise? This isn't the Hotel Bristol."

I wished she hadn't mentioned the hotel, because suddenly it was all I could think about. It soared above the heart of Warsaw and boasted an exquisite white stucco façade—a neo-Renaissance design, if I remembered what my parents had said. The stately belvedere on the rounded corner was my favorite part of the building. I imagined that I was at the hotel café for breakfast, feasting on eggs, sausage, apple-and-prune chutney, fresh orange juice, and assorted breads with jam, honey, and butter. I clung to the fantasy until a new voice broke through the desire lingering on my taste buds.

"How is she?"

"Awake," Hania replied. "Maria, this is Dr. Janina Ostrowska."

"Nurse, Hania, Nurse. My medical degree doesn't change the fact that I'm an incompetent Pole, remember?" Janina didn't mask the bitterness in her voice.

"An incompetent Pole, or an incompetent Jew?" Hania asked with a dry laugh.

"Both, I suppose. Take this, Maria."

Janina handed me pain medication, which I dutifully swallowed while she unwrapped the bandages.

Hania peered around Janina to glimpse my back. "*Merde*," she muttered, in what I assumed was French.

"I'm sure Maria appreciates the comfort," Janina said. "Keep comforting her like that and I'll throw you out."

Hania chuckled and said something in Yiddish, and Janina responded in kind while she checked my injuries. Her brow was furrowed in concentration, hovering above eyes that were light brown and flecked with gold, and the fuzz on her head had a red hue, reminding me of the chicory powder Mama and Tata added to their coffee when the drink became scarce. Although it was difficult to keep my eyes on her from my face-down position, I watched her while she treated my lacerations with expert care.

"You know, staring at the doctor is an excellent cure. That's what I always tell my patients."

The dry remark brought me out of my stupor, and heat rushed to my cheeks. "Sorry. I'm shocked to see another woman, that's all."

"You and everyone else. Hania saw me when I arrived last week, struck a deal with an SS man to spare my life, and secured a position for me here."

"Janina and I were neighbors before the ghetto," Hania said. "My family moved, but with the help of forged documents, she passed as a Gentile, remained in an Aryan district, and worked for the resistance."

"Until someone informed on me, and now here we are, neighbors again," Janina said as she finished applying fresh bandages. "You're as well as can be expected, but we'll monitor your progress over the next few days. Get some rest."

"Thank you, Dr. Ostrowska."

She flashed a wan smile. "Don't let the guards hear that. Call me Janina." She moved from bed to bed, a flurry of instructions and bandages and medications. When she'd gone, I braced myself against my bunk and pushed myself up.

"Where do you think you're going?" Hania asked, watching me.

"Block 11 for my labor assignment. Help me up, please."

"You heard Janina, you're not—"

"Father Kolbe is all I have," I whispered. "This is all the time I have left with him."

She remained silent. At last she voiced an unintelligible complaint in Yiddish before sighing. "Janina will have our heads for this."

I eased myself upright, but even with Hania's help my progress was painstakingly slow. By the time I was seated, I was already exhausted and lightheaded. Hania offered me a cup of water and a morsel of bread, and while I consumed them she stared at the back of my uniform. It was still open and exposed to my lower back, thanks to Fritzsch, barely clinging to my thin frame.

"I repaired your collar while you were unconscious, but I didn't have enough thread for the rest of the rip," she said.

"That's all right. I'll sew it later." I felt for the small hidden pocket until I found the beads contained inside, and I suppressed a relieved sigh.

After instructing me to meet her in the hospital block during free time so Janina could evaluate my injuries, Hania helped me to the door. The progress was even slower than my attempts to sit up, but determination drove me forward. Once outside, I paused to catch my breath.

"Hania, the last time we spoke, I—"

She held up a hand, cutting my apology short. "It's all right. Now, are you certain you can work?"

I nodded, and we pressed on. She supported me until we neared Block 11, then allowed me to continue alone. She watched me go, probably waiting until she was satisfied I could make it on my own, then I heard her walking away.

"Hania," I called after her, and she turned around. "Do you know how to play chess?"

"No," she replied, offering me a small smile. "But I'd like to learn."

* * *

When I reached Block 11 and staggered through the door, I insisted I was fit to work, and the kapo didn't dispute me. He assigned me to fetch waste buckets, so I spent my day in the basement.

As difficult as outdoor labor had been, Block 11 was worse. The prisoners crammed into the cells were condemned to terrible punishments and slow, torturous deaths. Moans, curses, and lamentations echoed down the dingy halls as I entered each cell. My progress was slow—even with pain medicine, every movement hurt. Some men glared at me, as if they resented my relative freedom; others begged for help, food, or water; others were too weak to acknowledge me. I evaluated the unfortunate faces long enough to look for Father Kolbe, then stared at the floor as I completed my tasks. Their tormented, hopeless gazes reflected my inability to alleviate their suffering.

It was the end of the day before I found him. Cell 18.

His gentle voice led prayers, accompanied by the other prisoners' murmurs, and I paused outside the door. They were reciting the final decade of the rosary. I closed my eyes, reached for the small pocket in my uniform, and grasped my rosary beads, listening as his familiar murmur rose above the rest and filled me with its usual peace. When the prayer was over, a reverent silence descended upon the cell.

Taking a deep breath to steady myself, I ensured the kapo wasn't nearby and pulled open the heavy door. The effort reopened a wound, making me gasp as it sent flames of agony across my back. The men turned toward the sound. Father Kolbe was kneeling in their midst, and he looked at me, eyes wide. He stood and opened his mouth to speak, but I went first.

"What you did for that prisoner, offering to take his place . . ." My voice caught, and it took me a moment to find it again. "You're an incredible man."

He shook his head. "That young man has a family. God willing, he'll return to them." Father Kolbe allowed the prayer to linger between us, then he took my hand and covered it with his own. "As for you, my friend . . ." The words trembled, and he swallowed hard.

I offered him a sad smile through eyes filled with tears. "How will I go on without you, Father Kolbe?" The answer was clear, but I had to hear it from him.

"You will live and fight, Maria." He gave my hand a small squeeze while he stepped closer and focused on my injuries. "Child, what have they done?"

I glanced at my lacerated shoulder, which had bled through the bandage hours ago. "A small price to pay for the reassignment I wanted."

As my words sank in and brought realization with them, I watched the shock register on Father Kolbe's face. I dipped my head in a single nod, confirming the unspoken question, and his eyes filled with grateful tears.

"Dear, clever girl, what a sacrifice you've made for me," he whispered.

He made a small sign of the cross over my wounds. When he was finished, I closed my fingers around his wrist, rotated his hand upward, and placed an item in his open palm. A pebble I'd picked up from the roll-call square, just like the ones he'd given me for a chess set.

Chapter 14

Auschwitz, 6 August 1941

H ANIA, WON'T YOU get in trouble for this?"
Because Hania and Janina insisted that I stay in the hospital to recover from my flogging and I was adamant about visiting Father Kolbe, we'd struck an agreement: I'd visit the hospital to rest and let Janina examine me, but I'd work in Block 11 enough to steal time with Father Kolbe. Hania dragged me back to Block 19 each day—she didn't trust me to uphold my end of the bargain—and as long as I kept returning, Janina was satisfied.

Janina had bathed my wounds in antiseptic—a process almost as painful as the injuries themselves—and bound them with fresh, clean bandages, and I voiced my question as Hania passed me my uniform. In response, she stole a glance around the room before dropping her voice.

"I had to translate some reports from this block anyway. I'll be fine, but if not, I'll take care of it."

The implications behind her words were clear. Fluency in five languages gave her an excellent advantage. She'd explained that she made deals with prisoners and guards alike, translating for them and receiving benefits in return, then kept the goods or used them for trade. Still, at the thought of bartering with our captors, I wrinkled my nose.

"My connections are the reason you're getting special treatment," Hania said, raising an eyebrow at me. "All the pain medicine you've received from Janina, for instance. Most prisoners are lucky to get half a pill. Thanks to my connections, Janina is alive, working here, acting as my hospital contact, and accessing additional resources through suppliers I've established inside and outside the camp, meaning she gives you proper dosages."

"Right, I'm sorry. I'm grateful for everything you've done," I replied with a sheepish smile while I put my uniform back on over my new bandages. "But you're Jewish. You should hate the Nazis even more than I do."

"If anyone hears you talking like that, all the hard work I've put into your recovery will be for nothing." She cast another wary glance around. "You can disagree all you want, Maria, but establishing connections with prisoners and guards alike has its perks. How do you think I got my own life spared? I have my younger brother to look after, too, so I'll welcome help in any form."

"Your brother is here?"

She nodded before sitting at the foot of my cot. "Izaak works as a locksmith. I have an SS connection who transferred him. When we first arrived, he was part of the road crew." One of the most arduous positions, where prisoners pulled heavy concrete cylinders to level the grounds.

"You can get labor reassignments?" I asked, genuinely impressed.

"As long as I offer the proper repayment. In a place like this, you have to give something to get something. It's not always pleasant, but I'll do anything to return to my *kinderlach*." A sad, fond smile tugged at Hania's lips, then she translated for me: "My children."

"How many children do you have?"

"Two, both sons. Jakub and Adam." A faraway look crossed her face, so I waited for her to continue. "They were three years old and four months old when my husband and I handed them over to the resistance. Eliasz, my husband, said it was for the best, but I wasn't so certain. Not until we were arrested."

"You saved their lives," I murmured. "How did you get arrested?"

Hania studied a small hole in her uniform before explaining. "In the ghetto, my elder sister, Judyta, lost her husband and newborn to dysentery. Her four-year-old daughter, Ruta, was all she had left, and she refused to give her up. One afternoon, my family and I were walking down the street, and four SS men were coming our way, so we kept to the gutter. My niece was chasing a pigeon, and when it flew onto the sidewalk, she followed. Judyta called to Ruta and tried to stop her, we all did, but Ruta wasn't paying attention. As my sister fetched her from the sidewalk, she apologized to the SS men for violating the law and assured them it was unintentional. It didn't matter. The officers didn't say a word before they threw them back into the street and started beating them."

"For being on the sidewalk?" I asked softly, and she nodded.

"Izaak, Eliasz, and my parents tried to protect my sister and niece, but they were attacked, too. As I watched, those men beat my family. I screamed at them to stop, but I couldn't move. I was paralyzed. All I could think about was the same thing happening to my sons if I hadn't sent them away.

"When the SS men relented, my niece was dead, right there in the gutter. They'd crushed her skull. Judyta wouldn't stop screaming over Ruta's little body, so the officers shot her and arrested us. My parents died in Pawiak from their injuries, then Eliasz, Izaak, and I were transferred here."

"I'm so sorry." My words sounded trivial and useless. No

apology could change such injustice. "What labor assignment does your husband have?"

Hania stared across the room, face blank, fingernails digging into her palms. "Eliasz died from a construction injury two months ago. I was in the process of striking a deal to have him transferred, but I didn't work quickly enough. My sons are all Izaak and I have left. We promised each other we'd survive so we can find them again." She ran a hand over her finger where her wedding band should have been. As I watched the simple gesture, a heavy ache settled in my chest.

"Hania, there's a guard looking for you," Janina said as she rushed by on her way to her next patient.

I knew she'd get in trouble.

The young SS man came into view, and the sight of Hania brought an easy smirk to his lips. My throat ran dry. It was Protz, the guard who had assaulted me when I first arrived. Before I realized what I'd done, I'd crossed my arms over my chest.

If Protz hadn't been so repulsive, his sharp, chiseled features could have been handsome. He ran a hand over dark blond hair styled in the typical SS undercut and took Hania in with pale blue eyes. Hitler's perfect Aryan specimen. His tall, muscular frame crossed the floor in long strides while arrogance radiated from him, both stifling and nauseating.

"You owe me for those cigarettes, 15177," he said.

"Let's discuss this outside, please, Herr Scharführer," Hania replied, an odd tightness behind her lilt.

As she led the way past him, Protz grabbed her arm and brought her to a sudden stop. She didn't look at him, but she closed her eyes for an instant and clenched her jaw. When she opened them, her expression was as controlled and emotionless as the words that followed.

"When shall I repay you, Herr Scharführer?"

Neither Hania nor Protz seemed to remember my presence, or that they were in the middle of the hospital block, for that matter. I searched my frantic mind for a way to intervene if necessary, but, for now, I watched and held my breath.

"Tonight." He stepped closer and tightened his grip enough to make Hania stiffen. "*Scheisse-Jude.*" Although she didn't react, he allowed the insult to sink in, then shoved her away.

Once Protz was gone, a flicker of revulsion cut across Hania's face before she replaced it with stony indifference. Clearing her throat, she pulled cigarettes and matches from a hidden pocket, placed a cigarette in her mouth, and took a few short draws as she lit it.

In the silence, I reviewed the exchange in my mind, not daring to believe I'd understood it correctly. But I had never forgotten the day Hania had counseled me on how to survive here, on one particular resource that could be exchanged for goods or services: yourself.

"You said you translate for them."

"I didn't say that's all I do. When I was separated from Eliasz and Izaak and sent to Block 11, I suspected execution was next. Protz pulled me aside and would have taken what he wanted anyway, so I suggested a deal. Myself in exchange for my life and whatever goods I request." She took a slow drag and gave a mirthless chuckle. "You'd be surprised how often they overlook their so-called 'race defilement' laws."

I shivered in disgust, so she offered me the cigarette, but I shook my head in refusal. "You warned me about taking risks, yet you're sleeping with a guard? You'll be severely punished if you're caught, and so will he. Don't you know that?"

"Of course, but Protz's family is heavily involved in the Nazi

Party. He has uncles, brothers, and cousins fighting, and his father is a high-ranking *Waffen*-SS officer who played a key role in some German victories. He stays here, evading the real danger, stealing whatever he pleases from transports, and using his family name to avoid trouble. We're careful, of course, but if we're caught, he'll protect me."

"Right, trust the man who considers us *untermenschen*." I spat out the German term.

"If staying alive for my brother and children means crawling into bed with a *schmuck*, so be it. Besides, he enjoys having a sub-human to call his own. He won't let anyone take that from him."

Though I could hardly fathom such bizarre logic, the over-whelming pity I felt after learning about her family returned, twice as strong.

Every moment came flooding back. Protz's tight hold on my wrists, my own helplessness, his sweeping, lascivious gaze. A stroke of sheer luck was the only thing that had prevented him from following through with his intentions. My experience had been repugnant enough, but the idea of agreeing to his demands was beyond my comprehension, particularly when the agreement could prove detrimental.

Hania was a female Jew, even lower on the hierarchy of un-termenschen than I. No amount of intelligence or skill changed her religion or the blood running through her veins. Appealing to man's carnality was all she could utilize to gain some perverted form of leverage, and even that could be insufficient. Although she'd found a man salacious enough to overlook the dangers of the forbidden exchange, the arrangement hung by a thread that could be cut the moment he gave the word.

She was in check. One wrong move, and it was checkmate.

Hania tossed the last of her cigarette onto the floor and stared deliberately at my arms across my chest. I removed them. Something glimmered in her eyes, something akin to concern or perhaps sympathy—or maybe I imagined it. The only thing I saw now was a knowing, macabre gleam.

"Gave you a warm welcome during registration, did he?"

It took some effort to relax my clenched jaw enough to respond. "That's not funny."

"Did he?"

"No."

"Don't lie to your elders, young one."

"Don't accuse me of lying, old one. Checkmate." I couldn't resist a triumphant grin while she chastised me in French. Besides, it wasn't a lie. Protz's welcome hadn't gone as far as she thought.

"Oy vey, you're insufferable," Hania said, shaking her head even as she smiled. After a moment, it faded. "You're not a *yenta*, are you, Maria?"

"Can I be a yenta if I don't know what it is?"

She chuckled. "Right, you're a Gentile, I almost forgot. You're not a gossip? Because Protz might be able to protect me if we're discovered, but I'd rather not have to find out."

"I won't say anything. But now that I know what *yenta* means, I'm tempted to be one so I can claim that title."

"That's what I get for opening my big mouth."

Hania accompanied me back to my block. Along the way, a breeze swept over us, carrying the faint, unmistakable scent of jasmine. Although the source must have been near, I failed to locate it. Perhaps it was beyond the barbed-wire fences. The fragrance took me away from the lingering ache of my injuries, but it reignited an ache of another sort, one that tended to flare unexpectedly before I subdued it. It was an ache of longing to be wherever the jasmine was, somewhere outside the gate.

Since we had time before the first gong, I set up a chess game with the twigs and gravel, and we began to play. Hania was no Vera Menchik yet, but she was learning. Even champions were beginners once.

We'd hardly begun when I waved a hand, indicating that she should stop. While I repositioned her pawns, Hania let out a huff.

"I've only moved two pieces," she said.

"Both of which weakened your king, so you've made it far too easy for me to win. Keep the king protected."

"Do you coach Fritzsch like this?" she asked, shaking her head while I made my first play. "How did you become his personal chess grand master?"

I shifted positions, trying not to upset my injuries. "Do you remember when you asked me why I'd been spared? So long as Fritzsch enjoys playing chess against me, he'll let me stay."

Hania nodded, then she gave a dry chuckle. "I suppose we were both kept for their pleasure." When I didn't respond, she sighed and reached for her knight. "It was a joke—"

I placed a hand over hers to prevent her move, and she drew back with sudden haste. She stared at me, as if unsure what to make of the gesture. Something wavered, something that seemed to pierce her wall and expose her to the fullness of realities that were too difficult to face, before she blinked and retreated behind her refuge. She laughed, though it sounded a bit forced.

"Don't tell me you're worried about me."

"All I have to do is play a game," I murmured.

"One that your life depends on, if I understood you correctly. In my case, Protz is an arrogant schmuck, but harmless as long as I keep him happy. Fritzsch, on the other hand . . ." She let her voice die and lifted a questioning eyebrow while she moved her knight.

I doubted that Protz was as harmless as Hania would have liked me to believe, but I held my tongue in that regard. Instead I leaned closer to her. "I can trust you, can't I?"

"That depends. Would you trust someone who saved your life?"

"You also took me to Janina, and sometimes I think I'd prefer another flogging to her treatments." I grinned while she smirked, then I lowered my voice. "Do you want to help me get Fritzsch transferred?"

She waited, as if expecting me to take back the words. When I didn't, her eyes grew wide. "*Oy gevalt*, Maria, did Fritzsch flog your back or your head?"

"I'm serious. My life depends on chess, like you said, but if I can get rid of him first, I might have a chance of surviving. Besides, I'm not the only prisoner who wants to see him gone."

"Of course everyone wants to see him gone, but unless Kommandant Höss decides—" Hania paused while her mouth dropped open. "Don't tell me you goaded him into that flogging just to get the kommandant's attention."

"Not exactly," I replied as I examined the board before selecting my queen. "That was luck."

"You and I have very different definitions of that word." She fell silent long enough to move a rook, which I captured. "What if Fritzsch figures out what you're trying to do?"

"He wants to kill me either way, so at least I'll have done everything I could. Please, Hania." I grabbed her hand again, and she didn't pull away this time. "You have access to the administrative offices, so all I need you to do is let me know if you hear Kommandant Höss will be in the main camp. Nothing to jeopardize yourself. Will you think about it?"

Hania played one more move and stayed quiet while I played my checkmate, but she looked pensive. "You're certain Fritzsch plans to kill you when chess no longer holds his interest?" she asked, and when I nodded she got up. "Well, we can't have that, can we?"

I grinned. "Chess tomorrow, but only if you've learned to defend your king."

After responding in Czech, Hania walked to the door and disappeared. I gathered the chess pieces and savored the comforting embrace of gratitude. With her help, my odds of getting Fritzsch transferred had improved considerably.

I was settling into my bunk when someone called my prisoner number. The häftling handed me a small slip of paper and left before I could ask for an explanation.

To the girl who told me to leave her alone,

I realize I'm disrespecting your wishes, but I haven't seen you in a while, so I wanted to make sure you were all right. If you'd write back and let me know, I promise to respect your wishes from this day forward. My family owns the bakery in town, so give your note to a prisoner who works there, and he'll pass it to me. I don't know if this message will reach you, but if it does and you don't respond, that's rude, and you should be ashamed of yourself.

Respectfully,
Mateusz Kolczyk

P.S. I'm really sorry about your black eye.

Well, the stupid boy wasn't so stupid. I could give him a chance. The odds of seeing him again weren't likely, but smuggling letters to a civilian seemed far less risky than speaking to one, and the idea of another friendship held a surprising appeal. I rummaged through some organized goods I'd gotten from Hania until I found a piece of paper and a pencil to craft my response.

Dear Mateusz,

I'm fine, but my labor assignment changed, which is why you haven't seen me. I've been employed on camp grounds for some time now, so I'm afraid our paths won't cross in the future. As for my black eye, it's long since healed. All is forgiven.

Your friend,
Maria Florkowska

P.S. It's rude to disrespect a girl's wishes, and you should be ashamed of yourself.

Chapter 15

Auschwitz, 14 August 1941

YOU CAN DO better than that, Maria. Ofenchajm."

"Ofenchajm." Laughter interfered with my attempts to insert additional phlegm into my pronunciation, which was the only way I could think to make it sound right.

"Ofenchajm," Hania said, more forcefully this time. Still laughing, I mimicked her, and she sighed. "You sound more like a Gentile every time. Do I want to hear the Shema?"

"If I can't say your surname properly, do you think I can say an entire prayer in Hebrew?" I asked, grinning as I moved my knight along the chessboard we'd drawn on the filthy floor. "Your turn. How much do you remember?"

Hania contemplated for a moment. "*Pater noster, qui es in cœlis, sanctificétur nomen tuum. Fiat volúntas tua, advéniat regnum tuum—*" She feigned offense when I failed to mask my chuckle, then seemed to realize she'd switched the order of the last two phrases. She waved a dismissive hand and moved her rook. "I was close enough."

As our chess game continued, we snacked on a small cup of mare's milk and some potato skins—payment Hania had received from a stable worker and kitchen worker in exchange for favors.

She'd insisted on sharing, though I tried to refuse, because she was the one who'd earned them.

When the milk was gone, I chewed two potato skins slowly, making them last as long as I could, and closed my eyes. These were no longer potato skins—they were *pierogi* stuffed with meat and cabbage, potatoes and onions, mushrooms, and, best of all, strawberries and blueberries.

Once the game was over, we gathered the pieces into a jewelry pouch, and I tucked it into the corner of my bunk. Hania brushed herself off.

"I'll practice the Our Father, and you study the mathematics we discussed today, then practice your Yiddish and my surname. You need all the help you can get," she said with a teasing grin. "We'll save the Hebrew for after your Yiddish improves."

"My Yiddish is coming along well, if I say so myself. I heard it all the time before the war."

"Your pronunciation says otherwise." This time it was my turn to feign offense, and she chuckled. "Get some sleep tonight and keep your wounds as clean as possible. They're healing nicely, but you need to rest and—"

"And make sure they don't get infected." It was what she told me every time. "You know, Hania, I think you fuss over me as much as Mama did."

"It's a mother's responsibility to fuss, Gentile or Jew."

Years ago, from frequent visits to the local Jewish deli, I had picked up the Yiddish word for *grandmother*, so I stole a mischievous glance at her while I tightened my headscarf. "Thank you for looking out for me, *Bubbe*."

Hania's eyes lit up with pride, even though she was quick to protest. "I'm twenty-three!"

As she departed, I pulled Mateusz's latest letter from my pocket and left it on my bunk. In it, he'd described a recent confrontation with a cantankerous old man on his paper route and mentioned that the bakery was doing well, but his parents hated that it had been overrun by SS officers. As I composed my response, I updated him on Hania's chess skills and her complaints about my Yiddish. The lighthearted parts of my day had become even more important to me now, as they were the only things I wrote to him about.

It was odd being friends with a boy I wasn't certain I'd see again, a boy who could have been my friend in Warsaw. If things had been different, we would have met our friends at the movie theater, ridden our bicycles through town, talked about our families, and shared our dreams for the future. Instead Mateusz had the freedom to do those things—or as much freedom as the occupiers permitted—while I wasn't sure I'd survive one day to the next.

"Maria."

The unfamiliar voice reached my ears the moment I left my block. Aside from Father Kolbe and Hania, no one called me by anything other than my prisoner number. The man who had spoken motioned for me to follow him into the alley between Blocks 15 and 16. I obeyed, but I closed my hand into a fist. It was never a good idea to follow a strange man into an alley.

Even among prisoners, it was difficult to know who could be trusted. When he paused and faced me, I studied his appearance. Red triangle, capital *P*, Prisoner 4859. Thin, but strong. Square jaw, slight cleft in his chin. Narrow nose, and the eyes on either side were as clear and blue as a cloudless sky, but sharp as ice, watching me beneath thick blond brows. Impeccable posture, scrupulous gaze, much like my father's. Perhaps he was a military man, too.

After this inspection, I felt better, but I kept my distance. "How do you know my name?"

"I heard you tell Fritzsch during your flogging," he replied. "When that priest volunteered to die in place of another man, you created quite a scene."

"Father Kolbe is my friend."

"Surely you knew begging for his life would get you punished."

"At the time, I wasn't thinking."

He smiled. Maybe he saw through my lie. "I've watched you play chess, and I've kept an eye on you outside of those public displays, too. You seem to be a smart girl. Very prudent. Not one to react without thinking."

"It's difficult to be prudent when your friend is sentenced to death."

The man nodded. "Indeed. It's even more difficult to successfully manipulate Fritzsch."

Even though I didn't react, he stayed quiet, and I suspected he was waiting for the silence to goad me into a confession, one that would confirm the accuracy of his assessment. I wouldn't tell him anything. If he knew he was right, he might tell Fritzsch, and if Fritzsch discovered my actions were intentional he'd never fall for a provocation from me again.

When I didn't say anything, the man chuckled. "Don't worry, your secret is safe with me. In fact, you're exactly the kind of person I need. We're alike, you and I." Before continuing, he closed the space between us, and I didn't move away. "You're a girl who has managed to survive in a men's camp, you knew how to encourage Fritzsch to reassign you, and you accepted the punishment that came with it. I went outside during a street roundup in Warsaw so I would be arrested and sent to Auschwitz."

Surely he hadn't said what I thought he'd said. "You came here on purpose?"

He nodded. "The Nazis have done an excellent job covering up what happens in these camps, so I wanted to uncover the truth and send reports to the resistance's military branch. The Home Army needs to know what's really happening. I've been gathering information since I came here almost a year ago, but I can't do it alone. That's why I need people like you."

This strange man was fascinating, but I couldn't resist a dangerous question. "How do I know you aren't working with the Nazis?"

"Because something tells you I'm not, just as something tells me you won't betray me. Now you know exactly why I'm here, and one word from you to the nearest guard means my death. But you won't betray me. We understand each other."

As strange as it was, he was right, but I reminded myself not to be too hasty. After what had happened the last time I worked for the resistance, I wasn't sure I wanted to do it again.

"Once they have enough information, the Home Army will help us. I'm sure of it. And we'll be ready when they do. We'll have weapons and numbers, we'll fight, and we won't stop fighting until we're free." The man fell silent, watching as I considered his words. *Free.* "You'd be a wonderful asset to my organization, Maria. Take all the time you need to consider it, and when you're ready, find me. My name is Tomasz Serafiński."

As he said it, there was the slightest change in his pitch, so slight I would have missed it if my senses hadn't been at their most heightened. I smiled. "That's not your name."

"Of course it is." When he leaned closer to me, I detected a knowing gleam in his eyes. "If you look for a man named Witold Pilecki, I'll tell you I don't know anyone by that name." He winked, then he left the alley and disappeared into Block 15.

Intrigued, I stared after him, but I pushed the encounter aside for the time being and hurried to Block 11. During the past two weeks, I'd visited Father Kolbe's cell every day to empty the waste bucket, even though it had been dry for days. Thirst had driven the men to desperation, prompting them to drink its contents. Each time, I'd found Father Kolbe standing or kneeling, lifting his voice in prayers and hymns. The tranquility that filled his cell never ceased to astound me, but not even his efforts could prevent death from claiming his fellow captives.

How Father Kolbe had survived immurement for two entire weeks was beyond my comprehension.

The moment I entered Block 11 and closed the door behind me, a familiar voice echoed down the empty hall.

"Prisoner 16671."

He stood near the stairs to the basement, and I couldn't bring myself to move away from the door. Above his head, the yellow lightbulb flickered, lending an eerie gleam to the vicious smile that spread across his features. That smile meant he had something terrible planned for me.

Fritzsch's boots thudded against the concrete floor as he closed the distance between us. I stood still, hoping he believed I wasn't intimidated, but in reality it was fear, not courage, that rendered me immobile. I was alone. Alone in the death block with the most wicked man in Auschwitz.

"I was hoping I'd find you here," he said as he reached me. "You've saved me the trouble of fetching you."

Something hard collided with me and forced my back against the door. The impact reignited the agony of my flogging injuries, and I cried out and looked down to find Fritzsch's pistol pressed against my chest.

"That priest is a stubborn bastard, isn't he? Two weeks without food or water, and he's still alive." Fritzsch grabbed the back of my collar, and I shrank away, but he pulled me close. "Well, I have something special planned for you and Prisoner 16670."

Even if I could have found words, I didn't have time before Fritzsch shoved the gun between my battered shoulder blades and dragged me downstairs toward the damp, dark cell. I bit my lip against the pain, but every time I stumbled, Fritzsch dug the barrel into my back, forcing me to move more quickly to alleviate the torment.

Voices came from the open door to Cell 18, indicating that a few guards were there. The older SS officer I'd noticed during my flogging stood outside the cell, alone, staring at the ground. Fritzsch forced me into the doorway, giving me an unobstructed view of the inside. Father Kolbe sat with his back against the wall. Despite the frailty of his tormented body, his face was serene, eyes as bright and kind as always. I looked from him to the guards, and I didn't understand what was happening, why the guards were here, why Fritzsch wanted me here.

Not until I noticed the guard preparing the injection.

"Father Kolbe—"

When I started toward him, Fritzsch jerked me back, and my collar cut across my throat and silenced my gasping cry. This reaction was exactly what he wanted from me. I knew it was, and I shouldn't have given him the satisfaction, but I didn't care. The only thing that mattered was saying goodbye to my friend. All I wanted was one moment, just one final moment.

Eyes brimming with tears, I turned to Fritzsch, my voice hardly a whisper. "Please, Herr Lagerführer."

As the plea escaped my quivering lips, his eyes gleamed with malice. Instead of acknowledging me, Fritzsch nodded at the guard with the injection, giving him permission to proceed.

I should have said something to Father Kolbe, especially since

Fritzsch wouldn't permit me to go to him, but I couldn't find words. When I met his gaze, suddenly I felt as if my presence was enough. Somehow the suffering, dying priest was still able to comfort me.

Fritzsch had brought me here for his own vindictive pleasure, and even though despair wrapped its relentless hold around me, a small part of me was grateful. Every day, I'd feared coming to this cell and finding Father Kolbe dead, and once his fellow prisoners died I was afraid he'd die alone. Now he wasn't alone.

Father Kolbe offered his arm to the executioner. The guard hesitated, clearly taken aback by the gesture; for a brief, foolish moment, I was convinced he wouldn't carry out the sentence. Then he glanced at Fritzsch, swallowed hard, and proceeded.

As the tears streaked down my cheeks and I sank to my knees, the guard administered the injection, and Father Kolbe's gentle voice lifted in one final prayer.

"*Ave Maria.*"

* * *

When Fritzsch tossed me from Block 11, it felt like coming out of a daze. The daze had been one of grief, raw and piercing, sucking up all my energy, but I emerged from it with a stronger clarity than any I'd ever known.

I'd promised Father Kolbe I'd fight to survive; until now, I hadn't realized the full extent of the greater purpose my promise would serve. Fritzsch was using chess against me, but to use my friends was a play so bold and aggressive that it left me no choice but to redouble my efforts and regain control of the board. The game between us had become far more ruthless, and it was time to adjust my strategy.

Rubbing the last of my tears from swollen eyelids, I made my way down the poplar-lined street before reaching Block 15, and I didn't slow down until I'd burst through the door and shouted his alias.

"Tomasz Serafiński!"

Pilecki turned toward me, and I spun on my heel and led the way to the alley between the blocks.

"I want to join the prisoner resistance movement," I said once he'd joined me.

Pilecki didn't look surprised or pleased, just pensive. At last the corners of his mouth turned into the slightest of smiles. "Welcome to the *Związek Organizacji Wojskowej*, Maria. We're called ZOW for short."

That was all I needed. I closed my eyes and savored the words while the energy inside me swelled to capacity.

Protocol violations were useful toward my goal, but, if the entire camp rose up in rebellion, Höss would have no choice other than to punish Fritzsch to the full extent of his power. Transfer and demotion, surely. Perhaps something even worse.

Chapter 16

Auschwitz, 20 April 1945

WITH EVERY PASSING move throughout this chess game, my throat gets tighter. I've spent years waiting for this conversation with Fritzsch; now that the time is almost upon me, suddenly I'm afraid I won't be able to voice everything I need to say. As we progress through the middlegame and Fritzsch's queen takes my bishop, he holds the captured piece between his fingers.

"You've done very little talking, 16671. I'm sure you didn't come here to bore me."

The words make me sit up straighter. I planned to keep quiet until our game progressed further, until I feel ready; now he's tired of waiting. Fritzsch sets the bishop beside the other pieces he's captured while I stay quiet, buying a few more precious seconds. When his thumb strokes the gun at his hip, I have no choice but to alter my strategy.

"You did it, didn't you?"

Fritzsch wipes rainwater from the back of his hand. "With a question so vague, I'm afraid I can't answer."

I clench my jaw to contain the fury he always manages to produce in me. If this game is going to end how I want it to end, I need to maintain control. "The execution wall, 1941. They were political prisoners. You killed them, didn't you?"

"Is that your purpose for this meeting? To badger me with senseless questions?" Fritzsch waits for my reply, but my tongue can't form the question I long to ask, and he narrows his eyes against the rain. "The next words out of your mouth had better be worth my while."

The question dislodges itself from my throat, so I release a slow breath and concentrate on each word to keep from blurting it out. "Did you kill my family?"

How long I've waited to ask that question, to find the confirmation I've sought all these years, to get justice for them. But, when my voice catches, Fritzsch snatches his opportunity as easily as he snatched my bishop from the board. The tension in his jaw releases, and he chuckles.

"Do you expect me to remember a few particular prisoners?" He sighs and shakes his head. "Besides, I was Auschwitz's deputy, not an executioner, remember?"

He's playing his game, extending control to the center of the board, positioning me exactly where he wants me. The heat racing through my veins won't be quelled, and I swallow hard.

"Tell me if you killed them."

"You'll need to be more specific. You were sent here with parents? Siblings? Grandparents? And none of them were registered?" He crosses his arms and settles back into his chair. "Fascinating. Such a shame I can't remember."

"Liar!"

The accusation comes out before I can stop it, then I'm halfway out of my seat and clutching the edges of the table. This is a feeling I recognize all too well, the one that always comes when I teeter on the edge, and if I don't pull back then there's no regaining control. With considerable effort, I relax my grip on the table.

Fritzsch acknowledges my outburst with nothing more than a heavy sigh. "Are you going to keep spewing nonsense, or shall we continue?"

As he gestures for me to move my next piece, a small smirk plays around his lips. He knows the truth, I'm sure of it, and he's going to admit it. I sink into my seat and move my remaining bishop without taking my eyes off him.

"An eyewitness told me everything. Remember that before you answer me again." I give him a moment to contemplate my words before asking once more. "Did you kill my family?"

"You seem to have made up your mind, so what I say isn't going to matter." Fritzsch leans closer to me. "Perhaps you can jog my memory. Why don't you tell me what you think you know?"

 Chapter 17

Auschwitz, 11 January 1942

WINTER IN AUSCHWITZ was a vicious beast. I'd never been as cold as I'd been these past few months. When it became unbearable, I thought of evenings spent drinking hot tea in our cozy apartment on Bałuckiego Street while playing chess against Mama and Tata or Monopoly and checkers with Zofia and Karol. Memories warmed me as no fire ever could.

Early one evening, during free time, Hania and I walked through the camp while snow fell around us and transported me to wintry family outings at Park Dreszera. The ARBEIT MACHT FREI sign above the main gate was quick to remind me that I wasn't in Warsaw. To its right, four bodies dangled, stiff from death and cold and covered in a dusting of snow. Hanged for attempting escape, left on gruesome display to deter anyone brave enough—or foolish enough—to follow their example.

I swung my arms at my sides, and my fingers bumped into Father Kolbe's rosary. I let my hand linger. Hania noticed my fingers brushing over the hidden pocket and offered me a small smile. She didn't know what I'd witnessed the day of Father Kolbe's execution, but she knew I always kept his rosary close.

"Maria, was it your idea to take a walk?" As I turned my head to acknowledge Hania's younger brother, Izaak puffed on the last of his cigarette, tossed it into the snow, and pulled his collar up for more protection from the icy wind. "You'd be the only one crazy enough to suggest going out in this weather."

In response, I scooped up a handful of snow and hit him squarely in the chest. Izaak retaliated, but I darted behind Hania, so his snowball found her instead. She cursed in Yiddish while he and I laughed, then she eyed us with disapproval before flicking snow off her shoulder.

Izaak pointed an accusatory finger at me. "She started it."

"You're the one who hit Hania," I replied. "Checkmate."

Before I could launch my next missile, Hania knocked the snow out of my hands. "Enough, kinderlach."

"Truce, Maria?" Izaak asked. "My sister is no fun."

Giggling, I nodded, and Hania and Izaak continued bantering in Yiddish and Czech. Listening to them reminded me of tugging on Zofia's curls or scooping Karol into my arms and kissing his cheek before he could run away.

Thoughts of my family reminded me of finding them outside Block 11, of the chess game that had taken place shortly after I joined the resistance. A memory so fierce it pulled me from this frigid day and shoved me into the roll-call square on that warm summer evening.

The sun sank low and washed over the chessboard, staining it blood orange. Fritzsch hadn't invited an audience, so we were alone. I attempted to focus on the game instead of him, and, when I moved a bishop, a little sound hummed in his throat. Impressed, or simply mocking me, I wasn't certain.

"You play well for a child," he said. "Who was your instructor?"

The query elicited recollections of home. Countless evenings playing chess against my father. His patience, guiding me from the most basic strategy to the most advanced. His fingers developing pieces across the board, eyes bright each time I begged for one more game.

His body, pale and glistening with raindrops, piled among dozens in the back of a truck.

The familiar clatter of a chess piece struck the board, never failing to seize my attention. Fritzsch held another at the ready. Before he let it fall, I hastily provided the answer to his question.

"My father." The words sounded too shrill. I drew a shaky breath and made a second attempt. "He taught me how to play."

Fritzsch nodded and selected a knight. "When we met on the arrival platform, you were looking for your family. Was your father with them?"

He hadn't dropped a chess piece, but I flinched as if he had.

I shifted in my chair, attempting to disguise my reaction, and played my nearest pawn. One he easily captured.

"I hope you managed to find them."

His words wrapped around my throat, preventing my response. Fritzsch held the captured pawn between his fingers, evaluating me with an intrigued gaze, the same one that had sent me to registration. The look that indicated something more, a deeper intention and purpose.

I closed my hand into a fist, though I didn't have my pawn from Tata to grip this time. Why now? Why ask of my family now? He controlled everything—my name, my punishment, my life, each move intentional, calculated. Fighting tremulous breaths, I dissected every word and glance as if studying a grand master. Something about my family had excited him. But what?

Then it hit me. His game. *This* game. He enjoyed seeing me react, seeing me remember. He knew something more than I, and this was his way of telling me: *Your move, Prisoner 16671.*

Could there be more to their deaths? Perhaps I hadn't considered the possibility because it had been easier to assume that their fates had been the same as countless others'. Now the possibility was before me. I peered at him, certainty filling my lungs. His words were a chess piece too easy for me to capture, baiting me, luring me into my next move. The only way to uncover the truth—to reveal what he knew—was to find someone in this camp who had witnessed my family's execution.

My strategy for our game forgotten, I made another rash play. This time he placed me in checkmate.

I hardly noticed the loss. I had a new mission: Recruit my fellow resistance members to help me locate someone who had seen my family following our separation. Someone who had been in Block 11 that day in May of 1941.

"Maria, if you knew the things Hania was saying to her own brother."

I escaped from Fritzsch's scrutiny and returned to the present, where Izaak shook his head in admonition.

"And you're as innocent as a sacrificial lamb, aren't you, Izaak Rubinstein?" she answered.

"Are you related to a man named Akiba Rubinstein?" I asked, catching on the familiar surname. "The chess grand master?"

"Your friend Irena, is she related to the author Henryk Sienkiewicz?" Izaak replied.

"When I asked, I believe her exact words were 'No, you idiot.'"

"I see. Now remind me of your question?"

"Are you related to Akiba Rubinstein, the chess grand master?"

"No, you idiot."

I darted out of Hania's reach and bent to scoop up more snow, but, before I could, Izaak cursed in Czech. As I straightened, he brushed snow off his arm while Hania smoothed her uniform with wet hands, composed and controlled amid my giggles and Izaak's wry smile. Hania didn't acknowledge us, maintaining her air of innocence until she slipped on a patch of ice and yelped.

Izaak steadied her. "You're going to fall and break a bone, *schlemiel*." He jumped aside when she attempted to smack his head in playful admonition.

"*Toi, toi, toi*," she replied, making the spitting sound three times.

He scoffed. "Don't bother warding off the evil eye. It has already caught up to us." He indicated our surroundings to emphasize his point, and Hania narrowed her eyes and responded in French.

"*Tu me fais chier.*"

Izaak waved an accusatory hand toward her and looked at me. "Now she's trying to annoy us because we can't understand her."

She flashed a smug smile. "*Je réussis, n'est-ce pas?*"

"How did you learn so many languages?" I asked.

"Our mother's family immigrated from Czechoslovakia to Warsaw when she was a girl, and our father was from Kraków. Growing up, my siblings and I spoke Czech, Polish, and Yiddish; we studied German in school, and Judyta and I studied French together. She and I were always better at languages than Izaak."

He laughed. "True, but neither of us were as good as Judyta. She spoke English, too."

Hania nodded in agreement. A wistful silence fell, remaining until Izaak complained about the cold and hurried away in search of warmth. He was right; it was too cold, but I didn't care. It was nice being able to walk without a particular destination in mind rather than rushing to the roll-call square or labor assignments. My feet crunched against the snow while Hania and I took a right at the next intersection, continuing our leisurely stroll past Blocks 6 and 7.

"You'll never guess what I got today," Hania said.

"Seven boxes of German chocolates and three bottles of the finest champagne after striking a bargain with Kommandant Höss himself."

"Oh, of course. Kommandant Höss always breaks his sacred rules, so he would be the one to barter with a prisoner, wouldn't he? And a female Jew at that." When I laughed, she smirked before continuing. "Since I don't have chocolates or champagne, now my earnings are going to sound much less impressive, so thank you for that. I got a comb, three toothbrushes, cigarettes, matches, and aspirins."

"That's almost as good as champagne and chocolate." The taste of chocolate lingered in my mouth, melted against the heat of my tongue. The tantalizing craving was unbearable. It was my own fault for teasing. "Last week, I translated a few men's letters into German, so I collected bread, lye soap, and a sausage," I said as we made another right, passing between Blocks 18 and 19. "And Mateusz sent us bread from the bakery."

Thoughts of my discreet exchanges with Mateusz always made me wish I could write to Irena. Official camp letters were permitted not as a kindness, but simply as a Nazi ploy to reassure family and friends who received them from deported loved ones—or sometimes from loved ones who were already dead, though those at home were unaware. To maintain the scheme, each letter was censored, so if I wrote, I couldn't tell her the truth of my situation or share fond memories of our resistance work. Besides, it would have been foolish to put her name before those in the censorship office. What if they investigated everyone and discovered her resistance involvement? The risk of exposing her was too great.

"Time to warm up, *shikse*," Hania said as she took another right toward Block 14.

"That means 'a Gentile girl or woman,' but isn't it an insult? Consider me offended."

"No need to teach me my own language." Hania gave me a light shove while I giggled through chattering teeth. "We've been out here long enough, and I have to meet—" She stopped, but I grabbed her arm to make her face me.

"Protz?" I shouldn't have bothered asking. I knew the answer.

"Don't give me that look, Maria. I won't tolerate people who *kvetsh* about repaying favors, myself included. And while we're on the topic of favors, do you need more medication?"

I shook my head. I'd had a fever for the past few days, but I refused to visit Janina in the camp hospital or miss work. Going to the hospital was one step closer to the crematorium. Hania had gathered medicine and additional helpings of soup, so my fever had broken this morning.

"You have a right to kvetsh about letting that *paskudnik* touch you," I muttered.

"When did you become a Yiddish dictionary?" Hania asked with a chuckle. "A deal with a paskudnik is still a deal."

"Not a fair one for you."

The words must have come across harsher than I'd intended, because her amusement transformed into a sudden glare. "I'd tell Kommandant Höss to drop dead if that's what Protz wanted, so long as he gives me what I ask for in return. We have an agreement, which is more than you can say about your paskudnik—or has Fritzsch started showering you with presents every time you win a chess game?"

Fritzsch was all it took to rob me of words. Hania must have regretted mentioning him, considering her scowl disappeared, but I crossed my arms against a gust of wind and took a few steps down the empty street. The snow had stopped, replaced by silence, as hazy as the gray sky above.

In a place where death was nearly unavoidable, we combatted

it however we could. Survival was the endgame strategy, but each prisoner played differently, and fairness was irrelevant. Death had no regard for fairness.

Hania sighed and intertwined her arm with mine. "*Je suis désolé*, shikse," she murmured, which wasn't fair, either. She knew French was my favorite of her languages. "No need to worry about me, though. All things considered, the price I pay is insignificant. Besides, Protz won't touch me unless I'm clean enough to meet his standards, so every meeting includes a proper shower and thoroughly washed uniform."

Although cleanliness was almost more enticing than food, even that wasn't worth the cost. I took her hand and made one final attempt. "Please don't go, Hania. Let's keep walking."

She scoffed. "How do you expect that to be received? 'Forgive me, Herr Scharführer, I didn't pay you back because I was on a walk.'" She imitated Protz's smirk and lowered her pitch to mimic his. "'No need to repay me, 15177, the pleasure is mine. Here's a dozen loaves of *challah* I baked with my own hands, five bars of lavender soap, and the warmest wool coat money can buy. Only the best for my untermensch.'"

I tried not to reward her with my laughter, but her impression was too accurate, so I didn't succeed. The humor vanished from her eyes, and the usual guarded look took its place.

"By the way, last night I hovered around the roll-call square so Fritzsch would see me and challenge me to a chess game. Kommandant Höss showed up, like you said he would, and he found us right as Fritzsch was celebrating his win," I said while she pulled me close once more, providing a slight buffer against the frigid wind.

"That makes the third time he's caught you two with that chess set, doesn't it?" she asked. "Not a complete protocol violation, considering Fritzsch insists your chess games boost morale and

Höss has permitted the arrangement, but everyone knows he feels Fritzsch has been abusing it. What more will it take to get him transferred? Maybe we should increase our efforts."

"If he's caught breaking the rules every time Höss visits the camp, Fritzsch will get suspicious. We have to space it out like we've been doing."

"And if you run out of ideas before Höss takes action? There are only so many new ways you can suggest to play chess."

"The next time Fritzsch tells me he's getting bored, I'm going to tell him I'll play blindfolded." I tucked my numb fingers into my sleeves. As long as chess held his interest in me, we could coax him into protocol violations. Höss was bound to do something soon.

"This is a risky game you're playing," Hania said, and she tightened her hold when a gust of wind tore across us. "Now you're going inside, understood? We can't have you catching pneumonia." The *toi* I expected didn't come. Maybe she agreed with Izaak more than she'd have liked us to believe.

"Always looking out for me, Bubbe Ofenchajm."

"If the real Bubbe Ofenchajm heard your attempted pronunciation, she would say it was all *fercockt*."

"I take it that's not a good thing?" I asked with a sheepish smile.

Hania patted my cheek as she guided me down the snowy street. "It's whatever you want it to be, little shikse. If you want it to be a good thing, it's a good thing."

Somehow I didn't believe her, but I appreciated the sentiment.

* * *

The next day, when the workday ended, I hurried from Block 11 on the way to Block 14. Hania was eager to share her latest bounty from exchanging favors, so we'd planned to meet in my block.

As I passed Block 16, Hania came down the main street, as I'd expected because she spent most of her time in the administrative offices outside the main gate. I hurried to catch her, but two prisoners appeared, shoving her off the street until all three stood in front of Block 15.

I darted down the alley between Blocks 15 and 16 and moved closer, searching my frantic mind for a plan to stop whatever they were about to do. As their conversation reached me, I paused. Pressing into the icy brick wall, I cupped my hands around my mouth and breathed against my fingers to warm them, taking small breaths so clouds wouldn't form and betray my presence.

"You're demanding payment from him?" one man asked, a German Jew.

"That's my business, not yours, yenta," Hania replied. At her use of the female term, the man bristled.

"Last month, when you gave me your soap, you said you'd ask me to return the favor when you needed something, so I agreed to the deal. When you came for repayment, you demanded three bread rations and left me no choice but to comply. Three bread rations for a tiny piece of soap? You swindled me, but I won't let you do the same to my friend."

The accusation made me press harder into the wall. He was mistaken, I was certain of it. I waited, anticipating the clarification that Hania would surely give. Instead she flashed a smug smile.

"You call it swindling, I call it a fair deal."

"When you offered to translate my letter, I thought you were helping me out of kindness," the second man said, his German heavy with a Czech accent. "How was I to know you'd want repayment?"

"Were you stupid enough to think I'd do something for nothing?" Hania asked with a laugh so harsh it sent a sudden chill through me. "The minute you accept something from someone, you're indebted to that person. If you didn't know that, now you do, and you can thank me for teaching you a valuable lesson."

The Jewish man pinned her against the building, and, as I took a breath to scream so I could distract him, I caught sight of the look on Hania's face. A hint of a smile danced around her lips, as if daring him to do more. The look stole the air from my lungs and kept me rooted to my hiding place while the man tightened his grip on her shoulders.

"You think you're so clever, don't you?" he said. "Well, I've been watching you, and I know how you keep your SS men close." He waited, perhaps expecting her to blanch during his dramatic pause, but instead she raised her eyebrows.

"Jealous?"

"I wouldn't be caught dead with the likes of you, and from now on, no one else will, either. You're nothing but a devious *nafka*." Given the way he snapped the Yiddish word that I hadn't learned, I could guess what he'd called her. "The commanding officers will be delighted to hear a Jew is contaminating their guards," he went on. "How does that sound for repayment?"

Both men stood tall, but their confidence withered beneath Hania's unrelenting stare.

"I have far more power than you realize, and I have eyes and ears all over this camp," she said. "If you don't keep your mouths shut, my SS connections will hunt you down and ensure your silence. They won't be hard to convince, because I know exactly how to persuade them." She flashed a suggestive, dangerous smile before continuing in Czech and Yiddish, perhaps relaying additional threats.

She finished in Yiddish, and whatever she said must have been a particularly heavy threat or weighty insult because the Jewish man raised an arm, but the Czech man grabbed it before he struck.

Hania didn't flinch. Only nodded toward his clenched fist. "Go on, if you'd like to be reassigned to the road crew."

The Jewish man didn't move, but he seemed to reconsider. Hania leaned forward as far as his grip allowed and focused a murderous glare on him.

"Take your hands off me."

He obeyed, even though he looked as if he wanted to close his hands around her throat.

The two men turned their backs on her and strolled past my hiding place. Once they'd made it a safe distance, they paused, and the Jew sent a withering glower over his shoulder.

"*A khalerye,* nafka."

"*A khalerye,* yenta."

As Hania watched the men go, I stared at her, frozen in my hiding place, but it wasn't the frigid temperatures that prevented me from moving. At last I forced myself into motion and sprinted down the alley. I took a left behind the block and came up another alley between Blocks 13 and 14, slipping on ice and filthy snow as I went, then paused long enough to peer around the corner. Hania hadn't moved, and she was holding a lit cigarette. Once inside Block 14, I rushed to my bunk and threw myself upon it. I steadied my breathing and pretended to study the various scrapes and bruises on my arms. A few minutes later, Hania arrived and smiled at me.

"Sorry I'm late. I had to take care of some things. Nothing important." She waved a hand, brushing the matter aside as if the scene I'd witnessed had been a trivial inconvenience. "Let me show you what I brought, starting with cigarettes. I know you hate them, but most people covet them, so take some for trading purposes."

While Hania went through her goods and we set up a chess

game, I did my best to seem engaged, but I couldn't shake the recollection of that small, arrogant smile she'd given the men. It was as though I had reached the endgame and ignored my father's counsel: *When few pieces remain on the board, the king's activation is necessary.* I had trusted her for no reason other than she had been kind, a woman, a friend; I had continued sheltering my king. A beginner's mistake, one I should have known better than to make. In Auschwitz, trusting too freely could be the difference between life and death.

After running my numb finger along the dirty floor to redefine the grid lines, I moved one of my knights and closed my hand into a fist to fight the sudden tremor that overtook it. Maybe I could blame the trembling on the cold.

"Are you sure your fever is gone, shikse? You shouldn't have done that." Hania flashed a teasing grin since my move had left me vulnerable to check.

"What do you want?"

When the query left my lips, she paused in the middle of reaching for the knight. Her hand hovered over the board for a moment, then she scooped up the pebble, set it on the ground beside her, and placed me in check.

"Right now? To win this chess game." Despite the jest, I detected a tightness in her voice, and a slight crease formed along her brow when she looked at me.

"I saw you, Hania. With those men." I let the words sink in before sitting up straighter. "Tell me what you want from me."

Her expression didn't change. Silence stretched between us, but the loud voice in my head demanded to know why I'd provoked her. The pounding of my heartbeat drummed against my ears while she took a moment to light a cigarette, exhaled a steady stream of smoke, and cleared her throat.

"When my husband and I handed our two sons over to the resistance, all we knew was that they'd be disguised as Catholics. I don't know their fake names, where they were sent, nothing. After the war, I'll need someone who worked for the resistance in Warsaw to get me in touch with the woman who took them." She watched a few ashes fall to the frigid floor, then raised her dark eyes to mine. "You're going to help me locate my sons when we get home."

"How long have you been planning this?" I had a feeling I knew the answer, but I wanted to hear it from her. I wanted her to be honest with me for once.

"Since I found out you were a resistance member from Warsaw."

"Right after I was flogged. You've had this in mind for the entirety of our friendship. And if I don't cooperate, you'll blackmail me like you did those men."

It was useless to pretend otherwise, so she didn't. Hania took a slow drag on her cigarette and reassumed the mask of stony indifference I'd seen on her before, but now I realized I'd never seen it. Not for what it was—detachment. From me, from herself, from everything.

"With SS connections, it's easy to make people cooperate," Hania said with a chuckle. "I thought it would be easy to strike a deal with you, given your position, but you never gave me much opportunity. Not until your flogging."

I lifted a hand to the back of my shoulder, feeling the uneven lumps of skin that suddenly throbbed as if they were fresh. "You helped me because I wasn't in a position to refuse."

A fresh stream of smoke surrounded us, thick and pungent, making it impossible for me to speak further even if I could have found words. Hania watched the smoke rise from the end of the cigarette, then looked to me. "I intended on getting a substantial repayment for saving your life, but after we talked, I decided this deal would be different from my others. I needed to help you stay alive and keep you close until the time was right."

The words stung more than the smoke, which had found its way into my eyes. "Is that why you're helping me get rid of Fritzsch?"

"Of course." She finished her cigarette and used the bottom of her shoe to extinguish the remaining embers. "If he gets tired of you and kills you, that would interfere with my plans."

"So, you're keeping your shikse alive for her usefulness." I spat out the word she'd taught me and stood up and marched past her toward the door. "I suppose I should be accustomed to that by now."

As I left her with the half-finished chess game and stepped out into the frigid evening, the bite of her betrayal was as acute as the wind lashing through my thin uniform. I was nothing more than her most prized deal. I couldn't comprehend why I had confronted her, but it was rash and foolish. Too late for regrets now.

Besides, I didn't regret it. If Hania attempted to hinder me in any way, I'd fight back with everything I had. Even without SS connections.

As I trudged down the frigid street, our conversation lingered in the air around me, echoing with each gust until a new shout pierced the wind whipping past my ears.

"Do you think you can walk away? It's far too late for that, Maria." Hania latched onto my forearm, and I attempted to pull away, but she held fast and forced me to face her.

"You won't hurt me if you need me alive." Though I made the claim, I wasn't certain it was true.

"I also need you to cooperate, and if I have to make you, so be it. Protz will do what I ask, and he won't be merciful, so unless you want to contend with him—"

"Stop, Hania!" This time I managed to twist out of her grasp. "If you think you have to force me to help you find your sons, you must not know me very well."

Upon those words, Hania gaped, then she narrowed her eyes, as if deciding whether or not to believe me. I took a deep breath to settle the heat racing through my veins. Threats didn't mask the unspoken plea behind her dark eyes, eyes that bore pains unlike any I'd ever known, eyes that betrayed the war raging within her. I was someone she'd chosen to use to her advantage, no matter what it took. But I was also someone she'd befriended, despite her initial intentions, and I was a girl who had lost her parents, just as her children had lost theirs.

She wasn't the same conniving woman I'd seen a moment ago. She was a young widow desperate to reunite with her children. My parents had felt this same desperation, surely, when they realized I was missing. When they realized my siblings were to suffer for my actions. When they realized all hopes of reuniting our family were to be stolen from them.

I crossed my arms against a burst of cold air, turned away, and spoke in a soft voice. "While working for the resistance, sometimes Mama and I would imagine life after the war. We were both looking forward to reuniting the children we helped with their parents. Such work would be an honor, but to do it for one of my closest friends . . ." I broke off with a shaky breath. "All you had to do was ask."

When I looked at her, Hania stared into the distance, gone to a place far from here. Her tears glistened through the darkness before she blinked, as if coming out of a daze, brushed a stray tear, and spoke in a whisper. "Maria, I—"

I shook my head to stop her. We were creatures of war, and sometimes we'd morph into unrecognizable imitations of our former selves. I didn't need her to apologize for something the war had created. I just needed her to be the woman I recognized again.

When I offered her my hand, she took it, and I stepped close enough to wipe another tear from her cheek. "We'll find them, Bubbe. I promise."

She gave my hand a gentle squeeze. "In a place like Auschwitz, it's easy to forget decent people still exist."

Back in my block, we sat on my bunk. As we huddled together with my thin blanket across our laps, life gradually returned to my fingers and toes, resurrected by a bit of warmth from the small wood-burning stove. It was insufficient for heating the space, but it was better than no heating at all. Other prisoners weren't so fortunate.

"When the war is over, I'll contact Irena and her mother, and they can help us," I said, once my teeth stopped chattering. "Would you tell me more about your sons? How long has it been since they were smuggled out of the ghetto?"

"Nine months. Jakub's birthday is in March, so he's about to turn four, and Adam is fourteen months." A sudden realization seemed to hit her, one I imagined she'd dwelled on so often before, but with fresh pain each time. "My son is growing from a toddler to a little boy, and I missed my baby's first words, his first birthday . . ." After a moment, she took a calming breath. "I'll never forget the night they were taken. It was late Saturday evening, the twelfth of April. We had one final Sabbath as a family. The rest of us were arrested a week later."

The date stood out in my mind. Something important had happened on the twelfth of April. It was a date I'd promised myself I'd remember because it was the day I completed a resistance errand by myself for the first time. I had delivered papers. Mama was supposed to have joined me, but I'd gone alone because she'd gone to the ghetto.

I sat up a bit straighter, reminding myself to breathe. It was a coincidence, that's all.

"What about the person who took your children?"

"They went with a woman I'd met a few times, and I had friends who let her take their children. She persuaded me into letting my boys go. She was kind and friendly, but I don't know much personal information aside from her name. I doubt it was her real name, but she went by Stanisława."

A resistance woman named Stanisława who rescued children on the twelfth of April. The same alias Mama used, the same night she went into the ghetto.

"What did Stanisława look like?" I kept my voice light. If my suspicions were wrong, I didn't want to get Hania's hopes up. After all, I was sure plenty of resistance women went by that alias and had gone into the ghetto that evening.

"She was a Gentile and older than me by ten years or so. Average height, blond hair, beautiful. She wore a wedding band, so I assume she was married." Hania was quiet for a moment. "Once, she said she had a son a bit older than Jakub, my three-year-old."

At the time, Karol would have been four years old. "Did Stanisława say anything else about her personal life?"

"No, but she spoke German like a native. She took my sons during curfew. Adam was sedated so he wouldn't cry, and Jakub was so confused. He asked me why, why wasn't I going with them, why was I sending them away, and I—" Hania broke off when her voice caught. "How was I supposed to explain it to him? Before I could say anything, Stanisława knelt down, held his hand, and said, 'Jakub, listen to me. Your mother and father love you and Adam so, so much. Will you promise to be a brave little boy for them?' That calmed him down. He nodded, and she never let go of his hand. That's the last I saw of them."

While Hania steadied herself, I considered everything she'd told me. It couldn't be, but it had to be. There were too many similarities for my suspicions to be incorrect. I closed my eyes, and I could picture Mama kneeling before Jakub, holding his hand so he knew she was there, murmuring reassurance, while he focused on her, only her, not sorrow, distress, or pain. It was exactly what she'd done so many times for me and my siblings.

Now I imagined Mama kneeling in front of me, and I met her bright blue eyes and felt the warmth of her hands over mine. She took me away from the cold, hunger, and fear that constantly surrounded me in this place. I clung to her, seeking the clarification she'd already given me. A slight smile played on her lips while she stood and placed a gentle hand on my cheek.

Please don't go, Mama.

I kept my eyes closed a moment more, clinging to warmth and peace, then opened them. Next to me, Hania was silent, lost in a world all her own.

"Stanisława Pilarczyk," I whispered. "That's who rescued your children, Hania."

"Oy gevalt, you know her? Are you certain it's the same woman?"

I nodded and ran my fingers over my cigarette-burn scars. "Her real name was Natalia Florkowska. She was my mother." I took a shaky breath and met Hania's incredulous gaze. "Which means I know how we can find your sons."

Chapter 18

Auschwitz, 15 January 1942

DESPITE HOW MUCH I loathed working in Block 11, where so many innocents were sentenced to punishments and executions, it had its perks on some days. At least I was indoors most of the time.

During a vicious January morning's appell, I stood as still as possible, teeth chattering, knees knocking, while the wind howled across the dark sky and snow and freezing rain pelted my emaciated form. When the häftling beside me collapsed, I kept my eyes forward and listened as his breaths weakened and then stopped.

The SS men were safe inside their guard towers, protecting themselves from the raging weather. When roll call was finished, I would have run to Block 11 if I hadn't been required to march with SS escorts. As I stood in line, waiting for the order, Pilecki appeared beside me.

"Do you remember the day you were registered, when you spoke to a man removing bodies from the death wall?"

I dipped my head in a discreet nod.

"That prisoner is one of our recruits now, and I asked him if he knew anything about you or your family. He remembers speaking with you that day, and he remembers an SS officer who didn't work in Block 11 often, but who was there when you approached the truck. He suggested you talk to him. The officer's name is Untersturmführer Oskar Bähr. Middle aged, gray hair. He's assigned to Block 11 today."

I remembered noticing a middle-aged officer when I'd found my family. I opened my mouth to voice my thanks, but Pilecki had already melted into the crowd. When the SS men ordered us to Block 11, the members of my kommando pushed, shoved, and tripped over one another to get indoors.

During my reprieve from the horrible cold, I performed miscellaneous tasks and hunted for the gray-haired SS officer; at last I found him. He was stationed at the end of a small hallway leading outdoors to the courtyard, calm and observant, watching the condemned men file past him. His uniform indicated he was an Untersturmführer, as Pilecki had said, but, to ensure that he was the man I sought, I cast my mind back, pinpointing the other places I'd seen him. Father Kolbe's cell for his execution. The roll-call square during my flogging. And the courtyard between Blocks 10 and 11 when I found my family.

Don't be too hopeful. I can't afford to be too hopeful.

Combatting my hopes was more difficult than I anticipated as I returned to work. The officer stayed near the washroom and courtyard all day. When it was over, the guards shouted for my kommando to line up outside. Ignoring the order, I rushed back to the hallway as the officer made his exit.

"Herr Untersturmführer, may I have a word with you?"

He paused, likely taken aback by my boldness, but before lowering my gaze I noticed his own held no anger as it assessed me. "What's this about?" he asked.

"My family. They were sent to the wall in May of 1941. I saw you there that day, so I have reason to believe you—"

"I've seen thousands of people march to that wall," he said with a bitter laugh. "Even if I'd seen your family, I wouldn't remember them."

When he turned to go, I grabbed his arm. "It'll only take a moment."

Oh, God, why did I touch an officer?

Gasping, I released him, anticipating the consequences of my brazenness. Instead of a blow, I noticed the officer extending a hand toward me before hesitating and withdrawing it. I'd already been far too daring, but there was no turning back now. I lifted my eyes to his and found they held something I hadn't seen in a long time—pity. My voice fell to a quiver.

"Please, I'll do anything. Please help me."

He chewed on his lip and grappled with his decision. At last he gestured for me to accompany him. The officer told his companions he needed me to stay to finish a few things, so he'd escort me to my block later. They seemed satisfied with the excuse. Once the block was empty, he led me to an interrogation room. He cast a furtive glance down the hall, ushered me inside, and closed the door behind us.

"What's your name?" he asked as he sat across from me.

What an unusual query, considering my prisoner number was on my uniform, easy enough for him to see. I waited for him to correct himself, but he didn't. He was genuinely asking for my name, my real name, and the realization was so baffling that I didn't know whether to laugh or cry. I enunciated each syllable, listening as my name rolled off my tongue, so familiar, yet so rare and precious to me now.

"Well, if I'm calling you Maria, you can call me Oskar," he said. "Tell me about your family."

"My father was tall, and he had light brown hair and a crippled leg, and my mother and siblings were blond. They spoke perfect German. Zofia was nine, and she was the only one with curly hair, and Karol was four. My parents were Aleksander and Natalia, and the surname was Florkowski. Like I said, it was May of 1941, and I saw you near the courtyard when I found them, so I was hoping you'd seen something."

He stayed silent, his expression unreadable; then he nodded. "There was a family around that time which matched your description. They stood out to me because they were together in the men's washroom, and I'd never seen females there. Someone said the woman had asked if they could stay together. Her husband couldn't walk on his own."

I blinked to clear my blurry vision. Of course my parents had found a way to ensure they stayed together.

"Fritzsch came into the washroom, but he didn't look surprised to see the woman and children there. Maybe he was the one who permitted them to stay together, I'm not sure. Once they'd undressed, he was eyeing the woman—" Oskar broke off, cheeks flushed, and cleared his throat. "I happened to be standing close to the family, and I was intrigued by them. The woman—Natalia, was it? She saw Fritzsch looking at her—"

"You're certain it was Fritzsch? And you're certain he saw my family?"

Oskar nodded. "He spoke to them." He opened his mouth again, then closed it. "Do you want to hear this?"

I nodded. "Please keep going."

"Tell me if you want to stop," he replied. "After Fritzsch went back into the hall, Natalia spoke to her husband, then she went after him. Like I said, I was intrigued, so I followed at a distance. I didn't hear their whole conversation, but I heard the last thing Fritzsch said before—"

"What did he say?"

Oskar's face fell. His chair groaned in protest as he shifted position, and he rubbed the back of his neck. "I'd rather not repeat it."

"What did Fritzsch say to her?" I asked with as much force as I could muster. "Tell me his exact words."

Oskar took a deep breath and ran his thumb across a nick in the table. "He smiled, then he said, 'I'm not doing a damn thing for your children, you filthy Polack bitch.'"

The words hung heavy between us, and I bit my bottom lip until I tasted blood. I was certain my parents had realized what fate awaited them, and their first thoughts would have been how to spare their children. They would have agreed that Mama should talk to Fritzsch, though Tata would have hated for her to put herself through that. They had to die knowing they'd done everything they could. Mama would have offered Fritzsch anything, anything at all, to spare her children's lives. Not her own, not even Tata's. Just her children's.

And Fritzsch would have delighted in her desperation before refusing her.

My parents had put forth their best efforts, but it wasn't enough.

"Fritzsch sent her to the holding cell where they'd placed the rest of the family, and when it was time to go to the wall, they went together. He went out, too, and I stood at the far end of the courtyard. I don't think the little boy was aware of what was happening. Your father was distracting him, but the girl—your sister, I suppose—looked panicked until your mother knelt beside her and said something. Then she calmed down. All four started speaking in Polish, and I couldn't hear very well or understand it, but it didn't sound as if they were voicing their patriotism, and they weren't singing a Polish national anthem. Whatever they were saying sounded . . ." He seemed to search for the right word. "Comforting. Prayerful, even."

My hand strayed toward the secret pocket in my uniform. They'd been praying the rosary.

"They held hands and faced the wall, and Fritzsch . . ." Oskar let his voice trail away.

"Fritzsch didn't let the executioner do it," I finished for him. "He killed them himself."

Oskar didn't look at me, but he nodded. "Your siblings first, one right after the other. It was quick; they didn't suffer." The words were apologetic, as if they were meant to be a small comfort. He cleared his throat and removed the SS cap from his head, but I already suspected what happened next.

"Fritzsch waited before killing my parents, didn't he?"

Oskar's head dipped into a small nod.

Of course he'd waited. He wouldn't have missed his chance to torment two parents with their children's lifeless bodies.

"Your mother fell to her knees beside the children," Oskar continued, suddenly absorbed in the Totenkopf emblem on his cap. "I thought she was going to faint, but she stayed there, silent, staring at their faces. Your father took her by the hand and pulled her into his arms for a moment. Then they turned to face Fritzsch."

Mama and Tata had comforted Zofia and Karol in the only ways they could, and they somehow managed to keep them calm until it was over. And, when it was time for my parents to face the same fate, they did so with courage and dignity. It was all they could do.

"Your father was next," Oskar said. "When he fell, your mother flinched, but she didn't waver beyond that. She knelt and kissed his cheek, then kissed each child's before guiding them into her lap, taking your father's hand, and facing Fritzsch. She held that bastard's gaze until the end."

In the silence that followed Oskar's words, I heard the wind howling outside, and through the small window I saw the snow steadily falling. A damp chill filled the room, and I shivered, but I wasn't sure whether it was from cold, anger, sorrow, or all three. My parents watched their children die. My mother watched her husband die. All because of Fritzsch.

I hope you managed to find them.

His voice echoed in my head, his mention of my family during our chess game. This couldn't have been what he was implying. He couldn't have known the family he shot was mine. Perhaps he guessed they'd been murdered, so his words were meant only to remind me of this fact. He didn't know he was the one who had murdered them.

But the look in his eyes had revealed something deeper.

What if he knew? What if he knew everything?

I traced my cigarette-burn scars.

Mama. Tata. Zofia. Karol.

When I managed to find my voice, it was hardly audible. "You saw me that day, didn't you? How long had they been gone?"

Again, Oskar didn't meet my gaze. "Minutes."

Minutes. I'd missed my family by minutes. Their final moments, my chance to save them, join them, say goodbye, whatever could've happened had I arrived in time, I'd missed it by minutes.

"I requested to be relieved of duty, so I'll be leaving at the end of the week," Oskar said, staring at his cap. "I know that doesn't change anything, but I hate what goes on here."

He was right. It didn't change anything.

"If I could have stopped it, executions or floggings or any of it, I would have, but I'm one man, and if I . . ." Oskar rubbed his eyes and cleared his throat, then spoke again in a soft tone. "If it helps at all, your siblings seemed at peace. And even after what they'd witnessed, so did your parents." He hesitated before returning the cap to his head.

I rose to my feet and gripped the back of the chair with both hands to steady myself. He waited, as if anticipating that I was going to say something. When I did, I didn't bother trying to keep the tremble from my voice.

"If you meant what you said about hating what goes on here, I need you to promise me something."

He didn't react right away, but at last he dipped his head in a small nod.

"Tomorrow, I want you to report to the kommandant and tell him everything you know about Fritzsch."

* * *

After my conversation with Oskar, I rushed to my block. Hania and I had plans for a chess game, but chess was the furthest thing from my mind. When I got there, Hania was lingering outside and hurried to meet me, but I passed her without slowing down.

"I'm going to find Fritzsch."

She grabbed my arm. "Wait, Maria, you can't."

"Yes, I can," I exclaimed, shaking her off. "He can flog me all he wants, but I'm going to find him. I have to—"

"Listen to me, shikse," Hania murmured, taking me by the shoulders. "You can't go to him because he isn't here."

"Fine, I'll wait until he comes back, and when he does—"

"He isn't coming back." She held my hands and gave them an excited squeeze, beaming. "This morning, the SS men in the administrative office said Kommandant Höss summoned Fritzsch for a long meeting, and he left the moment it was over. Höss had ordered an immediate transfer and sent him to a concentration camp in Flossenbürg. He's gone."

Impossible. Fritzsch couldn't be gone. Not yet. With Oskar's testimony and Fritzsch's numerous transgressions, I was almost certain Kommandant Höss would transfer him, but I had asked Oskar to give his report tomorrow so I could have time to confront him first.

"It's true, shikse, I promise." Hania's voice made me blink, and she stepped closer to me with a small smile. "You've done it. He's gone."

Fritzsch was gone.

I'd spent months working toward his transfer, but my own plan had ruined everything. If I'd known he'd killed my family, I could have demanded to know if it was true, if he had been aware that he had spared one member of that family even as he condemned the others. Survival was supposed to feel like justice—a way to honor my family, overcome this place that had claimed so many lives, defy Fritzsch and his plans for me. Once again, I was facing a move I hadn't foreseen, one that changed everything. Stripping Fritzsch of his position and fighting for my survival were not enough. Justice was hearing the truth from my family's murderer. Finding a way to make him pay. But it was too late; he was gone.

I'd lost my chance.

No, this game wasn't over; this pawn was still in play.

Even though the snow almost reached my knees and the relentless wind made my eyes water, I wasn't cold. The heat of fury thawed me and left me with the embers of my resolve—a slow, steady burn that would not die.

I will get out of Auschwitz one day. And when I do, I will find Fritzsch.

Chapter 19

Auschwitz, 20 April 1945

NOW THAT THE time has come to confront Fritzsch with everything I learned from Oskar, my conversation with him pours from my mouth, though it takes considerable effort to keep my voice steady. Once finished, I fall silent and take a breath. The truth is laid out before us, as clear and defined as the squares on the chessboard. Fritzsch has no choice but to make his play.

He stays quiet, watching me; then he takes my queen, so my knight takes his. "You were told I executed your family, and that's why you tried to ruin my career, isn't it?"

Though I suspected he was aware of my scheme by now, hearing him say so stirs a maelstrom of terror within me, as strong as if he'd discovered my involvement at the time. To calm it, I remind myself that I have nothing to fear. The endgame will unfold as I've planned.

"Answer me, Polack! Did you try to ruin my career?"

The shout startles me into focus. I didn't realize how long I'd been silent. Fritzsch glowers at me, unblinking, so I examine the board, but if I delay for more than a few seconds, he'll take action.

"My efforts began long before I learned what you'd done, but ruining your career was your fault. I gave you opportunities to break protocol, that's all. I didn't force you to take them."

"So you did cause the transfer," he says, his voice so low that I have to concentrate to make out the words. "And you planned your actions according to the kommandant's whereabouts, didn't you?" When I nod, he shakes his head in disapproval. "I gave you the chance to be useful, and you turned against me."

"Don't act as if you treated anyone with mercy," I reply, though my voice is strained. "Not me, and not my family."

"My job was to keep the prisoners under control, so that's what I did," Fritzsch says, calm once again as he moves a pawn. "It seems I should have focused on controlling the guards as well."

In the midst of reaching for my own pawn, I retract my hand. "What do you mean?"

Fritzsch removes his cap to wipe the rainwater from the Totenkopf emblem, then he replaces it on his head. "The one who told you about your family. Did you not consider the possibility that he lied to you?"

Rainwater trickles down my back, and I combat the urge to shiver. I search Fritzsch's face, looking for any indication of trickery, but he just waits, expectant, for my response. I clear my throat before attempting it.

"After speaking with me, Oskar reported the same story to the kommandant."

"If he lied to you, why wouldn't he have lied to the kommandant? I remember the man in question. He wasn't cut out for this line of work, but he disapproved of me. I'm not surprised he took the opportunity to sabotage me. He'd been relieved of duty, and I was already gone, so he had nothing to lose. By speaking with you, he presented me as he wished, then delivered the same report to Höss, likely praising the kommandant for transferring me and seeking to regain the favor he had lost by being too weak for his camp assignment, all while I was not present to address the accusations against me."

I shift in my seat, but the adjustment makes me even more uncomfortable. "He had no reason to lie."

"Ah, that's not true, is it? You were vulnerable, desperate for answers, and you went to this man begging for them. He told you the odds of him remembering your family weren't good, but since you insisted, he seized the chance to undermine me, crafted a story to satisfy you, and expected you to show your gratitude." Fritzsch leans closer, holding my gaze. "Did you make it worth his while?"

The lascivious murmur unleashes my fury. "No, I would never—"

"Didn't you tell him you'd do anything? You shouldn't make promises you don't intend to keep."

"He didn't ask me to repay him in any way."

"Certain rewards lose all value if you have to ask for them," he says with a smirk. "Besides, the other female prisoner participated in race defilement—"

"Leave her out of this."

"Don't act so shocked. I knew everything that went on in this camp."

"You didn't know I was working toward your transfer."

A wave of anger crosses Fritzsch's visage. "I suspected as much when the kommandant mentioned the protocol violations which caused it, and most involved you. Such a shame my relocation was immediate, otherwise I would've had time to address it with you prior to leaving."

The contempt in his voice is a small satisfaction, but my victory remains a marginal one. Oskar couldn't have lied to me. The suggestion prompts the memories, and I feel the pain starting, the slight ache that precedes the bouts of relentless, uncontrollable pounding in my head. I clamp my teeth together to fight it, but it persists.

"You said you hoped I'd located my family," I manage at last. "You wanted me to . . ."

When the headache intensifies and steals my voice, he lifts a patronizing brow. "Do you always make such drastic inferences from simple statements?"

I close my eyes as I fight the constriction that overtakes my breaths. Control has been teasing me this entire time, darting within my reach, letting me grasp it, then breaking away again. The more I wrestle it, the more it overpowers me.

"Had you focused on your family rather than having me transferred, I never would've gone to Flossenbürg. Instead, you waited too long to look into your family's deaths, and you trusted a man whose story couldn't be disputed. I'm the only one who can refute or confirm his claims. That's why you were determined to find me again, isn't it?" He nods to the board to indicate it's my turn and settles back in his chair. "If I didn't execute your family, you've wasted all these years chasing the wrong man."

Chapter 20

Auschwitz, 8 June 1942

LIFE IN AUSCHWITZ was unusual without Fritzsch. As scorching heat replaced the frigid winter, no one forced me to play chess against my will, and I no longer spent my days plotting against him or hoping he wouldn't tire of me. Though I welcomed the respite, I was left with a void, one that wouldn't be filled until I was free to pursue the plans I'd made to locate him.

On a warm summer morning, I hurried from Block 8 and made my way to roll call. Block 8 had become my residence in March, when transports of women started arriving, and the guards had transferred us to our own set of blocks separated from the men's by a concrete wall. As I walked, I checked my sleeve to make sure the tiny nick in my arm wasn't bleeding through my uniform. Hania had managed to obtain typhus vaccines for me, herself, and Izaak, equipping us to fight the epidemic, which worsened every day. She'd assured me that she'd come by the vaccines honestly, but I suspected empty threats had been involved—though she wouldn't admit they were empty or that the SS men were unaware she used their names to protect herself. She'd woven an intricate web, and it wouldn't come apart until she gave the word.

Following roll call, I walked with my kommando to Block 11

and resisted the urge to scratch my upper back. It was probably a
flea bite. Fleas had taken a liking to the women's blocks. When the
itching became unbearable, I succumbed and gave it a quick rub,
and my fingers passed over a hard lump of skin. One of my flogging scars. I moved toward the secret skirt pocket with my rosary
while a wistful smile played around my lips. *Father Kolbe.*

The smile disappeared as I entered Block 11. The first wave of
victims for the day would be executed soon: prisoners who had
been caught participating in the camp resistance, or underground
resistance members who had been sent here simply for death. As
I walked down the hall toward the women's washroom, I passed a
few rooms outfitted as barracks. Inside, civilians were being held,
awaiting trial. I didn't know why the SS men bothered putting
anyone on trial. They sentenced almost everyone to death anyway.

Ahead, I glimpsed shorn, dark hair beneath a headscarf, and
I craned my neck to get a better view as the owner navigated the
hallway. When the female prisoner approached, my hopes deflated. Not Hania. For her sake, I was glad she wasn't translating for
trials or interrogations today. Given the torture she was forced to
witness, she hated working in Block 11. For my own sake, though,
I wished it had been her.

When I reached the small washroom, I paused in the hallway.
Focus, I told myself, repeating the mantra I recited prior to every
workday. *Focus on living. Fighting. Surviving.*

But no amount of focus could take away my shock when Irena
Sienkiewicz walked into Block 11.

It was her; it was unmistakably her. She looked exactly as
I remembered, though more haggard because she would have
just come from Pawiak—and I knew how that felt. She was still
dressed in civilian clothing, and she lifted her chin with her
usual defiance, but her eyes roamed, quick and uncertain. The

guards directed some political prisoners into the courtroom or a holding room; then they sent others in my direction, including Irena. As she followed the crowd, she didn't notice me, so I hurried to meet her.

"Irena Sienkiewicz? Or should I say Marta Naganowska, so you won't yell at me for using your real name in front of the SS men?"

She stepped back and stared at me, but, as her wary gaze drifted from my face to my prisoner number and back, my words must have triggered recognition. Her eyes widened, then she grinned and shook her head. "Dammit, Maria. You're alive."

Never did I think I'd take comfort in hearing Irena swear at me, but it almost brought tears to my eyes. As much as I hated that she was here, I couldn't help how thrilled I was to see her. *After all this time—*

The thought stopped short. Irena had been sent to the women's washroom, the last stop before the courtyard. And no one sent to the courtyard emerged alive.

Yes, she was a woman, but she was young and healthy, and usually the young, healthy women were kept for labor. Why hadn't they kept her for labor? When I noticed her swollen stomach, the answer was clear.

"Irena, you're pregnant."

"Am I? I had no idea."

We followed the other women into the washroom, and a passing SS man ordered them to undress. While Irena did so, I mechanically accepted various articles of clothing the other women handed me. Once undressed, the women left the room or moved into the adjoining one to use the latrines.

"The baby's father?" I asked at last.

Irena pressed her mouth into a thin line. "A soldier who caught me during curfew. The son of a bitch said he wouldn't arrest me on one condition, but I didn't get to choose whether or not I accepted his terms. I would have chosen arrest." She removed her blouse and continued with a halfhearted laugh. "Some fights you just can't win, even if you fight like hell. As you can see, that was almost nine months ago, then I was caught taking a Jewish girl to live with a Catholic family outside Warsaw." She paused and folded the blouse with meticulous care. "Someone informed on us. Once I'd dropped the girl off, the Gestapo arrested me outside the house, locked everyone inside, and set fire to it. After making sure no one survived, they took me to Pawiak. Interrogation almost sent me into labor, but my little one is as much of a fighter as I am, so here we are."

I didn't know what I expected the explanation behind her pregnancy or arrest to be, but that wasn't it, and it was too appalling to process. Nothing I said could take away what she'd endured, so I asked the next question on my mind. "Your mother?"

As she stepped out of her skirt, a shadow crossed over her face, nearly broke her, before she swallowed hard. "Mama was fine a few weeks ago, but she'll know I've been caught by now, so I can't imagine how she's coping. Your family?" My expression must have given away the answer. She opened her mouth, then closed it.

Irena removed her undergarments and handed her clothing to me, and I added her belongings to the growing pile I'd created on the floor. The bruises covering her body took me back to my own time in Pawiak. Grief and anger tightened in my chest. The Gestapo had tortured a pregnant woman.

She washed her face and hands in the sink and started to exit the room, but she paused in the doorway. She placed both hands on her stomach now that it was exposed.

"They're going to kill me, aren't they?"

She knew the answer, I could see it in her eyes, but she had to hear it from me. I couldn't tell her the truth, how could I possibly tell her the truth—but she deserved the truth, and I wouldn't lie to her. I didn't trust my voice, so I nodded.

Irena didn't look surprised, but her hand moved to the crucifix around her neck. Only then did she seem to realize she had to take it off. As she grabbed the clasp, she hesitated. "This was the last gift my father gave me," she murmured, more to herself than to me. She hastily removed it and handed it to me. I should have put it with the confiscated jewelry, but when the crucifix and chain settled in my palm, I closed my hand into a fist. I couldn't let it go. Not yet.

An SS officer marched down the hall, shouting orders, and he focused on me and Irena. "Keep her moving, 16671."

Hearing the command made Irena's fate all too real, and I had to do something. I couldn't let her die. I didn't have time to develop a plan, only to beg.

"Wait!" I shouted, and I grabbed his arm. "She's going to give birth any day now, then she can work, for God's sake, let her work—" I broke off when the officer jerked out of my grasp and raised a hand to strike me, but, before he could, Irena grabbed my shoulders and shook me.

"Listen, you crazy bitch, I don't know who the hell you think I am, but I've told you we don't know each other, and I don't want to work with you. Leave me alone." She pushed me away and turned to the officer in exasperation. "Please tell me where I need to go to get away from her."

He gave her an amused smirk. "Take a left down the next hallway and continue into the courtyard." He gestured in the proper direction before moving away from us.

Once he'd gone, Irena turned to me. "I may have learned a

thing or two from Helena Pilarczyk." She flashed a small, teasing smile as she used my resistance name.

All I could do was follow her toward the courtyard, so I did. I would stay with her as long as I could. She stood tall, shoulders back, chin and chest lifted, a protective hand on her round midsection.

"Why did you stop me?" I murmured as we walked.

Irena took a deep breath before replying. "Because even if they let me work after giving birth, they'd take my baby. And I'll be damned if I let them take my baby." Her voice broke as a single tear escaped. She brushed it away hastily and swallowed hard; when she spoke again, her tone was as steady as always. "I can't save my child, but we can face death together."

We paused outside the men's washroom, a few meters away from the iron gate that led into the courtyard. The wall was beyond it to the right, out of our line of vision. This was as far as I could go without getting caught. When we stopped, Irena took my emaciated hand and pressed my palm to her stomach. I felt a slight yet powerful ripple as the baby moved.

"If I had a girl, I was going to name her Helena," she said, smiling at her round abdomen. "And a boy, Patryk."

Both names conjured such fond memories of our time in the resistance together, and I'd felt the life within her that was about to be snuffed out along with her own, and it was too much, it was all too much, but I didn't notice my tears until I heard a familiar annoyed rebuke.

"Good Lord, stop that. You're going to get in trouble."

But I couldn't keep the tears from cascading down my cheeks, and I buried my face in my hands. Every time I thought this place had thrown all the cruelty it possibly could upon me and my loved ones, it proved me wrong. My friend and her unborn child were about to die. And here I was, accompanying them to their deaths, powerless to save either one.

I felt her fingers around my wrists, and she guided my hands away. Through my tears, I looked into her face and attempted to speak clearly enough for her to understand me. "Irena, if only I could—"

She pulled me into a tight embrace and kissed my cheek, silencing me, then she released me before anyone caught us and placed gentle hands on my shoulders. She looked at me with glassy eyes full of strength, always strength, and more affection than she'd ever shown me before. I might even have called it love.

"Give these bastards hell, Maria Florkowska."

Without giving me time to reply, she walked toward the gate. When she reached it, Irena touched her right hand to the center of her forehead, chest, and each shoulder, making the sign of the cross, then rested her hand on her stomach. The hinges creaked as she let herself out and closed the gate firmly behind her. With her head high, she continued into the courtyard and took a right toward the wall, disappearing from my sight. I turned my back to the gate and didn't listen to the angry SS guards or look at the women filing past me to the courtyard, but I stayed where I was. I wouldn't leave her.

A few moments later, the familiar crack of gunshots sent me to my knees.

* * *

I sobbed for a few precious seconds before I somehow dried my tears and forced myself off the floor. I wasn't sure how I did it. Maybe because somewhere, deep in my subconscious, I knew my survival depended on it. I fastened Irena's crucifix around my neck and tucked it underneath my uniform, out of sight. I had a piece of my family through my cigarette-burn scars, a piece of Father Kolbe through his rosary, and now a piece of Irena. Then I got back to work.

The rest of the day passed in a blur. Once it was over, I rushed toward the main gate to wait for Hania. I was so distracted that I almost passed the black skull and crossbones, ordering prisoners to *HALT!* and *STÓJ!* The warning was painted onto crude wooden planks mounted on a cement pole, and I wanted to ignore it, to dart through the gate and burst into the SS administrative buildings and find Hania, but I wouldn't. Going beyond the sign was a mistake I knew better than to make.

Prisoners marched past me while I shifted my weight from one foot to the other, but I didn't have to wait long. When Hania arrived, I gestured for her to follow me. I led the way in search of somewhere private and settled on the alley between Blocks 17 and 18. It was out of the way, but not far from the gate, and I couldn't keep myself together much longer.

"What is it?" Hania asked once we got there. "Are you hurt? Is Izaak hurt?"

"Irena." Her name was all I managed before my sobs escaped, the sobs I'd contained all day, and they rendered me unable to speak. I pressed my back to the hard bricks, sank to the ground, and buried my head in my arms until I sensed Hania crouching beside me.

"Shhh, calm down, shikse." When I lifted my head, she brushed a tear from my cheek. "Tell me what happened."

"She was here," I whispered. "Irena was here."

"Your friend from home?"

I nodded. "Block 11. She was pregnant." I couldn't bring myself to continue, but Hania simply shook her head, assuring me there was no need. "You've said before that you can get prisoners reassigned," I went on. "Can you really do it? Please, Hania, I don't care where I work, but please get me out of Block 11. I can't do this anymore."

"Don't worry, I'll take care of it," she said, placing a reassuring hand over mine and bringing my frantic pleas to a halt. "I'll get you out as quickly as I can."

"Only if all you have to do is translate or trade organized goods. Nothing else," I whispered, my thoughts on Protz. Despite my desperation, I didn't want her to get hurt.

"It'll be a fair exchange, harmless for all involved," Hania replied, flashing a small, appreciative smile. "I promise."

When she produced a sedative and offered it to me, I shook my head in refusal. I wanted to allow myself to cry, to live fully in this moment, because as painful as it was, it meant my walls had come down in a way I hadn't permitted in a long time. The ache of love and loss pierced me to the core of my soul. And it reminded me that I was still human.

Everyone I loved had been taken from me. Irena had been my last piece of home, the last bit of the life I'd left behind, taken as easily and viciously as my parents, brother, and sister. She had prevented my attempt to help, had accepted her fate, yet overwhelming darkness struck me as it had after I had found my family. Failure. Despair. Everything I held no power to change, direct and fierce as the whip across my flesh. Father Kolbe had told me to live and fight, but the more I did the more I lost. And I wondered if I had anything left to live or fight for.

No, I couldn't allow myself to think that way. There were a few things I had left. I had my memories of them and a life to live in their honor. I had Hania and my promise to reunite her with her children. I had my vow to find Fritzsch, to hear from his own mouth how he had denied my mother's final request, refused to spare my siblings, and executed my family himself. I had the resistance.

When I managed to catch my breath, I lifted my head and looked at Hania. "I've been working with the resistance for almost a year, and you—"

"Don't start this again," she said, holding up a hand. She rose to her feet, and so did I. I'd attempted this conversation many times, but I wouldn't let her avoid it this time.

"What will it take for you to join?"

"That is enough. You've had a difficult day, you're upset, and I'm not discussing it," Hania said sharply, and when she spoke again it was with finality. "I have children, Maria."

"Children who haven't seen their mother in over a year."

She had started to leave the alley, but that was all it took for her to close the distance between us, fuming. "I've fought for my sons every day, and if I risk everything, if Protz finds out—"

"None of it matters if we don't stop this. They'll kill us eventually, and they'll keep killing until there's no one left." I caught her by the shoulders, but my voice fell as my tears returned. "When will it end?"

Hania released a breath; then she softened her glower and pulled me close. I wrapped my arms around her, combatting shaky breaths. Of course I understood her reservations, but the fastest way to get back to her sons was through liberation. It did no good to fight for daily survival if the end was inevitable. That's why we had to change the ending.

"If I'm going to do this," she murmured at last, "could I borrow some of your chutzpah?"

I looked up to confirm what I'd heard. "You'll join?"

Despite the lingering concern in her eyes, Hania offered me a small smile. "Don't you dare say 'Checkmate,' or I'll quit right now."

Chapter 21

Birkenau, 11 October 1942

O N A DREARY October day, I trudged through mud up to my ankles and bowed my head against the lashing wind and rain, making my way to the latrines. I should have grown accustomed to the lack of roads and drains in Birkenau by now, considering that the female inmates had been moved to Auschwitz's new addition in August, but each day I missed the minimal amenities of the main camp more than the last.

As I approached my destination, I blinked water from my eyes and made out the SS guard stationed outside. He took shelter against the building and grimaced as he wiped rainwater from his face, but when he saw me he brightened. He'd come to expect my visits. Without a word, I pressed a pack of cigarettes into his greedy palm, and he allowed me inside.

Janina, the redheaded Jewish doctor who worked as a nurse, motioned for me to sit beside her on one of the long concrete benches. I obliged, avoiding the cluster of holes that served as the toilets.

"According to my sources, Pilecki recovered from his recent bout with typhus and was released from quarantine last week," Janina murmured. "He transferred to the tannery kommando and has started organizing valuables hidden in leather goods."

As if to prove it, Janina offered me four small diamonds. Giving a silent, solemn thanks to whoever had left them behind, I tucked them into my pocket. They'd be useful for future exchanges.

"My next update isn't good," she continued. "We lost one, a woman named Luiza. She wanted to avoid transferring to another camp, so I gave her a false case of typhus."

"Injection or gas chamber?"

"Injection."

"You work in the hospital, Janina, you had to know it was over-crowded."

"Of course I did, but I never know when the guards will empty it."

Closing my hands into fists, I stood and turned away. This was why I hated when members entered the hospital under false pre-tenses. It was too risky. Now Luiza was dead for nothing. If we kept losing women this way, we wouldn't have anyone left when the rebellion happened.

When Janina and I parted ways, I retraced my steps along the unpaved road, stumbling over jagged pieces of brick, rock, and rubble. I reached a large, deep puddle and moved closer to a pile of decomposing corpses. I kept my eyes on the cold, slick mud, seeking camouflaged limbs so I wouldn't trip, and kicked muck at a rat in my path. My missile landed with a squelch, but it missed the rat, which rejoined its companions gnawing on the mass of blue-gray skeletal forms.

Upon reaching my brick barracks, I paused at the threshold and cast an envious glance over my shoulder, imagining that I could see three kilometers east, all the way to the main camp. Al-though Block 8 had been infested with fleas, it had level floors, latrines, and a water supply. This structure had none of those.

I shook off as much mud as possible, using the rain to my advantage, then utilized the raindrops to quench my ever-present thirst before going inside. Shivering and wiping off stray droplets, I skirted the rat lingering by the door and crossed the uneven floor toward the rows of wooden slats. When I reached my row, I climbed to the top bunk. The bunks didn't leave enough space to do much besides lie flat, but I had a few centimeters to spare, even when I extended my legs. I hadn't inherited Tata's height.

I selected a piece of bread from my stash of organized goods and tore off a chunk. Despite the rain trickling through the roof, it was my favorite day of the week, because it was Sunday. On Sundays, we didn't have to work.

I produced my camp letter form so I could compose another letter to Mrs. Sienkiewicz. Though I'd been afraid to write to resistance contacts, Irena's fate had left me no choice. Before crafting my response, I read hers again.

Dear Maria,

Thank you for telling me about the deaths of my daughter and grandchild. While the news was devastating, I appreciated it coming from my daughter's loving and trusted friend. It means so much to know she visited with you one last time. I'm glad you're doing well, my dear. Please write again soon.

Best regards,
Wiktoria Sienkiewicz

A simple, safe letter. As a resistance member, Mrs. Sienkiewicz knew how to write letters that would pass the Nazi censorship office. I had a feeling she also knew that Irena didn't die during a complicated childbirth and the baby wasn't stillborn, as I'd said in the message I sent her following Irena's death. Someday I'd relay the real story.

I killed the louse that found its way onto my arm, then I began writing. This time maybe I'd keep my tears from staining the pages and causing the ink to run.

Dear Mrs. Sienkiewicz,

Thank you for responding to my letter. Please tell me about yourself and everyone at home. I'm fine and doing well.

In my haste to share the news of your daughter with you, I forgot to discuss my own family. Sadly, we caught a terrible illness, and I was the only one who recovered. I miss them, but I'm fortunate to be kept busy through employment. I work in a weaving shop, and I spend my spare time translating for Poles who don't speak German.

Today is a beautiful day, and I hope the sun is shining over Warsaw, as well. I look forward to hearing from you soon.

I hated myself for the lies, feigned positivity, and, above all, the standard reassurance of my well-being. It was a line I was obligated to include to ensure that my letter passed the censorship office. If not for censors, my letter would have shared all the details of my work with ZOW and our hopes that the Home Army would agree that an attack was necessary to liberate Auschwitz.

The letter forms didn't allow much space to write, but I had room for one more line before my closing. As I read my words again, desperate for honesty, I thought of my time working for the resistance in Warsaw, and I knew what to say. Best of all, Mrs. Sienkiewicz would know what it meant.

Please give my love to my friends, Marta and Helena.

Best wishes,
Maria Florkowska

* * *

After I finished my camp letter to Mrs. Sienkiewicz and a secret one to Mateusz, two of my bunkmates remained absent, but Hania returned to our block. Fortune had favored us and assigned us to the same living quarters, so naturally she was the fourth member of my bunk. Muttering in Czech, she attempted to wring the rainwater out of her muddy uniform. On Protz's demand, she and her clothing received a thorough scrubbing during their meetings, so she tended to be shockingly clean when she returned. But after her trek across the drenched camp she was as filthy as I was.

"How did it go?"

Hania raised her eyebrows, chuckling while she settled beside me. "I realize you won't be sixteen until February, Maria, but you should know that by now. If I have to explain it to you . . ."

"I'm well aware of what happened between you and Protz. He treated you to a delicious dinner of roasted duck with rowanberry sauce and took you to an opera at the *Teatr Wielki* in Warsaw, and then . . ." I paused, as if searching her face for clues, then gasped. "He kissed you?"

Hania placed a hand over her chest. "A lady never tells. Such a shame you missed the opera, though. It was *The Barber of Seville*, and it was marvelous."

I giggled, but I didn't miss the sad detachment behind her amused smirk. "I was talking about what you've been meaning to ask him. Did you do it? Is he going to let you see Izaak?"

"Yes, I asked, and he agreed. Before escorting me back to Birkenau, Protz took me to speak with him. We only had a few minutes, and Izaak hates that he's in the main camp and we're here, but otherwise, he's fine."

"Thank goodness. Next time, tell Izaak I miss him."

She flashed a small smile. "I will, shikse."

Even though she had to go through Protz, seeing her brother seemed to have given Hania a much-needed boost of reassurance. A hopeful light had reignited in her eyes, outshining a bit of the worry that had been more present of late. Despite the improvement in her demeanor, I detected a new uncertainty, so I waited for her to voice it.

"Maria, if I keep asking Protz to let me see Izaak, that's the only deal he'll make. He won't let me see Izaak and give me necessities in the same exchange."

Of course Protz had inserted a caveat into the arrangement. That schmuck. Hania had given up exploiting other prisoners for goods, but Protz remained her primary supplier. Losing him would be a heavy blow, and I wasn't sure we could afford it. Still, as Hania waited in hopeful silence, I knew my answer to her unspoken request.

"Protz is your connection to Izaak. You don't need my permission to choose your brother."

"I didn't want to let you or the resistance down," she said, though she didn't hide her relief. "I know how much it'll affect our resources."

"You and Izaak need each other, Bubbe. Besides, you're the best translator in the whole camp, so we can find plenty of exchanges for you to make up Protz's loss," I replied with a teasing grin, though it didn't eliminate the knot in my stomach.

I knew better than to suggest finding another connection to Izaak and breaking off the arrangement with Protz. She would insist that decision was not hers to make, claim she was fine. But some evenings I found her lying in our bunk with a small, empty vodka bottle, usually pilfered from the SS barracks. Night was a safe haven for secrets lurking in the depths. They arose without fear until exposure to morning light forced a retreat. Once they were reburied, Hania awoke with no recollections of voicing them, so I concealed them within my own depths. Her emphatic curses, fragile whispers, eventually condensed into the simple truth: *I had to stay alive for my boys. But I never imagined it would go on this long.*

"Do you want to play chess?"

The question alleviated the knot slightly. When we'd moved to Birkenau, I'd brought my makeshift chess pieces along, and she had hardly finished the query before I jumped down from our bunk. I fetched the jewelry pouch from beneath a loose brick in the floor, where I kept it buried, and began setting up the game. I never said no to chess.

* * *

A few weeks later, I walked with my kommando to the basket-weaving workshop outside the camp grounds, where I'd been reassigned following the move to Birkenau. A cool morning breeze whipped around me while I tucked my last note from Mateusz into my pocket. Our covert letter exchanges became more difficult after the move, but we found ways to stay in touch. I hadn't seen him since our first meeting, but, after my most recent correspondence, I hoped to change that. I worked among civilians now, and if I could convince him to join me I could enact the next phase of my plan.

Sure enough, I walked into the workshop, and there he was.

The gangly boy I remembered wasn't so gangly anymore, but still the same as he stood among the civilian workers. His bright blue eyes scanned the prisoners filing in. The moment we were ordered to take our places, I hurried to sit beside him.

"You got my letter, Maciek," I said with a smile, and he chuckled upon hearing the nickname. "And I can't tell you how much better my workdays will be now that you're here. Your parents don't mind that you've left the family business?"

"I'll help when I can, but they know I want to go to a university instead of owning the bakery. Assuming the Allies win and universities are reopened to Poles, I can put the money I make here toward my education."

"And I hear making baskets is a necessary qualification for university acceptance."

Mateusz laughed, then he stopped weaving long enough to look at me. "It's good to see you, Maria."

I hid my smile and pretended to be absorbed in my basket's shape, though I'd hardly constructed enough for it to matter yet. "This doesn't mean you'll stop writing, does it?"

"Never."

An SS man strolled by, so we fell silent. As I waited for the guard to move out of earshot, I cast a sideways glance at Mateusz, who was bent over his work. His movements were quick and deft, and he didn't slow down as he watched the SS man pass from the corner of his eye. Once the guard was a safe distance away, Mateusz looked to me. I averted my gaze, though I hadn't intended to stare, but the flutter in my stomach came from more than almost getting caught.

He'd come, like I'd hoped he would, and now was my chance

to recruit his help in my most vital personal mission. I'd rehearsed what I was going to say for a while, but as I went over it again I adjusted the weave in my basket. No matter how hard I tried, I never got it quite right. Once ready, I leaned closer to Mateusz until I could smell the lingering traces of fresh bread from the bakery mingling with sweet grass from his walk and salt on his skin.

"There's a number of us who have joined a resistance movement within the camp, but we need information and resources from people outside," I said, keeping my voice low. "Would you be willing to help?"

"Of course," he replied without hesitation. "I'll bring you whatever you need, and I have friends who work for the resistance throughout occupied Poland and a few in Germany. I'll see what I can learn from them."

He'd said the words I'd prayed he'd say, and I hadn't even asked my next question yet. Resistance connections in Germany. This plan was coming together even better than I'd hoped.

I took a slow breath so as not to sound too eager. "Are any of your connections near Flossenbürg?"

"Yes, actually. Why?"

Instead of responding right away, I reached toward him. When he opened his palm, I dropped a small diamond into it. Mateusz gaped, as if unsure it was real.

"Maria, I don't want—"

"If you don't take it, the guards will. You'll make much better use of it, Maciek. Consider it a small token of thanks." I waited until he tucked it into his pocket, then I dropped my voice again. "Contact your resistance members in Flossenbürg. I need whatever you can find on a man named Karl Fritzsch."

Chapter 22

Auschwitz, 20 April 1945

IF I DIDN'T execute your family, you've wasted all these years chasing the wrong man.

As we continue the game, Fritzsch's claim fills my mind while I prop my elbows on the table and press my hands to the sides of my head, desperate to focus on the board, unable to succeed. I select a pawn, but I don't pay attention to whether or not it's the best move.

"You're a liar."

The words aren't much more than a whisper, and I'm not sure he can even hear them over the rainfall. I lift my head and raise my voice.

"You're a liar. Everything Oskar told me about you was true."

Fritzsch drums his fingers against the table while he surveys the board. "I never said his claims were true or false. I only said it's possible he lied to you."

"But he didn't, did he?"

The question hovers between us while I watch him. My beliefs aren't wrong; they can't be wrong. After a moment, Fritzsch moves his rook.

"Most women wept and begged for their lives and their chil-

dren's, but not your mother. She was calm and diplomatic, concerned only about the children. Not herself, not her invalid of a
husband, not you—in fact, she didn't mention a third child at all.
Just the little ones. It was strange, seeing a woman remain so collected while preparing for death. I knew the calm wouldn't last. In
the end, they're all the same."

There it is, the confession I've sought all these years, stated in
such a simple, matter-of-fact manner that it leaves me speechless.
Fritzsch examines the captured black queen, then waves it toward
me, as if urging me to make my move, but I can't think of chess.
I can picture the scene all too well, can imagine Fritzsch toying
with my mother as easily as he toys with these chess pieces. He
would have let her attempt to reason with him while he waited for
her to dissolve into the desperation and fear he craves. And when
she did, he refused her.

"Why?" It's all I can manage to say.

"Why would I spare two useless children? I had the same question. That's why I didn't."

He waits, perhaps giving me time to consider the words, perhaps expecting a response, I don't know. I can't do anything but
stare at him.

"Or are you asking why I executed them myself? Because when
I met you on the arrival platform, you had that little chess piece, so
I decided to make use of you, but you were in such a panic about
where your family had gone. I thought I'd help you find them."

As I comprehend the implications behind his words, I stare
into my lap, where I don't see the skirt I'm wearing—I see the
one with blue and gray stripes. And on the chessboard, I don't
see raindrops. I see glaring streaks of setting sunlight, feel the
humid breeze carrying his words to my ears.

I hope you managed to find them.

The images fade, but nothing feels different. I remain in the roll-call square, playing chess against Fritzsch, alone, his eyes confirming every suspicion.

"You knew who they were all along." I don't wonder this time, because he's already erased all doubt. But I need to hear him say it.

Fritzsch takes a pawn and presses it between his thumb and index finger. He twists it slowly, deliberately, before releasing it and letting it clatter against the table. "Didn't I tell you I knew everything that went on in this camp?"

The agony in my head is worse than it's ever been. He knew. He knew from the moment I found them at the wall; he knew when he made me play chess during my first roll call; he knew the entire time.

"When I went to Block 11 to locate them, one family spoke German, asked to stay together, and kept glancing around as if something were missing. I had a feeling they were the ones you'd been looking for, and your mother all but confirmed my suspicions when she approached me and started carrying on about the little ones. You favored one another so much in your desperation. And now, thanks to you, I have no doubts I was correct."

Even if he expects me to respond, I can't. I wish I'd never met Fritzsch on the arrival platform that day. I wish I'd stayed with my family . . .

Fritzsch stands and gestures for me to join him. "Let's take a walk to the courtyard. I'll show you exactly how it happened. Naked in the rain, a single shot each from the same pistol I have here. First the little boy, then the little girl, but I wasn't watching them. I was watching your parents, listening to the sound your mother made when the children fell—"

He's interrupted by a shriek, an unearthly shriek that formulates a word and emerges from my own throat.

"Stop!"

"There, that's almost how your mother sounded," Fritzsch says with a laugh. "Didn't I say you're all the same? The little brats died quickly, and then it was just your parents, standing in their blood."

The shriek comes again, and I press both hands to the acute thudding in my head. "Stop, please stop . . ."

"That's why you came, isn't it? To hear how I killed those Polacks? Or would you rather go to Block 11 and visit Cell 18, where we watched your priest friend die?" His voice rises into the crazed bellow I know so well. He slams both hands on the table, rattling the chess pieces before leaning toward me, and I wither beneath him and curl into myself while his words berate me and everything inside me swirls into a chaotic frenzy. "Shall I continue, or should we take a walk? Which will it be, 16671? Go on, tell me what you want."

Words fail me, despite everything I want to say, despite how I fight to conjure something, anything, but all I see are my family's bodies in the truck and the needle piercing Father Kolbe's arm, and the images aren't chased away until I close my fingers around the cold, hard metal in my pocket, spring to my feet, and aim my pistol at Fritzsch's chest.

Chapter 23

Birkenau, 9 February 1943

I WOKE TO THE sound of familiar voices raspy and hoarse from constant yelling. The SS-*Helferin*—the female guards. As I lifted my head—not too high so I wouldn't hit the roof—I blinked to clear my vision, but the darkness lingered.

"Oy, what now, a selection?" Hania's voice was heavy with sleep while our two bunkmates hurried to the ground. "Didn't we have one a few days ago?"

I shrugged and offered her the pale pink lipstick I'd organized a few months ago to bring more life into our pallid complexions, our secret weapon against selections. We dabbed our lips and cheeks—just a little so as not to be obvious to the guards or wasteful of such a precious resource—then blended it in. The hue was light and natural. I removed Irena's crucifix from my neck and tucked it into the pocket with Father Kolbe's rosary, making sure the button was secured so the items wouldn't fall out. Once satisfied, I followed Hania and the other women outside.

As the biting wind cut through my thin uniform, I dreaded the thought of taking it off in a few short minutes. It was hard enough to pass as fit for labor when the weather was nice, but worse on days like this one, when we'd be nude in fresh snow while the

SS men looked us over. The smallest flaw could get a häftling sent to the gas chamber, where inmates were murdered in massive numbers before their bodies were cremated. The last selection had ruled in Hania's and my favor, but this was a new day. Nothing was guaranteed.

"Watch out for the Beast," Hania whispered as we trudged through the snow and fell into line.

The head of Birkenau's female camp, Lagerführerin Maria Mandel, stood with our guards. As a macabre joke, Hania and I had dubbed her the Beast because the bitch was too vicious to be human, but somehow the name caught on. It was all over the camp, spreading from prisoner to prisoner as easily as the ashes from the crematoria spread on a breeze. As we assumed formation, Mandel cursed and beat any woman within reach. Her usual tight updo secured her hair away from her wide forehead, and her eyes were wild and bloodshot beneath heavy brows. Mandel was the Fritzsch of the women's camp, and she was almost as bad as he had been.

I took my place and scanned the faces around me. When I'd first come to Auschwitz, most prisoners had been non-Jewish Poles. Now the listless women surrounding me were mainly Jews from all over Europe, sent here as part of a demented plan to eradicate an entire race. As I studied them, I wondered which camp I would have been sent to a few weeks earlier if Hania hadn't found my number on a transfer list. She'd bribed the prisoners responsible to remove it. Thanks to her position in the SS offices, she kept a close eye on the lists and ensured that our numbers and Izaak's weren't included in relocations.

When the women were situated, the Beast contained herself after one final shriek. "Scheisse-Juden!"

The command against my ears was harsher and more vicious

than the wind chafing my skin. This selection was a Jewish one. Beside me, Hania didn't react, but I reached for her, slow and cautious, until our hands met. She stroked her thumb across the back of my hand, then started to move away, but I didn't let her go. I couldn't.

Hania jerked free and pinned me in place with a sharp glance, and I could almost hear her telling me I should know better. Of course I knew better. But that didn't make it easier to watch her follow the other Jewish women, who obeyed in petrified silence as they created a separate formation.

Undress, kneel, get up, lie down, don't move, again and again. Even from a distance, Hania looked more fragile than I recalled as she moved through exercises, though it had been only three days since the roll call that had somehow transformed into a selection. As the sky began to lighten, I counted the vertebrae along her spine as she lay facedown in the snow, motionless, then examined her protruding hip bones and shoulder blades when she got up. Most prisoners were just as skeletal and flat-chested, standing beneath a sky as gray as their skin, but others, recent transfers, retained a slight roundedness, perhaps even a faint flush of health. Time hadn't had a chance to rob them of either yet.

An unbearable whisper encroached upon my thoughts; when I held it back, it resisted, demanding to be heard. Suddenly I was immune to the cold, immune to everything but a heavy terror that pressed down upon me. The whisper asked whether or not lipstick would be enough for Hania this time.

While SS men conducted the selection with Mandel, a few female guards watched my group. I was on the outskirts of my row, so I studied the guards near me, considering my options, choosing my play. The one closest to me was young, maybe Hania's age, bright-eyed and attractive. Diamond earrings glittered against her earlobes, thick fur lined her boots, and I imagined that the nails beneath her leather gloves were neat and manicured.

Another guard patrolled ahead, eyes narrowed, shoulders stiff as she paced back and forth, tapping her riding crop against her thigh, as if eager to use it. Her opportunity arose when one prisoner shivered. The young guard was the more promising choice. I slipped an item from my pocket and waited for the strict guard to march to the front, away from me.

"Frau Aufseherin."

My whisper startled the young woman, but, before she could silence me, she noticed the gold bracelet in my palm. I closed my hand into a fist. A glimpse was all it took. Gradually she stepped closer, and I spoke without turning my head.

"Prisoner 15177 is in the selection. She's in line now, ten prisoners from the front. Make sure she isn't chosen."

The guard dipped her head in a discreet nod, then snatched the bracelet from my extended hand. Tucking it into her pocket, she moved toward the men conducting the selection. She took her time, as if with no particular purpose in mind. She exchanged a few words with various guards and approached an SS man who clutched a handful of documents. As they conversed, she whispered into his ear. Her hand lingered on his arm a bit longer than necessary, and she left him with a coy smile before returning to her place beside me.

When it was Hania's turn, she stood before the same man. She extended her arms to the side, and he jerked his thumb to the right, sparing her. As she joined her group, Hania's gaze found me across the snow-covered ground, her blue lips twitching into a faint, appreciative smile, as she likely suspected what I'd done.

"I have another bracelet identical to the first, Frau Aufseherin," I whispered. "If you'll bring me a loaf of bread, it's yours."

"Tonight," she muttered. She moved away before anyone caught us speaking.

I relished my success and blinked to clear the snowflakes obscuring my vision. Bartering with guards was a risk, but I was willing to take it.

When the selection was finished, the guards shoved the condemned into a truck. It roared to life and hauled them away, never to bring them back, while the rest of us marched to our labor assignments. Surrounded by vicious dogs, SS guards on horseback and on foot, and my fellow inmates, I followed my kommando across the frozen, snowy ground until we reached the basket-weaving workshop.

Each day in the workshop was as monotonous as the last, though far better than Block 11. It wasn't the worst job, but my fingers were made for chess, not meticulous weaving. Sometimes as I worked, I imagined twisting Zofia's hair into the basket patterns instead of our usual braids, though the mental images were always accompanied by a heavy ache.

The workshop was humid, thick with the stench of humans who hadn't had a real bath in God knew how long. At the far end of the room, Pilecki was bent over his own basket. He'd transferred into the kommando a few days ago, which made it far more enjoyable for me. Toward the end of the day, I stationed myself next to him. We kept our eyes on our individual tasks while I updated him on the morning's selection and the female guard willing to barter with me. He was particularly thrilled to hear I'd secured a whole loaf of bread, which I'd share among as many women as possible. I'd reserve a larger portion for Hania, but I wouldn't tell her I'd tweaked the proportions.

"Any news from the main camp?" I asked, once my narrative was over.

"No updates on the war, but a friend of mine recently escaped through the sewers, so I sent a report with him. I plan on transferring to the parcel office soon. The SS men take the packages sent to dead prisoners, so we have to organize those goods before they do."

Pilecki had an uncanny ability to secure the most advantageous labor assignments. Even without his numerous connections, his cleverness and confidence were enough to bend anyone to his will. He was in the basket-weaving kommando only because I worked here, and he wanted to spend time discussing the women's resistance with me before relocating. Sometimes I thought Pilecki could have convinced Kommandant Höss himself to step down.

"Do you miss Warsaw, Tomasz?" I asked as I finished my basket. I was proud of myself for remembering his alias, even though I knew his real name. For some reason, calling him Tomasz was much easier than referring to Irena as Marta had been.

"I miss the city and my family, but I won't go back until my work here is done." Pilecki paused to inspect his basket. "And you, Maria? Will you return to Warsaw when we're free?"

"Warsaw is home. I'd like to go back, but with my family gone, I don't know what I'll do when I get there."

"You'll establish a life for yourself beyond Auschwitz," he replied as he set his finished basket aside, then we separated to avoid drawing suspicion.

A life beyond Auschwitz was what I'd imagined these past two years. It was an encouraging thought, but, as I pictured myself back in Warsaw, I couldn't erase my family from the image. We were together, as we'd been before. It was a wonderful dream, but that was all it was. Survival was easier to fight for when all it required was living from one day to the next; when it required a new life in a place once familiar and reassuring, now devoid of loved ones, of security, of vivacity, of *home*, it felt impossible.

The space Pilecki vacated was quickly occupied by Mateusz. When he sat beside me, we didn't acknowledge each other, but, as he wove, he found my palm. I closed my hand around the pills he slipped me and tucked them into my pocket. In return, I passed him a sapphire, as dark blue as his eyes. Gems were worth a fortune to him, and medication was worth a fortune to me.

"I have news," he said under his breath, pushing a strand of dark hair away from his face. "I heard from my connections about that man in Flossenbürg, Karl Fritzsch. This news isn't public yet, but the SS is investigating internal corruption within their organizations, and he's a prime suspect."

Corruption. How fitting. "You mean to tell me the SS is concerned with such a thing?" It made sense, given that those like Höss were obsessed with order; then again, others, like Fritzsch, had no regard for rules of any kind. Still, as I focused on my next basket, the thought of the SS disciplining their own sent a little rush of warmth through my veins. "Is he going to be arrested?"

"Not yet. The investigation has hardly begun, so it'll be some time before they take action. My connections will let me know once something develops."

"Thank you, Maciek. You don't know how much this helps."

"Does it help enough for you to tell me why you're so interested in him?"

I should have known that Mateusz's lack of curiosity wouldn't last. I envisioned Fritzsch's vicious sneer as he fired the pistol at my family, recoiled as the whip cracked across my back, strained against his firm hand clutching my collar while the guard shoved the injection into Father Kolbe's arm. "He was our camp deputy at one time," I said at last.

"If he's facing a potential corruption charge, I can't imagine he was the best fit for that job. What was he like?"

How was I supposed to answer that? He was a man who used me for entertainment. He was a man who murdered my family. He was a man I had to find.

"He scared me." It wasn't a lie.

Mateusz stopped working, and I corrected my last weave, pretending not to notice, but he waited. I lifted my eyes to his, always surprised by the look I found there. Few people regarded me as if I was more than a number anymore.

"What's he done to you, Maria?"

If you only knew, Maciek.

"Nothing." The lie didn't make me feel guilty, even though it should have. "But he did hurt people. I'm afraid he'll be transferred back, that's all."

Mateusz placed his hand briefly over mine before returning to his work. For a moment I was too taken aback to listen to what he was saying. "If Fritzsch is sent back, I'll make sure you have a warning. Try not to worry."

How little he knew of the world I lived in. Worry was a constant companion. In the workshop, he saw a glimpse of how prisoners were treated, but it was nothing compared to what we experienced each day. And I didn't share details.

If he knew my history with Fritzsch or my plans for when I found him again, Mateusz wouldn't have helped me. He would have said confronting Fritzsch would be dangerous, which is what

Hania would have said, too. That was why I couldn't tell them. Anyone privy to the truth could interfere, and I couldn't have that. Besides, the less Mateusz knew, the safer he'd be.

Pilecki wouldn't return to Warsaw until his work was done, and neither would I. With Mateusz's help, I was keeping a close eye on Fritzsch, and, once I was free, I'd get justice. Sometimes my vow was the only thing that got mc through the day. I'd return to Warsaw and live the life I'd promised my loved ones I'd live.

But first, I would confront Fritzsch.

 Chapter 24

Birkenau, 26 April 1943

WHEN LAGERFÜHRERIN MANDEL announced that there would be no labor, I should have been relieved. But the Beast was never the bearer of good news.

I took my place with my labor assignment, but I would have almost preferred another arduous workday to whatever Mandel had planned. As she ordered this häftling to shut up and that häftling to straighten the line, she dealt ten times as many blows.

At last she stationed herself by the gate and ordered her beloved women's orchestra to play. The inmates, women forced to use their skills for survival as I had been with chess, struck up the *Horst-Wessel-Lied*, so we marched in time to the Nazi national anthem while the guards sang along. Thank goodness we weren't ordered to join in. When the music ended, the guards descended on us with curses and blows while their Alsatians growled and strained against their harnesses, herding us like cattle, ready to sink their bared fangs into our flesh at a word from their handlers.

A woman ahead of me turned around to look at Mandel. At once, a guard pulled her out of the ranks. She wouldn't be coming back. Those who turned to look at the Beast never returned.

As I marched, I drank in a crisp morning breeze. After a long, frigid winter, the earth was reawakening. Instead of trekking through snow and ice on the way to the workshop, now I passed wildflowers along the road and orchards and fields in full bloom. Springtime reminded me of Warsaw, where friendly street vendors sold roses, geraniums, crocuses, and poppies, and Mama would fill every vase and pot until our apartment was as colorful and fragrant as a garden.

Like buds bursting from the earth in springtime, the residents of Oświęcim were reemerging from their homes. Sometimes I'd catch glimpses of them seeking little moments of normalcy, as if the SS soldiers had never occupied this area and life was as it had been before the war. Gray-haired couples took leisurely strolls, young people turned their faces toward the warm sunshine, and children laughed as they raced across open fields.

What struck me most were the girls my age, girls with long hair, flowing dresses—thin from strict rations, perhaps creases of worry across their brows, but finding whatever joys there were to be found in wartime. Girls who picked wildflowers with friends or darted behind trees to steal kisses with handsome young men. An existence so different from my own. Sometimes I felt as if those girls didn't exist at all. They were just products of my imagination, the result of a fairy tale too idyllic to be true. They weren't reality. Reality was hunger, labor, suffering, death.

Then they would avert their eyes when we walked by, and I remembered that their lives were real. And so was mine.

It was my second spring in Auschwitz. While the world around me teemed with new life, my own deteriorated. Springtime was when the ache for freedom became most acute.

At last we reached the main camp, and they ushered us into Block 26, the same block where I'd been registered. Inside, the massive room was already packed with inmates. I didn't see

Hania, so I supposed I'd lost her somewhere in the crowd. I fell into line, but I was too far away to determine what was happening.

After I'd been in line for a few minutes, a familiar whisper came from behind me. "Have you noticed recent transports have been given prisoner number tattoos?" Its owner extended her forearm to display the ink etched into her skin.

"That's what they're doing to us?" I whispered, staring at the bubbles of blood mingling with the ink. "How badly did it hurt?"

"Not as badly as this."

At her words, I turned to look at Hania, wincing at the fresh gash on her forehead.

"Courtesy of the Beast," she said as she rubbed excess dried blood from the wound. "Well, I should get back to my kommando, but before I go, what are we going to do with our day free from labor, shikse?"

"Will you listen to my Yiddish? I've been practicing."

"Oy vey, if I must, but my head hurts enough as it is."

I narrowed my eyes in mock reproach, but a new voice wiped Hania's smirk away.

"Prisoner 15177."

Over her shoulder, I glimpsed Protz standing between the lines of prisoners. Hania muttered a Yiddish curse, so quiet that I was probably the only one who heard. I opened my mouth, though nothing I said would have convinced Protz to leave her alone, but a tiny shake of her head made me close it.

"We'll practice Yiddish some other time," she whispered. She closed her eyes and took a small breath, then she squared her shoulders and followed Protz out of the block. Once Hania was gone, I swallowed the lump in my throat and faced the line.

The hours ticked by until it was finally my turn. The tattooist placed my left forearm on the table. When his needle pricked my skin, I automatically pulled away, but he held me steady, despite a brief, apologetic glance. Guards stood near, and I had no choice but to yield, so I clamped my teeth together and tried to remain still while my fellow prisoner worked. The needle's sharp point injected blue-black ink into my skin, and I watched in numb silence. Worse than the pain was the knowledge of what it would leave behind.

When the process was complete, *16671* was forever branded into my skin. It lined up perfectly beneath my five cigarette-burn scars.

Following orders, I exited Block 26 to wait for the other women before returning to Birkenau. As I fretted over whether or not Protz had let Hania go yet, movement near Block 20, one of the hospital blocks, drew my focus. Pilecki motioned from the shadows of the building. After making sure no guards were watching, I hurried to meet him.

"It's time for me to finish my report and speak to the Home Army about the attack," he said as I reached him. "I'm getting out tonight."

"You're escaping?"

"Through the bakery in town during my night shift. I got myself admitted to the hospital a couple days ago and was informally discharged today. Those in my block think I'm still sick, but I switched to the bakery kommando and reported to Block 15 instead of my own." He flashed a sly smile.

"If you have trouble at the bakery, the owner's son is my friend Mateusz. They're on our side." A guard's distant shout reached my ears, so I moved deeper into the shadows to avoid detection before continuing. "And tell the Home Army when the time to fight comes, we'll be ready."

If Pilecki managed to speak to the Home Army, the battle we'd been anticipating for so long would be a real possibility. The idea stirred something inside me, something powerful and irrepressible, and I let it expand until it filled every part of me.

Soon, I'd be free. And once free, I'd make my way to Flossenbürg.

* * *

In the workshop the next morning, thoughts of Pilecki's freedom prompted hopes for my own, but I didn't dwell on them. My current reality was vastly different, and warping my perception of it could prove dangerous. A glimmer of hope, on the other hand, sometimes meant the difference between life and death. Striking the right balance was delicate.

When Mateusz sat next to me, I leaned as close to him as I dared. "Did he get out?" I asked before he could speak.

"You mean the three men who escaped from the bakery last night?"

"They were successful?"

He nodded as his fingers flew over his basket, weaving far more expertly than I ever could. Unlike me, he completed the meticulous work with exceptional skill. "By the way, the investigation against Fritzsch is moving forward, and my connections think he'll be arrested within the next few months. Assuming he's convicted, you won't have to worry about him returning to Auschwitz, Maria."

Good news, but also bad. Fritzsch deserved far worse, but if he were imprisoned it would be difficult for me to confront him. There was no sense in worrying about that yet. For Mateusz's sake, I flashed a relieved smile. One he didn't return as he paused from his work.

"My parents have friends in Pszczyna, and the hospital has a position available." He stopped to clear his throat and ran a hand across his chin. "Since I've been considering a medical field if I attend a university, I feel as if I should—"

"That's a wonderful opportunity." Forcing the words out was difficult, and forcing a smile was worse. He'd become a constant for me, a tie to the life I might have had, the girl I might have been. I couldn't bear to hear more, so interrupting him with feigned delight was my only choice. "Of course you should do it. I'm happy for you, Maciek."

"It's not far, so I promise I'll stay in touch. Especially if I hear anything else."

He looked as if he wanted to say more, but then refocused on his work, and so did I, distracting myself from waves of disappointment and panic. I didn't want him to go. I'd grown fond of the stupid boy who'd earned me a black eye, but I'd miss far more than his company. I was losing a friend, a source of goods, and the only aid in my mission against Fritzsch.

Chapter 25

Auschwitz, 20 April 1945

W HEN THE SURGE of rage pushes me to my feet, my chair clatters to the ground. But Fritzsch doesn't flinch as I produce my pistol. He calms at once, raising an eyebrow while his hand strays toward his own weapon.

"Don't."

He places a hand on his gun, but he doesn't draw it. He waits—as if daring me to pull my trigger—before taking his seat, lacing his fingers together, and propping his elbows on the table. "Does this mean you resign?"

His flippancy ignites the rage again, though it had never completely died. All this time, the pain and anger have ebbed and flowed; now they course through my body, manifesting in every word and deed, every twinge of pain in my head and quake in my voice.

"Stop talking."

"You're the one who has been carrying on about your family, and now this." He waves a hand at the gun before flicking rainwater from his sleeve. "Sit down and shut your mouth. If you get distracted, you'll get careless, and it would be a shame if you didn't play your best."

"I said stop talking." I grip the pistol with both hands, hoping it will steady my aim. "Put your gun on the ground."

Fritzsch sighs and rubs his temple. "Can't we finish the game? It's your turn."

Keeping my eyes on him, I take one hand off the pistol and reach for a rook. I recall every play we've made and every position on the board, and I don't need to look at it to know my next move.

Check.

Chapter 26

Birkenau, 20 September 1944

MOST DAYS, I felt as if I'd lived a thousand lifetimes in the camp. Others, it was as if my life were somehow frozen in time and, if I could emerge beyond the barbed-wire fences, perhaps I'd return as that fourteen-year-old girl with a loving family in Warsaw and girlish whims of chess championships.

By the fall of 1944, a new year was approaching and would bring my eighteenth birthday, an unusual and foreign realization because each passing year felt no different from the last. If not for the war, I would have been preparing to attend a university, maybe to study accounting like my father or social work like my mother. My siblings would have been clumsy adolescents, and we would have teased my parents about the streaks of gray creeping into their hair. I would have met friends in cafés and spent romantic evenings at the ballet with a handsome young man by my side. I'd have been a young woman by all measures. Instead my story was a different one.

As I left my block one September morning and readjusted my headscarf, I spotted a Jewish woman lingering outside the building. After making sure the guards weren't looking, I hurried to meet her.

"You know, Maria, if you'd ever like to transfer back to the Union Munitions Factory, we can arrange it," she said by way of greeting.

"You're the ones smuggling the gunpowder, not me," I replied with a smile. "All I did was work there for a time to lend my support."

"Which we appreciate, because we need those hiding it in the camp just as much as we need smugglers. But this time, instead of bringing you a capsule, I brought this." She pressed a slip of paper into my palm, then we parted ways.

As I followed the kitchen kommando to my work detail, I clung to the tiny scrap, certain that I knew who had sent it. When the guards were distracted, I stole a peek at the paper, which contained two hastily scrawled words.

Front lines.

According to the date, Mateusz had written the note a few months prior, which meant he'd had some difficulty getting it to me. As he'd said, Pszczyna wasn't far, but he sent or received letters only when he visited his parents' bakery, so our exchanges had been infrequent. Although he hadn't brought me many updates when we'd worked together, his presence had been a comfort, and I always knew he'd pass word along as soon as he received it.

I closed my hand around the paper and tucked it into my pocket. Anyone else would have been thrilled to hear that Fritzsch had been sent to the front lines. Not me. Had he been imprisoned, getting in touch with him would have been difficult but not impossible. He would have stayed in one place. Now his location was subject to constant change, and my plan to go to Flossenbürg after liberation was ruined.

Fritzsch couldn't fall in battle. Not before I'd had my say.

When we reached the kitchen, I assumed my place at the sink

to prepare for dishwashing, my typical morning assignment. I plunged my arms into hot soapy water, cleaning the ladles and large cauldrons that served our meager soup. If I blocked out the supervisors cursing and demanding we work faster, I could almost imagine I was washing dishes at home.

I was vigorously scrubbing a cauldron when a firm hand grabbed my collar and pulled me backward. Sometimes even my best efforts weren't enough to escape a guard's wrath. As I tensed and took a gasping breath, a contemptuous voice met my ears.

"You're not working very hard."

When the guard released me, I didn't turn around, but something in her voice sparked my curiosity. It sounded familiar. She must have yelled at me before. The insults, curses, and slurs came from so many people that they started to run together.

A shove against my shoulder indicated the guard wasn't finished with me. "Stupid bitch, look at me when I'm talking to you."

Drying my hands on a dirty dish towel, I obeyed, and the sight before my eyes made me clutch the countertop for support.

She was an SS guard I hadn't met, and her resemblance to Irena Sienkiewicz was uncanny. If Irena had lived to see her twentieth birthday, she would have looked like this woman—near twenty herself, with Irena's tall, thin frame, angular features, and bright eyes, but blond hair beneath her cap. If I hadn't known better . . .

Stop, it's impossible, I told myself. *Irena is dead. Shot and killed two years ago along with her unborn child.*

This woman's voice sounded familiar because it sounded like Irena's. A new guard who resembled my friend in appearance and speech. What a cruel irony. A daily reminder of my grief.

"Do you have anything to fucking say for yourself?"

The guard had Irena's mouth, too.

I looked into her eyes and found something behind the cruelty, something I couldn't place, but I dismissed it. It was all in my head. This woman was my enemy, not my dead friend.

"Forgive me, Frau Aufseherin," I murmured; then I faced the cauldron and resumed cleaning.

She grabbed my shoulder and spun me around again. It seemed I was doing everything wrong around this guard. "Did I say I was finished with you?" she asked.

"No, Frau—"

"Shut the hell up! Dammit, 16671."

And that was when I knew.

It was Irena.

It wasn't, it couldn't be, but the more I told myself I was wrong the more every wit and sense and fiber of my being told me I was right. Irena had survived. I didn't know how, but I didn't care because she was alive and she was masquerading as a camp guard. I looked into her eyes again and identified what I couldn't place before. Annoyance that I hadn't recognized her, then annoyance replaced by satisfaction.

We both knew exactly what needed to be done.

"You're not dismissed until I say so, is that clear?" Irena asked.

"Clear, Frau Aufseherin, and if you'll be so kind as to dismiss me, I have work to do," I replied, making sure I was loud enough for my kapo to hear.

At once, Irena grabbed my arm, sneering something about teaching my defiant ass a lesson, and ushered me past my kapo, who darted out of the way. I stumbled along beside her, too dazed to focus on where she was taking me, but, when we passed through a familiar gate and courtyard, I realized our destination. Block 25. Earlier, I'd overheard a guard saying Block 25 had been emptied, so Irena must have been privy to the same knowledge.

Inside, the bunks were vacant, but Irena kept her firm grip on me while she looked around. Once satisfied, she released me, and I fell away in disbelief.

"It took you long enough to recognize me," she said, seeming unfazed by my incredulity.

"How?" I whispered. "I heard the gunshots."

"They must have been someone else's. After I said goodbye to you, I went to the courtyard, where a guard said he'd been ordered to take me elsewhere for execution. He took me to a storeroom instead, gave me civilian clothing, put me in a car, and drove me out of the camp. The Polish resistance had gotten word to its camp contacts that I was coming, so they bribed him into saving me."

As Irena mentioned the camp's resistance, my heart swelled with sudden gratitude. Pilecki. His organization had saved her life.

Irena adjusted her black leather gloves and lifted her gaze to mine. "After we discovered your family had been caught, Mama and I spent weeks trying to determine how to bribe a Pawiak guard to break you out. By the time we found one willing to help, he said you'd been sent away. We thought they'd taken you somewhere and killed you, otherwise we would have kept looking." She paused and took a breath. "When the guard fetched me from the execution wall and said he was letting me go, I begged him to go back for you, but he said that wasn't part of the plan and if I didn't leave right away then he'd shoot me, and I . . ." She let her voice die, but she wrapped one arm across her midsection. I could picture it as round as it had been upon our last meeting.

"Your baby?" I murmured.

Those words brought a fond smile to Irena's lips. "Helena is a happy, healthy two-year-old. After she was born, I contacted our German resistance connections, and they taught me how to masquerade as a guard. I learned all the Nazi shit I needed to know, got the right papers, perfected my German accent, dyed my hair, and put on this damn uniform. Since you'd reported my death to Mama and stayed in touch with her, I knew you were still alive, but we decided it would be safer if you didn't know I survived. When I went to a Nazi women's organization to volunteer for camp employment, our contacts and a few well-placed bribes ensured I was sent to this one. Now here I am: Frieda Lichtenberg, daughter of dairy workers in Wrechen, a few years of primary education, staunch member of the *Bund Deutscher Mädel*, Aufseherin of Auschwitz-Birkenau."

Months of studying and preparation to infiltrate the SS-Helferin as a woman created by the Third Reich, and she had somehow succeeded. My brain felt as if it were trudging through mud. "If you survived and escaped, why are you back?"

"Why the hell do you think? Because I'm getting you out of here, you idiot."

Of course that was why she had come back, but I could hardly believe what I'd heard. She came back to save my life. To give me a chance at freedom. *Freedom.* A sudden, fierce yearning filled me to the depths of my being, but I shook my head in refusal.

"No, you have to go before you're caught. Go back to your mother and daughter. I won't let you risk your life—"

"You don't have a choice, because I'm already here, and there's not a damn thing you can do to make me leave. Especially not after all the shit I went through to get here. But speaking of my family, I need you to promise me something."

I opened my mouth to ask what it was, but the look on Irena's face made the query catch in my throat. A cold terror settled in the pit of my stomach, and I wanted to beg her to remain silent. Voicing it made it real.

"Mama and Helena are staying in Mother Matylda's orphanage in Ostrówek," Irena said. "Our Home Army contacts wanted Mama to stay in Warsaw to help with their planned uprising, but we agreed leaving was necessary to protect Helena. They got out a week before the uprising began, and thank God they did. After what those Nazi bastards have done in the Mokotów district alone, I know exactly what happened to a middle-aged woman and child. Now you know where to find them if necessary, which brings me to the promise I mentioned." At this, her voice wavered, so she paused for a moment. "If I'm discovered, you'll tell Mama. You'll look after her. And you'll adopt my daughter."

I'd expected the implications behind those words, but to say yes was to acknowledge a possibility too devastating to fathom, and I shook my head. "I can't—"

"Dammit, Maria, don't fight me on this."

Irena fell into expectant silence. Of course I'd do it, but I didn't trust myself to speak, so I dipped my head in assent. Suddenly my chest ached as it had in the railcar with my father, nodding as he reassured me after I apologized for what I had caused, though none of us yet knew the extent of the damage I'd done. Despite drawing constant comfort from Father Kolbe, and then his rosary, and resolving to fight for my life, neither had eradicated the truth. My failure had led to my family's deaths; now one of my dearest friends was here on my behalf. Another life to potentially be lost for my sake.

I was faintly aware of Irena saying something about bringing me food later and smuggling me back to my block; then she started toward the door. As she turned, I grabbed her arm.

"Listen to me. You can't do this, Irena. I've already lost everyone I love, and I won't lose you, too. Not a second time."

There was an unusual amount of emotion in her resilient gaze, but, when she spoke, her voice remained level and unyielding. "Then we'd better make damn sure we both get out of here alive."

I'd dreamt of freedom for so long. I'd promised myself I would attain it; I'd lived and fought for it, for myself and my family and Father Kolbe, but now I dared to believe it could happen. Something rolled down my cheek, and I touched it. A single tear. I stared at the moisture against my dirty fingertip. My fingernail was cracked and broken, skin torn and calloused, each groove and crevice coated in grime, yet there it was, the first droplet in years, sitting atop the filth, clear and pristine.

"Good Lord."

I hadn't realized how badly I'd missed hearing Irena's favorite complaint, and I laughed and blinked back the tears. "I'm sorry, but I don't know what to say."

"You should be cursing your bad luck, because Frieda Lichtenberg has officially made Prisoner 16671 her target. And Frieda is a real bitch."

Unable to speak, I pulled her into a tight embrace, and she wrapped long arms around my emaciated frame. It took me only a moment to remember that I was filthy beyond comprehension and covered in lice, fleas, and God knew what else. I hastily released her and stepped away.

Surely Irena knew why I was hesitating. But she guided me back into her arms.

It was the first time I'd embraced anyone other than Hania in more than two years. The last time had also been Irena. Right before her intended execution.

My body was starving, yet my soul was starving even more. Starving for kindness, compassion, love, everything I once took for granted. Raw hunger never ceased to gnaw at me, but the hunger for human affection was a sharp ache that pierced me to the depths of my being. One simple gesture was all it took to alleviate the agony. And in this moment, this one moment, the hunger within my soul was satiated.

* * *

No prisoners were transferred to Block 25 all day, so I spent my time alone and attempted to comprehend what had happened. Irena was alive. She had a daughter. And she was risking everything to help me escape.

She slipped me some bread and sausage at lunchtime—food from the SS supply, a rare delicacy—but she didn't linger. Seeing her a second time was enough to remind me that the day's events had been real.

When the workday ended, I sat on a bunk and peered through the bars on the window, watching as the women returned to camp. I stayed there until the door burst open, then I flipped onto my stomach, praying I'd remain undetected.

"Maria? Maria, where are you? First Izaak was transferred to the *Sonderkommando*, and now this—"

At the sound of the familiar, frantic whisper, I stuck my head out so Hania noticed me, and relief washed over her face. "Oy gevalt, shikse, I was so worried. I came as soon as I heard."

I quickly climbed down from the bunk. "Izaak was transferred to the Sonderkommando?" I asked as she reached me. The name tasted of ash on my tongue. Those prisoners were condemned to work in the gas chambers and crematoria and forbidden to interact with others—and frequently liquidated to prevent them from revealing the horrors they saw. If the work was so awful that the rest of us were not permitted to know details, I couldn't fathom what the Sonderkommando was required do.

"I was in the central office and saw the work record of inmates reassigned to Crematorium II, and his number was among them," Hania said. "Oh, and these are for you."

I opened my hand, suspecting what she'd brought. She pulled two small gunpowder capsules out of her mouth, smuggled to her from other resistance members who had gotten them from the women in the munitions factory. I'd pass them on to a woman in the clothing detail, another person in our long, complex chain. When the time to fight came, we'd be ready.

I grimaced as she dropped the wet capsules into my palm. "I always appreciate when you carry these in your mouth."

"There are worse places." A teasing grin accompanied the words while I tucked the capsules into my pocket, then it disappeared. "Here we are going on and on when we don't have time to waste. I'll get you out of here, I promise—"

The door swung open, cutting her words short. Gasping, she whirled toward the sound, and Irena stepped across the threshold.

At once, Hania moved in front of me. She would attempt a deal, as any prisoner might in such a desperate situation. To survive in this place was to depend on what others were willing to give in return. One prisoner might offer cigarettes for another's medication. A kapo might grant a woman a morsel of bread in exchange for a quick favor—the kind that took place behind the block or in the darkened barracks after curfew. As for bartering with the guards, even a request for a life might be granted for a suitable price.

I had no time to tell Hania that negotiations would not be necessary; she was already speaking, her tone filled with the confidence and determination she always adopted in these instances.

"Frau Aufseherin, in exchange for her release, I—" And then her voice broke, shattering her usual resolve as if her intended proposal had fled. Silence fell, broken only by a distant guard's faint shout, before she went on in an unsteady whisper. "Please."

Irena appeared too stricken to respond while I swallowed the sudden lump in my throat. I placed a hand on Hania's forearm. She glanced at me, her eyes dark with fear, desperation, as though unable to fathom two devastating blows—her brother's reassignment, then my supposed imprisonment. With a small, reassuring smile, I gave her an appreciative squeeze before stepping forward to address Irena.

"We can trust Hania."

Hania spun me around to face her. "You know a guard working both sides?"

"Not exactly," I said with a laugh. "Meet Irena."

At this, she looked at me as if I'd truly gone mad. "Your dead friend?"

"Right, I'm a fucking ghost. Can we go?" Irena moved toward the door; when I tried to follow, Hania caught my forearm.

"It's been over three years since you've worked together," she said, voice low, wary gaze on Irena's turned back. "She comes here as if to die for the resistance, then returns as part of the SS-Helferin?"

Before I could explain or dispute her concerns, Irena came to an abrupt stop by the window. "Shit."

A few guards crossed the courtyard with a group of prisoners, women who would remain in Block 25 until they were sent to the gas chambers. And if Hania and I didn't have a convincing reason to leave, we'd be joining them. Despite the imminent danger, an old, familiar thrill pulsed through me, and I imagined walking down the streets of Warsaw with Irena. Two resistance girls outwitting the Nazis. It was time for us to be those girls again.

When Irena turned to me, I gave her a small smile. "Are you ready, Frieda?"

Hania looked more confused than ever. "Frieda?"

"I'll explain later. For now, you're my interpreter."

"You don't need a—"

"Do you have a better excuse as to why you're here? Just follow my lead, Bubbe."

But Hania looked as if the betrayal she feared had been set into motion: that Irena would leave us with the condemned and walk out with her SS counterparts. She was wrong, I knew she was; I needed her to trust me enough to let Irena prove it.

The door creaked open, and the guards ushered the half-dead women inside. Some were so weak and sick that they leaned heavily on one another as they shuffled toward the bunks; others pleaded for their lives, insisting that they remained fit for work. One guard looked at Irena and opened her mouth, but we were already deep in conversation.

"I wanted to rest for a few minutes, Frau Aufseherin!" I exclaimed in Polish. "I lost track of the time, but I intended on going back to work, I swear." I turned to Hania, who stiffened. "Please tell her."

Silence. The guards waited, and, when all eyes fell on us, Hania's widened in renewed terror. I repeated myself in Polish, begging her to translate, silently begging her to play along. Without her, this plan was useless.

"Well?" Irena asked in German. "What is this Polack blabbering about? Hurry up, you stupid Jew."

Hania swallowed hard, this time looking at me with slightly more assurance before responding in German. "She swears she came here to rest and intended on returning to work. She didn't realize how late it was."

"I knew she wasn't sick," Irena said with a scoff. She grabbed my collar, so I let out an appropriate whimper. "You think you're so damn clever, hiding in an empty block to avoid your labor assignment, don't you? If you try that again, I'll have you moved to Block 25 for good."

She didn't wait for Hania to translate before shoving us toward the door. She shouldered her way past the guards and prisoners, not giving anyone the opportunity to question her, and dragged us into the courtyard. We crossed it in a few steps, passed through the gate, and continued without disturbance.

After dinner, Hania and I sneaked to the latrines so we could talk privately. Once I'd explained everything, I concluded with my decision. I couldn't let Irena attempt to smuggle me out.

"They don't enforce collective punishment for escaped inmates anymore," Hania said. "You have nothing to lose."

"Except our lives if we're caught."

"Irena is here undercover and could be caught just as easily if you stay."

"Which is why she needs to leave."

"She came back for you, Maria. She left her daughter and risked her life to save yours, and she won't leave until you do. Don't keep her from her child any longer than necessary." I didn't miss the knowing shine in her eyes.

After Irena had led us from Block 25, I was confident our joint scheme had proved that her intentions were honorable, but, once we reached our block, Hania had paused at the door and turned to Irena. My confidence fled, and I prepared to mollify them if an argument ensued. More guards were walking by, certain to overhear once they drew closer. I gripped Hania's arm, issuing an alert, but she was already speaking too intently to notice, voice low yet urgent.

"My sons. In Warsaw. Maria said a few years ago you and your—"

I tightened my grasp as my gaze flicked to the guards again;

though Hania missed my warning, Irena didn't. She caught Hania's collar, cutting her off and pulling her close.

"My mother has the information regarding where each child was placed," she said, barely above a whisper. "I will contact her the moment it's safe. I promise. Am I clear?" she added more loudly, as though finishing a threat.

While the group of guards passed, Hania dipped her head in an obedient nod, though her eyes glistened. Irena gave a tiny nod in return, then shoved us both into the block, but not before catching my faint smile.

I wanted Irena and Hania both safe, reunited with their children. Surely it wouldn't take us long to develop a plan, minimizing the amount of time Irena had to stay in such a dangerous position. As for myself, I would do whatever it took. The only way to get justice for my family was to leave this place. Freedom was worth the risk.

Now, in the quiet latrine, I released a slow breath. "If you're willing, so am I."

"Me?" Hania asked with a laugh. "What does my willingness have to do with anything?" The genuine confusion on her face was baffling.

"Because you're coming with us," I replied. "You and Izaak."

She didn't react for a moment, as if unsure that she'd understood me, then she took a few steps away and passed a hand over her headscarf. At last she sighed and turned to face me. "Sonderkommando workers aren't allowed to see anyone else. You know that. Protz managed to get me around the rule today, and since I can't get a Sonderkommando worker reassigned, he remains my only means of contacting Izaak, and we have to speak through the fence. It would be impossible to break him out."

"No, it wouldn't, because Irena can get access to him."

"The odds of four people making a successful getaway aren't good."

I didn't understand why she was making the plan so complicated, but I relented with an annoyed sigh. "Fine, we'll wait until the Home Army attacks and we revolt. There are reports of the Red Army advancing, too, so it can't be long until—"

"There's no time to wait. When Izaak and I are free, we'll meet you in Warsaw to find my sons, but you and Irena have to get out as soon as the plan is in place."

This time, I was the one who was unsure that I'd heard her correctly. After a moment, I shook my head in adamant refusal. "I'm not going unless you come with me. I won't leave you, Hania—"

"Enough, Maria."

The fading evening light slipped through the wooden slats and spilled across the floor and over the concrete benches while we regarded each other in silence. We tended to keep these private meetings brief due to the suffocating stench within the latrines; this time, neither Hania nor I wavered.

Sudden sobs broke me in a way I hadn't broken in so long. I closed the distance between us and wrapped my arms around her. If only an embrace were all it took to prevent us from ever being separated. Liberation called to me, and the temptation was so strong. Once free, I could find a way to contact Fritzsch on the front lines. Once free, I could confront him.

The opportunity to move forward with my plans was most tempting of all.

Hania held me close and kissed the top of my head, then she shushed me and took my face in her hands. As she searched my gaze, a small, affectionate smile played around her lips.

"Go with Irena," she murmured, brushing a tear from my cheek and blinking back her own. "Go home, shikse."

Chapter 27

Birkenau, 7 October 1944

IN THE TWO weeks following her arrival, Irena learned all she could about her SS coworkers and their routines. I promised I'd go with her when the opportunity arose, but I still hoped for the Home Army's attack or the Red Army's advance. Pilecki had been free for more than a year, giving him plenty of time to plan our liberation, and the Soviets drew closer every day. The revolt we'd been awaiting would come, and we'd fight from the inside while our allies fought from the outside.

I was so close, almost in a position to take control of my life again, to find the man whose name I heard in the echoes of every gunshot. The thought of getting to him was almost more enticing than freedom.

One October morning, while breakfast preparations were underway, I grabbed a cauldron and filled it with the grain mixture that served as our coffee. I didn't add water to the pot, then left it on the fire to burn. If my plan worked, I'd get sent out of the kitchen, and I could attend the brief meeting Irena and I had arranged to share our latest tidbits of information relevant to our escape.

I sliced old turnips and potatoes until a burning stench filled my nostrils, then the kapo threw a piece of rotting potato at me and ordered me to dispose of the burned coffee. With profuse apologies, I poured water into the cauldron to cool it off, attempted to scrape the burned bits clinging to the inside, then hefted my burden and let myself out into the crisp autumn morning. An orange-and-crimson carpet of leaves painted the ground, and I drank in a cool breeze, a pleasant alternative to the stuffy kitchen air, which smelled of filthy, sweaty bodies and rotting food—and now smoke, thanks to me.

Behind the kitchen block, the sight that greeted me almost made me drop the cauldron. Irena was there, as I knew she would be, but not alone. At the far end of the building, standing by her side—close, far too close—was Protz. They were smoking and smiling, but even from my distance I could sense Irena's discomfort.

"Aren't you supposed to be in the main camp?" Irena asked him as I moved closer.

"The prisoners aren't going anywhere, and if my absence is detected, no one will say anything." Protz gave her his stupid, smug smile, and Irena probably wished she could slap it off as much as I did.

"The rest of us don't have that luxury."

Though she failed to keep the sarcasm from her voice, Protz didn't seem to detect it. When she flicked her cigarette butt away and turned to go, he caught her by the waist. "Relax, I won't let them penalize you. What are you doing this evening, Frieda?"

Though she gave him a small smile, her words were venomous. "None of your damn business."

The response only encouraged him. He tossed his cigarette aside, tucked a loose strand of hair behind her ear, and pulled her close. "I'm making it my damn business."

He didn't notice when Irena stiffened—or if he did, he didn't care. As Protz pressed his lips to hers, he guided her hips into his, minimizing the space between them while Irena's hand drew back.

Before she struck, I pretended to stumble, bumped Protz aside, and tossed the ruined coffee all over Irena. They broke apart, gasping and cursing, while I scrambled across the ground to retrieve the empty cauldron, spluttering apologies.

"I'm so sorry, Herr Scharführer. I tripped—"

Though I expected the booted foot that met my stomach, it was still agonizing. For a moment, I coughed and drew painful breaths while Protz cursed my stupidity. I opened my mouth to apologize again, but, when I looked into the pistol barrel leveled at my head, the apology caught in my throat.

My plan was backfiring. I'd known it was risky because my plans were always risky, but I hadn't expected Protz to be so upset. After all, he wasn't the one doused in coffee. All I could do was cower, but I didn't miss the unmistakable snap of the gun's toggle, a sound that meant a bullet had lodged in his pistol's chamber.

"Please, Herr Scharführer—!"

"If you touch her, it'll be the last fucking thing you ever do."

At Irena's words, I cautiously looked up. Her jacket and skirt were drenched, and she shook liquid from her hands and glared at Protz.

Oh, God, she's defending me. She's acting like Irena, not like a guard, and now my plan has ruined everything, and he's going to kill us both.

"What the hell, Frieda?"

Protz's query broke through my panicked thoughts, but he fell into stunned silence when Irena grabbed his collar and pulled him close. Meanwhile, I watched in horror and prepared to wrestle the gun from his grasp.

"You heard me, you stupid bastard. Get the hell out of my way."

She pushed him aside and turned to me, her voice deep with rage. "This bitch is mine."

On the outside, I tensed, but on the inside I could have cried with relief. Of course she had reacted like Irena. She'd seized the opportunity to "give him hell," as she would have said, but used it to our benefit. How could I have doubted her?

For a moment, Protz didn't react, then he relaxed and put the gun away. He stepped back to watch our exchange; time for us to put on a good show. Irena closed the distance between us while I panicked.

"Forgive me, Frau Aufseherin, please, I didn't—"

Irena kicked the empty cauldron out of my hands, and I shrank away. "You made a big mistake, didn't you, 16671?"

As I apologized, I glanced at Protz. He looked convinced so far, but he seemed to be waiting for the inevitable. With him watching, Irena couldn't avoid it. It's what any guard would have done in this situation, and if she didn't she'd be exposed as a fraud.

She had to hit me.

I'd known this time would come. Amid my pleas, I lifted my eyes to Irena's, urging her to do it. So she obliged.

The back of her hand smacked across my cheek, bringing my frantic apologies to a halt and sending me sprawling onto the ground. The familiar numbness followed by pain spread across my face, then I realized I'd bitten my lip, so I spat the metallic taste of blood out of my mouth. While my mind cleared, Irena's shadow loomed over me. I drew myself in and raised an arm to shield my head, as if preparing for the next blow.

"Listen carefully, Polack. You're going to clean my uniform until every button shines brighter than the damn sun, do you understand?"

Before standing to do her bidding, I spat out another mouthful of blood. I was tempted to aim for Protz's shiny boots, but I dismissed the amusing thought and refocused on my part. Once on my feet, I stole one more glance at Protz, who appeared satisfied. I was satisfied, too.

You don't get both of my friends, you vile schmuck.

Next to me, Irena seemed tense, but I brushed it aside and maintained my timid act as she led me outside the camp. We reached her barracks, and to my relief every woman was out on duty. I followed her to a large room with bunks similar to those I'd had in the main camp, but these were far nicer, of course. The space was tidy and smelled of fresh bed linens, and Irena closed the door before directing me to a bottom bunk.

"Sorry I doused you with ruined coffee to get Protz away from you." I chuckled and wiped my mouth with the back of my hand, leaving a red streak. "Give me your uniform. Have you learned anything helpful from the guards?"

I expected her to answer the question and reprimand me for the rashness of my plan, but she didn't respond. Instead she took off her black gloves and checked her jacket's two large square pockets. After pulling out a watch and a white handkerchief she placed the items on her bunk and removed the jacket. Irena traced her finger over the eagle atop the swastika that adorned the upper left arm, then she threw it with as much force as she could muster.

"You can take this fucking uniform and let it burn in hell where it belongs!" When the jacket landed in a crumpled heap on the floor, she sat on her bunk with her head in her hands. All I heard were her heavy breaths. "Dammit, Maria," she whispered at last, her voice muffled.

Granted, I, too, would have been upset if Protz had kissed me, but I didn't think that's what had prompted the outburst. When

Irena handed me the handkerchief, she refused to lift her head, and I laughed and sat on a small stool at the foot of her bunk.

"Do you think I haven't been hit much harder than that? We did what we had to do, Irena."

"I don't give a damn about what we had to do. Those bastards make your life hell, and now I'm one of them." She refocused on the dirty uniform and dropped her voice to a mutter. "This was a stupid idea. I should've come back as a prisoner instead."

"No, you made the right choice. This way, you have access to places I don't, you can learn things I can't, and you're safe as long as they don't find out the truth. And even if something happens to me, you still have your freedom. You can get back to Helena."

"Yes, my daughter will be so proud to have a mother who slapped her friend in the name of *saving our lives*." The words dripped with contempt.

"We had to—"

"Don't tell me we had to do it. We didn't *have* to do anything, but it was that or be killed." Her laugh was harsh, bitter. "Do you realize how absurd that is?"

Her words surprised me, and I was even more surprised when I realized she was right. Of course it was absurd. Nothing made sense here. But I'd grown so accustomed to the absurdity that I hadn't noticed it until she said so.

A distant look filled Irena's eyes. She went to a world all her own, and I listened to her furious mutters.

"The guards have a resort on a beautiful lake nearby. They call it Solahütte. When I went on Sunday, Heinrich told me about his favorite restaurants, museums, and nightclubs in Salzburg. Johanna cried over a letter that said her brother had died from surgical complications following a battle injury. I hiked and sunbathed with them and many others. The next day, they were beating and shooting prisoners, shoving them into gas chambers, listening to their screams while they died, and cremating them in ungodly numbers. So many corpses piled everywhere . . . they can't even dispose of them fast enough. It's inhuman; it's absolutely inhuman." Her words faded, and when she looked at me tears shone in her eyes. "But they're people, Maria. The guards and the prisoners. They're people. And I don't understand how people can treat other people like this."

I'd seen her reaction many times in my fellow inmates, even in myself. The sheer insanity and wickedness of this place would break you if you let it. It almost broke me. And now I was watching it break her.

"Even though I was here when I was going to be executed, I had no idea it was like this. I knew the resistance had received reports but never learned what those contained. When I volunteered to come, the only training I received was a brief lecture. A regime obsessed with order and efficiency, and they failed to do something as simple as prepare me for a job? Or they were deliberately vague so I wouldn't refuse? I was praised for serving the Reich, told to supervise, maybe give punishments. Then, when I arrived, I was informed this work is important, *necessary*—" Irena fell silent again, stared at the wall, and closed her shaking hands into fists. When she spoke, she fought to keep her voice level. "I don't want to be Frieda fucking Lichtenberg."

I placed a gentle hand on her arm. "You don't have to be. Please go home, Irena. Don't put yourself through this on my account."

Despite the temptation, she drew an unsteady breath and shook her head. "I'm not leaving, especially not after seeing what I've seen. God knows I can't understand how you're alive."

I dabbed the handkerchief against my lip, stared at the vermilion stain, and took an unsteady breath of my own. Some wars were fought with guns, others with the mind and will. The fight against Auschwitz was deeper and more complex than any on the battlefront. It whittled away at the mind and will until it had robbed its opponent of all defenses. Auschwitz was a master, but each day of survival was a day we defeated it. I intended for us to see this game through to the end.

"Every day, I choose to live and fight, and every day, people around me choose to do the same. They give me the strength to go on. And together, we will live and fight through this." I paused and took Irena's hand. "And I hope you know you have one of the biggest hearts."

Her hysteria had subsided, but a tear glistened on her cheek before she brushed it away, cleared her throat, and smirked. "You don't get out much, do you?"

"It's true, and this . . ." I gestured to the wrinkled uniform on the floor. "I can never repay you for it. And I'll never understand why you came back."

Irena followed my gaze. "You know how I feel about self-preservation. I still think it's the smartest thing to do in these times. But what the hell do I know?"

I smiled, and she gave my hand a light squeeze before crossing the room toward a dark wooden wardrobe with mirrored doors. She kicked off her boots and selected another field-gray uniform, identical to the first. She exchanged one wool skirt for the other and smoothed the large pleat down the front, then made sure her white shirtwaist wasn't soiled before donning the clean jacket. After stepping into the boots, Irena regarded her reflection with disgust while she put the watch and gloves in one pocket. When I offered her the handkerchief, she waved it away, so I tucked it into one of my hidden pockets.

"Will you do me a favor and be incredibly particular about the standards of your uniform?" I asked as I picked up the stained garments. "The more time I spend cleaning it, the less time I have to spend in the kitchen."

Irena flashed a mischievous smile. "Frieda won't be satisfied until every button shines brighter than the damn sun, remember? If that takes all morning, so be it."

True to her word, Irena let me spend a leisurely morning cleaning her uniform, then escorted me back to the kitchen. As we walked, the afternoon was pleasant—or would have been if we'd been anywhere but Auschwitz. The breeze that surrounded us was mild and temperate, and the sky was clear and blue—except for the addition of smoke.

The sky was always filled with smoke and ashes from the crematoria, but the smoke on this day came with the familiar shriek of alarms, a sound that sent the guards into a frenzy. Something had happened.

As Irena and I neared the kitchen, guards ran around like mad, shouting, cursing, and waving weapons. Most were so distracted they didn't notice the bewildered prisoners who watched them or hurried to take shelter elsewhere. The scene was absolute chaos.

"Wait in your block until I come for you," Irena said under her breath. "I'll find out what's going on."

I nodded and hurried to the block, altering my course when the Beast rushed across my path, screeching and striking anyone unfortunate enough to be within reach.

In a place where every moment was strictly regimented, seeing it upended was more satisfying than I could have ever imagined. Guards were frantic, labor was forgotten, and prisoners wandered unsupervised, some confused and afraid, others unconcerned. Part of me wanted to join the fray or see what goods I could organize while the guards were so wonderfully distracted, but Irena was right. I needed to stay in my block until we knew what was happening.

There was only one reason the guards would be in such a panic. The attack I'd been anticipating had begun. I was sure of it. As I waited, the Home Army or Red Army—whichever had arrived first—would be surrounding the entire complex, destroying the electric fences, tearing down the gates, opening fire. Soon the guards would be occupied with the outside attack, and while they were fighting they wouldn't see the inside revolt coming. The wailing sirens, the cursing guards—all sounds of freedom, a freedom that meant Irena, Hania, Izaak, and I could leave this place.

A freedom that meant I was one step closer to finding Fritzsch.

Hania returned shortly after I did, and we watched the confusion and waited for Irena. It was late in the afternoon before she appeared. Compared to the hectic scene earlier, it was now much quieter, but SS guards were still prowling around, so we remained cautious as we slipped outside and darted behind the block, where Irena joined us.

I couldn't contain my questions any longer. "It's the resistance, isn't it? The uprising—"

"No, Maria, the Home Army isn't going to attack Auschwitz."

I snapped my mouth shut, taken aback by the news and the sharpness in her tone. That was impossible. After hearing Pilecki's report, the Home Army would help us. They had to help us.

"They said an attack isn't feasible." Irena sighed as she dug her heel into the dirt. "I heard from outside connections earlier this week, but I didn't know how to tell you. As for what caused today's uproar, the Sonderkommando planted explosives in Crematorium IV."

"Oy gevalt, Izaak, you *meshuggener*, what have you done?" Hania whispered. Without waiting to hear more, she rushed away, muttering something about finding Protz.

My pathetic hopes went up in flames. My hopes, my plans, my strategies, my rebellion, my freedom. Gone.

Dear God, no one is going to help us.

"We'll continue the fight ourselves," I said aloud, keeping my voice as even as possible. "We have willing participants, weapons, and gunpowder all over Birkenau, so I'll spread the word and—"

"It's too late, Maria. It's already a fucking massacre. Security has been increased, and the guards won't rest until everyone involved is caught. We can't rebel without getting killed." Irena swallowed hard, eyes glistening with dread. "And we sure as hell can't escape."

* * *

I lost track of how long I stayed outside after Irena departed. I couldn't make myself return to my block. No one was going to help us.

An angry shout brought me out of my daze, then a club sent me stumbling back to where I belonged. The guard shoved me inside my block, and as I climbed into my bunk a slurred voice greeted me.

"You didn't keep your promise, Maria." Hania lay on her back, staring at the ceiling. She lifted her blanket to show me a small empty vodka bottle and shook her head in disapproval. "Remember the last time I organized vodka? You said you wouldn't let me do it again. But it's all right, shikse, I forgive you." She rolled onto her side and gave me a reassuring smile. One eye socket was already discoloring with a bruise, and her lip was split and smeared with dried blood.

"What happened?" I murmured.

Hania's smile faded, then she touched a finger to her injuries. "I never told Eliasz," she said softly. "About Protz. Perhaps he knew; at the start of the war, we swore to protect the boys and try to survive for them, no matter what the cost. But I still didn't tell him. Why force him to bear a burden impossible for him to alleviate? When we found time with one another here, I wanted to discuss our family, our sons, Eliasz playing his violin for them. Not this. Then, one day, my husband was gone, so I told Izaak. I couldn't bear it alone any longer."

When she fell silent, I waited. My hands tingled and ached from cold, but not as severely as the ache of every pounding heartbeat while I studied her glassy, dark eyes beneath thick lashes. Often so reticent, now laid bare. These moments were infrequent but always a sign of a significant occurrence. At last she continued.

"Izaak refuses to let me visit anymore. He wouldn't admit if he participated in the plot or not, but he said it isn't safe for me to be seen with a Sonderkommando member. The guards will assume I was involved in the uprising. He didn't give me a chance to argue before he moved away from the fence, and when I asked him to wait, he only paused long enough to tell Protz not to bring me back."

"Don't worry, he'll change his mind once the danger has passed."

Rather than responding, Hania gripped the vodka bottle with both hands, closed her eyes, and spoke in Yiddish. The words emerged through her clenched teeth and sounded angry, almost frantic, but after a moment she relaxed and opened her eyes. Her next few breaths were small and tremulous while a single tear escaped, then they steadied and she blinked slowly, calm and dazed.

"After Izaak left, I'm not sure what came over me, but I broke things off with Protz. He wasn't happy." She giggled and pointed to her face, the sight a vicious reminder tempering my marginal relief. "Now he'll kill me, but it doesn't matter. My kinderlach don't need a nafka for a mother."

"You're not a nafka, Hania."

"No, Protz won't kill me," she amended as if she hadn't heard me; then she laughed again. "He said he won't, and he won't turn me in for race defilement or force himself on me, either, because our arrangement isn't over, not until he's finished with me, and his untermensch will come crawling back the moment she needs something, begging for help and forgiveness. All he has to do is wait. And he's right. It's only a matter of time, isn't it?"

"You don't need him. We've survived without goods from him for a while, and when Izaak lets you visit again, Irena will help."

She sighed and turned the empty bottle in her hands. "I wish I had your confidence, and I wish I had more vodka. But I mean it this time, don't let me organize alcohol again." It was what she said every time. "Do you promise?"

"I promise, and I want you to promise that you won't go back to Protz."

She giggled. "I can't, but even if I could, I wouldn't remember, would I?"

"Yes, you can, and you can do it again in the morning." I eased the bottle from her grasp and gave her hand a fervent squeeze. "If not for yourself, please do it for me."

A bit of warmth joined the inebriated haze in her eyes, and she patted my cheek. "All right, my little shikse. If it means that much to you, I promise."

We settled down for the night, but I couldn't sleep. I lay in the darkness, thinking of the failed rebellion, listening as Irena's words reverberated across my mind.

We sure as hell can't escape.

Chapter 28

Birkenau, 5 January 1945

THE WINTER THAT followed the Sonderkommando uprising was the coldest I could remember since coming to Auschwitz. The snow and ice were as relentless as the sorrow, guilt, and
frustration that had plagued me since the seventh of October. The
revolt had been crushed, the Home Army wasn't coming, and the
Red Army hadn't arrived. Everything I wanted was gone, reduced
to ashes like so many other dreams in this dreadful place.

One January morning, I was awake long before dawn, staring
at the frost on the windowpane. Hania wasn't next to me. Since
the uprising, she'd been increasingly worried about Izaak, making
sleeping difficult, so she often went outside to wrestle her nerves
alone. I pulled my blanket more tightly around myself, shivering
from the merciless cold, and clung to one of the small pebbles we
used as a pawn. Hania and I hadn't played chess in a while.

How had I believed rebellion and escape were possible in a
place like this? Despite the strength of the resistance's numbers,
we were a pathetic force against countless armed guards and electrified barbed wire. We wouldn't have stood a chance even if we'd
gotten help from outside the camp. Auschwitz was built for death,
not life. I'd been a fool for thinking life would emerge the victor.

The fourteen-year-old girl with too much confidence and blind faith was still deep inside me, and sometimes I let her influence me more than I should. Now even she knew to stop wishing for rebellion. It might have been a possibility once, but not anymore.

The game was nearing its end. It had been a long, hard battle, but my opponent had placed my king in check. And I wasn't certain that this was a game I could win.

It was still too early for anyone to be awake when the door to our block swung open, letting in a burst of wind. The slumbering women stirred, gasping and groaning as the frigid air tore across their skin.

"Prisoner 16671, come with me."

Irena's voice. Slowly I climbed down from my bunk and followed her from the block. We walked in silence through the dark, freezing morning, and the snow gave way under each new footstep. Once smooth and clean and white, now crushed and marred.

A lone guard passed and reached for his gun when he saw me, but when he noticed I was with Irena, he continued on his way. Word of Frieda Lichtenberg's claim over Prisoner 16671 had spread, so if Irena was around, most guards didn't touch me for fear of incurring her wrath. She'd made it clear I belonged to her and her alone.

We approached the gate, where a familiar figure waited for us—Hania. Without a word, she fell into step with me and tossed a cigarette butt into the snow. Tension emanated from her and Irena, as icy as the wind lashing across my body. Something was amiss. Once we passed through the gate and began trekking across the fields from Birkenau to the main camp, both opened their mouths to speak. Neither succeeded.

I didn't need an explanation. I'd been anticipating this day since the Sonderkommando revolt.

"The Political Department wants to speak with me about the rebellion."

When I'd heard that the guards had found remnants of gunpowder capsules in Crematorium IV and traced them back to the Union Munitions Factory, I'd also heard that four of our resistance women had been caught, interrogated, and tortured by the Political Department, otherwise known as the camp Gestapo. Since I'd been employed alongside those same women, I'd had a feeling my time would come.

"The bastards called me into a meeting last night," Irena muttered. "They want to see all prisoners who recently worked in the Union Munitions Factory. Since you're a special favorite of mine, I have the pleasure of overseeing your interrogation."

"And Irena told them you'd need an interpreter, so we'll be with you the whole time," Hania said.

I came to an abrupt halt. "No, I don't want either of you there. Witnessing it will be too difficult."

"If we're absent, how will I explain Frieda's sudden change of heart or my lie about the interpreter? We're staying with you," Irena said with finality.

Hania looked across the empty field toward the distant, dark outline of the forest, and I could almost see the plan formulating in her mind. "Maybe none of us have to go into that room. You two can escape—"

"Escape?" Irena's laugh was scathing. "Every part of this fucking camp is crawling with guards, including the perimeters near the forest. They'd catch us in a heartbeat. If it weren't for your damn uprising, we could've left weeks ago."

"*My* uprising?"

"It was your brother and his friends, wasn't it? He won't say as much, but it was."

"Is that so, yenta? Did you hear that from your SS friends?" As she finished speaking, Hania's glare abruptly shifted. She held up a hand to interrupt Irena's retort and brushed past us. "Delay the interrogation however you can, Irena. I won't be long."

I knew exactly what she was planning, and I grabbed her arm. "Don't, Hania. You promised, and I won't let you go to Protz on my account."

"Did I ask for permission?" She tried to pull away, but I held firm, so she rounded on me. "Let go, Maria."

"I doubt that bastard has any influence over a Gestapo interrogation," Irena said with a scoff.

Even if he could have helped, Protz would refuse out of spite. I was sure of it, and, somewhere beyond her familiar relentlessness, Hania must have known it, too. He'd make her atone for angering him, then say he was permitting her to implore forgiveness, and that was her repayment. She'd go through hell for nothing.

Hania's arm trembled beneath my grip, her eyes glistened despite their hard edge, and I didn't think the cold was responsible for either. She tried to push me away again, but she paused when I relaxed my hold and stepped closer.

"Please, Bubbe."

Hania looked from me to Irena. At last she cursed in Yiddish, sighed, and placed a hand over mine. "Maybe we can't get you out of this, but we'll get you through it."

My stubborn, darling friends. Every part of me wanted to order them away, to insist I could do this on my own, but the little voice wanted them, needed them, selfish though it may have been.

The cold air burned within my lungs, but I fought around it in order to speak. "Promise you won't give yourselves away. No matter what happens to me, I have to know you'll be safe, so please, please promise me—"

Hania pulled me close, her embrace as sure and comforting as my mother's and father's had once been. I held tight to the rough fabric of her uniform, let her soothe my trembling breaths, sensed her heart pounding through her thin chest. "We promise, shikse. Don't we, Irena?"

"Dammit, Maria," she muttered. I took it as a yes.

With every step, the chilling air grew colder, fouler, as if carrying the pungent odors of singed hair and flesh and dusting my skin with ashes. No matter how I chided my mind for playing tricks on me, because the crematoria were not currently running, the scent clung to me while the feeling of the particles lingered. I wrapped my arms tighter around my waist. Death was a constant, familiar assailant, poisoning the air while the sky wept snowflakes of gray ash, mourning each stolen life.

Through the darkness, I located the ARBEIT MACHT FREI sign above the gate. The sign triggered memories of following my family out of the railcar, lingering with Tata as he comforted me one last time. I nearly smelled the wax and pine from the polish he used on his cane, almost felt his gentle hands warming my frozen cheeks while his reassuring voice warmed me to the core.

True freedom comes from bravery, strength, and goodness. The only one who can take those from you is you.

I closed my hand, as though his fingers were wrapping mine around the tiny pawn.

I hadn't been to Block 11 since transferring out of the kommando, and when we arrived it felt as if I'd never left. It looked the same, stark and cold and bare, and smelled the same, like filth and death and bodily fluids. And it felt the same. Hopeless, desperate, agonizing.

We walked down the eerie halls until we reached an interrogation room, one where I'd spent numerous hours cleaning blood, urine, and vomit from the floor. As I entered, the Gestapo agent conducting the interrogation was sitting behind a small table, smoking a cigarette.

Sturmbannführer Ebner.

Sheer horror brought me to a sudden halt. Fortunately it was an appropriate reaction for my situation, so Irena pushed me farther into the room. I wasn't aware that Ebner had transferred from Pawiak to Auschwitz, yet there he was, and suddenly I was fourteen again. Almost naked, alone, terrified, immobilized by strong men, remaining as silent as possible while this man cursed and struck me, this man who had outwitted me, tormented me, and threatened my family. This man who had sent us to Auschwitz.

Irena didn't know my history with him, but she clapped a hand on my shoulder, as if pushing me into my seat, and gave me a quick squeeze. Reminding me I wasn't alone.

Once I was across from Ebner, I swallowed hard, suppressing my terror. *Think. Study him.*

I knew this man, but as I looked into his face he didn't appear to recognize me. He didn't seem to remember the girl he'd tortured all those years ago, likely because he'd tortured many more since me. Which meant I had an excellent advantage.

The last time I'd faced Ebner, he'd won. We'd matched wits, we'd fought long and hard, and he had emerged the victor. But the pieces had been set up again. It didn't matter who won last time; it mattered only how the game was played this time. And this time, I had two more pieces on my side, and I knew how to play Ebner's game.

Let him believe I'm falling for every trick he plays.

My strategy was in place, and it was time for a rematch.

"Prisoner 15177 is the interpreter, Frau Aufseherin?" Ebner indicated Hania with a nod.

"Correct, Herr Sturmbannführer."

He focused on Hania. "You will speak only to interpret. If you say anything else to Prisoner 16671, I'll assume you're encouraging disobedience and take necessary action upon both of you. Do you understand?"

She managed a small nod. "Yes, Herr Sturmbannführer."

Ebner placed a fresh cigarette between his lips and lit it before turning to me. "My name is Wolfgang Ebner. Would you care for a cigarette?"

When he addressed me, I watched him with no apparent recognition or understanding on my face, then waited for Hania to translate. Once she finished, I widened my eyes, as if surprised by the generous offer.

"Thank you, Herr Sturmbannführer. I don't smoke, but would you mind if I hold one?"

When I accepted the cigarette he offered me, my hand lingered above the table long enough for him to notice the tremble I inserted for his benefit. I twirled it between my fingers, and Irena snatched one without waiting for an invitation. Meanwhile Ebner smoked and watched me, allowing the suspense to drive me mad. So I gave him exactly what he wanted.

"Please tell me why I'm here, Herr Sturmbannführer," I exclaimed, tripping over the words in my haste. "It's because of the uprising, isn't it?"

Ebner held up a hand to silence me and looked to Hania, who stood beside me. She was quiet for an instant, as though reminding herself to treat this interrogation like all others she'd witnessed. It was another day at work, nothing more. When she spoke, her German was clear and precise, her expression neutral.

Ebner flashed a reassuring smile. "Yes, but if you cooperate, you have nothing to fear."

I released a breath, letting him know his words had produced their intended effect. "As a former resistance member, I know better than to make that mistake again. Actions have consequences, Herr Sturmbannführer. Sometimes the consequences only affect the guilty parties, but more often, they affect innocent people like myself. That's something many forget."

"Indeed." He took a long draw from his cigarette. "You're saying you were rightfully condemned for the resistance activities which sent you to Auschwitz, but this time, you weren't involved in the rebellion?"

"That's right." I turned the cigarette over in my hands while Ebner tapped ashes into an ashtray and consulted the papers on the table.

"You spent a few weeks working in the Union Munitions Factory during the spring of 1944. Why did you spend such a brief amount of time there?"

I drew a ragged breath and let my voice quiver. "Because I was young when the occupation began. Working with gunpowder and explosives reminded me of the bombings from the invasion."

"Were you involved in smuggling gunpowder for the uprising, and even if not, were you aware of the scheme?"

"No, Herr Sturmbannführer."

Ebner stayed quiet once Hania finished speaking. Despite her attempts at indifference, she seemed more tense with every passing moment. Irena had positioned herself behind Ebner, probably so she could play her role without the added stress of him watching the entire time. I didn't dare look at them too much, but their presence provided me with comfort.

The heavy silence was enough to drive me mad; fidgeting would serve my position well, so I didn't fight the urge. At last Ebner turned to Irena.

"Frau Aufseherin, I'm told you keep a close eye on Prisoner 16671. Do you recall detecting any suspicious behavior?"

"No, Herr Sturmbannführer, but I know where she was on the seventh of October. The clumsy bitch spilled coffee all over my uniform that morning, so I supervised while she cleaned it. And it took far longer than it should have since she's too incompetent to shine a damn button properly," Irena said with a condescending laugh as she exhaled cigarette smoke. "By the time I escorted her back to the kitchen, the camp was in an uproar."

After Hania translated the response, I seized her skirt and pulled her close with such force that she staggered. "The coffee was an accident! Tell Aufseherin Lichtenberg it was an accident, please—"

"Shut up!" Irena shouted, so I released Hania and flinched in anticipation of a blow. She tossed her cigarette butt on the floor and stepped on it, then held up a hand to interrupt Hania's translation of my plea. "Don't bother, Jew. I don't give a shit."

While we'd been talking, Ebner had moved to the back of the room, where the torture instruments were displayed in a case. He'd been calm, likely putting me at ease so I'd be even more startled when he flew into a sudden rage. It was about to happen. I could feel it.

When Ebner returned to stand across from me, he held a whip in one hand and a club in the other. He placed both on the table. One reminded me of my last Gestapo interrogation, the other of my flogging, but I wasn't afraid of either, because I remembered this stage of his interrogations. He wasn't going to torture me, because I was already cooperating. He just wanted to terrorize me.

We'd reached the most critical moment of our game. We'd made our opening moves and had established control of the board, strategizing and planning. Now we attacked.

I inserted a level of heightened urgency into my voice. "You said I had nothing to fear if I cooperated."

"Which is why you'll continue," Ebner replied, studying his options.

From her position behind him, Irena made eye contact with me, as though unsure how to proceed, but I hoped the look in my eyes urged her to stay in her role, as she'd promised. Meanwhile, Hania struggled to force her translations out.

"Frau Aufseherin, which do you suggest?"

Upon Ebner's prompting, Irena selected the club. Hania appeared too stunned to translate, but it didn't matter because I grabbed her arm. Even though I was pretending to seek protection, I gave her a small squeeze, urging her not to lose faith. She grabbed my forearm in response, and I could feel her pulse pounding, but she returned the gesture.

Ebner lifted the club toward me. "Unhand her at once."

I recoiled while Hania backed away and Ebner came to my side. Since I didn't have a braid for him to grab this time, his rough hand closed around the nape of my neck while the club lifted my chin.

"You're certain you knew nothing of the smuggled gunpowder?" he asked, tightening his grip while I gasped. "Why don't I leave you with Aufseherin Lichtenberg while you consider your answer?"

When he referred to Irena, I tensed, then he released me and passed the club to her. Before Hania had finished translating, I started begging, and I suspected Ebner didn't need a translation to believe his plan was working.

Lips curled into a wicked smile, Irena toyed with the club. "Did you hear that, Polack? Just us."

I fell into abrupt silence while Ebner looked between me and

Irena, waiting to see what we would do next. My shallow breaths were the loudest sound in the room, and I met Irena's gaze.

Your move, Frieda.

In a sudden explosion of motion, Irena slammed the club down on the table and lunged for me, and I released the most petrified scream I could muster and fled toward the locked door. With shrieks rivaling Mandel's, she caught me and forced me into the chair. Keeping me immobile, she hit the table again. Even as I let out another cry, I sensed the hope and urgency and desperation between us and Hania, whose back was pressed against the wall, panicking as much as her part required—though some of it seemed authentic, too.

Before entering my interrogation, we'd detoured to the women's washroom. I'd bent over the filthy sink and gulped mouthfuls of water, enough to take my terrified prisoner role as far as necessary. It was time to enact the next phase.

Amid Irena's threatening bellows, I cowered and pleaded and sobbed and released the tight hold on my bladder. The pungent smell of urine filled the small space while the warm wetness seeped into my uniform, puddled in my chair, and trickled onto the floor. Irena's jeers and threats were lost amid my continuous blubbering, and I buried my head with a final despairing cry.

"I told the truth, I swear I told the truth! Please don't leave me alone with her."

Aside from my weeping and Hania's trembling voice finishing interpretations, everyone fell silent. Ebner must have been pleased. And so was I. I heard him striking a match, then the smell of smoke reached my nostrils.

"Prisoner 16671, is there anything else you need to tell me?"

"I told you everything, Herr Sturmbannführer, I promise. Please get her away from me," I whispered, drawing farther from Irena.

Ebner allowed the tension to linger, and my panicked sniffles filled the room, as loud as the thoughts racing across my mind. *So close, we're so close . . .*

I jumped when Ebner's chair scraped across the floor, harsh and chilling, as he pushed away from the table. "We're finished."

Checkmate.

With a parting shove, Irena released me, so I reacted with a sharp intake of breath. I remained curled into myself, afraid to lift my head and risk looking at her or Hania. We couldn't ruin it now. I focused on the cigarette I'd dropped during the scuffle, now on the floor, soggy and saturated with urine. The sight was oddly satisfying.

"Frau Aufseherin, escort the prisoners back to Birkenau," Ebner said. "I'll see you tomorrow."

"Tomorrow?" Irena asked while I looked up.

He nodded and tapped his cigarette, watching the ashes fall to the floor. "We're conducting final interrogations today, but otherwise, we've caught the women responsible for smuggling the gunpowder from the munitions factory. Tomorrow the entire women's camp is going to watch them hang."

* * *

"I knew you had a lot of chutzpah, Maria, but not that much," Hania said, shaking her head as we traveled back to Birkenau. "I don't understand how you came out of an interrogation unscathed. That was a risky scheme." She'd spent the beginning of our walk carrying on in various languages to calm her nerves, so I considered this a step in the right direction.

Irena said nothing. Deep lines traveled across her forehead, a sign she had pushed Frieda away and was left with only lingering hatred toward her.

Shivering and silent, I wrapped my arms around my midsection as snowflakes descended around us. Of course I was relieved that I hadn't been implicated, but it didn't alleviate the familiar chill of guilt. While working in the munitions factory, I'd corresponded with the Jewish women who had been caught. They could have named me, Hania, or countless others, but they hadn't betrayed anyone. Tomorrow they would pay with their lives.

Hania must have sensed my thoughts, because she wrapped a comforting arm around me. "Even though the uprising failed, it gave hope to so many. Those women will die as heroes."

She was right, but I couldn't erase them from my mind. In this terrible place, so many heroic people had met death with unmatched courage. I would always admire their bravery.

Even though I'd emerged unharmed from my Gestapo interrogation, it rekindled memories I'd suppressed for so long. All day, I waited for Ebner to summon me, saying my role in the smuggling ring had been uncovered, that I'd be joining the condemned women. Whether or not he believed my lies was irrelevant. Lies hadn't saved me last time.

Last time, I thought I had protected my family. Last time, my false confession had spared them an interrogation but put us on a train. This time, I had no reason to believe I had protected myself or my friends any more than I had protected my family.

That night, in our bunk, when Hania and I were bundled under our blankets, I rested my head in her lap and produced the bottle of vodka I'd organized after my interrogation. I took a sip and let the heat build in every corner of my mouth before swallowing and passing it to Hania, who accepted it without a word.

When the bottle was empty, warmth tingled through my body while the room gently swayed. I was no longer so concerned that Ebner would come for me or that this interrogation would yield similar results to my last. Hania's hand rested on my head, but she was quiet. Somehow I'd ended up drinking more than she did. Maybe I'd have a headache in the morning. How could a tiny bottle of clear liquid give me a headache? The absurd notion made me giggle.

"Hania?"

"Hm?"

"Will you tell me a story?"

She chuckled and sat up as far as the space would allow. "A bedtime story for the girl turning eighteen next month?"

I grinned. "Precisely, Bubbe."

"Oy, I'm afraid I haven't told a bedtime story in a long time, Maria."

"Don't worry, I haven't heard one in a long time. Will you tell it in French?"

"You want a story you won't understand?" She laughed, but she knew how much I enjoyed listening to her speak the language. After I nodded, Hania traced her finger over a small cut on my cheek and spoke in a murmur. "*Il était une fois . . .*"

I closed my eyes while her lilt wrapped me in the finest French silks and filled my stomach with the most delectable pastries, perhaps a croissant, macaron, and mille-feuille from a quaint bakery in the French countryside. Hania's voice was one I could have listened to all the time without tiring of it, no matter the language, but her French captivated me. It was as delicate and beautiful as she was. I didn't know what the story was about, but as it lulled me to sleep I heard a familiar Yiddish word amid the French. *Shikse.*

Chapter 29

Birkenau, 17 January 1945

C HECKMATE AGAIN."

Hania exhaled and massaged her temple. "You've won four games in a row."

"Because you're a bit slow today, Bubbe." I giggled when she reprimanded me in Yiddish. "Rematch?"

"So you can continue gloating?"

"I'll only gloat a little this time, I promise."

We huddled near the small stove, desperate for the bit of warmth it provided. I started setting up the chess pieces, but Hania climbed to our bunk, so I collected them and joined her. We lay close together and watched a few prisoners trudge through the deep snow, their noses red and lips blue. A mixture of snow and freezing rain descended from the sky and pummeled the unfortunate women, urging them along until they disappeared into another block.

Two SS guards hurried by, wasting no time as they sought shelter. The guards had been in a strange mood during the past few days. They'd been more anxious than usual, and they'd destroyed various buildings and countless records, filling the air with the smell of burning paper rather than burning flesh. Irena had been busy, so I hadn't had the opportunity to ask what had prompted the shift.

As if on cue, the door swung open, and Irena slammed it behind her. "Good Lord, it's freezing!" she exclaimed, hurrying to the stove. She stood there for a moment before casting a disapproving gaze over the bedraggled women packed into their bunks. "You call this a fire? Prisoner 16671, fix this."

Irena never barged into our block without reason. Something had happened.

I hurried to do her bidding. I gathered kindling and stoked the fire, pretending to be absorbed in my work while she hovered over me and spoke in a hushed voice.

"The Red Army is near. Evacuations have already begun, and tomorrow the women's sector will relocate toward Loslau." A town west of Oświęcim, known in Polish as Wodzisław Śląski.

Irena didn't linger to hear my response. Once she'd gone, I relished the fire's warmth and considered the news. We were leaving Auschwitz. Surely that meant freedom would come soon. Once we were resettled, I'd have to get a note to Mateusz so he'd know how to contact me with updates on Fritzsch.

Upon hearing my whispered report, Hania laughed dryly. "Our liberators are coming, but there will be no one to liberate."

"We could come across Allied forces during relocation. If not, at least we'll be out of Auschwitz. That calls for a celebratory chess game."

She sighed, but it didn't prevent a smile. "More chess?"

"We can play by the stove, so we'll be warmer than we are here."

"Fine. One more game, shikse."

I jumped down and grabbed the jewelry pouch from its hole beneath the loose brick, and Hania followed more slowly, an odd, vacant expression on her face. Something wasn't right. I'd been too absorbed in our chess games to notice, but I saw it now as she descended from our bunk. When her feet touched the ground, she swayed, and her knees buckled.

Gasping, I caught her before she hit the floor. To my relief, she was still conscious. "Hania, what's wrong?"

"Nothing, nothing." She waved me away until I reluctantly released her. "I've had a splitting headache all day, so I got a little dizzy. And before you ask, no, I didn't organize vodka."

I touched her forehead before she pushed my hand aside. "You have a fever. Does anything hurt?"

"It's just a headache, and I don't have a fever."

"Answer the question."

"My joints ache a little, but that's because I'll be twenty-seven in a few months. Age is catching up to me," she said with a teasing smile. She led the way to the stove, but she used the bunks for support. When I lifted her uniform, she snapped a Yiddish curse, yanked her skirt from my hands, and turned to me, her brow furrowed. "What was that for? Stop fussing and set up the game. I'm not sick."

But I'd already seen what I'd been attempting to locate. The rash.

"Hania." I let her name hang between us as I struggled to keep my voice calm for what came next. "You have typhus."

She pressed her lips together and looked at me as if I'd been speaking complete nonsense. "We were vaccinated against typhus, remember?"

"That was a long time ago, and you—"

"Enough. I need rest, that's all, and I don't want to hear another word about it." She held my gaze, but when she spoke again she softened her tone. "I'm not sick, shikse."

Hania wasn't denying the illness to keep me from worrying.

She'd convinced herself she wasn't sick. I saw it in the obstinate set of her glassy gaze, in the newfound fear present in her dark eyes, despite what she was telling me and herself. She wouldn't relent, because to admit illness was to take one step closer to death. And she had children who needed her.

"You're going to be fine, Bubbe, but you have typhus." I wrapped my arm around her before she could protest. "You're getting rest, and I'm getting help."

Hania stumbled along beside me while I escorted her back to our bunk, but she carried on in multiple languages, and I caught a few stubborn mutters that emerged in Polish and German. "Impossible. I don't have typhus. I didn't survive this long just to die of typhus . . ."

Once she was settled beneath our blankets, I stepped outside. The frigid air stung like a slap to the face, but the bite of terror was far sharper. *Not Hania. Please God, not Hania.*

I pressed my back into the wall, sank into the shadows, and took a few slow breaths to keep my panic at bay, watching my breath form smoky puffs. After a moment, I began the arduous journey through the deep snow and ice. The hospital. I needed to get to the hospital.

When I reached the proper block, I hurried inside, shouting and ignoring the doctors and nurses telling me to be quiet. "Janina? Janina, where—?"

"I'm right here, Maria, now stop disturbing my patients." The words came from a familiar red head, which remained bent as its owner administered medication to a semiconscious prisoner.

By the time she was finished, I was already at the foot of the patient's bed, blurting out my story and begging for medication. Janina disappeared to check her supply, and I waited in agitated silence. When she returned, her grim expression crushed my hopes.

"I'm low on everything, and the guards have stopped providing me with supplies. This is all I have." She placed three pills into my outstretched palm. "That's not enough to cure Hania, not by any means. But a few doses are better than none."

Suppressing my disappointment, I clutched the precious pills and voiced a small thanks before allowing myself out. I retraced my steps across Birkenau's grounds.

Hania will be fine. A few doses are better than none. Hania will be fine.

I didn't know how many times I'd repeated the mantra before I spied a familiar face heading across the camp—Protz.

"Herr Scharführer!" I shouted and chased after him even though he ignored me. "Herr Scharführer, I need your help."

At this, he stopped to listen. If there was one thing I'd learned about Protz, it was that his greed was limitless. "What are you offering?" he asked.

"This in exchange for medication."

His gloved hand was already extended, and I dropped the biggest diamond I had into his palm. He inspected it while I waited, fighting the cold and my own impatience. Once satisfied, he looked at me, but, when I saw recognition in his gaze, his eyes narrowed.

"Is Prisoner 15177 sick?"

I'd been counting on Protz to not remember me, but he'd seen me with Hania countless times. Fortunately, I'd had a lot of practice lying.

"The medicine is for me."

"Prove it. Bring her here."

When I didn't move, he smirked, having gained the upper hand. I started developing another lie, but abandoned my efforts. Even if he'd been wrong about my motives, he seemed convinced he was right.

"I should shoot you for lying, but I'd rather adjust the terms of our deal. This," he said, showing me the diamond, "is in exchange for your worthless life. And if you're stupid enough to get medicine from anyone else, I will find out, and our deal will be off."

The diamond was so close to me, I could have easily snatched it back, but the little voice reminded me that I couldn't help Hania with a bullet in my skull. Relishing his victory, Protz pocketed the diamond and left me with a final taunt.

"Give the Scheisse-Jude my regards."

His words triggered the part of me that disregarded all potential consequences, the part that cared only about taking action, and words poured from my mouth so quickly I couldn't stop them even if I'd wanted to.

"Hania! Her name is Hania, you ignorant—"

Before I finished, something smacked against my cheek and knocked the breath from my lungs. As I landed amid the fresh snow, Protz loomed over me. He regarded me with his usual contempt, and I dropped my gaze to his feet in anticipation. The feeling of a boot colliding with my body was all too familiar, so if it was going to come, I wanted to be prepared.

"I'm sure you're aware Prisoner 15177 has a brother who works in Crematorium II. Lately, there's been no need to operate its gas chamber, but I can change that and give the lazy bastard someone to drag out of it. Another word out of your mouth, Polack, and he'll be burning the Jewish whore's corpse."

Whether or not Protz had the power to fulfill the threat, I didn't know, but it wasn't a risk I could take. There was no point in replying, anyway. Instead I watched a few drops of blood fall from my nose onto the white snow—he must have punched me. Sometimes I wondered why I wasn't better at dodging blows by now. Protz's footsteps crunched against the snow, growing fainter until they disappeared altogether. Then I was alone. I sat up but stayed where I was, clinging to the tiny pills.

It was during such times, when I'd failed, that I missed Father Kolbe most. When the misery overtook me, he'd always known what I needed, whether it was a kind word, his comforting presence, a chess game, or his rosary. I placed my hand over the hidden pocket, feeling the round beads through the thin fabric. It helped, but, no matter how hard I'd tried during the past few years, I'd never found Father Kolbe's resilience.

"What the hell, Maria? You'll freeze to death, and you're bleeding."

I wasn't sure if a few minutes or hours had passed when Irena's voice broke through the howling wind. As I stood up, I wiped the lingering blood from my nose and discovered it was frozen. That was when I realized how cold I was.

"Hania has typhus." Speaking through my chattering teeth was almost as difficult as voicing those words. "There's not enough medicine in the hospital block to treat her, and Protz refused to help. Do you have anything?"

Irena shook her head. At first the small pills in my palm had been better than nothing; now they taunted me, reminding me how helpless I was. I could provide her with some relief, but not enough. And the evacuation was tomorrow.

The same thoughts must have been on Irena's mind. She dropped her voice to a murmur. "Maria, the evacuation plan only includes the fittest. The sick will be left here."

It took a moment for her words to register. They were leaving thousands of sick people to die. As the realization settled over me, I shook my head. I wasn't surprised, not at all. Just angry. And I wouldn't let that happen to Hania.

People died every day in Auschwitz. Losing friends, strangers, and fellow resistance members was a normal part of the life I'd led for so long. But this was different. This was Hania, my oldest friend in the camp, the friend who had mothered me, educated me, and taught me Yiddish words, the friend I'd taught Catholic prayers and how to play chess. The woman whose children Mama had smuggled from the ghetto, the children she'd fought to remain alive for no matter how desperate the measure, the children I'd promised to help her find. We'd gone through too much for it to end like this. I wouldn't let it end like this.

I had a plan.

After making sure no guards were approaching, I stepped closer to Irena and lowered my voice. "Go to Crematorium II and find Hania's brother. His name is Izaak Rubinstein, and he's Prisoner 15162. Bring him and meet me in the latrines as soon as possible."

She nodded, and we parted ways. Once I returned to my block, I gathered fresh snow into my small cup, melted it over the stove, and took it to Hania. She was more delirious now, but I roused her and coaxed her into taking a pill. After drinking the melted snow, she settled back into her feverish stupor.

We were supposed to be in bed, so I was forced to bide my time until the SS guards finished prowling outside the blocks. I nestled close to Hania, providing some additional warmth, voicing gentle reassurance in a hushed tone. After the barks of both the guards and their Alsatians had fallen silent, I slipped out into the frozen night, avoiding the searchlights, cloaking myself in darkness. My journey was maddeningly slow, but, between the frigid temperature and the guards who would shoot at any movement, speed was impossible.

Inside the latrines, two familiar figures waited in the shadows, and the sight of one brought me to an abrupt halt.

Izaak had changed. He looked as if he'd aged ten years, but that wasn't what shocked me. It was his eyes. I'd expected to find relief and happiness upon seeing me after all this time. Instead the eyes that once held richness and warmth now displayed a haunted, painful darkness and anger. So much anger.

"Why am I here, Maria, and who is this?" He pointed an accusatory finger at Irena.

"A friend, but there's no time to explain. It's Hania."

At the mention of his sister, I hoped a bit of worry or love or something, anything, would chase away his hostility. Instead he shifted into an even deeper fury. "What did that bastard do to her?" Izaak didn't need to name Protz for the implication to be clear; I refrained from lifting a hand to the tender imprint his fist had left around my nose, certain to develop a bruise.

"Nothing. She's sick. The camp is being evacuated tomorrow, and the sick will be left behind." I swallowed hard, unnerved. "I . . . I thought you'd want to stay with her. You can hide in the latrines, and when everyone is gone, you can care for her until the Soviets arrive."

"I've already added your number to the list of dead," Irena said. "Your absence won't be detected."

Izaak was silent. He looked between me and Irena, then jerked his head in a quick nod. Once I'd voiced my thanks and promised to visit him in the morning, Irena escorted me back to my block. As we walked, I felt as if his eyes remained upon me, and I crossed my arms to suppress a shiver.

"I've only been near the crematoria and gas chambers a few times, but it was a few times too many," Irena said. "If you were allowed to see what the Sonderkommando has seen, you'd understand."

Back in my block, I lay in silence, unable to sleep. Hania's shallow breaths hovered around me while I moved my fingers along my rosary beads. Almost four years of my life had been spent in this place. Tomorrow, they would come to an end. The thought should have brought me comfort, but it didn't. Not now that I was leaving Hania and Izaak. And I was leaving liberation. The Soviets would arrive any day, but I would be gone. Freedom dangled just beyond my reach—and with it my ability to confront Fritzsch. Until I had heard the truth from him, my fight for survival—for justice—would continue. Justice alone held the power to ease the ache in my chest—one that longed for my family, prompted me to imagine them standing in the courtyard between Blocks 10 and 11. Their confusion; their grief; their terror.

I gripped the rosary tighter, pushing the thought away while I drew a shuddering breath. Someday, escape would come; for now, the bars on my prison were no weaker.

My captivity wasn't over. Just changing.

Chapter 30

Auschwitz, 20 April 1945

DESPITE MY ORDER to disarm, Fritzsch hasn't touched his gun. Instead he glances at his king in check before settling back into his chair and watching me, watching the pistol in my shaking hands. "Do you plan to kill me like I killed those Polacks? Watch me die like you watched Prisoner 16670?"

Every part of me wants to shoot him, to pull the trigger and bury a bullet in his skull. Pain urges me to do it. But my wits, my final piece in this game, urge me to play a different move. The weight of Father Kolbe's rosary is heavy in my pocket, and I can almost hear his gentle voice guiding me as he did so many times before, removing me from the darkness within this dreadful place, within myself. My cigarette-burn scars tingle, five marks for the five Florkowskis, aligned above five tattooed numbers, 16671, the brand upon my skin like the brand this place left upon my soul. And here, so close that the barrel of my gun is hardly a meter from his chest, the man who murdered everyone I loved.

Fritzsch waits for my answer, so I choose my play. I choose my wits.

"I didn't come here to kill you. You have the rest of eternity to burn in hell. Put your gun on the ground, and after I take you to the authorities, you'll confess to everything you've done. You'll be arrested and charged for your crimes, and I'll verify your confession and show everyone the scars you left on my back. You'll be sentenced to death or prison, but I hope it's prison so you'll live a long and miserable life in captivity. And you'll never escape."

The rain has stopped. The only sounds are my unsteady breaths, the heartbeat pounding in my ears, and the names playing over and over in my mind. *Mama, Tata, Zofia, Karol, Father Kolbe.*

Fritzsch laughs. "Deranged rants and a few scars won't win a trial. Why go through all that trouble when you could simply pull the trigger?"

The suggestion banishes everything else—everything but the chorus of names keeping pace with my racing heart. As if of its own accord, my finger moves toward the trigger. One bullet. That's all it would take.

"If you attempt to testify before a court, you won't make it through without an outburst, then you'll lose all credibility. No one will believe a word you say." Fritzsch pushes his chair away from the table and stands, exposing the front of his body to me. "You've managed to get this far, Prisoner 16671. Don't let it fall to ruin."

The trigger is smooth and slick against my wet, cold finger. One bullet.

Just one bullet.

Chapter 31

Death March, 18 January 1945

AFTER A FITFUL night's sleep, I slipped from my block while our nighttime curfew was still in effect. Armed with a bundle of belongings, I hurried to the latrines.

Though it was still dark as I slipped inside and eased the door shut, I found Izaak sitting with his back against the far wall. As I tiptoed closer, he didn't stand; suddenly I felt like an intruder.

"Is Hania dead?"

The question sounded so impassive. I blinked and cleared my throat.

"Um, no, but her fever is worse. I've brought the last two pills, so make sure she takes them. Here, this will help until the Red Army arrives."

I offered him my bundle. Wrapped inside a blanket, I'd stashed the additional organized goods Hania and I had saved: food, the pills, socks, mittens, soap, an extra toothbrush, a small bowl, a broken comb, matches, cigarettes, and coal. Izaak accepted it with a terse nod.

Mumbling a farewell, I returned to my block before my absence was noticed. Huddled on our bunk, Hania looked smaller and weaker than ever. I climbed in next to her and wrapped my arm across her midsection and watched the fluttering rise and fall of her chest. My only reassurance that she was alive.

Outside, a hum of voices indicated the SS guards had started to gather, and when I glanced out the window I saw that the sky threatened snow. It was almost time.

I flipped onto my stomach and rose on my forearms so I could look at her face. "Listen to me, Bubbe," I whispered. "I have to leave, but Izaak will take care of you. You're going to live, and we're going to meet in Warsaw and find your children. Jakub and Adam need you. And so do I. Stay alive, Hania, do you understand? Stay alive."

Her eyes remained closed, brow creased, lips cracked and dry, but as I tucked the blanket around her frail body I prayed some part of her heard me. I kissed her burning forehead, studded with beads of sweat even in this frigid block, and brushed away one of my tears that had fallen onto her cheek.

Then the shouts started, the shouts that had greeted me upon arriving at Auschwitz, the shouts I'd heard every day since. *Raus, schnell!* I didn't obey.

Countless innocents would never escape this terrible place. One whose limp represented a bravery and compassion I'd dreamt of emulating, another whose fervent spirit had ignited my own. One whose curiosity had been as boundless and unrestrained as her golden curls, another whose youthful exuberance had found constant joy even in simplicity. One whose selfless nature had brought me out of suffocating darkness. Here, before me, one fighting against the poisonous clutches of sickness and death, left with the promise of a liberation that could come too late. What right did I have to leave when so many had been denied the chance?

I barely felt the club or heard the voice ordering me to move.

I'd delayed as long as I could. Releasing Hania and climbing down from my bunk was one of the hardest things I'd ever done.

After receiving a small bread ration, we lined up in rows of six to march to the main camp. I found a place at the back of the throng, where Irena hovered in my vicinity. We moved toward the gate, and I lifted a hand to my neck to feel Irena's crucifix through my uniform, then found the skirt pocket where I'd tucked Father Kolbe's rosary. But there was something I'd forgotten to add to that pocket.

My chess pieces.

I'd intended to bring them when I left. If I hurried, I could return to my block, grab them, and rejoin the group before anyone noticed. It wouldn't take long.

When I turned around to enact my plan, Irena grabbed me. At the same time, another woman hesitated, and an SS man shot her in the head.

Irena dragged me a few paces forward, making it look as if I'd kept up, then released me before anyone saw us. I had no choice. That woman's fate would be mine if I didn't stay in line. With a final glance toward the clusters of brick and wooden buildings stretching across the grounds, where Hania and the chess pieces remained, I swallowed past a sudden heaviness in my throat and kept walking.

After joining more prisoners in the main camp, we walked a few kilometers to Rajsko, where more columns awaited us. From there, we pressed onward. The cold was merciless. I had a few layers of organized clothing beneath my uniform, but those weren't enough to combat the blizzard that assaulted us from every angle while we trudged through its fury.

Because I was toward the back, countless rows marched ahead of me through the howling wind and snow. Even if I hadn't been following the crowd, the trail was obvious. The longer we marched, the more people fell behind or collapsed from cold or exhaustion. New prisoners and old, friends and strangers. And they were all shot. Some begged for their lives; others didn't bother. Dead bodies littered both sides of the road, and red blood soaked into the snow. One body stood out to me as I marched by and noticed short, familiar red hair. Janina.

When the bread ration was gone, we didn't receive anything else. Ahead of me, a man spent all day consuming handfuls of snow, plants, rotten vegetables, anything he could find alongside the road, and slipping morsels of organized food into his mouth. He hid his resources from guards and prisoners alike, eating with a ravenousness that I recognized. I had miscellaneous items tucked inside my secret uniform pockets, but I'd left my organized food with Hania and Izaak. I combatted piercing hunger in silence.

As I dwelled in envy while watching him eat, it didn't take long for the inmate's stomach to betray him. I could tell by the way his gait became more labored, how his arms wrapped around his midsection, how he stopped searching for food. My envy transformed into sympathy, and I willed him to keep going, to resist the pains assaulting his insides, but the situation was beyond his control. After a few agonizing minutes, the häftling crouched in the road, unable to keep going, while others moved around him until the final column passed, leaving him exposed to the guards. A bullet ended him before sickness had a chance.

Keep walking. Live. Fight. Survive.

Despite the severe cold, we maintained a vigorous pace all day. I clustered around my fellow prisoners for warmth and stayed toward the edge of the group so I could be near Irena. When the woman beside me fell and told me to leave her behind, I pulled her to her feet and draped her arm across my shoulders before the guards saw us lagging. Together, we pressed on.

I supported the woman until she gingerly released me. We walked in silence for the next few minutes. Then she ran.

One of the SS men drew his pistol and aimed at her. The woman broke into the woods, where she tripped and collapsed with an agonized scream. Her face contorted in pain, and I caught sight of a glistening bone protruding from her leg while her desperate shrieks carried across the open road.

"Shoot me, please shoot me!"

The man aiming at her lowered his gun. None of the other guards drew theirs. The woman's pleas drowned in the sound of footsteps.

Keep walking. Live. Fight. Survive.

Outside Miedźna, we stopped for the evening. Covered in snow and ice, skin chapped and raw and bleeding, delirious, little more than walking corpses, we stumbled into a large barn, our shelter for the night. As I fell onto a makeshift straw bed, the throbbing pains that assaulted my body were unbearable, but exhaustion took over, pulling me into its murky depths.

I'd hardly closed my eyes before someone ordered me awake again. The only thing on my mind was hunger. The ache was familiar, but there was no getting accustomed to it, and it overpowered everything, even the debilitating cold and my exhausted, blistered feet. I didn't want to move, I wanted to stay on the filthy, itchy straw and let starvation or cold or a bullet bring this dreadful existence to an end. But I got up and filed out of the barn.

Irena stood outside the barn door, watching as we exited. When I passed her, she grabbed my arm to hurry me along. As she did so, her free hand brushed mine, so briefly no one noticed. I closed my fingers around the morsel of bread she'd slipped into my palm.

The second day was even more arduous than the first, but the pattern remained the same. Walk, hunger, cold, gunshot, live, fight, survive.

More prisoners attempted to escape. A few were successful. Most weren't. Some were shot as they ran; others were caught and brought back so we could witness their executions. Blood and death. So much blood, so many deaths.

To attempt escape would have been reckless. But, as every step became more difficult, escape was ever-present on my mind. And when I stole a moment to meet Irena's gaze, I suspected it was on hers, too.

The only SS personnel surrounding us were a few men and women, including Protz. He rode a motorcycle and traveled up and down the column of prisoners, shooting at every given opportunity. No one was paying attention to me, so I glanced at Irena again. She looked to me before moving her eyes to the road ahead, then gave one small, swift nod. And our mutual agreement was made.

When the opportunity arose, we would escape.

* * *

By the time we reached midday, I felt as if we'd walked for weeks. I wiggled my toes to alleviate the painful swelling and numb cold, then I scooped up another discreet handful of snow. When I straightened, I slipped it into my mouth. The snow melted against the heat of my tongue, the only part of me that was warm, and I savored it as long as possible. When it was gone, the emptiness in my stomach didn't feel better, but I tried to convince myself it did.

I slipped my frozen fingers into my sleeves, hoping to warm them. Ignoring the shouts and gunshots around me, I felt the rough, uneven skin of my cigarette-burn scars and traced my prisoner number, even though I couldn't see or feel the tattoo.

When my fingers were warmer, I hugged my arms around myself and bowed my head against the wind, pressing onward. I stepped over a fallen body in my path. The snow had ceased for now, a slight blessing on this cursed evacuation. I was at the edge of my row against the left side of the road, so my front and right side had a small buffer thanks to fellow prisoners, and there was one row of inmates behind me. Not an ideal position, but it was the best way to stay close to Irena without drawing suspicion.

A familiar sound disturbed the rhythmic tramp of footsteps. The man behind me had stumbled. He hadn't fallen, but now he was a few steps behind the row, which meant I knew what to expect next. The gunshot.

When the crack pierced the air, something collided with my back and threw me to the ground. The landing was hard and painful, enough to knock the breath out of me. Dazed, I blinked to clear my vision. Had I been shot? I didn't feel injured, and I didn't think I'd been behind the column, but my lungs couldn't expand enough to draw a proper breath.

No, it wasn't a wound affecting my breathing; something was on top of me, pinning me down. The dead man.

We'd landed halfway on the road, halfway along its side. From my position, I didn't think anyone could see me. I'd be shot if a guard saw me hurrying to my place, and I'd be shot if a guard found me underneath this corpse. But if I remained hidden and avoided discovery, then I would have successfully managed to escape.

So I didn't move.

Holding my breath, I peered through the gap between the road and the dead man's shoulder, watching the columns of prisoners. None of the SS men or women stopped, no one wondered where I was, no one cast a second glance at the dead man. No one noticed at all.

All I had to do was alert Irena.

She walked along the left side next to the final row of prisoners, and I watched her feet as they passed. Protz hovered in her vicinity. Once she was a few meters ahead of me and the dead man, she sent a deliberate glance over her shoulder. Of course I didn't need to alert her. She already knew.

When no eyes were on her, Irena collapsed and grabbed her right leg. "Shit!"

At her cry, Protz parked his motorcycle and dismounted. "Damn this weather. Is it your ankle?"

Irena nodded, grimacing. He moved closer, but she bit her lip and waved him away, as if in too much pain to speak.

The prisoners had continued marching, growing smaller and smaller in the distance, but one guard turned around. "Protz, Lichtenberg, let's go!" he shouted.

"Right, I'll start crawling," Irena replied, glaring at him.

"We'll catch up," Protz said. "Frieda's hurt."

The guard nodded and returned to the group. Protz sat next to Irena, who was nursing her supposedly injured limb, wincing and cursing. I had a feeling she enjoyed the theatrics that accompanied our charades, though she never would have admitted it.

When Protz leaned closer, she slapped his hand. "Bastard, don't touch me."

Of course she found a way to give him hell.

Protz didn't dispute her, and she ignored him, absorbed by the injury, while the rows of prisoners disappeared down the road. At last, after the gunshots had grown distant, she sighed.

Protz seemed to decide it was safe to engage her. "Does it feel better?"

"Not at all."

"Good, you'll be riding with me for a few days."

"Well, I'm glad you derive such pleasure from my misfortune, Ludolf," she said with a sardonic laugh.

I grimaced. *Ludolf?*

Irena turned back to her ankle, but Protz grabbed her chin and pushed his lips against hers. At once, she tensed, and it took everything in me to remain hidden. Somehow she endured it, but the moment he placed a hand high along her inner thigh she pushed him away with a strangled gasp.

"Get away from me!" The frantic cry emerged in Polish, not German.

No, no, no.

"What the hell did you say, Frieda? Since when do you speak Polish?"

For God's sake, Irena, recover.

She didn't respond right away. At last she forced a nervous chuckle. "Good Lord, I've spent too much time around the Polacks. Help me up."

Protz rose to his feet, leaving her where she was. "Are you a Volksdeutsch? Why didn't you say so?"

Irena could have said yes. That would have been the easiest and safest answer. But when she looked at me, so briefly that Protz didn't detect it, I suspected that her response would be risky. Stupid. Reckless, even.

Her choice should have terrified me. But, as I eased myself from beneath the dead body, it calmed me instead.

From her place on the ground, Irena looked at Protz and smiled. "I'm not a Volksdeutsch. I'm not German, either. And I sure as hell am not Frieda Lichtenberg."

While Protz reached for his gun, I sprang to my feet. He fired at the sudden movement; at the same time, Irena kicked his legs out from under him. The shot went into the woods, and when Protz landed on his back, the gun flew from his hand. She dove for it, but he wasn't far behind. He caught her leg, and she attempted to kick him while they wrestled toward the pistol.

Clutching two rocks I'd grabbed while in hiding, I ran toward them, but by then Protz had Irena pinned down, preventing her from drawing her pistol. While she writhed, he reached over her, his fingers centimeters from his gun.

"Get off her, you stupid son of a bitch!"

My cry distracted Protz for only a moment, but it was enough. He looked over his shoulder at me, giving Irena the space she needed to drive her elbow into his chest and draw her pistol. Protz lunged again while I pelted him with my rocks, and as his fingers closed around his weapon, Irena raised her gun and hit the back of his head. He collapsed.

Irena pushed him off her. I wasn't sure if Protz was dead or alive, but we didn't linger to find out.

We ran. The prisoners were long gone, but it was only a matter of time before another guard would return to see why Protz and Irena hadn't caught up. We darted through the woods, fighting bushes and shrubs that snagged our clothes, trudging through snow, slipping on ice, tripping over branches, putting as much distance between ourselves and the road as possible. When we couldn't run anymore, we stopped. For a moment, we were too breathless to speak.

By no means could this be counted as a successful escape yet; still, a strange combination of tension and elation rose in my chest. It was a step closer to freedom. To finding Fritzsch and taking action against him now that Germany's position in the war was weakening. If the Nazis were defeated, they would be made to pay for their countless crimes, surely; once Fritzsch admitted that he killed my family, I would see to it that he was held accountable.

"That was a spectacular performance, Marta Naganowska," I said, giving Irena a teasing smile after using her old resistance name.

"Thank you, Helena Pilarczyk, I learned from the best. And if I'm not mistaken, that was the first time I've heard you curse."

"I learned from the best."

Irena flashed a pleased smirk before removing her overcoat and offering it to me. When I hesitated, she heaved an exasperated sigh. "Are you going to pretend you're not cold in that pathetic excuse for clothing? Put on the damn coat. And yes, I'll take it back later," she added, rolling her eyes.

Satisfied with the arrangement, I obliged. The coat was heavy and woolen, warmer than anything I'd worn in a long time. I wrapped it around myself and eased Irena's leather gloves over my numb hands. Now that we'd caught our breath, we kept walking.

It had been years since I'd been in a forest. Even though it was freezing, the cold, once nothing but my enemy, also became a source of awe. Icicles dangled from twigs and branches, catching the light from the setting sun peeking through the trees. A frozen spiderweb glistened against a bush while a blanket of snowflakes covered a fallen log. Flashes of movement indicated small creatures taking shelter, so quick that I didn't get a good look at them, but I saw their tiny tracks. The ground was snow-covered and frozen but layered with fallen leaves and twigs that gave way beneath my feet, far softer than the frozen mud I'd walked on for the past few winters.

I'd stepped out of one world and into another entirely new. One suffering and death, the other beauty and tranquility. It was difficult to imagine the same winter creating both.

"Why didn't we steal Protz's motorcycle so we could drive closer to the nearest town?" Irena muttered after we'd been walking for some time. She crossed her arms more tightly as a frigid wind swept over us, so cold it stung my eyes.

"You couldn't have suggested that before we ran?"

"I didn't think about it until now. Why didn't you suggest it? You're the one who comes up with the ridiculous plans, not me."

"Right, so sorry. By the way, how is your ankle?"

Irena narrowed her eyes but didn't mask a small smile. She cursed when she tripped over a root camouflaged by snow. Despite the harsh climate, I was glad we hadn't spent a moment longer than necessary on the open road. Had we fled closer to town, we would have risked exposing ourselves to civilians, SS men, anyone who could potentially have seen us. Here at least we were alone. But with a town came warmth, food, and shelter, and those would have almost made the risk worth it.

"Do you even know how to drive a motorcycle, Irena?"

"No."

As we pressed onward, blue and gray stripes caught my eye. When I returned Irena's overcoat and gloves, as it was now her turn to wear them, she followed my gaze to the body and turned aside as I inspected it. A young man, near my age, stiff with cold, covered in ice and snow. Tattered uniform, too tattered to be useful. Empty pockets. I knelt beside him and lifted his bony wrist. Something was ensnared within his frozen fingers, something I recognized right away—half a bread ration. He must have saved it and was attempting to eat it when the cold rendered him unable to put forth the effort. With some difficulty, I pried his fingers apart to access the offering and pressed the sacred morsel between my palms, affirming its existence.

Survival was a selfish instinct. Desperation didn't allow time for gratitude. Still, when good fortune found me, I did my best to recognize it, as if my acknowledgment of the favor would encourage fate to shower more blessings upon me. Even when survival depended on it, taking advantage of another's sacrifice never felt like a fair play.

I whispered a thanks to the dead man before returning to Irena's side. Once I managed to tear the bread in half, I offered a piece to her. She shook her head as her mouth warped in disgust.

"All yours. I'd rather not eat something that came from a corpse."

A valid claim, but when I met her gaze she averted her eyes, proving it wasn't the entire reason behind her refusal. "I've seen the way you look at me, Irena. You can't treat me like I'm fragile."

"Good Lord, Maria, you are fragile. After what you've been through, you should know that better than anyone."

"Hunger doesn't pick and choose. You're no better equipped to fight it than I am, and unlike you, I don't have a child who needs her mother."

At this, she drew an unsteady breath and broke an icicle from a birch limb. "I have a far better chance of getting back to her than you do. You know that. And I'll be damned if I let you die after surviving that hell."

I was silent for a moment, letting my irritation go. "You said we'd both get out of Auschwitz alive, remember? I have no intention of losing now."

This time when I offered her the bread she accepted it. After swallowing, she looked at the corpse, and the color drained from her face. I pulled her along, cursing my own stupidity. Why hadn't I made her walk away first?

Keep the bread down, Irena, please keep it down.

She did with great difficulty.

We pressed on. Our search for food was futile, so we ate snow and various roots. The frigid air ached as it touched my lungs and enveloped me in its frozen embrace, tighter and more painful with every step, sucking what little energy I had left from my body. We wouldn't survive the night in this forest.

Daylight was almost gone when the trees started to thin. I prayed it meant we were nearing the edge of the woods, so we kept walking until a welcome sight confirmed my hopes. Before us, a quaint farmhouse sat on an open stretch of land. Wisps of smoke rose from its chimney, and an elderly man—the farmer—emerged from the barn, wielding an ax. He spent a few minutes chopping the pile of logs gathered beside the barn until an elderly woman called to him from the house.

Their voices carried across the field and reached my ears. German. I noticed the flag billowing on a pole near the house, and I didn't need daylight to recognize the white circle, black swastika, and red background.

"Dammit, they're Volksdeutsche. Why couldn't we have found a nice Polish couple?" Irena muttered, then she laughed. "Well, I suppose we can knock on the door and ask for a bed instead of sneaking into their barn."

"I'm glad you're thinking what I'm thinking."

Irena looked from my sly smile to the farm and back, eyes wide. "I wasn't serious."

"You're a camp guard, remember? A guard would demand a place to stay, and since they're Volksdeutsche, they'll be happy to oblige. We'll be warm and have a proper meal."

"Doesn't dining with the enemy sound wonderful?"

I ignored her sarcasm and continued with our story. "You and your colleagues were relocating inmates to Loslau, and I attempted escape, but you caught me. Since we got separated from the rest, we need somewhere to stay for the evening. And remember, you don't speak Polish."

When I offered an amused grin, she glared in mock reproach. "If you tried to escape, why didn't I shoot you?"

"You couldn't get a good shot, you didn't want to waste a bullet, I don't know," I replied with an impatient wave. "They won't question why you made the decision you made. Draw your gun and let's go."

Irena held the pistol loosely and led the way. When I didn't follow, she looked back. "What?"

"Is that the best you can do, Frieda?"

She clenched her jaw. "They can't see us."

"Not now, but if they happen to look outside and see us walking to their door like two friends on an evening stroll, do you think they'll believe our story?"

"Good Lord." She sighed, brushed a loose strand of hair aside, and closed a hand around my upper arm. When I looked at her again, she tightened her grip begrudgingly and pushed the gun barrel between my shoulder blades.

"Much better." I nodded in approval as Irena forced me to walk in front of her. "Don't forget to be convincing."

"Shut up."

"Forgive me, Frau Aufseherin."

"Dammit, Maria."

When we reached the farmhouse, Irena pounded on the door until the woman answered. Irena said nothing, waiting for her to speak, but the woman looked so surprised that I had to remind myself not to laugh. The farmer joined his wife by the door and immediately raised his right arm in salute. The woman blinked, as if coming out of a stupor, then imitated him.

"*Heil* Hitler," they said in unison.

"Heil Hitler," Irena said with the faintest hint of force, though her hold on me gave her a reason to avoid raising her right arm. "Frieda Lichtenberg, Aufseherin of Auschwitz-Birkenau."

"Hermann Meinhart, and my wife, Margrit," he replied. "What can we do for you, Frau Aufseherin?"

After Irena relayed our tale, Frau Meinhart stepped aside and shooed her husband out of the doorway. Inside, I took in my surroundings. This was the first time I'd been inside a home in almost four years. We crossed the wooden floor in the living room, where there was a sofa, rug, and two armchairs. A cheerful fire danced in the fireplace while a small mantel displayed a framed wedding photograph and a few baby portraits. An enticing aroma of meat and vegetables wafted from the stove as we reached four chairs and a square table set with a floral tablecloth, a small loaf of bread on a platter, two white cloth napkins, two spoons, and two bowls.

I didn't know why the simple home overwhelmed me and brought tears to my eyes. Thankfully, crying was appropriate for my part in our charade. As Frau Meinhart indicated two empty chairs, I swallowed my tears and prepared to sit, but Irena held me back. She kept me at arm's length, as though too repulsed to come nearer.

"Where do you think you're going, you filthy creature? You're not doing anything until you've scrubbed every bit of grime from your body."

I could have kissed her on both cheeks.

Herr Meinhart placed two wooden tubs before the fireplace—one for me, a smaller one with a washboard for my uniform—then fetched water from the well, which Frau Meinhart heated over the stove. Once finished, they disappeared into the back of the house, allowing me privacy while Irena made as if to stand guard; instead she sat at the table with her back to me. Even in the camp, she had always managed to avoid seeing me without my uniform on. Perhaps she didn't want me to feel as if I were being inspected; perhaps she doubted her ability to bear what lay underneath.

I disinfected my uniform first, killing every insect and using the washboard to lift away layers of filth. By the time I finished, the garment remained dingy and stained, but it looked a bit better. I hung it over the edge of the tub to dry, close to the fire's warmth.

The wooden floor was cold beneath my bare feet as I moved to the larger tub, then stepped into the hot water. With a bar of soap—an entire bar of real soap—I cleaned myself and scrubbed my shorn head, inhaling the soap's faint yet sweet scent of apple blossoms. It was a sensation I hadn't felt in so many years: clean.

Once finished, I dried off with a soft white towel and donned my uniform—still damp, but the house was warm enough. When Irena joined me and saw the sudden tears in my eyes, a soft smile played on her lips.

Then, sighing, she lifted her gun to my back before summoning the couple. Herr Meinhart carried the tubs outside while Frau Meinhart reheated dinner. Irena led me to my chair. I sat straight, breaths shaky, tensing when she pressed the gun more firmly between my shoulder blades.

"Behave yourself."

"Yes, Frau Aufseherin," I whispered, then heaved a small sigh when she released me and removed the gun.

Frau Meinhart placed steaming bowls of stew before us. No one spoke throughout the meal, but the painful silence didn't bother me. My one serving of stew held more pork, carrots, onions, and cabbage than ten servings in Auschwitz. The broth warmed me from the inside out while the tender vegetables, thick, juicy cuts of meat, and sliced bread dispelled the ever-present ache of hunger. It was the most wonderful meal I'd ever had.

But mine was a small portion, only a thin slice of bread and a few spoonfuls of stew. As I finished and rose in search of more, a hand grabbed my bowl. At once, I snatched it back, and though the other inmate's grip remained firm, so did mine. Such audacity, stealing from one of the oldest numbers in the women's camp. She wouldn't get away with it. Experience had taught me how to win this game, so I would resist until she gave up, searched for an easier target, and gave my seniority the proper respect—

Her free hand closed around my wrist, so tight it forced my grasp to loosen, and I looked up to see if I recognized this häftling who had overpowered me.

Irena stood above me, one hand on my wrist, the other on my bowl. She wrenched it away. "Enough."

This wasn't my block; this was the farmhouse. Herr and Frau Meinhart kept their eyes on their own meals while Irena removed my bowl from the table. Irena wasn't a Nazi or another inmate. She was supposed to be my friend, so why was she starving me?

When she left my bowl by the sink, Irena placed both hands on the counter before looking over her shoulder. Given the way she'd suddenly turned on me, I expected her to regard me with hatred and disgust; instead her eyes glistened before she blinked and swallowed hard.

We'd seen what overeating did to prisoners in my condition. My body couldn't take it. Even if I'd been thinking properly, the temptation to consume my serving and countless more was too great. Frau Meinhart had given me a safe, manageable portion; now Irena was saving my life.

Once she'd composed herself, Irena returned to her seat. Tears sprang to my eyes, but I suppressed them. I wasn't sure why I'd been crying so much.

While the couple cleaned up after the meal, Irena and I stayed where we were. In keeping with my act, I'd kept my eyes down, but it was difficult. Because I couldn't watch their faces, it was almost impossible to determine whether the Meinharts believed our charade. Since their backs were turned as they bent over the sink, washing and drying dishes, I chanced a quick look at Irena. She toyed with her pistol, as if to ensure my obedience, but she was tense, likely thinking what I was thinking. If our ruse was discovered, they'd turn us in.

The couple led us to a small room with two beds on either side of a window, and after bidding us goodnight they closed the door. I waited with bated breath, listening. Their footsteps grew fainter as they retired to a bedroom down the hall, and I relaxed when the door closed.

In her haste to get rid of it, Irena almost threw her gun on the nightstand, then she sighed and sat on the edge of her bed. Meanwhile, I stayed where I was, staring at the second bed. A strange feeling came over me, much like I'd felt upon walking into the home. I still couldn't pinpoint what it was, but again I struggled to draw a proper breath.

"What's wrong?" Irena whispered.

"Nothing." I kept my head down to hide the tears, which had returned. Again. "Stop talking, they'll hear us."

"If they can hear us whispering from down the hall and through two closed doors, they must have damn good hearing."

"We can't take any chances."

To my relief, Irena didn't dispute me. She didn't even bother removing her boots before collapsing on the bed and pulling a blanket across her midsection while I moved to the window. Snowflakes, illuminated by the silvery gleam of moonlight, floated down and settled over the open fields. I wondered how many times I'd crossed snow-covered fields on my way to and from Birkenau. Thousands, probably. Maybe more.

If I'd been at home, I would have leaned over the iron railing on our small balcony or joined my siblings by the window, watching the snowflakes collect on the cobblestones and buildings along Bałuckiego Street while Mama and Tata drank tea and told stories. But I wasn't at home, and, when I thought of trudging through fresh snow again, dread joined the strange feelings that had overtaken me since we'd arrived. As I sat on the hardwood floor near the foot of the second bed, I prayed the snow would stop.

Irena propped herself up on her forearm. "What the hell are you doing?" she whispered.

"Going to sleep."

"On the floor?"

"Where else would Frieda have me?"

"Frieda has retired for the evening," she said, getting up and pulling me to my feet. "And Irena says sleep on the damn bed."

I shrugged her off and returned to the floor, ignoring her muttered curses. The day had taken its toll, and I was too tired and overwhelmed to argue. Besides, I couldn't explain feelings I didn't understand myself. I certainly didn't understand why the wooden floor quelled a bit of the chaos swirling inside me. As I sank into the familiar depths of slumber, I was faintly aware of Irena tossing a blanket over me.

Chapter 32

Pszczyna, 20 January 1945

MY EYES FLUTTERED open when something touched my shoulder. At once, I sat up and looked around to see if my bunkmates were still breathing. But they weren't there. Neither was Hania, and someone hovered over me, a guard preparing to force me from the block—

I blinked to clear the drowsy, confused fog surrounding me. The evacuation. Our escape. The farm.

Frau Meinhart put a finger to her lips and guided me to my feet. She led me into the living room, where faint light streamed through the window. It was almost sunrise. I supposed she'd awakened me for breakfast. I looked back to see if Irena was following us; instead I saw Herr Meinhart disappearing into the bedroom, wielding a rifle.

Gasping, I stopped short while Irena's surprised, furious voice reached my ears.

"What the hell? Get your hands off me!"

She continued spluttering curses while Herr Meinhart's angry voice joined hers, and she stumbled into the hall, half-asleep. Herr Meinhart had secured one arm behind her back, and he prodded her along with his rifle. Her pistol was at his belt. As he shoved

Irena into the living room, both still yelling, I swallowed hard against my dry throat.

It was over. They knew the truth, and now we were at their mercy; they'd kill us or turn us over to the closest SS man they could find.

No, we'd sacrificed too much to let it come to this. Ignoring the possibility of being shot, I struggled against Frau Meinhart's firm hold. I would break free, I would get to Irena, and we would run. For so long, death had been in constant pursuit, nipping at our heels while we eluded its grasp. This was not the day we would succumb.

While I thrashed, Frau Meinhart's grasp tightened. "Shhh, it's all right, dear," she said in soothing Polish.

At this, I stopped fighting. The firm grip must have been meant to protect me, not restrain me, and she was murmuring reassurance. And now, as I assessed the situation, I realized Herr Meinhart's gun was pointed at Irena, only Irena.

"Filthy Nazi," he spat as he forced her to the nearest chair. "Shut up and sit down."

We hadn't been found out—on the contrary, we'd been convincing. But we were wrong about this couple. They may have been Volksdeutsche, but despite appearances they weren't Nazi sympathizers.

"Don't worry, you're safe now," Frau Meinhart said to me, still speaking Polish. Maybe she believed my native tongue would calm me. She consulted her husband and directed a murderous look toward Irena. "What are we going to do with her?"

"Exactly what needs to be done." Herr Meinhart poked Irena with the rifle barrel. "Outside."

"Listen, you stupid bastard, if you touch me with that gun again—"

I opened my mouth to protest, but before I could, Frau Meinhart shushed me and gave my back a comforting pat. "You poor girl. I can't imagine what you've been through, but you're not in danger, do you understand? We won't hurt you, and she'll never hurt you again."

"Hurt her?" Irena asked with a scoff. "You don't know what you're talking about, so take your hands off her before I take them off myself."

I made another attempt to reason with them, but it was no use. My words were lost in the uproar of arguing voices. Amid the shouts, the front door swung open, ushering in a burst of cold air. Everyone fell silent, and a young man stepped across the threshold. He didn't bother to take in the scene before him as he shook snow off his belongings, hung his hat and overcoat on the hat stand, and voiced an absentminded query.

"Why the hell is everyone yelling?"

At the sound of his voice, Irena leaned forward to get a better look. "Franz?"

The young man lifted his head, and he scrutinized her as he crossed the room. "Irena? Is that you?"

Herr Meinhart placed a hand on Franz's chest, stopping him before he got too close. "You know this Nazi bitch?"

"Tell these morons I'm not a Nazi."

"Right. Irena, meet these morons, Hermann and Margrit Meinhart," Franz said, as his amused smile blossomed in full. "My parents."

Her cheeks turned bright red, and she ran a flustered hand through her hair. "Good Lord," she muttered.

"Papa, Mutti, allow me to introduce this Nazi bitch, Irena, who isn't a Nazi bitch at all. She went undercover to help a friend escape from Auschwitz. She contacted the German resistance for help to infiltrate the SS-Helferin, and I was her primary connection while I was spending more time in Berlin helping Elsa—my sister, heavily involved in the German resistance alongside her husband," he supplied for me. "We prepared Irena, then she entered the SS-Helferin training base north of Berlin near a village called Ravensbrück, home to a women's concentration camp of the same name. And this—" Franz paused as he looked at me again. "I assume she's the friend."

Irena nodded. "This is Maria."

The five of us stood in silence, though Franz seemed thoroughly entertained. At last Herr Meinhart lowered his rifle while Frau Meinhart released me. Still, none of us moved.

"Well, this isn't what I expected upon coming home from my night shift at the hospital. And finding my father holding you at gunpoint isn't how I envisioned introducing you to my parents, Irena," Franz said, his wide grin bringing dimples to his cheeks.

"You're certain this is the same girl you met, Franz?" Herr Meinhart asked. "And you're certain she's not a Nazi?"

"Completely."

"You didn't see what we saw last night," Frau Meinhart said. "I don't trust her."

Franz sighed. "For God's sake, Mutti, if she'd behaved in a way that made you trust her, she wouldn't have been a very convincing Nazi, would she?"

Frau Meinhart seemed unsettled by this logic. She didn't protest, but she didn't look convinced, either, and neither did her husband. Even though his gun was lowered, he hadn't relaxed his arm, and he hadn't returned Irena's pistol.

I stepped forward. "I understand how this looks, but it's true. No one has sacrificed more for me than Irena has."

Silence followed. Herr and Frau Meinhart exchanged glances. At last he allowed Irena to stand, though he stayed between her and Franz. He handed her the pistol, and she reluctantly accepted it.

With a satisfied nod, Franz addressed Irena. "How did you get here?"

When she acknowledged him, an unspoken accusation resided within her steely gaze—but, if I knew Irena, it wouldn't remain unspoken for long. "You're a damn Volksdeutsch? All three of you are registered, aren't you?"

He clenched his jaw while a flicker of guilt and disgust crossed his face. "Our choices were to acknowledge our German ethnicity or be branded traitors and persecuted."

"And you'd rather be branded traitors by the Polish untermenschen instead of the Nazis."

"If that's how I felt, would I have spent most of the war helping the German and Polish resistance organizations? Neither I nor my parents wanted to sign the Deutsche Volksliste, but church and resistance leaders said to do it for our safety."

"Well, thank God you could hide behind your heritage," Irena said with a scathing laugh. "Others weren't so damn fortunate."

A thick silence followed her words. I sensed all eyes on me. None lingered, but I felt like I was in the middle of a selection. Their scrutiny was suffocating, and I could hear the SS doctors ordering me to turn, lift my arms, open my mouth—

"Maria, we're leaving."

The gruff voices faded, the clothes returned to my body, a bit of anxiety vanished. I'd been spared. This time.

Irena marched past Franz without looking at him, but she didn't wait for me to follow before slamming the door behind her.

* * *

When ten minutes had passed and Irena hadn't returned, I persuaded Franz to let me talk to her before he did. Outside, the early morning sun lent its soft golden hue to the fresh snow that covered the house, barn, fields, and trees. The pastoral scene should have filled me with tranquility, but, as I crossed toward the wood pile where Irena was sitting, I was seized by a sudden unease. No one was ordering me to walk faster or shoving me toward my labor assignment, and I wasn't sure what to make of the sensation.

I sat next to Irena, who didn't acknowledge me. "Are we going to sit here until we freeze to death, or are we going to talk about your lovers' quarrel?"

"There's nothing to talk about, and it was *not* a lovers' quarrel," she said, glaring. "I knew you'd be obnoxious, which is exactly why I didn't tell you about him."

"A wise decision, lovesick idiot."

Muttering a stream of expletives, Irena got up to walk away, but I grabbed her arm to prevent her departure. Falling quiet, though visibly annoyed, she sat while I cast jokes aside.

"I'm finished, I promise. Didn't you know Franz was German?"

"Of course, but aside from that, I only knew his first name, because it wasn't safe to share personal information. I assumed he was a German who didn't support the Nazis. Instead, he's an ethnic German who grew up in Poland and used his ethnicity to save his own ass." She dug a hole in the snow with her booted foot, sighing. "I didn't think he was a coward, that's all. Or a traitor."

"So are you, Frau Aufseherin."

Irena stopped digging and stiffened. She waited, probably expecting me to retract my statement; instead I gestured to her uniform.

"You did this to help me, but you swore loyalty to the Third Reich and pretended to be a guard, didn't you? If Franz is a traitor for being a Volksdeutsch who doesn't actually support the Nazis, what does that make you?"

She opened her mouth, but no sound came out, so I made my final play.

"You even hit me."

At that, Irena sprang to her feet. "If I hadn't, we would've been killed, you know that—"

"Checkmate."

She fell silent while her fury dissipated. "Dammit, Maria, you're such an idiot," she whispered, sinking back onto the log pile.

"Would you have listened to me otherwise?" I asked with a small smile, but I gave her hand an apologetic squeeze. "Now, are you going to make Franz get frostbite, too, or can we go back inside?"

We trudged to the farmhouse, where Frau Meinhart was scrambling eggs for breakfast while Herr Meinhart stoked the fire. Franz sat in the living room, then stood and waited for Irena. When she reached him, they didn't speak.

"I guess I understand why you're a damn Volksdeutsch," Irena muttered at last.

He smirked. "That was the worst apology I've ever heard, but I'll accept it."

"Good Lord, don't make me take it back," she replied with a huff, but as she stepped away I saw the smile she was attempting to hide.

I drew closer to the fire, enjoying the heat prickling my skin. I'd forgotten what a real fire felt like, as opposed to the pathetic heaters that warmed our blocks. As I studied the dancing flames, I inhaled the smoky air, smelling of wood chips, but when I closed my eyes I choked on the familiar stench of singed hair and burning flesh—

"Maria, are you listening?"

Startled, I opened my eyes, and the reek went away. It took me a moment to comprehend where I was, though I couldn't fathom why. Maybe because the memory hadn't felt like a memory at all. The realization was as chilling and brutal as a winter night in Birkenau.

When I turned to face Irena and Franz, they looked as if they were wondering what had been on my mind. Thank goodness they didn't ask.

"I'm going back to the hospital to get a few things," Franz continued. "You're not the first resistance member or escaped inmate my contacts have directed here, though you *are* the first to stumble upon us by chance." He flashed a little smile. "Some of my colleagues at the hospital can be trusted, but it's best we keep you hidden."

I nodded, combatting an unsteady breath. First I was an inmate, now a fugitive.

After putting his hat and overcoat back on, Franz crossed toward Irena, caught her waist, and pulled her into a kiss—one she returned with the same enthusiasm. "Well done," he murmured, glancing at me before releasing her.

As the door closed behind him, she met my small smile. This time she returned it.

Frau Meinhart joined us. "Elsa's old clothes are in the room where you stayed last night, so you can change while you wait for Franz. You'll find a suitable selection."

Not selection, anything but selection.

Irena was already unbuttoning her jacket, seeming eager to shed her uniform and never touch it again. I followed her to the bedroom. From a crude little wooden dresser, she picked a skirt and blouse for herself and tossed a few options onto the bed for me. I surveyed the dresses, blouses, skirts, and trousers, knowing none would fit me, feeling as if I were sifting through organized goods. Before making my choice, I pulled Irena's crucifix from under my uniform and unfastened the chain, then I touched her shoulder to get her attention. When she faced me, I placed the necklace in her palm. Her breath caught in her throat. She stared at it in disbelief and traced a gentle finger over the crucifix before fastening it around her neck.

We continued changing, and I removed my striped uniform.

Behind me, Irena gasped.

There was a full-length mirror in this room, something I'd been too exhausted to notice last night. Now I studied the reflection I found. A slight form, every bone exposed, covered in various bruises, scars, cuts, and insect bites. Blue-gray skin; small, deflated circles where breasts should have been. A shaved head that made the ears stand out. A sharp jaw, small nose, concave cheeks, jutting cheekbones, and thin lips within a gaunt, sallow face absorbed by sunken eyes. Eyes that were haunted and vacant, but also bright, almost wild and desperate, clinging to the shreds of life that remained. And on the left arm, an arm that looked as fragile as a bird's wing, were five round scars and a tattooed number, 16671.

I hadn't seen my reflection since I was fourteen, but the number proved that this figure looking back at me was me. Maybe I should have felt something, but I felt nothing. This figure was no different from every other figure I'd seen during the past few years.

But it wasn't my emaciated form that had made Irena gasp. Her horror was concentrated upon my back, so I turned and craned my neck, getting a first look at them myself.

My flogging scars. Some were pinker than others, some long, some short, some thick and raised, others thin and less protruding. The gruesome web covered me from shoulders to lower back. The scars were hideous, but, at the sight, I smiled. *Father Kolbe.*

My body told the story of my life during the past few years. I was feeble and broken, a shell of a human, but when I looked at these scars I saw life. My life. The life I'd almost given up.

I folded my striped uniform and placed it on the bed. Then I donned a simple dress, which hung on my body like a sheet.

Irena stepped closer, so I allowed her to take my wrist. She rotated my forearm upward and brushed her thumb over my prisoner number. When she spoke, her voice was hardly audible.

"We did it, Maria. You're alive, you're safe, and you're free."

Alive. Safe. Free. Simple words, words that had once seemed nothing but a distant memory. Now that they'd become my reality again, I expected to feel joy or relief, but I didn't feel any different. Just tired and hungry, as usual.

Maybe when I was truly free, those words would evoke some sort of feeling, but I wasn't truly free yet. I was away from Auschwitz, but I'd made vows while I was there. To live, fight, and survive; to reunite Hania with her children, find Karl Fritzsch, and get justice for my family. Until I'd done those things, my business was unfinished. The game wasn't over.

Someday I'd be free, and someday that word would bring me the proper peace and comfort it was supposed to bring. But not today.

* * *

While we waited for Franz, I settled in bed at Irena's insistence. She stayed in the room with me—perhaps afraid I would return to the floor if she left—and I nestled into the pillows. I hadn't had a pillow in almost four years.

When Franz returned, he announced that he had brought a fellow resistance member and hospital employee who often helped his family care for those taking refuge with them. And when his companion entered the room, my heart thudded in a way I had almost forgotten possible. The new arrival came to a sudden stop, as he had on that day before dropping his bicycle alongside the road and falling into step with me. A stupid boy drawn to an imprisoned girl, he was now a young man and resistance member; I in many ways was that same girl, shackled to guilt and grief yet finding in him an unexpected refuge.

I was acutely aware of the stark contrasts in our appearance. Me, starved, bruised, and barely alive, and him, a tall, broad young man whose deep blue eyes sparkled with vivacity. But, if he was as distracted by our differences as I was, he didn't show it. He looked at me as he always had—as if I was more than a number.

I gave him a small smile. "It's good to see you, Maciek."

After exchanging introductions and pleasantries, Irena left to fetch me a glass of water and Franz went to wash his hands before tending to me. The door had hardly closed behind them before Mateusz sat on the edge of my bed, regarding me with such rapt attention it was almost daunting.

"I was sworn to secrecy, otherwise I would have told you my additional reasons for moving to Pszczyna," he began. "Franz asked me to work with him in caring for resistance members and escaped inmates sheltering with his parents. I couldn't pass up the opportunity, and I thought he might help me get you out. When I gave him your name and prisoner number, he informed me that he was already working with a young woman from Warsaw who planned to smuggle the same prisoner out of the camp."

My next breath was suddenly shaky, almost smelling of sweat and straw from our days in the weaving shop. He had left me only to try to liberate me.

"You helped me survive," I said at last, my voice soft. "And I don't mean by providing information or bread."

His eyes met mine, two azure pools beneath dark lashes, ones I had spent many nights fearing I would never see again.

After a moment he passed a hand across the stubble on his chin. "Speaking of information, since I last wrote, I discovered more news about Fritzsch's arrest. During the investigation, a former Auschwitz guard testified to various instances of corruption he'd witnessed. I don't know details, but his testimony and a murder charge were the reasons Fritzsch was transferred to the front lines."

A former guard who had witnessed Fritzsch's wickedness and viewed it as such. I knew exactly who that was. Oskar, the middle-aged officer who told me about my family. He'd seen Fritzsch whipping me almost to death without following protocol. He'd seen Fritzsch forcing me to witness a private execution in Block 11 when prisoners were to witness only public hangings. He'd seen what Fritzsch did to my family. Though he had delivered his report to Höss after Fritzsch's transfer, that report must have led to Oskar being called to testify at the trial, then to a verdict sentencing Fritzsch to the front.

Mateusz shifted, and the bed creaked. Even though I'd told him I was hunting Fritzsch because I was concerned he'd return to Auschwitz, I detected an uncertainty that was dangerously close to suspicion. Why had I ever thought he was a stupid boy? I couldn't let him start asking questions, so I had to assuage his fears. He needed to believe I wasn't connected to the corruption case. I was just a girl concerned about a cruel man. I took his hand.

"When you told me Fritzsch was under a corruption investigation, it didn't surprise me. I'd seen him treat inmates poorly, even by SS standards. That's why he scared me."

Mateusz placed his free hand over mine. "You don't have to worry about him anymore."

"It's not that simple," I murmured. "The war isn't over yet."

"Fritzsch is still on the front lines far from here. He can't get to you."

There it was, the information I'd been hoping for. Fritzsch was still alive somewhere on the front lines. And now that I was free, I could move forward with my plans.

"If I write a letter, could your connections take it to Fritzsch?" I asked, before releasing Mateusz and hugging a pillow to my chest. "I need to hear directly from him that he's on the front lines. I know it's foolish, and I don't expect a response, but I'd feel better if I tried."

The more I lied to Mateusz about my intentions with Fritzsch, the more surprised I was when the lies didn't concern me. I didn't have any other choice. If I told the truth, I'd put Mateusz in jeopardy and risk losing his help; I'd lose my chance at justice for my family, Father Kolbe, and myself. And until I got justice, I wouldn't go home. I couldn't.

He gave me a small, reassuring smile. "It's not foolish, Maria. One of the men in Fritzsch's battalion has been working both sides and supplying a friend of mine with information. I'll bring you paper, a pen, and an envelope for the letter, and once you've written it, they can help us get it to Fritzsch. Whatever it takes to help you find peace."

Mateusz believed me. He always believed me.

Chapter 33

Pszczyna, 19 April 1945

A FEW SCATTERED WHITE clouds chased one another across the pale blue sky as the sun warmed my skin and a cool breeze tugged at my skirt. Grass stretched across the field, emerging after winter like the deep blond hair emerging on my head. I stretched out on the soft blanket and closed my eyes with a contented sigh.

Three months. I'd spent three months without forced labor, beatings, disease, and the constant threat of death, and it still didn't feel real. Every morning I expected to wake up in Auschwitz. Every night sleep took me there.

When laughter reached my ears, I opened my eyes and rolled over toward the sound. Farther into the field, Irena held a line while Franz ran with a kite, its tail streaming in the wind. As the wind picked up, he released it, and the kite plummeted to the ground. Cursing, Franz tried again—they'd been at this for at least twenty minutes—but Irena was laughing too much to be of help, so he wrapped the line around her instead. Her laughter transformed into protests; even amid her complaints, she pulled him close and welcomed his lips against hers. They'd kissed in front of me many times, but this time I saw Protz's arms around her, Irena's reluctant lips against his, she squirming to escape his touch—

I blinked and dismissed the image. Disgusting.

Reminders of Auschwitz came when I least expected them. The thud of Herr Meinhart's boots against the wooden floor, the smell of burning skin when Frau Meinhart suffered a minor cooking injury last week. Franz's strong, heavy hand on my shoulder this morning, trying to get my attention, feeling too similar to the men whose hands found my shoulder before their fists found my face. A little while ago, Irena serving our picnic lunch, reminding me of measuring portions of organized food.

I didn't know why the memories came. When they did, it took time for me to realize that was all they were. Memories.

I plucked a few blades of grass, broke them into various lengths, and set them up like chess pieces. When a breeze blew them away, I abandoned my efforts. On my path to recovery, I'd had books, friends, and games, but not chess. Even if I'd had pieces, Irena didn't know how to play, and neither did Mateusz, Franz, or his parents. I could have taught them, and I could have made pieces like Father Kolbe did, but somehow it didn't feel right. That part of me was missing, and I didn't know when I'd find it again.

Or Hania. Her absence was another missing piece, one I needed desperately. When would I find her again? She was alive; she *had* to be alive. If I had left her to die as I had left my family—

"You know, I never thought basket weaving would be a skill I'd acquire."

I turned to acknowledge Mateusz beside me. He'd spent many afternoons on the farm. Sometimes we took walks or picnicked with Irena and Franz, and sometimes we just talked. We'd gone from exchanging simple letters and having whispered conversations in the basket-weaving workshop to spending entire days together.

When Mateusz held up the tiny, crude basket he'd made from grass and straw, I wrinkled my nose. "After all the baskets we made, why would you ever want to do it again?"

He shrugged. "It wasn't so bad."

"Not when your employment was voluntary."

The words came out far more harshly than I imagined they would. Whenever the memories were on the cusp of overwhelming me, somehow I lost all control.

I gathered the blanket into shaking hands and closed my eyes. Memories, just memories. The debilitating migraine would follow if I couldn't get ahold of myself. I had to recover before I succumbed, before my friends discovered how the memories crippled me, because if they did, they'd start asking questions . . .

I managed to push the memories down, and the trembles subsided. With a sigh, I opened my eyes and plucked another blade of grass. "I'm sorry, Maciek, that wasn't fair."

"War isn't fair." He examined his work, then threw it with as much force as he could muster. The tiny basket sailed a few meters across the open field until it disappeared in the tall grass. Mateusz looked as if he wanted to say more, but he noticed Irena and Franz approaching, so he refrained.

"You owe me a new line, Irena," Franz said. He held up the broken string and looked to us for support.

"It's your own fault, you idiot," Irena replied with a grin. She tucked a loose strand of hair behind her ear—its natural brown color, not dyed blond—and sat beside me.

"As a witness to the scene, I agree with Irena."

Franz shook his head. "I knew I'd get no sympathy from you, Maria."

"Let me see," Mateusz said. When Franz passed the broken kite to him, he ran his nimble fingers over it. "It's an easy fix. Do you have more line?"

"In the barn," Franz replied. "Help yourself. I've got business in town."

"The hospital, Dr. Meinhart?" Irena asked while Mateusz took the kite and made his way toward the barn.

"Always," he said with a wry smile.

"Any news on Hania or Izaak?" I asked.

Franz released a slow, sympathetic breath. "You know I looked all over the camp for them."

While Franz had cared for me on Irena's and my first day here, I had implored him to go to Auschwitz to find Hania and Izaak—an impossible task at first, as a few SS personnel had remained to guard the camp. A week later, when the Red Army arrived, he had joined the Polish Red Cross and other medics to tend to the inmates. Although he hadn't found my friends, I'd hoped some of the other medical volunteers might have discovered something by now and passed word to him.

When he didn't supply further information, I sighed. Irena and I never should have abandoned them.

"They didn't disappear," he said. "I'm sure someone found them and took them to another hospital. I promised you I'd locate them, and I will." Franz picked up his fedora from where he'd tossed it on the blanket, placed it on his head, and kissed Irena's cheek before crossing the field toward the barn, where he'd parked his car. After the engine rumbled to life, he drove down the dirt road and disappeared along the main street.

Irena watched him go, a thoughtful expression on her face, until she noticed the small smile playing around my lips. "Why are you looking at me like that?"

"Because I'm happy for you."

"Good Lord, don't start." She plucked a tall blade of grass and fiddled with it before tossing it aside. "He's German."

"I thought you'd gotten over the fact that he's a Volksdeutsch."

"It's more than that. Some Volksdeutsche barely have a drop of German blood, but Franz is only a second-generation Pole, and even though his parents grew up here, they're both full-blooded Germans. He's *German*."

"Your point?"

"You know my point!" she exclaimed, running a hand through her hair while I sat up. "What would Mama do if I brought him home?"

"Your mother isn't judgmental, and Franz isn't a Nazi."

"It's not that simple. People see an unmarried Polish mother, and they assume she's either a victim of war or a treacherous slut who collaborated with the soldiers, then they judge me and hate my child. I see it in their eyes every day, and if I married a Volksdeutsch—" She broke off with a huff, shaking her head in vehement refusal before dropping her voice. "I'll be damned if I make it worse."

I stayed quiet while Irena got up and paced back and forth in agitated silence. I'd had a feeling this decision had been plaguing her for the past few weeks, but she'd done well keeping it from everyone—especially Franz.

At last she stopped and faced the small farmhouse. "I won't put Franz in that position, either. After we leave, he'll find a nice girl, and Helena and I are fine on our own."

When she looked at me, I nodded. "All right."

She waited, but I didn't elaborate. "That's all you're going to say?" she asked.

"What am I supposed to say? It's your life. You decide what's best for you and Helena."

I sliced a piece of *gołka* and chewed it slowly, savoring the cheese's touch of saltiness while silence lingered. Irena probably knew what I was doing, but I won every time we engaged in this particular game, so I didn't relent. Sure enough, she heaved a sigh.

"Dammit, Maria, you're so annoying."

Although I grinned and she couldn't resist a small smile, a glimmer of concern remained in her eyes. Unfounded as some of her fears may have been, only time could eliminate them.

After a moment, I spoke in a soft voice. "You can leave whenever you want, Irena."

"How many times are you going to tell me that?" she replied as she sat down again.

"I know how much you miss them and that you didn't expect to be away this long."

"We talk on the telephone, and Mama and Helena are back in Warsaw now that it's been liberated. You're nearly well enough to leave. We'll use the papers Franz got us and keep you as covered up as possible, and he'll accompany us to make sure we arrive safely. We'll be home soon."

Silence fell, comfortable and familiar. Birds chirped in the distance and wind whistled past my ears. The tranquil farm had become our refuge, far different from the hustle of Warsaw or the wickedness of Auschwitz. The war was drawing to an end, but it wasn't over yet, so the farm was a welcome shelter from the horrors beyond it. Still, agitation consumed me.

I'd given my letter to Mateusz a day after asking him for writing supplies, and I was still waiting for answers. The wait was almost more maddening than my wait for liberation had been.

"Franz doesn't know about Helena," Irena said after we'd been quiet for a while. "I've shared very little of my personal life with him." She poked her finger into a small hole in the blanket. When she spoke again, her voice was quiet. "Mama doesn't know, either."

"I hope she does, considering Helena is her granddaughter and she's caring for her," I replied with a small smile, but, when Irena lifted her head, the look in her eyes chased away my lingering humor. "You didn't tell her how the pregnancy happened?"

She winced, then attempted to hide it behind a wry half smile. "Lovesick idiot, remember? I never thought I'd use that damn story, but it worked. When I couldn't hide the pregnancy any longer, I told Mama I'd been seeing a young man who worked for the resistance, but he'd been caught and executed, leaving me with his child. Since Tata's death, my dear mother has tried to make me stop swearing, because girls who swear are whores, right?"

"Don't, Irena, that's not fair. Not to your mother, and certainly not to you."

Despite the sharpness in my tone, Irena raised her shoulders in a dismissive shrug. "She was upset, of course, but I assured her I'd learned from my mistakes, and she never held my actions against the baby. Since Helena's birth, everything has been fine between us. Mama loves her."

"And she loves you. Why do you want her to believe a lie?"

"Good Lord, it's not important." The forced indifference in Irena's voice wasn't convincing. "The Nazis killed her husband, and she doesn't need to know what they did to her daughter, too. Let me worry about my mother, Maria, and you worry about yours." It took her only a moment to realize her mistake. "Shit, I didn't—"

I held up a hand to stop her, a hand that no longer displayed every bone. I was still thin, though. My body seemed to have forgotten how to retain weight. Irena fell into pensive silence while she toyed with her necklace, though I caught her eyes drifting to my forearm.

We hadn't spoken of my time in the camp. Not my arrest, not how I'd earned the five round scars she looked at when she thought I wasn't paying attention, not the story behind my flogging, certainly not Fritzsch. She was concerned that I was being too quiet—I'd overheard her telling Franz, who assured her I'd be fine—but I was quiet because I had a lot on my mind. Otherwise, our friendship had returned to normal.

I reclined, slipped my hand into my front pocket, and passed my fingers over the rosary beads. Sometimes I forgot I wasn't wearing my blue-and-gray-striped uniform. Since we'd come to the farm, we'd purchased a few items from town, including new clothes. If any of my garments didn't come equipped with pockets, I sewed them on.

Brushing flecks of grass off my skirt, I stood, and we cleaned up the remnants of our picnic. I was folding the blanket when I heard Franz's car parking near the barn, then a shout floated across the field and reached my ears.

"Are you going to say hello to me or not, shikse?"

At once, I dropped the blanket. I'd have known that voice anywhere, but I had to see its owner to believe it. Sure enough, there she was, standing next to Franz and grinning, and I sprinted across the field and didn't stop until I'd caught her in my arms.

"Careful, you'll knock us both over," Hania said, laughing as she returned the fierce embrace. "Let me look at you."

She took my face in her hands, and I held on to her wrists, reassuring myself that she was real. Releasing her felt like it would wake me from a better dream than any I'd had in a long time. But she was here, truly here, as real as I was. Her familiar dark eyes sparkled with vibrance, and her thick, dark hair was short, but growing back even faster than mine. She wore a simple dress, and it hugged a frame that was reshaping into delicate curves.

After a moment, Hania stroked her thumbs across my cheeks, as if reassuring herself that I was real, too, before kissing them. "You're more beautiful than ever, Maria."

"So are you, Bubbe," I whispered. "Franz, you knew Hania was alive all this time?"

"I spent my whole first day in the camp looking for her, and when I found her, I said shikse sent love to Bubbe, like you told me to. That's all it took to convince her to trust me."

"Why didn't you tell me?"

"That's my fault," Hania said before he could reply. "Izaak cared for me as well as he could, but when Franz found me, I still had a terrible case of typhus. I told him not to tell you in case I died. I recovered but caught pneumonia a few days later. By the time I was finally regaining my health, I decided to wait until I was well enough to surprise you. Franz has been taking care of me in the Pszczyna hospital."

I flashed a grateful smile at him, then asked the next question on my mind, praying I didn't know the answer. "Where is Izaak?"

She pressed her lips together before replying. "As soon as he'd recuperated, he and some Sonderkommando workers left together. I coaxed him into telling me where they were going, and all he said was looking for war criminals." She looked past me for a moment and took a deep breath. "I don't want to know what that means. He promised to meet me in Warsaw by the end of the summer."

Mateusz emerged from the barn, likely alerted by the commotion. "You were in almost every letter Maria sent me, Hania," he said, grinning. "I'm—"

"No need for introductions. I've heard so much about you, Mateusz," she replied, and his smile widened. When he turned to give Franz the kite he'd repaired, she studied him before leaning closer to me and speaking in a sly whisper. "*Mazel tov.*"

I gave her a light, discreet shove and pretended I didn't hear her chuckles. Still, at the sound, one that had seen me through the darkest moments during the past four years, my throat tightened. At last one of my missing pieces had returned. One I never should have lost in the first place. When I caught her hands in mine, she sobered.

"Not once did you leave my side," I managed, swallowing hard. "But I left yours."

Hania shook her head. "You and Irena gave me my brother, perhaps saved both our lives. My boys won't have their father, cousins, aunt, or grandparents, but they will have their mother and uncle. For that, I can't express my gratitude. And now the three of us are together again, aren't we?" she added as Irena joined us and pulled her into an embrace. When they released each other, Hania gave her a small smile. "Irena," she said, emphasizing her name as her eyes swept over the darker hair and civilian clothing that had replaced Frieda's blond locks and SS uniform.

"Hania," she replied with the same emphasis, grinning before addressing Franz. "You've been caring for her for weeks?"

"A doctor never breaches his patient's trust."

"I already have papers, too, thanks to him." Hania barely contained her delight as she turned to me. "He said you wrote to your friends about my sons. It's all right if we go home tomorrow to see what they've found, isn't it?"

Tomorrow. I'd promised myself I wouldn't return to Warsaw until I'd found Fritzsch, but I'd made a promise to Hania, too. It would have been cruel to make her wait any longer, but I wasn't ready. Not until I'd heard from Mateusz's connections.

"Of course. It's time we went home," Irena said before I could reply. She led the way toward the farmhouse without waiting for a reaction.

Franz watched her go, then started after her, saying something about telling his parents they'd have another guest for the evening.

As we caught up to Irena, I took a deep, calming breath. Mateusz would contact me as soon as he heard from his connections. We'd go to Warsaw tomorrow and see what Mother Matylda and Mrs. Sienkiewicz had discovered about Hania's children, then I'd refocus on Fritzsch. The order of my plan was changing, that was all.

I inserted myself between Irena and Hania and wrapped my arms around their waists. The two friends I loved most in the world, both with me, alive and well. It had been a long time since I'd had this feeling, a feeling I might have described as akin to true, unbridled happiness.

As I released them to follow everyone inside, a familiar grasp caught my hand and pulled me to a stop. I turned to face Mateusz, expecting news of Fritzsch until his sober expression told me otherwise.

"There's no sense in me trying to come up with another way to tell you this," he said with a half smile once the door closed behind our friends. "I'll be attending an American university in the fall. In the United States, to be exact. My uncle lives in New York, so I'm staying with him."

America. I blinked, letting the idea roll around inside my head, before voicing the first thing I could think to say. "You don't speak English."

He chuckled. "I've started learning. I leave next month."

Even though I smiled and told him how happy I was for him, I couldn't help feeling as I had when he'd moved to Pszczyna. Once again, I was losing my friend and my aide in my mission against

Fritzsch. Staying in touch from Warsaw would have been challenging enough, but America added a new level of complication. My plan couldn't be ruined now. Not when I was so close.

I often wondered what might have been if we'd met under different circumstances. These past few months had given me glimpses of it. Long walks across the fields, his hand in mine; baking *pączki* together and filling the balls of sweet fried dough with strawberry jam; sitting in the tall grass and watching the sunset, serenaded by chirping crickets, his arm around my waist, my head on his shoulder. Each moment, I almost felt like one of those girls I once passed on my walk to and from Birkenau. The kind of girl I might have been. I had believed that our time together would continue, perhaps would take us to Warsaw for breakfast at the Hotel Bristol café, followed by a walk down the *Krakowskie Przedmieście* and past Saint John's Archcathedral. Now the moments were coming to an end, taken by a play I hadn't foreseen.

I wasn't ready to lose either one—our future moments or my plans.

"One more thing," Mateusz said, and he handed me an envelope. "A response to the last letter you wrote me."

As quickly as my concerns flared, they receded when he placed the envelope in my palm. Although we'd kept exchanging letters during the past few months, I didn't have to open this one to know that it wasn't from Mateusz.

It was from him. I felt it in every fiber of my being.

"I had a feeling you wouldn't fall for it," Mateusz said, grinning. "My contact brought it to me today, and since you're leaving tomorrow, the timing couldn't have been better. But even if I'd had to do so from America, I would have made sure you received that letter."

I ran my fingers over the unbroken seal. "My thanks isn't enough, Maciek."

"Open it. Your peace of mind is waiting inside that envelope."

"Later." I took his hand and gave it an appreciative squeeze, erasing the bemused furrow in his brow. "Will you stay for dinner?"

"I can't. I have the night shift at the hospital."

"Then you'll come by tomorrow morning before we leave for Warsaw, won't you?"

His gaze softened. "As soon as my shift is over."

I nodded and wrapped my arms around him, holding on to the strength of his embrace, the reassuring beat of his heart, his small sigh as he tightened his grasp. I clung to him, all of him. To one of our last moments.

When we released each other, Mateusz returned to his bicycle and rode away toward town. I watched him go, though it required significant effort to wait until he was out of sight. The envelope burned in my hand like the sting of the whip against my flesh.

Once I was certain he'd gone, I examined the envelope. It had no markings, meaning the letter had retraced its predecessor's steps along the resistance line until reaching me. I opened it, and golden light from the late afternoon sun fell across a single sheet of folded paper.

Heil Hitler!

I received your letter, in which you mentioned having information regarding my transfer. I've been eager to address that matter with you, and as your letter states, you have an additional concern which would be better revealed in person. After considering your request to have

a discussion to resolve both, I've decided I can make use of you one last time. The Führer's birthday will be the perfect day for a meeting, don't you agree?
You'll know where to find me, Prisoner 16671.

Hauptsturmführer Karl Fritzsch
SS-Totenkopfverbände
Lagerführer of Auschwitz

Thank God for Mateusz. Despite being transferred to the front lines, Fritzsch hadn't fallen in battle. The Führer's birthday was tomorrow, and I knew where he wanted to meet.

My plan was unfolding exactly as I'd hoped, after all.

The door opened, and I folded the paper as Franz stepped out. "Are you coming inside?" he asked.

"Yes, I was reading a letter from Mateusz." I indicated the envelope. "Franz, would you do me a favor?"

He nodded, and I took a deep breath, not because I was hesitant, but because this moment had felt beyond my reach, and now it was here. As I clutched the letter, a surge of energy pulsed through me, more powerful than anything I'd felt in so long. I'd waited for this meeting since I was fourteen. At last I would atone for what I had brought upon my family, even if I never granted myself complete forgiveness. Even if it meant returning to that place my mind had never permitted me to escape.

"Tomorrow, I need you to take me to Auschwitz."

Chapter 34

Auschwitz, 20 April 1945

"MARIA, ARE YOU sure about this?" Franz asked for what must have been the hundredth time.

We were driving along the same roads I'd walked, roads once covered in snow, blood, and mud and littered with dead bodies. The snow had long since melted and the bodies had long since been removed, but, as I watched the roadside pass by, they were all I saw.

It wasn't yet dawn. At my insistence, Franz and I had left to drive to Auschwitz before anyone else awoke. We were almost there.

"Are you sure you want to go back? And are you certain you want to be alone? I don't mind staying."

"I told you, since we're leaving for Warsaw today, I want to see it once more to give myself closure. It'll be difficult to visit, so I didn't want Hania and Irena to feel obligated to come. That's why I didn't tell them."

Despite his questions, it had been easy to convince Franz to drive me. He'd believed my reason, even though it baffled him, and he'd thought it was considerate of me to look out for Hania and Irena. Then again, he knew nothing of Fritzsch and little of my time in captivity, so of course he didn't suspect anything.

Poor Franz. Irena would be furious when she found out, and I could almost hear the Yiddish curses Hania would spit at him. I would have bribed a neighboring farmer to take me if I hadn't needed Franz to know where I was. Perhaps Irena and Hania would have guessed once they noticed my absence, but I needed to be certain they knew. I needed them to come, just not right away. Not until I was ready for them.

I didn't expect them to understand. How could they? This was between me and Fritzsch. I didn't want them endangered, and I wouldn't allow them to stop me. This was something I had to do—to hear the truth at last, to get justice for my family, to hold Fritzsch responsible, to put an end to the nightmare I had lived for the past four years. Facing him alone didn't concern me. I had a long history of recklessness.

"I'll be fine," I added to silence Franz's questions.

That part wasn't a complete lie. Before we'd left, I'd organized Irena's pistol.

Chapter 35

Auschwitz, 20 April 1945

WHEN MY FINGER touches the trigger, Fritzsch pushes his shoulders back, as though inviting the bullet into his chest. One bullet, and I won't have to battle through a trial or attempt to speak of what took place here. I'll bury the memories, never to unearth them again, and this will be over. I just want it to be over.

But a bullet isn't part of my strategy.

Killing Fritzsch is not my plan; that's never been my plan. He deserves to spend the rest of his life paying for what he's done. By now, Franz must have returned to the farm, where Irena and Hania will have demanded to know where he'd taken me. They'll think something is amiss, and they'll come for me. Surely I've kept Fritzsch occupied long enough. My friends are on their way, I know they are. Once they arrive, we'll take Fritzsch to one of Franz's connections, who holds the power to formally arrest him. He'll confess to each atrocity and face the consequences.

Or I could shoot him.

I grip the pistol tighter so I can focus on the ache rather than the overwhelming desire to move toward the trigger again. A confession is enough to win a trial. My testimony won't be necessary.

I've spent the entirety of my imprisonment anticipating this game, and I will control the board. I can't lose now.

"Do it."

The croon almost makes me reconsider, but I resist the urge. A few more minutes. I held his interest in this camp for almost eight months. I can do so again for a few more minutes. My friends will be here before he tires of me, I'm sure of it.

"Put your gun down and finish the game." The quiver in my voice is worse than ever before, making my words sound more like a plea than a demand, but I don't break eye contact.

Fritzsch doesn't react. The familiar hunger lights his eyes while he watches me, and I use both hands to steady the gun. My aim remains level with his chest as I combat unsteady breaths, but with some effort I take my finger off the trigger.

A few more minutes.

His chuckle breaks the eerie silence. "What did you expect upon coming here, Prisoner 16671? All this time, you've planned to escort me into custody and make me confess during a trial? That would require me to comply with your wishes, but you've forgotten one very important thing, you useless little Polack bitch." He steps closer and smiles. "I don't follow orders."

He pulls the gun from its holster before I even blink.

The pain in my head is blinding, and I hear a scream that must be my own as I squeeze my finger against the trigger and one shot follows another, then I'm splattered in warm blood.

Smoke and blood, such familiar stenches, surround and suffocate me, and I wait for the pain to come, but I feel nothing. The blood isn't mine. I'm not wounded, and Fritzsch, like so many who stood upon this cursed ground, is on his back in a pool of his own blood, dead.

No, no, no, it can't end like this.

Runnels of blood and rainwater cover the chessboard, and the pieces are painted with tiny crimson droplets. With a sweep of my arm, it crashes to the ground, where the board breaks with a sharp crack and the pieces scatter.

He was supposed to stand trial, the world was supposed to know the truth, he was supposed to rot in prison, he wasn't supposed to die—

"Maria—oh God, what the hell have you done?"

"Put the gun down, Maria, please!"

Voices, familiar ones, though I hardly hear them. He was supposed to stand trial. Instead I pulled my trigger.

"Dammit, Maria, put down the fucking gun!"

"Listen to us, shikse. Please put it down."

I turn away from Fritzsch's body to face the voices, which belong to Irena and Hania. They came. But now it's too late.

The moment I whirl toward them, they tense, but I'm not sure why, and I'm not sure why they've stopped so far from me. Maybe they don't understand that Fritzsch is dead. He can't hurt them, and he can't be brought to justice. Hania and Irena move closer, still talking, and even though I'm not paying attention I think they're trying to soothe me. Maybe it's because I can't stop screaming.

"He was supposed to stand trial, he wasn't supposed to die—"

"The gun, Maria," Irena says fiercely, bringing my cries to a jarring halt.

The pistol. I forgot I was holding it.

I turn back to Fritzsch's body. My bullet tore through his lower abdomen and bloodied his perfect uniform. Somehow his had missed me. Fritzsch's pistol lies on the ground, next to his hand, and blood spills from the circle of mangled flesh at his temple, where a second bullet had struck. The death blow.

No, that can't be right. I pulled my trigger once, but a bullet to the stomach wouldn't have killed him so quickly.

And I heard two shots.

I fired once. I know I fired once, and so did he. The head wound killed him, the wound I couldn't have inflicted, not from my angle. And in all the time I've known him, Fritzsch's bullets always found their intended mark.

He hadn't fired at me at all. The head wound was self-inflicted.

"You stupid, cowardly bastard, you were supposed to go to prison, you weren't supposed to kill yourself!"

Amid my screams, the gun flies from my hand because I suppose I throw it, but I don't know. The migraine worsens, and my cries fade into sobs as my knees hit the gravel, where I press my hands against my temples to alleviate the pounding, but I succeed only in smearing the sticky droplets of blood that stain my skin like they stain the broken chessboard.

One mistake, one fatal mistake is all it takes to ruin an entire chess game. The mistake I made is so obvious now. Throughout my years of playing chess, I've never discussed my strategy, but this time I chose pain before wits, I moved my queen too early and my king too late, and I told him how I was going to play and how I wanted this game to end. This stupid pawn cleared the path for her own king's check, but I have to get out before the checkmate. There has to be a way; it can't end like this.

Gentle but firm hands lift me up and pull me away from Fritzsch's body, while two pairs of comforting arms encircle me. My own carelessness provoked his final move, and now he's dead.

When my tears and the pain in my head lessen, I'm vaguely aware of Irena and Hania leading me through the gate; then I hear Franz's voice. "What the hell?"

"Exactly!" Irena shouts, rushing ahead until she's pounding her fists into his chest. "What the hell, Franz? How could you leave Maria here?" She doesn't wait for a response before grabbing my shoulders now that Hania and I have joined them. "Explain yourself, you fucking idiot."

Whatever Franz attempts to say is lost in the uproar while Hania curses in Yiddish and pushes Irena away. She stands between us, yelling in various languages, but Irena is undeterred, and the more everyone yells the more I want it to stop.

"Go on, explain yourself! I know you had a plan, you always have a fucking plan—"

"Irena!" My shout comes out in a surge of fury, and the moment she hears it her tirade ends. She pulls me close, holds tight.

"Dammit, Maria," she whispers, barely able to formulate the words before she breaks down into sudden, fierce sobs.

Franz folds Irena into his arms while I walk a few meters away and face the sign above the gate. Three German words, one simple sentence. Somehow the phrase looks even darker and more ominous than usual. The tears return, leaving hot, angry rivers that tingle against my cheeks, but gentle hands turn me away from the sign.

"It's over, shikse." The comforting murmur breaks through the echoes of Fritzsch's taunts and the screams of frustration that fill my head. Hania's thumb brushes a tear mixed with blood from my cheek, then she holds me against her chest and presses her lips to the top of my head.

Over. It's not over. Not like this. The barbed wire still surrounds me, and the current still races through it.

When we leave, we drive in silence. My tears have ceased, and my pain has dissipated. I'm hollow again, as hollow as I was during those first months of captivity, when I chose to feel nothing. As I stare at the blood splatters on my clothing and skin—Fritzsch's blood—I return to that place. I choose to feel nothing again.

Chapter 36

T HE NEWSPAPER HEADLINE is almost one week old, and I've memorized it by now. I read it every day, reassuring myself that I didn't imagine it. Adolf Hitler killed himself. The Führer is dead. Another criminal took his own life so he wouldn't have to face the consequences of his deplorable actions.

I'm still furious with Fritzsch for what he did. I spent an entire week in bed dwelling on it, even though there was no sense in doing so. Sometimes I can't help thinking about it. No one talks to me about him, but the day after Fritzsch's suicide I overheard Hania and Irena discussing what they'd done. Franz returned to Auschwitz and burned everything—the table, chairs, chess set, and Fritzsch's body. He disposed of the ashes in a location he wouldn't disclose, not even to Irena. All he said was it wasn't among the Auschwitz victims. Because Fritzsch was supposed to be on the front lines, his disappearance will be classified as a battle casualty. No one will miss him, and no one will find him.

He's gone from this world, but not from me. I see his face, hear his voice. *Your move, Prisoner 16671—*

I stand abruptly from the bed to banish his jeers from my mind. It was as Hania had said when I refused to leave the bed, when she'd shared her own recurring memories with me: *All the cigarettes and vodka in the world aren't enough to make the past go away.*

Maybe we aren't meant to leave the past behind. Maybe we're meant to bring it with us so we can join others weighed down by the same burdens, and we can carry them together. Maybe that's how we find peace.

After placing the article in the open valise on the floor, I stare at the clothes piled on my bed. Everyone else has gone into town, but I stayed behind to finish packing. I pick up my folded prisoner uniform. Another object I look at every day. It's stayed at the foot of my bed since I changed out of it. Irena has told me numerous times to *get that damn thing out of our room*, but I haven't.

When I pick it up, it comes unfolded. My uniform is even thinner than it was when I received it, so thin it's virtually transparent. The gray and blue stripes are dingy and worn, the hems and cuffs frayed, the garment tattered and stained. The white strip bearing my black prisoner number is faded and dirty, as are the red triangle and capital *P*. A seam travels halfway up the back where I repaired the rip after my flogging. In the interior, I find the various pockets I added throughout the years for organized goods, but my favorite is the one with the button flap. The one for Father Kolbe's rosary.

I pull up the sleeve of my robe to trace my scars and the dark ink that stands out so prominently against my pale skin.

My given name was Maria. My resistance name was Helena. My new name is Prisoner 16671.

The familiar twinge creeps into my temple. Concentrating on slow, steady breaths, I press my fingers to the side of my forehead to suppress it. After a moment, the twinge dissipates.

Finish the game, Maria.

I'm beginning to wonder if I ever will.

Someone knocks, so I cover my forearm, refold my uniform, and tuck it under the dresses, trousers, and skirts I've tossed into my valise. Irena always bursts in without knocking, so it must be Hania. I tighten the robe around me and invite the visitor inside.

Mateusz steps into the room. He keeps his distance, the tightness of his jaw accentuated by a shadow of stubble. I haven't seen him since passing him briefly when I staggered into the farmhouse, shaken and covered in Fritzsch's blood. As promised, he had come to say goodbye to a dear friend and was met by a girl who had used him, his kindness, his trust. The look he gave me—concern, confusion, shock, sorrow, betrayal, combined into one, shattering me as I had shattered him. Since that day, he's never tried to visit, and I certainly didn't send for him.

For a moment, I'm unsure what to say, but I'm certain why he's come.

"You haven't left for America yet?" Thank God the valise gives me something else to look at.

"Next week. Franz said he's driving you to Warsaw tomorrow since the original plan . . ." He pauses, as if nothing could adequately capture what had happened to the original plan. ". . . changed," he finishes at last.

A simple conclusion, one that sums up the entirety of what had happened—to the original plan, to me, to him. To us.

He waits, perhaps believing his recognition of the change is all it will take to prompt me into revealing why it occurred. Maybe this is my opportunity to salvage the last of our remaining moments. But to do so requires an impossible play. I clear my throat.

"I'm doing a terrible job of packing. If you'll excuse me, I should finish." I rummage through the dresser drawers, pretending to sort the pieces.

The silence is oppressive. Part of me wishes Mateusz would say what he's come to say, but another part would rather dwell in this instant forever than move forward to the next.

"I wouldn't have given you that letter if I'd known what it contained."

Though I'd been waiting for those words, they stir something within me, pushing me toward the familiar brink. Shoving the dresser drawer closed, I turn to face him.

"That wasn't your decision. The letter was mine."

"You had this planned all along, didn't you? Why did you involve me?"

"I trusted you, and I needed help."

"And I trusted you, but you lied to me. For years."

He waits, probably expecting me to admit or deny it, but I don't. There's no need to confirm a truth he already knows. Maybe he's hoping for some sign of remorse.

When I don't react, he steps closer, rigid with tension. "You said you were worried. You never said you were going to confront Fritzsch. I helped you find him, I gave you his letter because I thought it would give you peace of mind, but instead it could've gotten you killed. Don't you realize that?"

"I had to do it."

"Why? What lie are you going to tell me this time?"

The sharpness in his tone inflames my fury more. "You can't understand."

Mateusz shakes his head and backs toward the door, as if he sees no purpose in disputing me. "Well, Maria, you found Fritzsch. You got what you wanted."

That's all it takes to prompt the memories. I see my family's bodies, Father Kolbe's arm humbly extended and awaiting injection, the whip dripping my blood, the chessboard in the roll-call square, Fritzsch's vicious smile, and I hear his jeers, feel every bit of terror and fury and agony he's inflicted upon me, then I hear the shriek, the one that always takes me aback when I realize it's my own.

"What I wanted? Do you think this is what I wanted? Everyone I loved was murdered because of him! *This* was because of him."

I turn and allow my robe to fall and display my back, from shoulders to hips. The crack of the whip rings in my ears while my gasping cries mark the sting of each laceration, *eins, zwei, drei—*

Mateusz's sharp intake of breath lifts me from the scorching, dusty ground in the roll-call square and brings me back to standing half-naked in this cold bedroom. I cover myself and face him again. He looks at me as if seeing me for the first time.

"I won't make excuses because I don't have any, but don't ask me to explain myself. I can't. Not even to Irena or Hania."

My voice quivers; the twinge creeps into my head. Rage and pain have become as much a part of me as these scars.

I retreat to the window and wait for Mateusz to say that my words aren't good enough, to demand an explanation because I owe him that much, given the extent of my deception. I crave his fury, crave something to push me into hating him as much as he surely hates me. But, when he speaks, his voice holds no fury, no hatred.

"Maybe you can't explain yourself today, maybe not tomorrow. But someday, the words will come, and when they do, we'll listen."

The windowsill is firm and unrelenting against my grip, the glass pane smooth and cold when I press my forehead against it. The sobs descend upon me in a fierce, sudden onslaught; though I don't loosen my hold on the windowsill, I sink to my knees. His hands find my shoulders and coax me to my feet. I should turn away, but instead I surrender to his embrace.

We stand at opposite ends of a chasm, one that will never go away. It can't, not when the past few years of our lives have been so vastly different. But, despite my inability to help him understand, I think the gap has narrowed.

"All I wanted was for you to find peace," he murmurs when I lift my head and wipe the moisture from my cheeks.

"I'm closer to it. And if I could do all of this again, there's one thing I would've done much differently, Maciek." I swallow the sudden quaver in my voice and raise my eyes to his. "I never would have done what I did to you."

Mateusz's finger traces my cheek beneath my eye, the same one that was discolored and bruised after our first meeting, then along my temple, where a pistol barrel once pressed so firmly that it left a mark. From his pocket he produces a worn, tattered piece of paper, but when he unfolds it I recognize the handwriting. Mine. It's the first letter I wrote to him, and he quotes the line before my closing.

"All is forgiven."

I shake my head, feeling the strange need to fight him as I fight forgiveness every time it's offered to me, but I've learned that this is one game I never win. If I'm going to lose with dignity, I should accept defeat now. So I do.

Mateusz rotates me and guides my robe down until it's fallen around my waist, and I close my eyes while he takes in the mangled mass of exposed flesh that stretches across my body. When he runs his fingers over the scars, the simple gesture slows the pounding beat of my heart. Once he re-covers me, I turn to face him. He draws me closer, and I lift my head, following his sharp jaw to the bow of his lips and slope of his nose until I reach his eyes. Such deep blue eyes. He's always seen the girl, not the prisoner.

When his lips meet mine, I abandon myself to everything except the gentleness of his touch. Somehow he quells the hectic flurry inside me.

Between kisses, he whispers my name, whispers for me to come to America with him and leave all of this behind. A familiar longing pierces the comfort of his embrace and the tingling warmth his fingers send across my skin. Longing for him, longing to be something other than what I've become, a thing created by that place. The loud voice interferes, telling me to ignore the little voice, and I'm tempted to listen to its deafening cries. But the little voice knows best. So much of me remains scattered, a jumble of chess pieces on a board where strategy has come apart, leaving confusion and chaos in its wake. Sorting through the mayhem is a challenge only I can overcome.

Once more, I rest my head against his chest and close my eyes. How I wish things could be different.

"You know, Maciek," I murmur, "I think Americans have post offices."

A chuckle rumbles in his chest and vibrates against my ear. "Is that so?"

"I can't be certain, but it's a strong possibility." I lift my head to look at him. "Maybe I'll write to you someday. But if I do, and if you receive my letter and don't respond, that's rude, and you should be ashamed of yourself."

"Don't worry, I'll write back. It's rude to disrespect a girl's wishes."

I pull his lips to mine once more. The loud voice makes one final attempt, reminding me how easy it would be to never let him go.

I gently release him. Instead I cling to this moment and the promise that, someday, perhaps I'll find the next.

Once Mateusz is gone, I stay where I am, looking at the letters tucked into the corner of my valise. He really isn't a stupid boy after all.

Chapter 37

Warsaw, 7 May 1945

I RENA WARNED US that Warsaw wasn't the same, but no warning could have prepared me or Hania to return to what's left of our city. Buildings that were once grand and ornate lie in crumbles of dust, ash, brick, and glass while other ruins have been cleared, leaving gaping holes. The emptiness reminds me of the hollow spaces in our bunks following selections. The streets, once thriving, are all but abandoned—the result of countless civilian deaths, deportations, and escapes. Warsaw has been almost obliterated.

Of course my city is beaten, bruised, nearly destroyed. Even if I had found the justice I'd sought, finding it would not have buried the past as I had hoped; now I face my past and present. Those who made Warsaw beautiful—made it my home—lost their lives. My actions ripped the beauty from my life and left me in ruins just as bombs, bullets, and blood ravaged my city. The home I left no longer exists; it has become a reflection of the life I created.

Despite the hopeless state of the city, Hoża Street is still beautiful. As Hania and I stand on the corner, it reminds me of the times I traveled up and down this street to the convent. Each fond memory is a small comfort, though tinged by the ache in my chest, so familiar to me now, one I no longer expect to ever fully leave me.

"Four years," Hania murmurs, more to herself than to me. "It's been four years since I've seen my sons. And I never imagined I'd face this day without my husband."

I place my hand on her forearm, but I'm not sure she notices. "You're certain you'd like me to stay?"

She nods without pulling her eyes away from the convent.

Our heels clack against the cobblestones as I lead her down the street. When we ring the doorbell, a sister takes us into the courtyard, where birds chirp and a breeze rustles through the trees. The tranquil atmosphere is a sharp contrast to the nerves raging within me. We wait near the Saint Joseph statue while she fetches her superior.

Hania stands beside me, face lined with worry, hands clasped, as pale and motionless as the Saint Joseph statue. She looks far older than she should. Old, tired, hopeful, petrified. Four years of unspeakable suffering have brought her to this moment. I extend a hand; she latches on to my arm and doesn't loosen her grip.

When Mother Matylda appears, alone, Hania's grip tightens.

She clutches me for an instant, then releases me, rushes to meet Mother Matylda, and grabs her hand. Her grasp looks so strong that I'm afraid she's hurting the elderly mother provincial, but Mother Matylda clings to her just as tightly.

"Tell me they're safe," Hania says, the words sharp and urgent despite the break in her voice. "Please, they can't be—"

"Oh, my dear child, forgive me. I didn't intend to frighten you," Mother Matylda replies, placing a soothing hand on Hania's cheek. "I wanted to share what my sisters and I have learned since Maria contacted us. Maria's mother, Natalia, brought your sons to us. Adam and Jakub were transferred to our orphanage in Ostrówek." She offers her a small smile. "And they are alive."

For a moment Hania looks too stunned to react, then with a

sob, her knees buckle. Her head droops under the weight of the news, and she presses her lips to the mother provincial's wrinkled hand. With surprising agility, Mother Matylda kneels with her, head bowed, eyes closed, cradling Hania as if she's one of the children the sisters have saved.

I close my eyes, returning to my family's living room, where Mama and I had so many whispered conversations, imagining moments like this, helping to reunite families that had been torn apart. *We cannot imagine what they have suffered, but we must do our part to ease it.* The advice she had always given. As I whisper a silent thanks to her for her tireless efforts, her enthusiasm, her compassion, I sense her relief and joy as surely as my own.

When Hania has calmed herself, the mother provincial wipes a lingering tear from her cheek. "Would you like to see your sons?"

Hania takes a moment to find her voice. "They're here?"

"After locating them, we brought them here as quickly as we could. I've explained the situation to them, so they realize they're Jewish. And they *are* Jewish," Mother Matylda adds, giving her hand a reassuring squeeze. "No one who has come to us has been baptized against his parents' wishes."

Hania blinks, seeming too overwhelmed to process everything she's heard. Another tear rolls down her cheek. She's still clinging to Mother Matylda, as if releasing her would take away everything the mother provincial has returned to her.

"Before you see your children, Hania, you must remember they were very young when you were separated, and they—"

"They don't remember me." She dips her head in a small nod even though her voice wavers. "I understand, Mother. Please bring me my kinderlach."

Mother Matylda beckons me. Once I've joined them, she coaxes Hania to her feet and disappears inside.

Hania's shaking hand finds mine—hers a rich olive, mine as pale as Mama's porcelain tea set. I imagine my mother holding Jakub's hand, leading him through the sewers while cradling Adam in her arms, and I picture them here, in this very spot, filthy and exhausted but alive. The sisters would have cleaned and fed the children while Mama changed and bundled up her filthy garments to mask her work and then hurried home before my siblings awoke.

If only Mama had known that those children she rescued belonged to a woman who would one day rescue her own daughter.

When Mother Matylda returns, she leads two dark-haired boys by the hand. A small gasp emerges from Hania's lips while her tremor reverberates in me as strongly as if it were my own. Jakub's dark eyes evaluate us, first Hania, then me, then back to her, while Adam's are large and curious. She takes a few steps closer to her sons, stops with apparent difficulty, and waits. Mother Matylda guides Jakub's hand into Adam's. Both wait for her direction, so she gives them an encouraging nod.

Slowly Jakub leads Adam across the courtyard. When they reach their mother, they pause while she sinks to her knees. I imagine she's longing to wrap them in her arms and smother them with kisses, but she's waiting for permission, afraid of overwhelming them. I watch with bated breath, praying Jakub will reach into the depths of his memory, will recognize the poor woman who has lost everything and has spent four agonizing years dreaming of this moment. Surely he'll recall something, anything, about the mother who loves him so much.

Hania studies the little boys who emerged from the toddler and infant she once knew, drinking in every detail. "Do you know who I am?"

"Your name is Hania, and you're our mother. That's what

Matusia Matylda said," Jakub replies, and I smile at his use of the endearing title. "She said my name is Jakub, not Andrzej, and Henryk's name is Adam."

Hania nods and fights to contain a fresh wave of tears while she murmurs in Yiddish. Jakub's eyes narrow, and he looks at Mother Matylda for an explanation. The mother provincial casts a sympathetic glance at Hania; again my heart twists into a painful knot. None of the sisters could help Jakub retain knowledge of the language. The one Adam hasn't had the chance to learn.

The same understanding must come over Hania, and she pauses midsentence. She swallows hard and produces the family portrait she kept throughout our time in the camp. After handing it to her sons, she points to their faces. "That's me, and that's you."

Her sons consult the image, then Jakub assesses her. "You look different."

She chuckles. "So do you. This photograph was taken four years ago. And this is your father, Eliasz."

"Where is he?" Adam asks.

"We'll see him again someday," Hania says softly, but her voice wavers. She takes their hands in her own. Adam takes a trusting step closer to her, and though Jakub still looks uncertain, he doesn't pull away. "You were so small when your father and I sent you away to keep you safe. We missed you terribly, but Matusia Matylda could protect you in ways we couldn't. Even though we weren't together, I kept you with me each day because I thought of you, I missed you, and I loved you. Do you remember the day you left?"

Jakub shakes his head. Adam shakes his head, too, as if he feels left out. I expected the response, but it's still disappointing.

"That's all right, because I remember it. Adam, you were a baby—"

"Like this?" He points to himself in the photograph.

"Yes, exactly like that. Jakub, you were hardly three years old, but you promised to be a brave boy. I can see you've kept that promise. Will you continue being brave?"

After considering the query, he nods.

"And Adam, will you be brave, too?"

Adam wraps his arms around Hania's neck in an exuberant embrace. "Yes, Mama!"

* * *

I allow Hania to get reacquainted with her sons, promising to return after I visit Bałuckiego Street. I'm not sure our apartment building survived the destruction or if there's anything left of the home I once knew. But I need to find out.

Outside the convent, I reach the end of the street and catch sight of Irena, on her way to meet us after introducing Franz to her mother.

"I'll join you in a little while," I say as I walk past, but she grabs my forearm, pulling me to a stop.

"Don't."

Startled by the urgency in her voice, I turn toward her. From the look on her face, she knows exactly where I'm going.

"Is it gone?" I whisper, though I'm not certain I can bear the answer.

"Yes—well, the building stands and the apartment was pillaged, but to answer your question, yes, it is gone." She relaxes her hold, and I meet her eyes, brimming with sympathy. "It was gone the moment the Gestapo invaded and took you into custody."

A lump rises in my throat. Of course it's been gone. *They* have been gone. But to hear Irena say it makes it final.

I need to go back. To face what I've done. Confronting Fritzsch was supposed to bring a semblance of peace, but Warsaw is noth-

ing more than another reminder. Every happiness I once knew here
has been erased. Why should I be spared the consequences of my
actions?

Bałuckiego Street and its loose cobblestones that always tripped
my sister. The tap of my father's cane on the stairs leading to our
apartment. My brother begging to go to Park Dreszera. My mother picking geraniums from her little garden on our balcony, arranging the pink and white blooms in her favorite crystal vase. My
beautiful Staunton chess set in our living room.

The home destroyed by the Gestapo. By my failure.

When I try to leave again, Irena holds firm. Perhaps she's right;
perhaps there's no need to see it, not when I can close my eyes and
revisit that day with fresh agony every time. Four years I dedicated
to justice, expecting it to assuage me. I had left Warsaw a broken
girl; now I returned a broken young woman. Broken things, even
if reconstructed, remain cracked, imperfect, never fully whole.

A cool breeze sweeps over us, so I cross my arms against it while
Hania emerges from the convent, leading a son on either side. As
they approach, I take a shuddering breath and look to Irena.

"What do I do now?"

She laughs. "Dammit, Maria, you're such an idiot."

Now isn't the time for flippancy. I open my mouth to protest,
but Irena is already setting her usual brisk pace toward her family's apartment. She doesn't slow down, but she calls to us over her
shoulder.

"Come on, we're going home."

* * *

When we enter the Sienkiewiczes' apartment, I remember the girl
who came here with her mother, anticipating her first day of re-

sistance work. How young she was, how eager. In many ways, it remains the same comforting, inviting home, though a newfound heaviness lingers in the air. The war has impacted this place as it has all of us—battered, almost ruined, yet fighting on.

Irena directs Hania and the boys to the living-room floor, where Franz sits with a little girl, surrounded by toys and games— each showing signs of age, likely having belonged to Irena as a child. The girl hugs a doll close and turns a page in her picture book, which she's too young to read. A pink ribbon holds golden brown hair away from her face, and she wears a simple dress, paying the skirt no mind as she sits with her legs wide apart. Beneath the girl's lingering roundness, I recognize her mother's long, lean frame, but, before Irena can summon her daughter, Mrs. Sienkiewicz emerges from the kitchen.

She's thinner than I recall, the work of something far more severe than meager rations. Each line on her face and crease in her brow tells a tale of suffering, fighting. From losing her husband and nearly losing her daughter to protecting her granddaughter, all while smuggling Jewish children to safety and playing an integral part in the resistance. This brave, selfless woman, my mother's dearest friend.

Without a word, she bestows three alternating kisses on my cheeks and pulls me close, and I wrap my arms around her. She shudders beneath my grasp; upon releasing me, she takes in Tata's eyes, Mama's nose, all the pieces of my family that melded into me.

Tears glimmer in her eyes, sympathetic and affectionate; I lower my gaze, unable to bear it. Not when the truth still lurks inside me, as it has for so long, coming free only when I revealed it to Father Kolbe. One day, they will hear everything from me. One day, if I can ever manage to reveal the truth without bringing the memories with it.

After kissing her daughter, Mrs. Sienkiewicz takes Irena's tiny crucifix between her fingers. She heaves a wistful little sigh before Irena covers her mother's hand with her own.

"We've nearly done it, Mama," she says, a sudden break in her voice. "It's nearly over."

"God willing," she replies softly, blinking back her tears while watching Franz point to an image in Helena's book. Her lips turn in a little smile. "Witold said Patryk would have adored both of them."

I look at her in surprise. "Pilecki?"

She nods. "During the invasion, he served in the Nineteenth Infantry Division alongside my husband. They were dear friends."

"Through the resistance, Mama stayed in touch with Witold and the Home Army, and when I was caught, she got a message to him," Irena says. "He arranged the bribe which saved my life."

"Yes, and he came by today to—" Mrs. Sienkiewicz breaks off. "Never mind, I'll let you get settled first."

She excuses herself, and Irena motions for me to follow her. When we reach Helena, she crouches next to her, and the little girl looks up from her book and grins.

"Helena, this is Mama's cousin," Irena says with a playful smile, reminding me of our favorite resistance scheme. "You can call her Aunt Maria."

Helena looks at me and focuses on my tattoo, visible since the sleeves of my floral shirtwaist stop at my elbows. Before I can explain, she tugs on Irena's arm.

"What are you doing, silly?" Irena laughs as Helena wrestles her forearm toward the ceiling.

"Where is the number?"

"What number?"

"The number, Mama! Like Aunt Maria's."

Irena's smile fades while her cheeks flush. She grabs her daughter's hand to end the eager search. "Enough."

Startled by the sharpness in her mother's voice, Helena freezes, as if unsure what she's done wrong.

"Your mother doesn't have a number, Helena, but would you like to see mine?"

Following the rebuke, the little girl casts an uncertain glance at Irena, who nods her consent. With her confidence renewed, Helena approaches me and studies the tattoo. "Why did you draw on yourself?"

"I didn't, but someone else did. Look, it doesn't come off." I rub my finger over the numbers to prove my point.

Wide-eyed, Helena runs a pudgy finger over the markings, confirming my statement, before placing a finger on each number and naming it aloud. "One. Six. Six. Seven. One. One-six-six-seven-one." Her triumphant smile fades when she evaluates the numbers again. "Mama says to draw on paper."

"Good. If you were to draw on yourself, it might not come off, like mine, right?"

Helena nods solemnly, then scampers toward Irena, who catches her in waiting arms and kisses her cheek. Over her daughter's head, she gives me a small, appreciative smile, and I brush my thumb across the tattoo. When Helena announced the sequence, I expected the headache to follow, but it hasn't.

Someone knocks on the door. Brow furrowed, Irena motions for Franz to answer, so he obliges, and standing in the hall is Izaak.

His face is one I hardly recognize—still fighting for recovery, as we all are, yet a vast difference compared to four months ago. His skin, leathered from years of labor, radiates a newfound warmth, his hair is dark and shiny, he's grown a thick, full beard, and the places that once held mere skin and bone now boast muscle. The strange darkness remains in his eyes, but as Hania gasps and throws her arms around him the hard edge softens.

"I thought you weren't returning to Warsaw until the end of the summer," she says as she releases him.

"We found the war criminal I was looking for and took care of him," Izaak replies. "I came back to Warsaw and reconnected with Witold. He told me you'd be here."

Izaak doesn't reveal the war criminal's name, but, based on the look he gives Hania, I know exactly who it was. Protz. The blow to the head didn't kill him after all. Hania steps back and lifts a shaking hand to her mouth as her eyes well with tears. Izaak pulls her close, murmurs something in Yiddish, and kisses her cheek.

"Come in, Izaak, make yourself at home," Mrs. Sienkiewicz says. "To think you and Hania are related to these sweet boys." She casts a fond smile at Jakub and Adam. "When Helena and I stayed at the orphanage in Ostrówek, she played with Jakub and Adam all the time. That was before we knew Maria's mother had taken them from the ghetto or that their mother was Irena and Maria's friend. Quite a coincidence, don't you think? It's as if everyone here was meant to find each other."

When I wrap my arms around Izaak's midsection, he returns the embrace, tentatively at first, then tightens his hold. "The organized goods you left me and Hania saved our lives," he says.

"Hania was responsible for most of those items. She was better at organizing than I was." I nudge him in his sister's direction. "Now, I think your nephews would like to get reacquainted with their uncle."

Smiling, Hania takes Izaak by the hand and leads him toward the boys. Mrs. Sienkiewicz bustles around, fussing over adults and children alike, and prepares beef goulash with the meat and vegetables Franz brought from the farm. After dinner, she gathers everyone in the living room. As she faces us, she draws an unsteady breath before speaking.

"Today, Germany signed a total and unconditional surrender, and the Allies will formally accept it tomorrow. The war is over."

Silence falls. This long-awaited news felt so far off for so long; now it's here, real. A few relieved sighs and breathless prayers of praise fill the quiet even as a sudden tightness seizes my chest. This nightmare of a war is over, but mine lingers. Sometimes I feel closer to the end, surrounded by these people whose presence strengthens and sustains me. Other times I feel as I did that first day in Auschwitz, finding my family and realizing that the life I had known was shattered beyond repair. What is life after war? Returning to the lives we left is impossible, yet creating a life anew feels nearly as insurmountable. We live, fight, and survive while the memories—and the past—endure.

As murmurs and chatter take over, Irena leads me to her bedroom. Once there, she pulls a box from underneath the bed and runs a finger along the closed lid.

"I've had this since the twenty-seventh of May, 1941. When you didn't meet me for our resistance work, I went by your apartment. I didn't think you'd be alive to claim any belongings, but I gathered these before pillagers had a chance. That way, if anyone came looking for you, I'd have a few items to offer them. It's not much, but it's something."

Irena places the box in front of me. Slowly I remove the lid and pull each item out, one by one. Three of Karol's toy soldiers and two of Zofia's hair ribbons. Tata's favorite gray fedora with the wide brim and blue Petersham ribbon and Mama's favorite crystal vase. Our rosaries. Best of all, a framed family portrait. It's the last photo we took together, and I clearly remember that April day in 1941. We dressed in our finest clothes and spent hours with the photographer, taking picture after picture so we could get the perfect shot. That was a few weeks before everything changed.

I look at Irena, but I can't speak through the tears that close my throat and blur my vision.

"Don't forget these."

She produces the items I didn't notice, too distracted by the keepsakes. A few large stacks of zloty, money my parents likely withdrew from their bank account and kept hidden in the apartment. I hardly glance at them.

"This didn't fit into the box."

Irena reaches under the bed and produces Tata's cane. The wood is as dark and rich as I remember, and though the silver head is tarnished, it's as beautiful as I recall. I clutch the handle, smooth from his grasp, and tap the cane to the floor, then grip it with both hands. Suddenly it's the only thing keeping me on my feet.

"One more thing. This didn't fit into the box, either."

I place Tata's cane on the bed while Irena reaches under it once more. This time she pulls out my chess set.

I trace my finger over the checkered board before lifting the lid to reveal the green felt–lined interior, where the wooden pieces are nestled into individual compartments. Each one is there, even more beautiful than I remember, and I turn the delicate carvings over in my hands. The last game I played with these pieces was against my parents the evening before our arrest. I pick up a white pawn. The lacquer is chipped, probably from when the piece crashed to the floor during the Gestapo invasion. Somehow that makes me tighten my hold.

"Dammit, I should've said something first." Irena sighs and pushes a loose strand of hair away from her face, perhaps taking my silence as discomfort. "If you don't want it anymore after . . ."

She lets her voice fade, likely recalling the blood-splattered chess-board from the roll-call square, then starts over. "If chess—"

I shake my head to stop her. Despite everything, chess is still my game. It always will be. This chess set reminds me of a father who gave his daughter this board and taught her this game, and of a girl fortified by a tiny handmade pawn.

"You know what this means, don't you, Irena?" I ask, smiling through my tears. "Now you have to let me teach you how to play."

"Shit," she mutters, but I'd like to think I hear a certain fond-ness in her tone, and she doesn't complain when I wrap my arms around her neck and kiss her cheek.

A gentle rap sounds against the door before Hania steps across the threshold. "Wiktoria is wondering why you two disappeared, so if I'm interrupting, let me be clear that she's the yenta and not me."

"Good Lord, she's never going to let any of us out of her sight again," Irena says with a sigh.

Hania chuckles and starts to turn away, but pauses when she notices the items on the bed. She comes closer and cradles the portrait in both hands, then brushes her finger over each face, ending with Mama's. "Could I show this to the boys?" she asks. "I don't want them to ever forget her. Or any of you," she adds, glancing between us, eyes bright.

Another reality of war: those who survived together may be forced apart at its conclusion. This war has already taken my family; I refuse to accept any more losses, no matter what the future holds. If any-thing comes between us, we will find our way back to one another.

Irena looks to the door. "We should join everyone before Mama thinks I've run off to become a fake Nazi again," she says, but I place a hand on her forearm to prevent her departure.

The little twinge returns to my head as I anticipate what I'm about to say. I take a small breath to alleviate it. "You both deserve so many explanations from me, and I want to give them to you, but I don't know if I can yet. I promise I'll keep trying."

"When you're ready, shikse," Hania says as she takes my hand in hers.

Irena nods. "And not a moment before."

I intend on saying more, but the words don't come, so I don't force them. Instead I pull my friends close, and the scattered pieces of my life cease to matter. When our arms encircle one another, peace dispels chaos and my heart recognizes its home. Together we will help one another pick up all the fallen pieces.

When we return to the living room, everyone gathers in a wide circle around the coffee table, where Hania sits across from me, flanked by Adam and Jakub. Irena sits beside me with Helena in her lap, and Franz settles next to them. Izaak and Mrs. Sienkiewicz sit on the sofa, watching as Hania and I set up the game.

"This is a horse," Adam exclaims, holding up a black knight.

"That's right. There should be two black ones, and you can put one here, and the other here." Hania points to squares B8 and G8.

Helena scrutinizes her chosen piece and shows it to Irena. "A tower."

"Those are called rooks, and they go in the corners." I point to the spaces. "You can put the two white ones in these corners by me, and the two black ones go in Aunt Hania's corners."

"How do you win the game?" Jakub asks as he sets Hania's final bishop in place.

"That's the only question I can answer," Irena says. "You put the opponent in checkmate."

I set up my last pawn. "Watch us play, Jakub, and I'll demonstrate a checkmate in a few minutes."

"Oy vey, gloating already, Maria?" Hania asks, flashing a competitive grin. "It's a bit early for that, even for you."

As Hania and I begin our game, we explain the rules to our curious onlookers. The children watch with wide eyes, interrupting to ask questions or voice exuberant suggestions about our next moves. When we reach the endgame, I make my final play, share its significance, and smile at her.

"Checkmate, Bubbe. And just for you, that's all the gloating I'll do."

She chuckles. "Excellent game, shikse. Your turn, Irena." She moves over and pulls her sons into her lap, allowing Irena to take her place across from me, despite her visible apprehension.

Once the little ones have set up the pieces, we begin. I allow Hania to act as coach—after all, it's Irena's first game. I might enjoy winning, but I enjoy a challenge even more. As my fingers navigate the familiar board, strategizing and planning and predicting her next play, I feel more like myself than I have since liberation. Most of all, I feel alive.

I'm alive. I'm safe. And I'm free.

The game I've played for so long still feels unfinished, but, when I learned to play chess, one of the best pieces of advice Tata gave me was to take my time. Consider each move, then make the play when the time is right. *Finish the game, Maria.* No matter how long it takes.

From terrible suffering and crippling loss rises a special kind of resilience, one unique to those who endure. Every tap of a chess piece against the board, every whisper and peal of laughter fills the room and sends a flicker of warmth into my chest. These are voices that evil attempted to silence, voices of bravery, kindness, strength, intelligence. Voices of resilience. Those ravished by hatred will be healed by love, and their courageous spirits and compassionate souls will lead them through the darkness to a life beyond.

 Epilogue

Auschwitz, 12 October 1982

T HIS PLACE. THE place I never thought I'd revisit.

    We hadn't returned to Europe since immigrating to New York a few months after the war ended. Together we had survived; together we would rebuild. Although the headaches and memories had become less frequent once I told my friends why I'd returned to Auschwitz after escaping, we didn't speak of anything else that had happened during the war. We'd endured it once, and once was more than enough. But a few months ago, while planning the trip to Vatican City for Father Kolbe's canonization, Hania suggested visiting Warsaw, too, and the little voice whispered that I needed to come back to this place. The loud voice protested, but I listened to the little whisper. I always do.

    Light fog and misting rain settle over the early morning. It's been thirty-seven years since I stood in this same spot, an eighteen-year-old girl, wounded and broken and desperate for justice, and forty-one years since I first stood here, a fourteen-year-old child who had no idea what horrors waited beyond the gate, the same gate staring at me in the distance.

ARBEIT MACHT FREI.

I pull Father Kolbe's rosary from my pocket and pass my fingers over the pale blue beads. It's worn from decades of use, but it's one of my most treasured possessions. I close my hand around the silver crucifix, recalling the night Father Kolbe—now Saint Maksymilian Kolbe—pressed it gently into my palm. Those first weeks in Auschwitz were the darkest days of my life, but this rosary is from a man who gave a tortured girl the courage to live, fight, and survive.

After tucking the rosary away, I draw a breath until the chilly air fills my lungs, warding off the reminders encroaching upon my mind. The memories will come. And when they do, I'll face them.

Visitors from all over the world file past, murmuring in their native tongues, taking photographs, asking questions, and listening to tour guides. Instead of continuing through the gate, I begin the journey three kilometers west, one I've made so many times before. A guide attempts to convince me to wait for the shuttle that travels between camps, but I shake my head. If I could walk this distance as a starved and battered child, I can walk it as a healthy, middle-aged woman.

I reach the women's sector in Birkenau and don't stop until I've returned to my block. Unlike some of the other barracks, mine hasn't been destroyed. A few tourists file out as I enter. I cross the uneven floor until I reach the top bunk where Hania and I spent so many nights, shivering and huddled together against the relentless cold. A rose and a stone rest on the wooden planks, both in remembrance of the dead.

Taking a deep breath, I kneel before the loose brick and pull it free. The hand holding it is pale, yet flushed pink, slightly wrinkled and peppered with a few age spots, lined with remnants of old scars. This hand has clutched this brick so many times before; in those days, my hand was gray and cracked, covered in calluses, scrapes, and bruises, unrecognizable beneath layers of filth. How things have changed.

Now that I've revealed the depression in the dirt, I look inside. There it is, exactly as I left it. The jewelry pouch I organized for my chess pieces.

With shaking hands, I pour the pebbles and twigs into my palm. Each one is here. A wistful smile plays around my lips while I set up the game on my old bunk; then I return the pouch to its hiding place and re-cover it with the brick.

I go back to the main camp, still on foot, but I stop before passing through the gate. Already I feel my heartbeat picking up its pace. I'm not certain I can make my feet continue. As I hesitate before the sign, two women appear on either side of me, and I don't have to turn my head to recognize them. My heart will always recognize those who hold it together.

"You didn't have to come."

"And you don't have to do this alone. We decided to give you the opportunity to change your mind."

A gentle warmth spreads over me, and I turn to Irena while she pushes a loose strand of hair away from her forehead. Her locks are dyed brown, a bit darker than what was once her natural color. According to Irena, the gray that has overtaken all of us makes her look old as hell. On my other side, Hania adjusts her raincoat. Her eyes, with wrinkles around the corners, glimmer even as they pierce the bleakness of this place. She won't go even if I order her away.

More footsteps greet my ears. When their owner reaches my side, I kiss his lips, but if I nestle into his embrace then I won't have the strength to emerge from it. I pull back at once.

"Maciek," I start to say, but it's all I manage before I meet his familiar blue eyes and the words catch in my throat. This gaze, the one that has always known me; this gaze, my refuge for so many difficult years, bringing moments of light into the darkness. This gaze and those moments, both found again when I set foot on American soil.

"Did you really believe we'd stay in Warsaw while you came here alone?" Mateusz asks with a small smile. The humor fades when he brushes a gentle hand over my scarred shoulder and drops his voice. "We've shared so little, Maria. All of us. Isn't it time for that to change?"

He glances over his shoulder, and I follow his gaze to find our family waiting a few meters away. When we turn to them, Jakub and Adam, in the midst of conversing in Yiddish, fall silent. Izaak and my son, Maks, take in our surroundings with furrowed brows, while my daughter, Marta, stops pacing and faces us. Helena stands between Marta and Franz, and she takes a step closer.

"We'll look around on our own if you'd prefer, Aunt Maria, but we . . ." Although the words trail away, the look in her eyes is no different from the others.

They don't know why Aunt Hania struggled for so long to break her smoking habit or why Aunt Irena never removes the gold crucifix around her neck. Why Uncle Izaak occasionally sits alone, uttering faint whispers about how *it could have been any of us*. Why Uncle Franz insists that food should never be wasted, because *they were skeletons, every one of them*. Why Uncle Mateusz carries a faded scrap of paper in his wallet. Why Aunt Maria experiences debilitating headaches and sometimes wakes in the middle of the night, gasping *Jawohl, Herr Lagerführer* . . .

Our children know so little when they long to know so much.

Leaving me with a kiss on my cheek, Mateusz rejoins our group. When I look at the gate again, the twinge slips into my head, threatening to overtake me. The burdens are simultaneously too horrific to speak of and yet necessary to divulge. History is the grand master, and only by studying his game can the pupil learn and improve.

I allow the twinge to pass before glancing between Irena and Hania. "You'll stay with me?"

Hania intertwines her arm with mine. "Have we ever left you, shikse?"

Years ago, I confronted my past alone. Today I will face my past alongside those who helped me through it. Together, Irena, Hania, and I walk through the gate, and our family follows.

We go slowly, relaying our experiences along the way. When we turn right toward the roll-call square, images of countless chess games and Fritzsch's dead body flit through my mind, but they don't torment me further. My feet know where to go as I traverse the rocky, uneven road and file past the familiar redbrick buildings.

Inside Block 11, we descend the stairs to Cell 18. My family has heard many stories of Father Kolbe, but none from the time I spent visiting him in this cell. Conjuring the words is difficult at first; then they come, passing over my lips like rosary beads passing between my fingers. When I'm finished, everyone waits for me outside while I stay at the cell, holding Father Kolbe's rosary, hearing his prayers and hymns that brought light and comfort into this place of darkness and despair. I reach into my handbag and pull out my childhood rosary, the one Irena recovered from my family's apartment. I slip it through the bars. Father Kolbe gave me his, so it's only fair that I return the favor.

Once outside, we stand before Blocks 10 and 11, facing the courtyard's open iron gate, where I stood on my first day here. The day I spoke to the prisoner filling the truck with bodies.

The wall is there. It's a new wall, because the original was taken down, and this one is covered with flowers, stones, prayer cards, and memorials. The gray structure stands out so prominently against the red bricks. As we enter the courtyard, their names echo with every step.

Mama. Tata. Zofia. Karol. Father Kolbe.

We pause a few meters away from the wall, and I close my eyes. How I miss them.

"Oh, excuse me." The apology comes from an American girl who had obscured my view in her efforts to photograph the wall. She steps back, seeming unaware that my eyes were closed anyway.

"It's all right," I reply in English, and her eyes widen. My English is decent, but despite the many years I've spent in America I can't shake the heavy Polish accent that accompanies my words. Hania takes great pleasure in pretending that my English is as poor as my Yiddish.

The girl looks to my forearm, where I've unwittingly pushed up my sleeve to brush my fingers over my cigarette-burn scars. When she notices my tattoo, her eyes widen even more. I study her while she studies me. She's so young.

"How old are you?"

Startled, she looks down, perhaps embarrassed to have been caught staring, but the gentleness in my tone must assure her I'm not angry. She tucks a loose strand of blond hair behind her ear and answers in a shy voice. "Fourteen."

I run my thumb over my prisoner number, 16671. "So was I."

The girl hovers near my family and watches as I approach the wall. Once there, I reach into my handbag and push aside the folded striped uniform. I usually keep it in a box at home, but I wanted it with me today. Beneath the familiar garment, I find what I'm looking for—a copy of the family portrait Irena saved so many years ago. On the back, I've written our names, birthdays, and the date of my family's execution. I have their rosaries with me, too.

Some say the life I led for almost four years wasn't a life at all, but I don't believe that. It wasn't a life I'd wish upon anyone, but it was still a life. My life. And my life was worth fighting for.

Even after all this time, it hasn't felt over. Not really. But now, standing in this place, this place that was the most vicious opponent I've ever faced, the game I played here is drawing to an end. It's time to make my final play.

I kneel and place my family portrait in front of the wall, and I weight it down with the remaining four rosaries and a pebble from my chess set. A pawn. I offer a prayer for my family, Father Kolbe, the Jews, and all who suffered and lost their lives during that terrible, terrible war. Irena and Hania join me on either side. As I take their hands and stand up, I wait for the headache, the trembles, the memories, but, for now, they don't come.

Checkmate.

"No one in the world can change Truth. What we can do and should do is to seek truth and to serve it when we have found it. The real conflict is the inner conflict. Beyond armies of occupation and the hecatombs of extermination camps, there are two irreconcilable enemies in the depth of every soul: good and evil, sin and love. And what use are the victories on the battlefield if we ourselves are defeated in our innermost personal selves?"

—St. Maksymilian Kolbe

Author's Note

THE FOLLOWING CONTAINS extremely important information and significant spoilers. I implore you to read it, but not until you have read the book. You have been warned!

First, allow me to clarify that the Auschwitz portrayed in this novel is not an entirely factual representation of the camp. To study Auschwitz, I relied heavily on Danuta Czech's *Auschwitz Chronicle* and Yisrael Gutman and Michael Berenbaum's *Anatomy of the Auschwitz Death Camp*, but I took various creative liberties for story purposes, some detailed below. My hope is that this book will encourage you to dive deeper into history. Auschwitz is where real people—more than a million of them—lived, suffered, and died, the overwhelming majority being European Jews. My own two feet have walked its grounds, and I have no words to describe the experience—the sorrow, cruelty, and injustice, yet the bravery and resilience of the victims. Sadly, some claim the Holocaust never happened, despite mountains of evidence to the contrary and eyewitnesses who still live. Bear in mind, the Second World War ended less than eighty years before the time of this book's publication. That is not very long ago. Please look to survivors, their testimonies, and listen and learn from them. Please turn to experts who have dedicated their lives to educating the world on these horrors—the Auschwitz-Birkenau Memorial and

Museum, Yad Vashem, the United States Holocaust Memorial Museum, and many others. Please do not forget.

This book began with Saint Maksymilian Kolbe, one of my favorite saints. Father Kolbe was a Conventual Franciscan friar and Polish Catholic priest who sheltered Jews in his monastery and published anti-Nazi materials. He was arrested and sent to Auschwitz in 1941; beginning in 1939, Auschwitz was a labor camp for male political prisoners before the Final Solution—the Nazi's plan for the genocide of the Jews—was implemented in 1942, transforming it into an extermination camp for Jews. According to eyewitness testimony, Father Kolbe was a positive, supportive influence on his fellow inmates and ultimately offered his life for one of ten men chosen by the camp deputy, Karl Fritzsch, to starve to death in reprisal for another inmate's escape. I learned so much about him through Patricia Treece's biography, *A Man for Others*. This novel came to me as the idea of a young female prisoner visiting Father Kolbe in Block 11, Cell 18, where he spent two weeks without food or water before being murdered by lethal injection. This girl had an intense need to be with him, so much so that she was willing to risk this visit, to try to comfort him as, I sensed, he had comforted her. Because women were not imprisoned in Auschwitz until March 1942, when the first transport of Jewish women arrived, I asked myself if I could come up with a way to make this impossible scenario possible.

As I got to know my fictional Polish resistance member, Maria, I studied *Church of Spies* by Mark Riebling. The Vatican's position on Nazism remains heavily disputed, but this fascinating account is rich with primary sources detailing work Pope Pius XII did in secret to combat the Nazis and overthrow Hitler—though his intended plot ultimately failed. To learn more about occupied Warsaw and the Polish resistance, I relied on *Irena's Children:*

The Extraordinary Story of the Woman Who Saved 2,500 Children from the Warsaw Ghetto by Tilar J. Mazzeo, the story of a Polish woman named Irena Sendler who smuggled Jewish children from the Warsaw Ghetto and is credited with saving more than two thousand five hundred lives. Through Sendler's work, she crossed paths with Mother Matylda Getter and the Franciscan Sisters of the Family of Mary. Although many of the details included about the sisters and resistance are factual, my portrayal has been condensed and fictionalized for story purposes.

Maria told me very quickly that she was a chess player, and I soon realized that chess would play a central role in her story. By diving into chess history, I discovered women such as Vera Menchik, who won the first Women's World Chess Championship in 1927, defended this title six times, and, in 1944, was killed alongside her sister and mother in a V-1 bombing attack on London. She was thirty-eight years old and remains the record holder as Women's World Chess Champion, with a seventeen-year title. In researching Auschwitz, I learned about Maria Mandel's prized creation: the Women's Orchestra, comprising Jewish women who were spared death but forced to entertain their captors through music and play for roll calls, selections, transports, and executions. I combined these concepts for my reasoning behind why Maria, a girl sent to Auschwitz while it was a prison camp for men, would be spared: the camp deputy, Karl Fritzsch, described by historians as a man who resented authority and often broke rules, was not always under the watchful eye of Kommandant Rudolf Höss, who was a firm believer in order and obeying superiors, as indicated in his autobiography, *Commandant of Auschwitz*. In my story, Fritzsch rebels by registering Maria, a female, so he can force her to play chess to entertain the SS guards.

When the reader first meets Maria in April 1945, Auschwitz

has already been evacuated—before being liberated by the Red Army—but the war is not over, as it did not end until May. She returns to Auschwitz for a final chess game against Fritzsch, seeking to confirm what she discovered during her imprisonment—that Fritzsch murdered her family. After the Soviets liberated Auschwitz in January 1945, the Red Cross cared for prisoners and took them to hospitals and displaced-persons' camps. Auschwitz did not officially become a museum until 1947, thanks to the efforts of, among others, Kazimierz Smoleń, a survivor. Following liberation, many former prisoners returned to the camp seeking family or friends. In other cases, "diggers," as they were called, came seeking valuables, so a protective guard—made up of, among others, former inmates interested in preserving the camp as a historical site—was eventually set up to watch over the camp and its artifacts. When that guard was established, I'm not certain, but I was compelled by the piece that mentioned prisoners seeking family and friends—or, in Maria's case, news of the circumstances surrounding their deaths, because she already knows their fate.

As for whether or not there was a time when the camp was completely abandoned, the simple answer is I'm not sure, so this is a fictionalization on my part. From a dramatic perspective, I wanted this pivotal scene to take place in Auschwitz for obvious reasons. This is where Maria and Fritzsch met, where she lost her family, and where she went through a horrific, life-altering experience that left her with crippling PTSD, which is severely triggered by returning, far more than she bargains for. Also, with Karl Fritzsch described by eyewitnesses and historians as a man fond of psychological torture, I was certain he would like nothing more than to bring Maria back to Auschwitz to further remind her of what she'd suffered at his hand. Finally, considering that there was a gap between Auschwitz's liberation in January 1945 and the end of the war in May, it left me wondering if, during that time, maybe a few prisoners like Maria had recovered enough to return seeking family or friends, but maybe the protective guard had not been set up yet, and maybe former inmates had not thought about preserving the camp and its artifacts, thus giving Maria and Fritzsch the ability to return to this space without interference.

Another more obvious liberty, as noted, was imprisoning a girl in a men's camp. Non-Jews were not subjected to a selection process as Jews were; however, in these smaller, earlier transports prior to the Final Solution, most men were spared. A few exceptions— including men unable to perform hard labor and a rare handful of women or children sent with the men or arrested in surrounding towns—were shot at the death wall in the courtyard between Blocks 10 and 11. By contrast, later, massive transports of Jewish men, women, and children were heavily scrutinized and the unfit sent to gas chambers. I made Maria's transport larger and busier than it likely would have been historically, making it easier for Maria to stray from her family.

When women first arrived at Auschwitz in spring 1942, they were given their own numbering system and kept in separate blocks in the main camp before moving to the women's sector in Birkenau when the camp was expanded. I learned much about what those first women experienced from *Rena's Promise: A Story of Sisters in Auschwitz* by survivor Rena Kornreich Gelissen with Heather Dune Macadam. Maria arrives in 1941, during a time when women and girls would have been executed.

I felt that it was only right for a Jewish woman to be the lone female prisoner in the camp before Maria's registration, a small, symbolic way to recognize and commemorate that the first female inmates were Jewish. This led me to Hania. Regarding Hania's registration, I created an SS guard whose prominent, fictional German family name gives him significant power, so he secures permission to register her (after she offers to prostitute herself to him in exchange for her life). Many women used their bodies for survival, often with prisoners in positions of authority rather than with SS guards. I wanted Hania involved with a guard to heighten the stakes, because this would have defied race defilement laws, and to demonstrate how much she was willing to risk to survive for her sons. She and Maria are housed with men and given prisoner numbers in the same groupings as the men's. The first female transport received the uniforms of executed Soviet POWs, not the blue-and-gray-striped garbs commonly recognized as camp uniforms. I put my characters in stripes for symbolic purposes. Since the series of numbers for women had not been created yet, Hania's number comes from a transport of twenty-seven prisoners registered on April 18, 1941, sent by the Gestapo from various cities. Warsaw is not mentioned, but I took creative liberty. Maria's number is consecutive with Father Kolbe's. I reasoned that Fritzsch wouldn't go to the trouble of granting separate quarters or establishing different number sequences for two women who, frankly, should have been dead, and whom he doesn't expect to survive long.

Another important liberty to note is Irena's infiltration of the SS-Helferin, or SS-Helpers, to become one of Auschwitz's female guards. To explain this, first I must address Witold Pilecki, a prominent Polish military and resistance figure who compiled a report on Auschwitz and the camp resistance organization he formed, since translated into *The Auschwitz Volunteer: Beyond Bravery*. This invaluable primary source helped me with camp life and his resistance organization, though I simplified it for story purposes, and his intention to stage a rebellion. Because Pilecki infiltrated Auschwitz as a prisoner, it gave me the idea to have

Irena infiltrate as a guard. Though far riskier and more difficult, I thought perhaps she could find a way to make this work given her family's connections to Pilecki, the Home Army, various resistance organizations, and the way the SS recruited camp guards.

When recruiting women for camp service, the SS advertised in newspapers, asking women to show their love of the Reich, and even hired criminals and prostitutes. Other women were recruited based on data the SS had already gathered in various ways, such as girls who joined SS organizations growing up. One of these, the Bund Deutscher Mädel (BDM), or the League of German Girls, was the female wing of the Hitler Youth, the youth organization and indoctrination program of the Nazi Party.

Under her false identity, Irena presents herself as a young woman who spent years in the BDM, a history that would have made her extremely pro-Nazi. Many of these women (and many of the female SS guards I studied to craft this persona) came from lower classes and were not highly educated, were not overly intelligent or skilled, and were eager to serve their country. When training for camp employment, some received no more than a brief lecture on their responsibilities, others a little more guidance, but none were fully prepared for the actual evils taking place. Once they took up their positions, many were shocked by what they encountered, but they were brainwashed by their ideals and were reassured that everything being done was for the good of the Reich. It wasn't long before they were participating in these horrific acts and even felt them necessary.

With help from her German resistance contact and love interest, Franz, Irena spends months learning how to be the kind of young woman the Third Reich would have formed and responds to a recruitment advertisement. Then, with additional help from the bribes that made up a huge part of camp and resistance life, she ensures she's sent to Auschwitz so she can help Maria escape. However, given how much mystery surrounded the camps and how the SS was deliberately vague when training these brain-washed men and women volunteering for camp service, she doesn't entirely realize what lies in store for her. While a historical stretch on my part, this was how I theorized such an infiltration might have been possible, and, if anyone were going to attempt it, I had no doubt that Irena would.

Another significant point to address is the fate of Karl Fritzsch. Although many guards defied rules while working in the camps, the SS did conduct an investigation into internal corruption, so Fritzsch was arrested, convicted, and sent to the front lines as punishment. It is believed that he fell during the Battle of Berlin (April 16–May 2, 1945), but his remains were never recovered, so his actual fate is unknown. By having Fritzsch return to Auschwitz to face Maria and commit suicide to rob her of the justice she seeks, I wanted to illustrate that the vast majority of camp perpetrators were never caught or convicted. Not holding these men and women accountable denied their victims the justice they deserved.

I attempted to stay true to actual dates, and many of the historical events included in the story did happen, including the Sonderkommando Uprising. I learned so much about this prisoner rebellion through *Eyewitness Auschwitz* by Sonderkommando survivor Filip Müller. Although I could have spent pages and pages describing every historical detail, I hope I've clarified some of the liberties I took and have encouraged you to uncover more of this fascinating, important history for yourself. Finally, I cannot recommend *Night* by Elie Wiesel or *Man's Search for Meaning* by Viktor Frankl enough, because both survivor accounts provide invaluable insight into the camp experience and its impacts on mental health. Any errors in history or setting are entirely my own.

 Acknowledgments

MY ENDLESS THANKS to everyone who supported, encouraged, and assisted me in writing this book. My agent, Kaitlyn Johnson, for your brilliant insight and unending faith in me. My editor, Lucia Macro, Asanté Simons, and the entire team at William Morrow, you are a dream come true. My dad, who was my first reader and research trip companion, and my mama, who ignited my passion for literature and history. My brothers, sisters, grandparents, aunts, uncles, and family for their love and enthusiasm. Adrian Eves, one half of the Guild. Olesya Gilmore, dear friend and incredible writer. Mary Dunn for being an early reader, and Melanie Howell for helping with Yiddish and Judaism. The Franciscan Sisters of the Family of Mary in Warsaw, Poland, for answering my questions, and the Auschwitz-Birkenau Memorial and Museum for such important, necessary work. Amanda McCrina for wonderful feedback and historical insight. Finally, to my grandfather. "If I could dedicate this story to the man who encourages me to keep reading, learning, and creating, it would mean more to me than all the success in the world." Words I never shared with you, part of an academic admissions essay stating that my career goal was to write a historical novel.

Within that essay, I described how you never doubted that I would achieve the dream I started chasing as a little girl. As I developed this story, you assisted with research material and planning my trip to Poland. Every Sunday, you called me from the bookstore to suggest historical novels you thought I'd like—many published by "that publisher you love," William Morrow. This book, in unpublished manuscript form, was my last gift to you, though neither of us knew it would be. So, Poppy, this story is as much yours as it is mine and is my very small thank-you. Dedicating this book to you truly does mean more to me than all the success in the world. I love you, I miss you, and I am forever grateful to you.

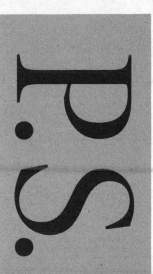

About the author

About the book

Insights,
Interviews
& More . . .

Meet Gabriella Saab

Janie Long Photography

GABRIELLA SAAB graduated from Mississippi State University with a bachelor's of business administration in marketing and now lives in her hometown of Mobile, Alabama, where she works as a barre instructor. While researching *The Last Checkmate*, she traveled to Warsaw and Auschwitz to dig deeper into the setting and the experiences of those who lived there.

This is her first novel. ❧

Historical Figures in the Novel

About the book

Karl Fritzsch

On July 10, 1903, Karl Fritzsch was born in Bohemia; in 1930, at the age of twenty-seven, he joined the Nazi Party and the SS. He held a position at the Dachau concentration camp from 1934 to 1939, then moved to Auschwitz in May 1940 to serve as camp deputy under Rudolf Höss.

Actively involved in the prisoners' lives, Fritzsch—described as small, slight, unintelligent, and sadistic—became known for brutality and psychological torture. According to testimony from Höss, Fritzsch suggested using Zyklon B, a poisonous gas, for mass murder and tested it on Soviet prisoners of war (POWs). On January 15, 1942, he was transferred to Flossenbürg concentration camp.

After the SS conducted an internal corruption investigation, Fritzsch was arrested in October 1943 and charged with murder; whether he murdered an inmate without authorization or a fellow SS man is not clear. He was sent to the front lines as punishment (SS-*Panzergrenadier-Ersatzbatallion* 18). According to *For He Is an Englishman: Memoirs of a Prussian Nobleman* by Captain Charles Arnold-Baker, an MI6 (British foreign intelligence) officer, Arnold-Baker arrested Fritzsch in Oslo, Norway, after the war: "We picked up, for example, the deputy commandant of Auschwitz, a little runt of a man called Fritzsch whom we naturally put in the ▶

3

custody of a Jewish guard—with strict instructions not to damage him, of course." In a 1966 report from the German Central Office of the State Justice Administrations for the Investigation of National Socialist Crimes, Berlin inhabitant Gertrud Berendes claimed that on May 2, 1945, Fritzsch shot himself in the basement of a house at Sächsische Strasse 42 in Berlin. Berendes said that her father and a neighbor buried Fritzsch in the Preussenpark and that she sent his personal belongings to his wife. In a separate 1966 report by the *Kriminalpolizei* Regensburg, Fritzsch's wife stated that she had received his wedding ring and personal letters and was convinced of her husband's death; however, Fritzsch's true fate has never been determined.

Matylda Getter

Matylda Getter was born in 1870 and grew up to become the mother provincial of the Franciscan Sisters of the Family of Mary in Warsaw. The sisters ran orphanages and educational facilities for children in Warsaw and its surrounding towns, including Anin, Wilno, and Ostrówek. During the war, they aided civilians and members of the Polish underground; arranged work, shelter, and false documents; and smuggled children from the Jewish ghetto. In this work they cooperated with Irena Sendler and members of *Żegota*— an underground Polish resistance organization tied to the Polish Underground State, established specifically to aid Jews. During the Warsaw Uprising, the provincial house at Hoża St. 53 became a paramedical station, a soup kitchen, and later a hospital.

During the war, the sisters rescued more than five hundred Jewish children from the Warsaw Ghetto. To determine if someone was willing to accept a Jewish child, Mother Matylda would speak in code by asking, "Will you accept God's blessing?" The Jewish children adored Mother Matylda and called her Matusia, a term of endearment similar to "Mommy." The sisters never forced conversions on Jews, unlike some Catholic civilians or religious, though forcing conversions was never an official practice of the Catholic Church during this time. As Mother Matylda simply stated, "I'm saving a human being who's asking for help."

Mother Matylda died in 1968 and was recognized by Yad Vashem as Righteous Among the Nations, an honorific used by the State of Israel to describe non-Jews who risked their lives during the Holocaust to save Jews from Nazi extermination.

Rudolf Höss
Rudolf Franz Ferdinand Höss was born on November 25, 1901, in Baden-Baden and grew up in a strict extremist family that emphasized the central role of duty in moral life. During World War I, at age fourteen, he enlisted in the German Army's Twenty-First Regiment of Dragoons. After the armistice of November 11, 1918, he joined the *Freikorps* (German military volunteer unit), then joined the Nazi Party in 1922 after listening to Hitler speak in Munich.

Höss joined the SS in 1934, then the Totenkopfverbände, and served at Dachau and Sachsenhausen before joining the Waffen-SS in 1939 after the German invasion of Poland. He was appointed commander of Auschwitz on May 1, 1940. He served for three and a half years and was responsible for the Auschwitz-Birkenau expansion. In June 1941, Heinrich Himmler told Höss that Hitler had ordered the "final solution of the Jewish question" and that Auschwitz had been chosen for a mass extermination site, so Höss began testing extermination techniques. According to his autobiography and eyewitness testimony, Höss accepted anything, even violence and brutality, as long as it was ordered by an authority figure.

Höss was described as cold and unemotional, though in his autobiography he claimed that he'd hoped to lead by example to encourage prisoners to work hard but that his "good intentions" were dashed by "the inadequacy and sheer stupidity" of the men posted to him. He thought it ". . . might have been possible to control men and bring them to my way of thinking if those in charge of the prison camp"—i.e., men such as Karl Fritzsch— "obeyed my wishes . . . this neither they could nor would do, owing to intellectual limitations, obstinacy, and malice." Höss constantly emphasized that he was the only one competent enough to get anything done, but prisoners were left in the hands of Fritzsch and other "distasteful persons" who didn't run the camp the way Höss wanted.

Obsessed with his position, efficiency, and order, Höss would ▶

burst into occasional fits of rage, particularly when he observed his subordinates bending his rules. Regarding the Final Solution, Höss said, "the reasons behind the extermination order seemed right," "I had been given an order, and I had to carry it out," and "what the Führer or his second-in-command ordered was always right." He claimed that the gas experiments made him "uncomfortable," but the killing "did not cause much concern." He felt that gassing was the most effective procedure because the guards were spared "blood baths" and the victims were "spared suffering." This was not true: it took the victims up to fifteen minutes to die, and the guards knew everyone was dead "when the screams stopped." The only regrets Höss ever expressed in his autobiography were not spending more time with his family; he never expressed any regret about his camp crimes.

As the war came to an end, Höss went into hiding before being arrested on March 11, 1946. He was put on trial for war crimes at Nuremberg and wrote his autobiography in prison. He was sentenced to death by hanging on April 2, 1947, and the sentence was carried out on April 16 in Auschwitz next to a crematorium near the camp's Gestapo building.

Maksymilian Kolbe

Raymund Kolbe was born in 1894 to a humble, poor family. In 1907 he joined the Conventual Franciscans and took the name Maksymilian in 1910 when he entered the novitiate, then Maria in 1914 when he professed final vows. He was ordained to the priesthood in 1918 and maintained a strong devotion to the Blessed Mother. After the German invasion of Poland, he stayed in the monastery in Niepokalanów to organize a temporary hospital. He was arrested in September 1939 but released in December; he sheltered refugees, hid two thousand Jews in the friary, and published anti-Nazi materials. The testimony of a Niepokalanów local stated, "When Jews came to me asking for a piece of bread, I asked Father Maksymilian if I could give it to them in good conscience, and he answered me, 'Yes, it is necessary to do this, because all men are our brothers.'"

On February 17, 1941, the Germans shut down the monastery. Kolbe was arrested by the Gestapo and sent to Pawiak, then transferred to Auschwitz on May 28. He arrived on May 29 and received prisoner number 16670. Even in the camp, he retained his humility and compassion and performed priestly duties in secret. On July 29, 1941, an inmate from Block 14, Father Kolbe's block, escaped. As punishment, Fritzsch sentenced ten prisoners to immurement. One young man, Prisoner 5659, Franciszek Gajowniczek, said he had a family and begged for mercy. Father Kolbe stepped forward and said in German, "I'm a Catholic priest. I'd like to take this man's place, because he has a wife and children." Everyone, even Fritzsch, was speechless, but Fritzsch permitted the exchange, because religious were some of the most hated prisoners.

Father Kolbe spent two weeks in the starvation bunker in Block 11, and eyewitnesses could hear him praying, singing, and calming his fellow captives. According to a janitor who worked in the block, Kolbe was always calmly standing or kneeling in the middle of the cell each time the guards checked on him. After two weeks, Father Kolbe was the only one still alive, but the guards were impatient to empty the bunker so it could be used for other prisoners. On August 14, 1941, he was killed by a lethal injection of carbolic acid. Kolbe offered his arm to the guard, and some say his final words were "Ave Maria."

Maksymilian Kolbe was elevated to sainthood by Pope John Paul II on October 10, 1982. The man he saved, Franciszek Gajowniczek, was present at his canonization.

Maria Mandel (also spelled *Mandl*)

Born on January 10, 1912, in Münzkirchen, Upper Austria, Mandel served at Lichtenburg and Ravensbrück concentration camps, rising through the ranks until she succeeded Johanna Langefeld as SS-Lagerführerin of Auschwitz-Birkenau. She reported only to the kommandant and participated in selections and other abuses. It is estimated that she sent half a million women and children to die in the gas chambers. At Auschwitz, Mandel was known as the Beast. She was fond of Irma Grese, a guard whom prisoners nicknamed the Hyena of Auschwitz and the Beautiful Beast, and promoted Grese to head of the Hungarian women's camp at Birkenau (Grese was accused of war crimes during the Belsen trial and hanged at the age of twenty-two). Mandel created the Women's Orchestra of Auschwitz and was awarded the War Merit Cross Second Class for her services. ▶

Historical Figures in the Novel *(continued)*

In November 1944, Mandel was assigned to the Mühldorf subcamp of Dachau and Elisabeth Volkenrath replaced her at Auschwitz. The US Army arrested Mandel on August 10, 1945, then handed her over to the Polish People's Republic in November 1946. She was tried in Kraków during the Auschwitz trial and in November 1947 was sentenced to death by hanging. The sentence was carried out on January 24, 1948. She was thirty-six years old.

Witold Pilecki

Pilecki was born on May 13, 1901, to a noble, devoutly Roman Catholic Polish family. He served as a captain in the Polish army during the Polish-Soviet War, the Second Polish Republic, and World War II. During the German invasion of Poland, he served in the Nineteenth Infantry Division as a cavalry platoon commander; then his division was incorporated into the Forty-First Infantry Division, where Pilecki served as second in command.

In October 1939 his division was disbanded and parts of it began to surrender, so Pilecki and his commander went into hiding in Warsaw, where they cofounded the Secret Polish Army, one of the first underground organizations in Poland. This resistance group was later incorporated into the Union for Armed Struggle, later renamed the Home Army. Pilecki later authored Witold's Report, the first comprehensive Allied intelligence report on Auschwitz and the Holocaust.

In 1940 he presented his plan to enter Auschwitz to gather intelligence and organize inmate resistance. His superiors provided him with a false identity: Tomasz Serafiński. On September 19, during a Warsaw street roundup, he was caught, detained for two days, then sent to Auschwitz and assigned prisoner number 4859. Pilecki organized the underground Union of Military Organizations (ZOW) at Auschwitz, and many smaller organizations at Auschwitz eventually merged with it. ZOW improved inmate morale, provided news from outside, distributed extra food and clothing to members, set up intelligence networks, and trained detachments in the event of a relief attack by the Home Army, arms airdrops, or airborne landing by the Polish First Independent Parachute Brigade, based in Britain. ZOW provided the Polish underground with information about the camp and sent reports to Warsaw starting in October 1940. Beginning in March 1941, the

Polish resistance forwarded those reports to the British government in London. When the organization began, Pilecki organized its members into cells of five, so each member was in communication with only four others. If one member was caught, this limited the number of men he could potentially expose under torture.

Pilecki worked in various kommandos, including carpentry, a weaving workshop, the tannery, and the parcel office. In 1942 Pilecki's resistance movement used a radio transmitter to broadcast arrivals, deaths, and inmate conditions, then dismantled it that autumn, fearing the Germans might discover it. Through civilian workers, Pilecki sent out coded messages and obtained medicine and typhus vaccines. He hoped that either the Allies would drop arms or troops into the camp, or the Home Army would organize an assault; meanwhile, the camp Gestapo under SS-Untersturmführer Maximilian Grabner captured and killed many ZOW members.

Pilecki decided to break out of the camp and personally convince the Home Army leaders that a rescue attempt was possible. After a clever plan involving faking a case of typhus and getting himself transferred to the bakery kommando, Pilecki and a few inmates enacted their escape on the evening of Easter Monday in 1943. At the bakery in town, they changed into civilian clothes provided by friends, took the back door off its hinges, and ran, carrying powdered tobacco to hide their scent from SS tracking dogs. While sheltering with a trusted contact, Pilecki contacted his Warsaw connections, saying he would remain near Auschwitz and form a detachment while he waited for permission to attack the camp; however, if his plan was denied and he was ordered to desist, he would return to Warsaw. In July, the Home Army commander was arrested, so Pilecki realized he wouldn't get an answer yet. He went to Warsaw and exchanged letters with men in Auschwitz to keep up their spirits. In the fall of 1943, he presented his full plan of attack and wrote his final Auschwitz report. In 1944, he took part in the Warsaw Uprising. Despite his efforts, the Home Army did not have enough manpower to successfully attack Auschwitz.

In Communist Poland after the war, Pilecki continued working for Polish military intelligence and collected evidence of Soviet atrocities. In May 1947, the Ministry of Public Security arrested and charged him with crimes including espionage, illegal border crossing, use of forged documents, and planned assassinations of ▶

Historical Figures in the Novel *(continued)*

ministry members. He pled guilty to all except the assassination plans and espionage, though he admitted to passing information to the Second Polish Corps; he considered himself an officer of the corps and claimed he wasn't breaking any laws. He was tortured, and some reports claim he said that his time in Soviet custody was worse than his time at Auschwitz. Following a show trial, Pilecki was sentenced to execution and was shot in the back of the head in Mokotów Prison on May 8, 1948, at the age of forty-seven, leaving behind his wife and two children.

In September 1990, Witold Pilecki and others sentenced in the show trial were rehabilitated. He was posthumously awarded the Order of Polonia Restituta in 1995 and the Order of the White Eagle in 2006, the highest Polish decoration. On September 6, 2013, he was promoted to colonel by the Minister of National Defense. ᕰ

Miscellaneous Facts and Info

- Maria's Gestapo interrogation was heavily based on survivor testimony, including such occurrences as doors and windows left open so prisoners could overhear torture, secretaries taking notes, young women and girls being stripped to undergarments, and entire families being tormented to force confessions from the interrogated prisoner. Interrogations were typically carried out in the prisoner's native tongue, which is why Ebner, Maria's interrogator, offers to provide an interpreter. I wanted the exchange to remain between Maria and Ebner, so I didn't include one. In contrast, during her second interrogation, Maria feigns ignorance of German so Hania can act as interpreter while Irena poses as a guard, thus allowing Maria their support and comfort.

- In Pawiak, prisoners used their bread rations to make chess pieces, rosaries, and trinkets to entertain themselves and boost morale. They combined bread with dirt, wire, hair, or whatever else they could find. I saw one of these chess sets when I toured the Museum of Pawiak Prison in Warsaw, and that's where I found the inspiration for Maria's father to make a pawn for her.

- Höss's return from a trip to Berlin alludes to his actual meeting with Himmler in Berlin in June 1941, where he learned that Hitler had ordered the Final Solution to the Jewish question. I probably extended his actual absence, because I have him returning in July. Himmler had selected Auschwitz as the extermination site for Europe's Jews "on account of its easy access by rail and also because the extensive site offered space for measures ensuring isolation." Himmler described it as a "secret Reich matter," so I use the same phrasing.

- The tattooing process was implemented a few years after the camp's creation. Incoming Jewish transports were tattooed in the main camp starting in autumn 1941 and Birkenau in spring of 1942, and inmates who were incarcerated prior to those dates were tattooed in the spring of 1943. Certain groups were exempt, such as Polish civilians deported after the Warsaw Uprising in 1944. I took some liberty with the date and location of Maria's tattooing and included her in the group of existing inmates who were subjected to the process. The date ties in historically with ▶

Miscellaneous Facts and Info *(continued)*

Witold Pilecki's escape plan, and the location (Block 26) is the same as where she was registered. I wanted to take her back to the main camp to revisit her registration block and have a last encounter with Pilecki before he escapes. In actuality, she probably would have been taken to a female tattooist in a registration block in Birkenau. In the early days of the tattooing system, a metal stamp was pressed into the skin on the prisoner's upper-left chest, then ink was rubbed into the wound. This method was abandoned in favor of a needle, and the location of the tattoo changed to the outer-left forearm, the inner side of the left upper forearm, and the lower left forearm. I wanted Maria's on her inner-left forearm, right below her cigarette-burn scars from interrogation, though she might have been more likely to have been tattooed on her outer forearm.

- The reader learns that Hania's sister and niece were killed in the ghetto because they walked on the sidewalk rather than in the gutter when a group of SS men were approaching, so the SS men threw them back into the street and beat them. This was based on a Warsaw Ghetto survivor's testimony, which described the punishments for walking on the sidewalk rather than in the gutter; the survivor mentioned a specific encounter where a group of SS men didn't even say a word before throwing a Jew into the street and mercilessly beating him.

- Maria mentions a typhus epidemic and the women's blocks being infested with fleas. If you look at the chapter dates containing those references, they tie in historically with a real camp typhus epidemic and a flea infestation in the women's blocks. Similarly, prior to a selection, Hania mentions a roll call that had taken place three days before and had transformed into a selection, and if you were to check the date, you'd find that a roll call took place on the date Hania mentioned and then became a selection.

- When Maria seeks details of her family's execution, she talks to Oskar, an SS guard who didn't approve of what was happening in the camps but felt powerless to stop it and feared reprisal should he speak out. All Germans were not sadists like Fritzsch, who delighted in cruelty; many were brainwashed into believing they were operating with Germany's best interests at heart, or they recognized that what they were doing was wrong but felt helpless to prevent it and resolved that duty to country stood above all else. The reader learns that the Florkowski children were killed first, which is often what the executioners did to torment parents, and that Maria's parents faced Fritzsch rather than the wall, something many prisoners did as an act of defiance.

- I wanted Maria to establish a civilian resistance connection, which is how Mateusz came to be. His family owns the local bakery, and this was inspired by Pilecki's escape plan. The Nazis took over many businesses, but in some cases civilians worked alongside prisoners. I imagined that Mateusz's family owns the bakery through which Pilecki escapes, so he reports its success to Maria.

- When Irena is captured and sent to Auschwitz, she says she was caught taking a Jewish girl to live with a Catholic family. The Gestapo locked the girl and the family inside, set fire to the house, and made sure there were no survivors. That fate of the Jewish child and the family harboring her was a fictional version of eyewitness testimony.

- There's a small detail in one scene where Maria is working in the kitchen and the kapo throws a piece of rotten potato at her to get her attention. This moment was inspired by a survivor's testimony. The survivor described an occasion when a kapo threw a rock at him to get his attention, and he said it felt even more demeaning than beatings and curses, because throwing a rock is something a man would do to get an animal's attention, not a human's.

- The reader learns that Pilecki is responsible for the bribe that spared Irena's life when she was sent to Auschwitz for execution. Guards were often easily bribed, and the nature of Irena's escape was inspired by real events. She was given civilian clothing and driven out of the camp; a real prisoner named Kazimierz Piechowski, together with a few fellow inmates, stole SS uniforms and a car and drove out of the camp, right past the guards in the towers and those who opened the gate for them.

- When Irena returns to the camp disguised as a guard and tells Maria that she intends to help her escape, they end the conversation with an embrace, which takes Maria aback and ▶

Miscellaneous Facts and Info *(continued)*

causes her to reflect on what that embrace means to her. That scene was inspired by a quote from Eva Moses Kor, a Mengele twin who died on July 4, 2019: "Being so alone, a hug meant more than anybody could imagine because that replaced the human warmth that we were starving for. We were not only starved for food, but we were starved for human kindness."

- Irena mentions that her mother and daughter left Warsaw because the Home Army planned an uprising. A collection of Warsaw Uprising survivor testimonies describes what occurred in the Mokotów district, where Irena and Maria's families lived. When the uprising occurred in the Warsaw Ghetto, Himmler ordered the entire city and its population exterminated. Although the Mokotów district and Bałuckiego Street survived with minimal damage, it was a key district for the Home Army and fell during the suppression of Mokotów; then the Nazis carried out a string of rapes—including gang rapes—robberies, and murders in homes and hospitals. Irena is relieved that her mother and daughter fled to safety and says she knows what would have happened had they stayed, meaning both would have fallen victim to rape and murder.

- Jews and non-Jews were supposed to live in separate blocks, but the guards often disregarded this rule. This is how Maria and Hania end up being bunkmates in Birkenau.

- At one point, Maria learns that the hospital block has been "cleared" and that a resistance member was there and died. When the hospital grew overcrowded, the guards would order everyone executed in gas chambers or with phenol injections. Prisoners were often afraid of transfers because they didn't know if the new camp would be better or worse than the current one. To avoid transfer, they'd bribe prisoners to take their name off the list or bribe a hospital staff member to admit them. Hospitalization was risky because if the hospital was ordered to be cleared, the resistance member would be killed alongside the sick, which did happen according to survivor testimonies.

- When Maria and Hania smuggle gunpowder capsules for the rebellion, Maria mentions passing the capsules to "a woman in the clothing detail." This is a reference to Róża Robota, who

14

worked in the clothing detail adjacent to one of the crematoria. Jewish women smuggled gunpowder from the Union Munitions Factory, where Maria takes a brief position so she can extend her support to these women; later, this employment is why she's interrogated by the camp Gestapo. Robota and others passed the gunpowder to the Sonderkommando workers. On October 7, 1944, the Sonderkommando workers in Crematorium IV (near where my character Izaak is employed) heard a rumor that they were going to be liquidated. They panicked and planted explosives in Crematorium IV. This killed and injured a few guards, but the rebellion was crushed and hundreds of Sonderkommando workers were killed in reprisal. The gunpowder capsules among the destroyed crematorium were traced to the munitions factory, so Róża Robota, Ala Gertner, Estusia Wajcblum, and Regina Safirsztajn were captured and interrogated, but they didn't betray anyone else involved. They were sentenced to hang, as Maria learns following her camp Gestapo interrogation, and were executed on January 6, 1945, in the presence of the entire women's camp, a few short weeks prior to liberation.

- The death-march scene in which Maria witnesses a woman attempting to escape is inspired by a combination of survivor testimonies. One reported a man with a broken leg being left to die, and another reported a woman who ran into a field and got caught in a snowbank. A soldier drew his gun to shoot her, but when she realized that she was trapped, she begged him to do it. When he heard her pleas, he put the gun away and none of the other guards drew theirs; instead they ignored her and left her to die in the snowbank.

- Franz and his family signed the Deutsche Volksliste under the advice of church and resistance leaders. Many German-descended anti-Nazis did this to protect themselves and secure better rights, which helped them travel more freely and access better goods. They often used their elevated status to support the resistance.

- Following liberation, Hania mentions that her brother, Izaak, went to hunt Nazi war criminals. Later the reader learns that Izaak tracked down Protz to avenge everything Hania suffered at his hands. Izaak's mission was inspired by groups like *Nakam* (Hebrew for "Revenge"), a group of Holocaust survivors who, ▶

Miscellaneous Facts and Info *(continued)*

in 1945, sought to kill six million Germans in reprisal for the six million Jews killed during the Holocaust. Many rogue groups like this hunted Nazi criminals and did so for years following the war, because many Nazis escaped without consequences.

- Many mental health issues were not well understood or addressed in those days, and post-traumatic stress disorder (PTSD) was not diagnosed. Survivors had difficulty readjusting to normal life, and people either didn't know how to help them or didn't know that they needed help. Maria's postliberation symptoms (flashbacks, headaches, restlessness, nightmares, mood swings, etc.) are now categorized as a type of PTSD specific to Holocaust survivors. After the war, she has no idea why she's developed such issues and fears them, which contributes to the difficulties in her final confrontation with Fritzsch. She's determined to keep the symptoms at bay and remain in control of herself, yet the environment—and Fritzsch himself—easily triggers her. Once he's dead, the symptoms still won't leave her alone, and Maria feels she's the only one haunted by the past until Hania confesses that she experiences flashbacks, too. Maria learns how to cope, but even in the epilogue, we learn that the symptoms never leave her. Many Holocaust survivors were plagued by PTSD for the rest of their lives, even those who eventually found the help they needed.

- Many survivors didn't speak of what they'd endured. This, coupled with the lack of therapy and other mental health resources, made it difficult for them to come to terms with what they had experienced. Some realized that sharing their story helped them cope, but most stayed silent for years, even their whole lives, and never wanted to revisit Auschwitz. When they did, many found that speaking of their experiences and going back to Auschwitz actually brought them peace. This is why Maria has such trouble speaking of her time in the camp, then starts to share her story, but she doesn't feel a real sense of peace until she returns to Auschwitz many years later. ∾